Helen Hollick lives in Lon[...]
between researching the ba[...]
and her pirate series about][...]
helping with her daughter's [...]
She has a university diploma in early medieval history – and a passion for pirates.

For up-to-date information visit Helen's website: www.helenhollick.net

Praise for Helen Hollick's novels

Some real midwifery, harrowingly accurate, beautifully written. Just glad I'm practicing in the 21st Century!
Nicola Witcombe, Midwife

Hollick's enormous cast and meticulous research combine to create a convincing account of the destructive reign of the hapless Edward and the internecine warfare that weakens England as William prepares to invade. Thanks to Hollick's masterful storytelling, Harold's nobility and heroism enthrall to the point of engendering hope for a different ending to the famous battle of 1066.
Publisher's Weekly

Don't miss Helen Hollick's colourful recreation of the events leading up to the Norman Conquest in Harold the King.
Daily Mail

An epic re-telling of the Norman Conquest
The Lady

If only all historical fiction could be this good
Historical Novels Review

Hollick joggles a cast of characters and a bloody, tangled plot with great skill
Publishers Weekly

Most impressive
The Lady

Also by Helen Hollick

The Pendragon's Banner Trilogy

The Kingmaking: Book One of the Pendragon's Banner Trilogy
Pendragon's Banner: Book Two of the Pendragon's Banner Trilogy
Shadow of the King: Book Three of the Pendragon's Banner Trilogy

The Saxon 1066 Series

A Hollow Crown (UK edition title)
The Forever Queen (US edition title)

Harold the King (UK edition title)
I Am The Chosen King (US edition title)

The Sea Witch Voyages

Sea Witch: The first voyage of pirate Cpt Jesamiah Acorne
Pirate Code: The second voyage of Cpt Jesamiah Acorne
Bring It Close: The third voyage of Cpt Jesamiah Acorne
Ripples In the Sand: The fourth Voyage of Cpt Jesamiah Acorne
(published autumn 2011)

To My Readers

A personal message from Helen Hollick

Writing can be a silly occupation. Solitary, often hard, tedious work for few rewards. But it is compulsive, and those few rewards can be great indeed: seeing your novel on a shelf in a bookstore; receiving an e-mail from an appreciative fan; a fabulous review; a nomination for an award. There is the sheer pleasure of starting with a blank page and experiencing the excitement of bringing a character to full and glorious life. Of delving beneath the facts of what happened and when, and filling in all the missing bits of why, how and with whom. That is the joy of writing!

Having a book published, however, is not always plain sailing. Several years ago my backlist was dropped by William Heinemann – historical fiction had gone out of fashion – and simultaneously my agent abandoned me. I was on my own and facing the prospect of not writing another novel. I spent two weeks sobbing, then pulled myself together and set out to find an alternative publisher.

I discovered an independent company who, as a part of their small mainstream imprint, took my backlist and my new venture: the first of the *Sea Witch* voyages. There were hiccups, but the office staff were enthusiastic and I had high hopes for the future. Sadly, the current economic climate is not kind to small firms, and for a second time I found myself facing the prospect of being out of print. I had four choices:

Give up writing
Find an alternative mainstream publisher
Go self-publish (produce my books myself)
Find a company that provided assisted publishing

For me, 1 was not an option. I cannot give up writing, not while I still have a story in my head to share. Choice 2: I am mainstream published in the US and other countries, but approaching a similar UK publishing house, with their full lists and tight printing schedules, could have resulted in my novels being unavailable for several months. I have many friends who would be so disappointed to see them temporarily disappear, as would I. Lacking the technical knowledge, or time, to go self publish was not viable or practical, although the thought of running my own company was tempting. However, excited by the prospect of being in control of my destiny – and my books – I decided to opt for choice 4.

I have known Helen Hart of SilverWood Books for several years and it was therefore an easy choice to send my precious novels into her good care, confident she would produce quality editions, quickly and efficiently.

Transferring my list of seven books has been hard and dedicated work, not just for me, but for the team at SilverWood Books, my graphic designer Cathy Helms of AvalonGraphics, and my editors Jo Field and Michaela Unterbarnscheidt.

Nor have the production costs been cheap – more on the 'gulp' level – but the quality result has been worth it…I love my characters and have great respect and fondness for all my followers, fans, friends and readers. Your encouragement and enthusiasm was all the incentive I needed to make the decision to keep my characters alive and well. And in print.

For that, I thank you.

Bring it Close

Helen Hollick

Being the Third Voyage of
Cpt. Jesamiah Acorne & his ship, *Sea Witch*

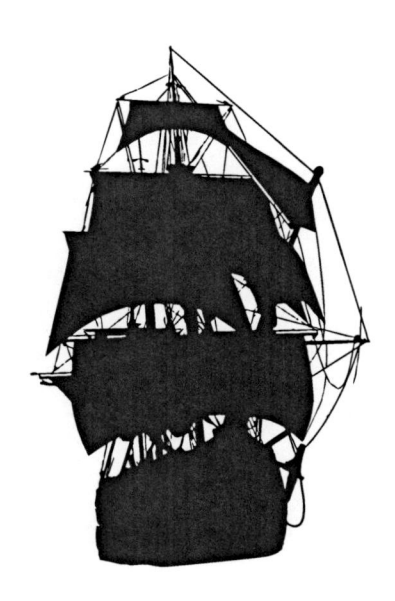

Published in paperback 2011 by SilverWood Books of Bristol
www.silverwoodbooks.co.uk

Text copyright © Helen Hollick 2011
Illustrations © Avalon Graphics 2011

The right of Helen Hollick to be identified as the author
of this work has been asserted by her in accordance
with the Copyright, Designs and Patents Act 1988.

All rights reserved. No part of this publication may be reproduced,
stored in a retrieval system, or transmitted in any form or by any means, electronic, mechanical,
photocopying, recording or otherwise,
without prior permission of the copyright holder.

ISBN 978-1-906236-62-5

British Library Cataloguing in Publication Data
A CIP catalogue record for this book is available from the British Library

Set in Palatino Light by SilverWood Books
Printed in England on paper from responsible sources

SilverWood

To Jo Field,

*author, editor
and such a very dear friend.
Jesamiah and I do not know what we would do without you, m'dear.*

Acknowledgements

As always I have many people to thank for their help, guidance and encouragement. Especially my husband, Ron, and daughter Kathy. After all these years of my demented scribbling, they still do not complain that I appear to live almost entirely in my study.

Thank you to Judy who undertook some essential Colonial Williamsburg research, and to John F. Millar who told such absorbing tales of Virginia history – and who welcomed me to a wonderful evening of Old English Dancing at Newport House, Williamsburg. To my veterinarian, Sean, for his advice about colic in horses, Wendy who suggested ideas regarding Samhain, and Nicola who advised me on midwifery.

My gratitude to authors James L. Nelson who, once again, gave me his expert advice with the sailing detail and to Peter St John who translated the French. Additionally, my appreciation to authors Elizabeth Chadwick and Sharon Penman and Bernard Cornwell and Suzanne McLeod for their ongoing support. Thank you also to my friends, Julie Malone of NewWriter's UK who writes as Karen Wright, Michaela, Kelly and Mal who have all helped in one way or another to aid in getting this book under full sail, and cheered me up during bouts of the doldrums. My gratitude to the many Jesamiah fans who have been so patient with the wait between books. I am trying to write Voyage Four as quickly as I can!

Thank you to Helen Hart and the entire Bristol-based SilverWood Books Team and thank you to Jo – *Bring it Close* is for you, with my love.

Finally, my thanks to Cathy Helms for her stunning artwork for the covers and marketing material for the *Sea Witch* Voyages – and for her patience with the nit-pick alterations from a fussy author; to Simon Murgatroyd for his photographic skills, and Ray and Anne for posing as various characters.

Helen Hollick
2011

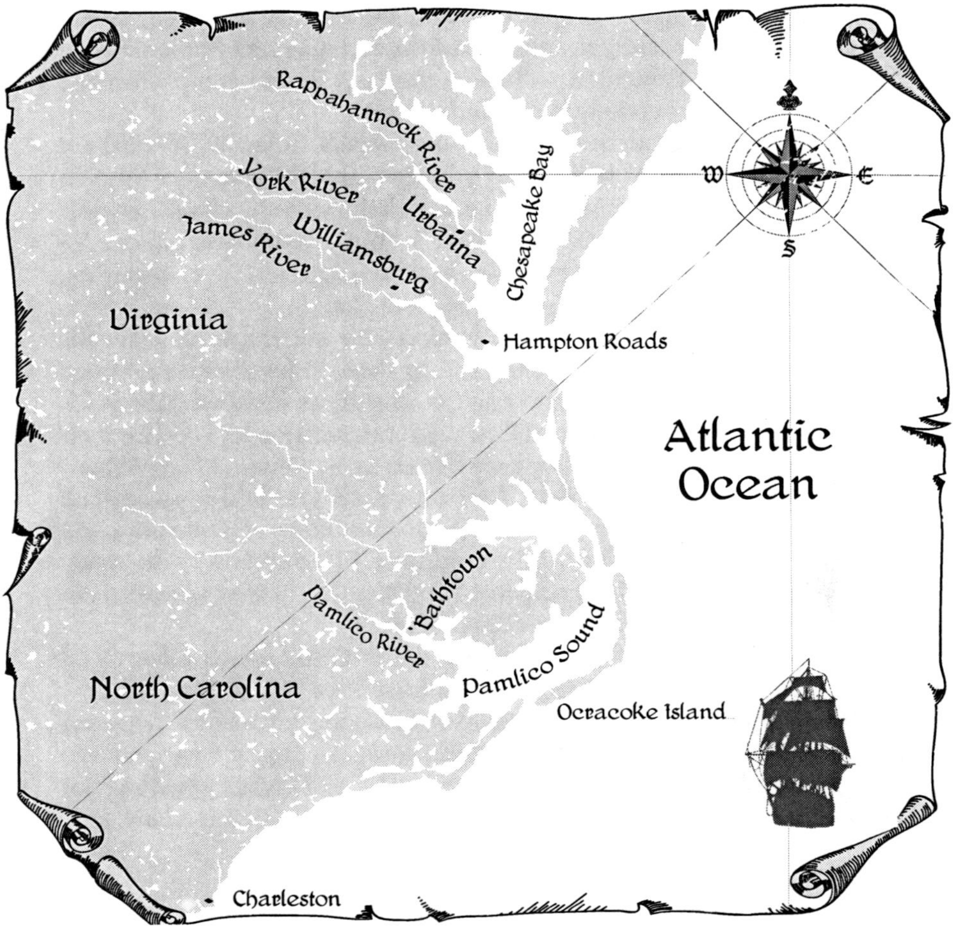
Rappahannock River
York River
Urbanna
Chesapeake Bay
Williamsburg
James River
Virginia
Hampton Roads
W
E
S
Atlantic Ocean
Bathtown
Pamlico River
Pamlico Sound
North Carolina
Ocracoke Island
Charleston

Plan of the sails and masts of a square-rigged ship

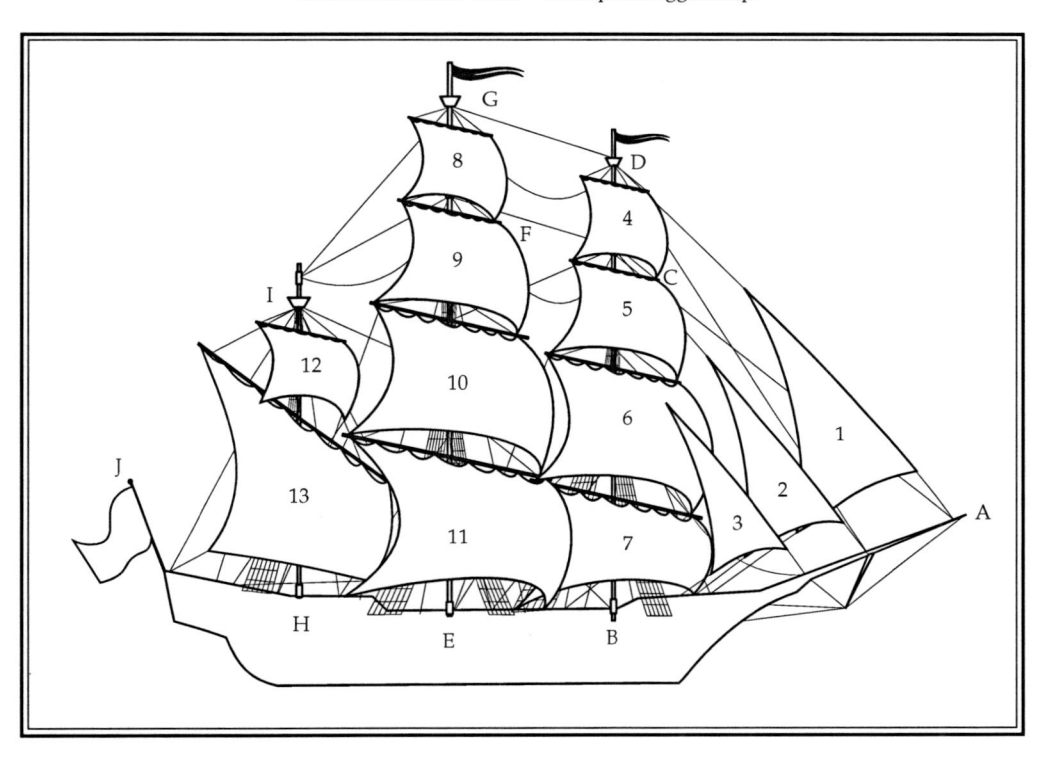

Sails

1	Flying Jib	8	Main Topgallant Royal
2	Jib	9	Main Topgallant
3	Fore Staysail	10	Main Topsail
4	Fore Topgallant Royal	11	Mainsail or Main Course
5	Fore Topgallant Sail (pronounced *t'gan's'l*)	12	Mizzen Topsail
6	Fore Topsail (pronounced *tops'l*)	13	Mizzen Sail
7	Foresail or Fore Course		

Masts

A	Bowsprit/Jib-boom	F	Main Topmast
B	Foremast	G	Main Topgallant Mast
C	Fore Topmast	H	Mizzenmast
D	Fore Topgallant Mast	I	Mizzen Topmast
E	Main Mast	J	Ensign and Ensign Staff

Bring it close
– an old term for a telescope.

An instrument used to bring what is far away nearer,
or to make that which is indistinguishable, clear.

October 1718

Part One

Nassau, the Bahamas

Thus it began…

In the place where the living are not dead and the dead are not alive, Time ceases and blends with the void of Forever, the two merging like painted colours weeping in the rain.

In that place there are many, but all are alone. Those who have no reason to be there cross the still, deep River and step ashore into the peace that is Eternity. Others sink into the desolation and oblivion of the Nothing. Some stand and shout their anger, or shed tears for their weak frailties, but learn nothing from their mistakes.

Some endure their regrets, and a few, just a few, choose to be patient and to wait and watch, and hope for a chance to return.

There, in that place, stood a man who waited, and while he waited he watched his son, who was among the living. And as he watched, he remembered. And in remembering he grieved bitterly for what he had and had not done.

"I would that I could speak to him," the man said to the ageless woman who stood a pace behind. He turned to her, anguish corrupting his tired face. "I would that I could undo what was done."

"It would be difficult. He is alive and you are dead," the Witch Woman said, with an ache of pity and compassion in her heart.

"Difficult?" He paused and gathered the courage to say what was in his thoughts. "Difficult. But not impossible?"

The Woman, the Witch, smiled, the power of her love sending the comfort of Light through the dismal shroud of Darkness that was tormenting his troubled soul.

"Difficult," she said, "but not impossible."

One

Tuesday, 1st October

Jesamiah Acorne, four and twenty years old, Captain of the *Sea Witch*, sat with his hands cradled around an almost empty tankard of rum, staring blankly at the drips of candle-wax that had hardened into intricate patterns down the sides of a green glass bottle. The candle itself was smoking and leaning to one side as if drunk. As drunk as Jesamiah.

For maybe ten seconds he did not notice the two grim-faced, shabby ruffians sit down on the bench opposite him. One of them reached forward and snuffed out the guttering flame, pushed the bottle aside. Jesamiah looked up, stared at them as vacantly as he had been staring at the congealed rivers of wax.

One of the men, the one wearing a battered three-corner felt hat and a gold hoop earring that dangled from his left earlobe, leant his arms on the table, linking his tar and gunpowder-grimed fingers together. The other, a red-haired man with a beard like a weather-worn, abandoned bird's nest, eased a dagger from the sheath on his belt and began cleaning his split and broken nails with its tip.

"We've been lookin' fer you, Acorne," the man with the earring said.

"Found me then, ain't yer," Jesamiah drawled. He dropped his usual educated accent and spoke in the clipped speech of a common foremast jack. He was a good mimic, had a natural talent to pick up languages and tonal cadences. Also knew when to play the simpleton or a gentleman.

He drained his tankard, held it high and whistled for Never-Say-No Nan, a wench built like a Spanish galleon and whose charms kept her as busy as a barber's chair.

She ambled over to Jesamiah, the top half of her partially exposed and extremely ample bosoms wobbling close to his face as she poured more rum.

"What about your friends?" she asked, nodding in their direction.

"Ain't no friends of mine," Jesamiah answered lifting his tankard to sample the replenished liquor.

The man with the earring jerked his head, indicating Nan was to be gone. She sniffed haughtily and swept away, her deep-rumbled laughter drifting behind as another man gained her attention by pinching her broad backside.

"Or to be more accurate, Acorne, Teach'as been lookin' for yer."

Half shrugging, Jesamiah made a fair pretence at nonchalance; "I ain't exactly been 'iding, Gibbens. I've been openly anchored 'ere in Nassau 'arbour for several weeks." Since August in fact, apart from a brief excursion to Hispaniola – which Jesamiah was attempting to set behind him and forget about. Hence the rum.

"Aye, we 'eard as 'ow thee've signed for amnesty and put yer piece into Governor Rogers" and," Gibbens sneered, making an accompanying crude and explicit gesture near his crotch.

"Given up piracy?" Red Beard – Rufus – scoffed as he hoiked tobacco spittle into his mouth and gobbed it to the floor, "Gone soft 'ave thee? Barrel run dry, 'as it? Lost yer balls, eh?" Added with malice, "Edward Teach weren't interested in fairy-tale government amnesties, nor 'ollow pardons." He drove his dagger into the wooden table where it quivered as menacing as the man who owned it.

That's not what I've heard, Jesamiah thought but said nothing. He had no intention of going anywhere near Edward Teach, better known as Blackbeard, though Black Heart would be as appropriate. Even the scum and miscreants who roamed the seas of the Caribbean in search of easy loot and plunder avoided the brute of a pirate who was Blackbeard.

Aside, Jesamiah was no longer a pirate. As Gibbens had said, he had signed his name in Governor Rogers' leather-bound book and accepted His Majesty King George's royal pardon. Which was why he had nothing better to do than sit here in this tavern drinking rum. Piracy, plundering, pillaging, none of that was for him, not now. Now, Jesamiah Acorne, Captain of the *Sea Witch*, had a woman he was about to marry, a substantial fortune that he could start using if only he knew what to spend it on, and the dubious reputation of becoming a respectable man of leisure.

He was also bored.

"You owe him, Acorne," Rufus said. "Teach wants the debt paid."

Jesamiah raised the tankard to his mouth pretending to drink. He had been drunk but he had become stone cold sober the moment these ruffians sat down at the table. Only he was not going to let them know it; safer to pretend otherwise, for Gibbens, Teach's boatswain, and Rufus, were trouble. Anyone who willingly sailed with Teach was either as crazed as a man who had quenched his thirst with salt water, or had brains boiled dry by the sun. In the case of these two dregs both instances applied. They were lunkheads who punched first and asked questions after. If they assumed Jesamiah was drunk they were less likely to err on the side of caution.

Two more men slithered from the smoke-grimed shadows and sauntered up to stand behind Jesamiah. He could smell the nauseating stink of their unwashed bodies and the badness of their breath. He winced as one of them prolifically farted.

Gibbens sneered, showing a ragged half set of black teeth. "Our Cap'n wants what you owe, Acorne. You sank our ship. You'll be payin' us for 'er. One way or t'other." He nodded, a single discreet movement towards the two men behind Jesamiah – and all hell broke loose.

As one of them went to grab at his shoulder Jesamiah was coming to his feet, his right hand drawing the cutlass at his left hip, the blade slung from a bronze-buckled strap aslant across his chest. The bench he had been sitting on tipped over, and with his left hand he lifted the table, crashing it onto Rufus and Gibbens who were a heartbeat too late in reacting

Jesamiah's reflexes were honed to a quick and precise speed. Half turning to his right in one fluid movement, he swung the cutlass upward and slashed the face of one of the men behind. Blood fountained in a gush of sticky red accompanied by a cry of pain and protest. He continued the turn, the blade, reaching the end of its arc, came down and forward again through the weight of its own momentum, amputating the arm of the second man as efficiently as a hot knife goes through butter.

Stepping aside to wipe the blood from his weapon on the coat of one of the fallen men, Jesamiah dipped his head in acknowledgement to Gibbens and Rufus, who were scrambling, furious, from where they had been pinned behind the table.

"Tell Teach if he wants to speak to me he'll 'ave to come in person. I don't deal with his monkeys." Jesamiah sheathed the cutlass, bent to retrieve his hat from where it had fallen and, flipping a coin towards Nan, sauntered from the tavern as if nothing had happened. His mind, however, was racing.

Teach was not a good enemy to be having. He was unpredictable, savage and vindictive. Rumour had it that he had shot his own mother for the price of a bottle of rum. Once a week, to keep his crew in order, he hanged or shot one of them. But Jesamiah was an optimist where the sea and piracy were concerned. Teach had one failing – he was usually as drunk as Bacchus. If he shot you, you were unlucky – nine times out of ten he was aiming at the blurred image of his inebriated double vision. All Jesamiah had to do was stay sober, keep out of the way and watch his back.

Hah! All!

Outside in the cool air of the starlit night he leant against a wall, his head back, eyes closed, willing the breath that was catching in his throat to calm, waiting for the pulsing blood flow scampering around his body to ease.

~ *Are you all right luvver?* ~

Into his mind, the voice, with its lilting Cornish accent, of his woman, Tiola – said not as *Tee-oh-la*, but *Teo-la*, short and sweet. Like her. She had been helping the wife of the captain of the Nassau Militia give birth to a first child. Had been there all day, all evening. Would probably be there all night.

She had been with another woman last night – one of the beach-dwelling whores. And the night before that with one of Governor Woodes Rogers' servants who had taken a tumble and broken his leg. Two days and nights and Jesamiah had not seen Tiola. It was all very well, her being a healer and a midwife, having this gift of Craft – witchcraft, for all that she did only good and not harm. These prolonged absences were not doing *him* any good though, were they?

~ *A minor disagreement. It was nothing. When are you coming home?* ~

He was used to this way of communicating with her now; telepathy, she called it. She was full of fancy words and ideas that no one else had ever heard or thought of. And he had no comprehension of, half the time.

~ *A few more hours.* ~

~ *I want to talk.* ~

~ *We will.* ~

When? he thought to himself, shielding it from her. He was practised at that too, not permitting her to hear all that he was thinking. *When will we talk?* ~ *I need answers, Tiola. I need answers to these questions that will not lie still in my head.* ~

He wanted to know about his father. His dead father and the bastard of a half-brother who had turned out not to be a brother at all. He had discovered part of the truth, exposing the deceptions he had grown up with only a handful of weeks ago. The pain that the knowledge was causing and the hurt inside him were spreading like a canker. But how did you uncover the invisible and discover the impossible?

Tiola's voice in his head shared his grief and understood his feelings of betrayal. ~ *I cannot answer your questions, my luvver. Your past is yours not mine, I am not able to reveal it. Only you can search for and find what you seek.* ~

Disgruntled at her refusal to help, he shoved himself from the wall and wandered along the dim-lit alleyway that reeked of pitch and smoke from the few sparsely placed torches set in the wall sconces, and of other more unsavoury smells that were best not identified. He kicked at a discarded gin bottle, shattering it with a tinkle of breaking glass against the far wall. Said aloud; "This has got to stop, Tiola. I never see you."

He neither heard nor saw the flicker of movement rushing from a darker, narrower alley to his left. Felt the crunch of a fist making contact with his belly and a boot connecting with his ribs as he sank to his knees, gasping for breath.

Sod it, he thought as he realised he could not fight against four men, two of whom were already pinning his arms behind his back with such force that he cried out. He closed his eyes, clenched his teeth and braced himself for what was to come.

Bugger, he thought again as another blow thudded into his side. *M'ribs still ain't bloody mended from the last drubbing I got.*

Two

There was nothing he could do except grit his teeth and take it. When the pressure on his arms eased and his captor released him, Jesamiah slumped forward face down waiting for the kicking or battering that he guessed would be coming next.

What he did not anticipate was the sound of running feet, an authoritative call of "What's goin' on 'ere?" More running feet as his assailants hoofed it, and then the close proximity of a woman's perfume.

A linen kerchief dabbed at the blood dribbling past his eye and down his cheek.

Fleetingly he hoped it was Tiola, but she never wore exotic perfume or expensive silk gowns that rustled as she moved. He opened one eye, squinted at the very pretty woman kneeling beside him.

"You 'appened t'be 'ere and the militia were fortuitously passin' by just in time eh, Alicia m'darlin'?" he croaked, the breath heavy in his aching belly. Added, "You'll get that fancy 'ankie all bloody, y'know. Ouch!"

She continued to dab. "Tch. You always were a baby, Jesamiah Acorne." She put her arms around his waist, helped him to his feet and guided him to a side door near the well-lit end of the alley. "You had better come to my lodgings: that cut needs tending."

Another fleeting thought. It would be better to return to the *Sea Witch* and wait for Tiola to patch him up. Shrugging the sensible thought aside, Jesamiah did not resist as the woman guided him up a flight of back stairs and ushered him into a front bedroom overlooking the late evening bustle and noise of King Street below.

The luxury and expense of the newly built King George Boarding House. The best in Nassau, the best in the entire Caribbean, or so the owner boasted. Jesamiah would not have expected Alicia Mereno, wife to his half-brother Phillipe, to be staying anywhere else. Except, Phillipe, as it turned out, was not a brother at all and Alicia was now a widow.

She sat him on the bed, poured water from the laver into the bowl on the washstand and searched for some linen she could use. Found an under-petticoat and tore it into strips, fetched a brown glass phial from a valise.

Jesamiah batted her hand away as she once again began probing at the cut above his right eye.

"Please Alicia, leave me alone. It will heal without you proddin' at it."

Alicia sniffed disdainfully and ignored him.

"What you doin"ere in Nassau?" Jesamiah winced as she persisted with her administrations, sucking air through his teeth with an indrawn hiss of stinging pain as she poured the tincture of seaweed into the cut. "For bugger's sake, leave it, woman!"

"What do you think I am doing here?" she retorted as she eased the cork stopper back into the bottle and tossed the bloodied linen into a corner by the door. "I came to discover why you had murdered my husband and left me destitute into the bargain."

Jesamiah grunted a bark of amusement as he flapped his left hand at the expensive room and then pointed at her fine gown. "You don't look in financial need, Madam, nor did I murder Phillipe. It was self-defence." Scowling he brushed at a dribble of the yellow-coloured tincture and insolently wiped his finger on the bed's white sheet, where it left a smeared stain. "The bastard you so fondly called husband had kidnapped and tortured me. Only fortune ensured the pistol he fired direct at my heart was not loaded." He grinned at her, lopsided, for his lip was sore. "I finished 'im off before 'e' ad chance to try again."

Leaning over him, her bosoms rounded and tempting beneath the tight fit of her bodice, Alicia inspected the wound, satisfying herself that the bleeding had stopped. They had known each other long before she had married Phillipe, in the days when she'd had a different upstairs bedroom in the more wretched surroundings of Port Royal's Love Lane. She had been good at her profession, but good had never paid as much as she craved. Rich husbands provided a better bargain and she had found herself two. The first had died of old age and a heart seizure, leaving her a rich widow. Phillipe Mereno had then swept her off her feet, married her and taken her to his tobacco plantation in Virginia. Where he promptly spent most of her fortune and what was left of his own.

She was just as pretty now as she had been when Jesamiah had bedded her as a whore, though. Prettier, for her figure had pleasantly filled out in all the right places. Whores starved, wives blossomed. And Jesamiah could never resist a pretty woman. He caught her wrist, slid his hand behind her neck and coaxed her to come close; put his lips on hers. A light kiss, intended as nothing more than a thank you, but ignoring the sting to his sore lip, he followed it almost immediately by one that was harder and more insistent.

Between the two kisses he murmured, "An' I very much doubt you're no more sorry t'see the end of 'im than I am." He pulled her onto his lap, picked at the lacing to expose those round, tempting ripe fruits that were craving to escape. "You set all this up, didn't you, darlin'?"

Alicia looked offended. "Set what up?"

"Those buggers in the tavern, the other lot in the alley?"

She was undoing the ties of his shirt. Trailing her fingers through the light covering of dark hair on his chest; murmured, "What buggers, what tavern? I have no idea what you are talking about."

So, denial about Teach's men. That Jesamiah could believe. But the other? She was up to something. The only way to find out what was to play along and see what happened. And as something else at this precise moment was all too clearly up, it seemed a bit of a pity to waste a given opportunity.

"If you really want to administer aid, darlin', I can think of a more effective way to dull the pain."

As he pushed her to the bed and rolled on top of her, Alicia smiled to herself. Jesamiah Acorne had always been so very predictable.

Three

The Past – 1683

In the place where he patiently waited, and watched with grief the son he had treated so wrong, the memories that in life he had set aside and tried to forget came back to him. They were tangled and confused at first, like trying to see through the grey of a morning sea mist that would not lift, or through an unfocussed telescope. But the more Charles St Croix remembered, the clearer he could see. The brighter and closer the images came.

St Croix had been his birth name, though he'd always known it was not the name of his father, for his mother had told him so. On reflection, he wished she had not, for his anger at the English lover who abandoned them, to whom she had referred but rarely and then only by the affectionate name of 'Magpie', had festered, disrupting his childhood. As a youth, when their paths had unexpectedly crossed, he had not known the man was his father. Only after his mother's death had he discovered the Magpie's true identity. But by then he no longer cared; had denied his birthright and later, taken another name for himself, the name of a friend. Mereno. Musing on this now, remembering it all, all the twists and turns of the past, the fog of regret and confusion slowly began to clear…

…The fighting was fierce, almost animal in its intensity, both sides desperate to win; to lose meant dishonour, for when you were fighting for your King, to die was preferable to giving up your honour. Honour was more important than life; or so the young captain of the English vessel, St Croix, had believed.

The deck beneath his feet was slippery with blood; the damage inflicted to ship and crew by three consecutive broadsides hurling grape shot and langrage had been horrendous. Then chain shot had brought down the rigging and main mast. The English were crippled. Finished.

Once the Spanish had come alongside and boarded – there had been no possibility of stopping them, too many of his crew were dead or wounded – it had seemed to be almost over. There were more Spanish than the English, and this, the waters of the Gulf of Mexico near Portobello, was their home territory; they knew the winds and the currents. But many of the English privateers had learnt their trade under the leadership of Henry Morgan, and none of them was prepared to surrender. Death or victory were the only options.

Now it was hand-to-hand, man pitched against man. St Croix knew this was his end. His right arm was broken, blood spilling from above his left eye partially blinded him. His energy was spent and he had nothing in reserve. He stood there on his gouged and splintered quarterdeck, a shattered cutlass in his hand, waiting for death. Did it matter if he died? He had no reason to live, nothing and no one to live for. His natural father had abandoned him to the stigma of illegitimacy, had not wanted to know him, or so he believed; his mother was dead – of a broken heart, some had said. A woman he had swived in England, Betsy, had cursed him for getting her with child. It had been years ago and he only eighteen, but the shame of her vindictive scorn and his guilt at abandoning her – like father like son – still tore into his soul. There had been no one to capture his heart; he had no one in this world to care for. And no one to care for him.

Perhaps, *he thought as he watched the man in front of him raise his sword for the final blow,* perhaps I will find peace, and someone to love, in the next world.

Better to die here, in a blaze of glory fighting for England than to lose his vessel and his honour to the Spanish.

His opponent, too, was tired. Grunting with effort the Spaniard began the downward arc that would end in St Croix's decapitation. But it was the Spaniard whose eyes widened in surprise as the lifeblood dribbled from his mouth; the Spaniard who toppled forward, dead.

Charles St Croix stared at the youth before him. Tall, thickset, only fifteen years old. His face handsome in a firm, rugged way. Black hair. Black eyes. The foremast jacks said he had a black heart too, for he was not well liked among the men: he was harsh on discipline and intolerant of fools. But he was a good sailor; he never shirked, never slacked, did his duty and did it well. Too well, maybe?

He came from Bristol. Some said he had killed his mother to obtain the money for his midshipman's commission. St Croix did not believe it. The circumstances of how the lad had come to be aboard a privateer vessel of His Majesty King Charles II's fleet were his own business. He would not remain midshipman long; promotion would fall easily to Edward Teach. If he lived long enough to achieve it.

The stiletto-blade dagger, driven deep, had pierced the Spaniard's heart. Teach, even at fifteen, knew how to kill. The Spaniards behind him faltered, began to drop their blades, to raise their hands in surrender. Without their captain there was no enthusiasm to fight. The Spanish did not share Captain St Croix's rigid code of honour, it seemed.

Teach bent forward, put his foot on his victim's back and retrieved the long, thin blade, the sound of its withdrawal making a sucking and squelching sound as it pulled free of the flesh. He wiped it on the man's soiled breeches. It was disrespectful. Not the action of an honourable gentleman – was any of this almighty mess respectful or honourable?

Charles nodded at the lad. "I owe you, Edward. Thank you."

Someone called out; "Do we take prisoners?"

Teach answered before St Croix could speak, his West Country accent strong and recognisable. "Nay quarter I b'lieve we sai'. We bain't t'give nay quarter aboar' this'n ship."

As Captain, St Croix could have countermanded the order, but that would have seemed weak, and Teach was right; there was no room aboard a ship for prisoners during a time of war. A quick death by sword, dagger or even the noose was preferable to being cast adrift or being marooned on an island with no food, water or shelter. But still, the murder of those who had surrendered sickened him.

Aye, his young midshipman had saved his life, for that he would grant a lieutenancy and be grateful. But Teach had no honour, he enjoyed killing, and for St Croix there was no pleasure in the bond. From the day the boy had come aboard he had recognised the lad for what and who he was. An evil bastard who should never have been born.

Four

Wednesday 2nd October

"Oh. Tiola. You're here." Jesamiah stooped beneath the low beam of the door lintel and stopped momentarily baffled, a step inside his great cabin. He removed his hat, coat, pistol and cutlass; hung them on their pegs.

Resorting to his usual flippant banter to mask the moment of discomfort, said with a laugh, "I was beginning to think you had decided to jump ship."

Tiola looked up from where she was kneeling beside a clothes trunk, pressing a gown into the already cramped space within. "If you want breakfast you will have to call for Finch. I ate an hour ago. There is some cold chicken left I believe. I doubt he'll re-light the stove and cook you something."

"I've already eaten," Jesamiah lied as he strolled to the table, opened the coffee pot lid, peered in and simultaneously felt its silver side. Stone cold. He poured a cup anyway. "When did you get back then?"

Tiola closed the lid of the trunk and began to buckle the straps. "About an hour after we spoke last night." She sounded calm, no hint of anger, but her words were crisp and succinct. Jesamiah knew her well. This was a lull in the wind before the storm broke.

"Oh," he said, frowning, puzzled, at the baggage. She had been here all night then. While he had been…Bugger! He lifted the pot, attempted a placating grin: "Coffee?"

"No thank you." The air was almost crackling with her in-held fury. She knew. Just how was beyond his comprehension, but then, when you had a witch for a fiancée and you spent the night making love to another woman, perhaps it was unwise to dwell on the details.

"I'm sorry, sweetheart." He shrugged; made a lame excuse, "I got detained."

Tiola went to the wall cupboard where she kept some particular medicines and salves, those that were expensive and hard to obtain; laudanum, quinine, mercury. Transferred them to a round leather valise that had compartments designed for the safe carrying of glass bottles and phials. Said nothing.

Jesamiah cleared his throat."Er? You goin' somewhere?"

"I am."

Puffing his cheeks he sat, sipped the cold, black coffee. It tasted revolting, Finch must have been making it last longer by adding ground rats' turds and dust again. He peered into the sugar bowl. Empty. He thought about calling for his steward. Thought better of it. Finch would be in as much of a strop as Tiola was – and she was about to erupt with all the force of that Roman volcano he had learnt about in his history lessons as a child. He was damned if he could remember what the darn thing had been called, now. He pondered a moment; Popocata…something or other. He stroked his fingers down his moustache; no, that was the Smoking Mountain of the ancient Aztecs in Mexico. Vesuvius! Ah, that was the one.

"So where would you be goin'?" He tried to keep his tone casual, to make it sound as if he was not much concerned.

"I have been asked to attend a confinement. The Governor's niece had a difficult time at her last birthing, he does not wish her to suffer so again."

That sounded ominous. Tiola would not be talking about Governor Rogers of Nassau for, as far as Jesamiah knew, his only family here in the Bahamas were his wife and unmarried children.

"Which governor would that be then?" Once again, no answer.

"You're packing quite a bit of dunnage; planning on being gone long?" When she did not reply, added, "Where would this governor's niece be then, eh? In England?" He forced a laugh. England was more than a good few weeks' sail away.

"North Carolina. Bath Town."

"What!" Jesamiah splattered coffee down his shirt and waistcoat. He dumped the cup on the table, spilling more on to the cloth. Finch would grumble for days about the resulting stain. "Bath Town? *Bath* Town!"

"*Ais*, Bath Town." Tiola shut the lid of the valise, looked around to see what else she should take with her.

"Are you out of your mind? No. Absolutely not. There is no way I will be permitting you to go there! No!"

In front of the mirror Tiola patted her raven's-wing-black hair, pushed a few pins more securely into place. Until a few months ago she had worn it loose, draped across her shoulders and down her back but since she had become a respectable wife to the Dutchman, Stefan van Overstratten – and recently, his widow – she had taken to wearing it piled in this neat, prim style. Jesamiah hated it; his fingers continuously itched to tweak at the pins and set it free from shackled confinement.

"I will be gone a while. She is not due yet." Tiola turned, smiled an irritating smile that held nothing of humour or sympathy. "I am sure you will not find cause to miss me."

She knew. Definitely knew. She was like a fuse, an innocent length of tarred cordage, benign until attached to a barrel of gunpowder and lit.

Beneath her apparent calm she was fizzing. Would blow at any moment.

Jesamiah Acorne, five feet ten, tanned, lean, muscular; dark-haired, dark-eyed. A respected seaman. Jesamiah Acorne, a pirate for ten years from the age of almost fifteen, an ex-pirate for less than two months. Quick to laugh, formidable when angry…aware he was up to his crotch in shite. And what did a man do when he knew he was in the wrong?

Losing his temper, he thumped his fist on the table then kicked the chair aside. More coffee spilt on to the cloth. "I said no – you are not going! I forbid it!"

"Do you indeed?" Tiola answered primly.

The door opened, Finch's squawked protest shrilled as a woman brushed past his vigorous attempt at barring her entrance. She raised an eyebrow as she glanced around at the light-oak panelling and the extreme elegance. The cabin was twenty-four feet by twelve, with only the space beneath the skylight high enough for Jesamiah to stand upright without a slight stoop. But with most of its furnishing – desk, cupboards, lockers that doubled as seating – fitted flush with the curved panels of the bulkheads, its five stern windows and the skylight, it was light, airy, and surprisingly spacious.

"So, this is the *Sea Witch*," she said, peering in at the neat side cabin that was Jesamiah and Tiola's bedroom. "Cosy, very cosy."

"Beg pardon, Sir, I couldn't stop 'er!"

"Thank you Finch, don't worry about it. You may go."

"Came aboard wiv'out askin'; swanned in 'ere as if she owns the bloody place."

"I said thank you, Finch."

"'T ain't proper."

Jesamiah glared at him.

Without acknowledging the woman's presence, Tiola swung a cloak around her shoulders and put on her bonnet, tying the ribbons beneath her chin. "If you would be so kind as to take these trunks, Finch, I would be grateful. They are to be sent over to the *Fortune of Virginia*, the Captain is expecting me."

Touching the shine of a forehead where the line of his thinning and grizzled hair was slowly receding, Finch piled the lighter two and the medication valise one atop the other and returned almost immediately for the third. Grumbling a few impolite remarks about the intruder as he shuffled past her, adding with an indelicate sniff, "The *Fortune* sails with the tide, Ma'am. Less than 'alf an 'our." He turned to his Captain, "If 'n your fancy piece wants coffee you can get it yer bleedin' self. I'm busy."

Jesamiah willed aside the red tinge that was threatening to blush into his cheeks. Fancy piece? Hell's grief, did the entire crew know where he had been last night?

For nearly a minute the two women glared in silence at each other.

Alicia stood aloof and patronising, Tiola, rigid with fury. How dare he invite his doxy aboard? How dare he!

Alicia broke the awkward silence. "Are you not to introduce us, Captain Acorne?"

Clearing his throat, Jesamiah indicated Tiola. "May I present my affianced, Mistress Tiola Oldstagh – Madam van Overstratten as was. Tiola. Mrs Phillipe Mereno, Alicia."

~ *I know perfectly well who she is. The whore you swived last night, you fuckster.* ~

The words slammed into Jesamiah's mind; he winced at the force of her anger – her hurt – hit him like a cannon ball. Tiola so rarely used impolite language.

Retaining her outward dignity, however, she dipped a slow and elegant curtsey. "Mistress Mereno."

Returning the formality, Alicia masked a flare of intense jealousy. She had heard this woman was comely – no, girl, not woman, for surely she was barely seventeen? And 'comely' was an understatement. Miss Oldstagh was a beauty. Beyond the two spots of red anger dimpled into her cheeks she was unflawed; perfect, apart from the lack of a rounded bosom, but even Alicia had to concede that as she was so petite, little more than a few finger-widths above five feet and as slender as a willow, full bosoms would have spoilt the faery image.

Her eyes were black and wide with long, thick, lashes. Not a hint of lead paint, cochineal rouge or coloured makeup anywhere on her face. Her bold stare, a direct challenge, had a fearless intensity that belied the apparent fragility. Alicia had the distinct impression that Tiola Oldstagh merely appeared to be the sapling willow, but was as indestructible as oak – and as potentially dangerous as yew.

Defiant, Alicia tipped her chin higher and fingered the gold crucifix dangling into her cleavage. Beneath this girl's piercing gaze she felt vulnerable and utterly exposed, as if she were standing, skirt and petticoats hauled up to the waist, lower half naked, waiting for the obligatory monthly examination by the pox-men. Even the experienced, tired old whores dreaded those intimate brothel inspections. Oh, she did not wish to go back to that kind of degrading, brutal life!

She forged a light, careless laugh and walked further into the cabin, and indicating permission, settled herself beside the table. "I have merely come on business," she explained. "Captain Acorne's unwarranted disposal of my husband has left me in somewhat of an altogether unacceptable position."

~ *What position be that?* ~ Tiola snapped into Jesamiah's head. ~ *Flat on her back, legs waving in the air as she screamed her ecstasy? Or did you thrust in from behind?* ~

He blanched. "Look," he protested, "I've known Alicia a long time, Tiola. This is not what you think." He patted the air with both hands, trying to dampen the sparks that were shooting, invisibly but none the less potently, from Tiola's eyes.

"I know what to think, Jesamiah Acorne." Tiola yanked his sapphire betrothal ring from her finger, tossed it to the table where it rolled and settled in front of Alicia. "I know full well what to think, and do not you dare lecture me contrariwise!"

A gust of wind swirled through the cabin and caught her cloak that rustled like bats' wings as, without a backward glance, Tiola swept out. Neither of the two remaining occupants noticing that the skylight and the stern windows were shut firm, that no wind could possibly have wafted in.

Jesamiah heard Tiola calling for Rue, his quartermaster and second in command. Through the windows a moment later, saw the gig heading for the *Fortune of Virginia*, Tiola in the stern, her back upright and towards the *Sea Witch*. She did not turn around. His heart was thumping, throat dry, and his stomach felt hollow, sickness in his guts. What in all the names of idiocy had he done? He'd had an itch and he'd scratched it; where was the harm in that? But women viewed it differently, he knew. How could he have been so utterly, totally, stupid?

~ *Tiola? I am sorry, love. So sorry.* ~

Silence. Jesamiah had never been able to initiate their private conversations, and even if he had, he was acutely aware that she was too angry to be answering him.

Five

Alicia Mereno smoothed the pink petticoat of her gown that was rouched and ruffled into delicate frills, the pleating held in place by tiny bunches of yellow roses, the colour exactly matching the over-gown. At the hem, a glimpse of lace from the under-petticoat, and protruding beneath, leather slippers and fine-knit stockings. Jesamiah knew full well those stockings would be held in place by yellow or pink ribbons halfway up her thighs.

Removing her bonnet Alicia lightly shook her head, evocatively jiggling the cascade of elaborate blonde ringlets. She had another ribbon laced into her hair. A blue one. Royal blue – Jesamiah blue.

What in the world had possessed him to give it to her last night as a keepsake? Had Tiola seen it?

Of course she bloody had!

"Your bruises are not troubling you this morning? I had no opportunity to enquire, leaving as you did before I awoke."

Jesamiah swung away from the windows and lifted his hands in exasperated surrender; "Very well, Madam, you have succeeded in embarrassing me and outraging my woman. What is it you want? Money? An apology for my killing your husband? I assure you neither will be forthcoming."

Again she smoothed her gown where it fitted trimly into her waist and across her stomach. "I could say I wanted to conceive your child, but as you have so eagerly obliged, I may already have done that."

Opening his mouth to protest Jesamiah firmly shut it again. With child? From the one bedding?

Seeing his doubt she fixed her gaze on his eyes, held their dark depth with her ice-blue. "Men have this misguided notion that they cannot father a child with but the one poke. A notion that suits them admirably in order to sidestep their lack of responsibility. The fault is always the next man's. Or the woman's carelessness." She inspected a broken nail, her forehead creasing into an annoyed frown. "You impregnated me before. The time you took me in my son's nursery. In Virginia; at la Sorenta. Do you recall? You were playing the part of a Spanish gentleman. The Spanish disguise was most convincing. You could never pass as a gentleman, however."

If the jibe was meant to sting it missed its target. Jesamiah recalled the event very well. The spending of lust with Alicia and the delight of cuckolding his brother in his own home had been a triumph at the time, but something had jogged Phillipe into recognising Jesamiah's true identity and the hatred between the two men had burst into the clash of a sword fight. Jesamiah had never discovered how Phillipe had seen through the disguise. Alicia, the bitch, had been about to betray him anyway, so cause was irrelevant.

"I should have run the bastard through there and then," Jesamiah said with a snarl. "You too. For some unfathomable reason my soft heart bade me spare the pair of you. I've hardened somewhat in the months between. If you expect me to believe I fathered a cuckoo on you, expect again, Madam. You enjoyed the encounter; you were and always will be a whore. You flutter your lashes at any fellow who can serve your purpose with loose buttons and a hard prick."

The bluster was to mask his doubt. How soon did a woman know she was carrying? Immediately? One month, two, three? He had never asked, never bothered to find out. Such things were women's matters, women's business.

Moving to sit on an upright chair, Alicia crossed her feet primly at the ankles, rested one elbow on the table and balanced her chin on thumb and finger. "Your daughter died soon after birth. I trust your seed is not weak, Jesamiah Acorne." She tossed a contemptuous glance at the bedchamber alcove, "From what I hear you and the Dutchman's widow have not been virgin-pure together, yet I do not see her belly swelling." She patted her flat stomach again. "The little one I may be nurturing in here as consequence of our liaison I will claim as Phillipe's, not yours. I need his son because I want la Sorenta."

Jesamiah laughed as he sat on the red cushions topping the lockers beneath the windows, his fingers curling into the blue shawl Tiola had left there. Her favourite. She would be sorry to have forgotten it. "A son? You already have two! One by your first husband and one of Phillipe's. I gave the child a gold coin as a christening gift, you will recall."

Alicia shook her head, dabbed at a genuine tear. "Yellow Fever took them both. Phillipe also nearly succumbed." Her sorrow changed rapidly to bitter venom. "He survived only for you to tip him overboard to drown."

Jesamiah shook his head, folded his arms. "Not so. I strangled him. With one o' those." He pointed at the blue ribbon in her hair. "They ain't just for prettyin', darlin'." He stood abruptly, walked to his desk that fitted neatly into the curved shape of the bulwarks, yanked open a small drawer and removed a pristine length of ribbon. Swiftly his fingers tied a killing knot at its centre and striding across the few yards between them he was suddenly behind her, had it looped around her elegant, ivory-pale neck. He crossed his elbows, wedging one into the other for purchase and with the ribbon ends clenched into his fists began to pull, the pressure on the silk squeezing against her windpipe.

Frantic, terrified, she clawed at the ribbon, panic storming through her; breath and spittle gurgling in her choking throat. As rapidly, he released her, opening his fists and throwing the garrotte aside. She collapsed onto her knees, hands clutching at her bruised throat, unable to speak, gasping air into her restricted lungs.

"You bastard!" were the first croaked words she managed.

"That's me," he said with a nod. "I'm the bastard, you're the bitch. We're even."

As she scrambled back onto her feet he turned away from her, bored with the charade. Watched as the *Fortune of Virginia* dropped canvas and began to glide with the tide towards the narrow channel between the sand bars that formed the entrance to Nassau harbour. Without a telescope he could not clearly see the figures scampering on deck, but he knew they were only crew hurrying about their business to get the ship under way. Tiola would not be there, looking back at him.

Swinging round he turned his attention to Alicia. "So what is it you want? You'd best tell me now and tell me quick for I have things to do – and playing Tom Fool to your self-indulgent games is not on the list."

"I told you; I want money. The law of inheritance is inconvenient. Without specific arrangement a woman cannot receive her husband's estates, they may go only to the nearest male relative. The plantation and all its assets have therefore passed to you. They should be mine. La Sorenta is my home. I want you to give it to me, or pay me suitable recompense."

Head tipping backwards, mouth open, Jesamiah roared with laughter.

Not understanding the jest, Alicia scowled. She did not like being mocked. Too many men had used, abused and humiliated her. And she needed money. Desperately.

"There are official papers waiting for you in Virginia. Your father's lawyer holds them in Williamsburg. He will legally cede the land to me when you sign them."

Sobering, Jesamiah wiped his left hand beneath his nose, displaying the tattooed letters of Tiola's name arrayed across his knuckles. "Let me get this right: you want me to come to Virginia to sign some bloody papers so you can get the estate – and no doubt immediately sell it?"

Her throat was aching, she could feel the uncomfortable bruising every time she swallowed, all the same she lifted her head high and stated, "Sell it. Yes."

Striding to the cabin door Jesamiah flung it wide; "I'll ask you politely t'leave m'ship." As often, when aboard or agitated, Jesamiah lapsed into a seaman's vernacular: "You 'ave the choice to do so under y'own sail or I'll 'ave Finch 'aul you off. I ain't p'tic'lar. You will not get one penny piece from me. Even do you put a noose roun' me neck and 'ang me, you will not get a penny."

Obstinate, she plumped herself down on the chair beside his desk. Folded her arms. "I will not leave here, Jesamiah. By right of marriage la Sorenta is mine. I want it."

Nostrils flaring, Jesamiah raised one hand and tapping each finger counted off a list of objections.

"One, I have no desire to sail to Virginia. Two, I cannot sail without approval granted by Governor Rogers' office. Three..." He paused. Three. He strolled to her side, put both hands on the chair arms and leant forward, his face close to hers. To her credit, she did not flinch away. He smelt of rum, wet hemp, tar and masculine sweat. He needed a shave: bristles sprawling above the black hairs of the short-trimmed beard that framed his jawline, were making his moustache ragged.

"Three," he repeated slowly. "Phillipe was never my brother. He was a bastard foisted on my father by the woman who spawned him. He has never had legal claim to that tobacco plantation." He paused, whispered, "And therefore, darlin', nor do you."

Alicia was a survivor. A Port Royal whore who had dragged herself from the gutter to become wife, and widow, to two men in succession. The husbands and children she could manage without. Her home, or more accurately, the wealth its sale would generate, she could not.

Clamping her nails into his wrist she removed one of his arms from the chair and with her other hand pushed him aside. "One," she retaliated as she stood up, "you will not be permitting your little bedmate to scamper around Bath Town unprotected because, as you are well aware, Bath Town is where Edward Teach has decided to anchor his flatulent backside. He does not treat women well and is attracted to a pretty-faced wench. For all I dislike her, if your doxie steps within range of his pizzle she will be used and dumped dead into the sea faster than you can get a hard cock. So you will be wanting to go after her. Two." She reached into the linen poke she had left with her bonnet, handed Jesamiah a folded and sealed parchment. "I took the liberty of asking Captain Jennings to write you a Letter of Marque. He was more than willing to grant it when I told him you were planning on going pirate hunting."

Before Jesamiah could protest that he had no intention of doing anything of the sort, she raised a hand for his silence. "Three. Among those papers concerning the estate and waiting in Williamsburg to be signed over to me, is a sealed letter from your father addressed to you. It reads: *'To be given to my son, Jesamiah Mereno, upon the death of Phillipe Mereno.'* Your birth name was Mereno, I therefore take it that this intriguing document is for you. I wonder if the contents have aught to do with that scandalous statement you have just made about Phillipe?"

"If it is for me," Jesamiah snapped irritably, "why did you not bring the damn thing with you?"

To his annoyance, despite thinking he did not want to have anything to do with this, he suddenly realised he desperately did want to know what was written in that letter. What his father had to say to him from beyond the grave. It had to be about Phillipe. Had to be.

Alicia walked to the door, her hips swaying provocatively, and paused a half pace over the threshold. "The letter is sealed and addressed to you. The lawyer would not give it to me. As for Phillipe, he was recognised by his father as his firstborn son. So whatever you claim, until you can prove otherwise, la Sorenta was legally his and therefore mine. Shall I have Finch bring my baggage in here, or have you another suitable cabin? I expect comfort on a sea voyage."

"You're not bloody sailing on this ship!"

She laughed coyly and sashayed back to him, sensuously kissed his mouth.

"Oh but I am. You are going to run like a lovesick boy after your black-eyed, black-haired mistress. And you want that letter as much as I want the estate."

Six

Tiola Oldstagh. A name chosen by herself, for rearranged it spelt *all that is good*. Created at the dawn of time with other entities of power, she was adept at hiding her feelings and at showing a bland mask of indifference to the world. She'd had eternity in which to practise.

Most of those of Power were gone, either forgotten and faded into non-existence or destroyed, for their abilities had not been so immense after all. A few remained, among them the Gods of Belief and Faith, their names used in wondrous variety, and the Old Ones of Wisdom – the Immortals of Light. Their purpose: to defend human life against the cruelties and hatreds of the Dark Power; to protect against the Malevolence that sought to destroy without qualm or pity.

Her ability of Craft enabled the full control of her body; she could govern every muscle, every nerve. The flow of blood, the pace of her heart and the breath in her lungs. She chose to repress her fertility, and although her present form was not immortal she could, in certain instances, cheat death. She was able to stand as still as stone for hours, or run for miles with the stamina of an ox and the speed of a gazelle. Had the strength of iron tempered by the delicacy of a cobweb. What was to be seen she could see, what was said, she heard. The wind obeyed her command and she could make the earth be stilled or quake. She had the Craft, a wisdom that bound and united the elements of nature – air, earth, fire and water. But not the salt seas. She had no jurisdiction over the ocean worlds where one of the few surviving Elementals from that early Time, Tethys, ruled with selfish indifference.

Tiola's inherited skills and wisdom had passed down through the alternate female generations, her limits were an inability to observe the future and to commit any action of intentional harm or hatred unless she was in mortal peril. There were few who possessed the old gifts of Craft now, for although the soul was immortal, the body was not, and too many of her sisters had failed to survive the predations of the Dark.

The Dark Power had always been strong and it so easily manipulated the frail and vulnerable human emotions of jealousy, hatred, spite and greed. So easily manipulated superstition and the fanatical beliefs of religion. All her sisters had died in the name of a God – along with the many innocents condemned wrongly as witches. Poor wretches who had no gift, beyond a knowledge of the healing herbs or of Sight, or were merely old, their only crime to live alone with a cat or a goat as a companion. So much suffering and misery caused by those corrupted by the unseen influence of the Dark.

Sitting in the lamp-lit gloom of a below-deck cabin, Tiola fought to repress her anger against that blonde-haired, blue-eyed cunny who had bewitched the man she loved. Bewitched him! *Ais*, yes! Did the Dark not empower its own witches and warlocks who lusted for the giving of pain and grief? Who sold their souls to the Dark for the promise of immortality? A false promise, for the negative energy of the Dark never fulfilled promises or set truth among the whispered lies.

She slammed her fists on the hard wooden cot, no more than a two-foot wide plank slung from ropes and covered by a thin mattress stuffed with straw. This was stupid jealousy, the green-eyed Malevolent which wormed into the heart, consuming to the core.

Alicia Mereno was nothing more than an ambitious woman who held the acquirement of material wealth as her ultimate goal. She was no Dark Witch. Her assets were her bosoms and the allure of the slit between her legs. To be sexually attractive was not the work of the Dark. The act of love when given with pleasure – or even indifference – was a natural thing. Rape, sexual violence and sadism, *ais*, that fed the Dark Energy, but Jesamiah took pride in his ability to make love. There was never anything brutal about his passionate couplings.

Smiling at the thought, at the memories, the rise of anger left Tiola. Jesamiah was a man who had a weakness for enjoying a woman's body. His attention to the ladies made no less of his love for her. Or did it? Was he already becoming tired of her? He had, when all was said and done, once admired Alicia. Even loved her?

One arm across her eyes Tiola lay back on the bed. Her deep love for a human ought not to have happened; she had control of her body, her existence, but not her soul's adoration for a damned pirate! That it was perhaps meant, that possibly her unity with Jesamiah Acorne was for some as yet unrevealed purpose may well be, but at this moment as the wind filled the sails of the *Fortune of Virginia* she could not give a bent penny for meanings, explanations or predictions. For the Good of All with Harm to None. The mantra of the Old Ones, the Immortals of Light. She loved him. Loved him with every fibre of her being. But did he love her? Had he ever loved her?

Oh this was nonsense! Less than two hours at sea and already the headache and the doubts were invading her senses and exaggerating her weaknesses, making her think foolish thoughts!

It was the sea causing it, she was sure, the mere presence of the sea. Tiola was a creature of the land, surrounded by salt water she was vulnerable to the pull of the tides that were draining her of energy and rational, sensible thinking. She had to learn how to master this debilitation! Had to!

But what if they were not so foolish? What if he wanted Alicia?

A solitary tear trailed down her cheek. Jesamiah did not understand that she had her duties to attend, that she was honour-bound to put others before herself. Her Craft, her knowledge and her wisdom, would all be for naught if she turned aside from what she was, a healer and a midwife, a Wise Woman of the Old Ones of Wisdom – a witch. To be nothing except Jesamiah's wife would be to give everything away. And she could not do that. Or could she?

Tiola felt so safe when she was with Jesamiah; safe and protected, for he was strong and brave. Invincible. Almost!

And she did so love him.

Seven

The cask only scraped the wall, barely touched it, but the wood burst open and foul, stinking water gushed out. The fourth cask to break.

"For fok sake!" Jesamiah yelled, looking up from the ship's list of required supplies and shoving the sheaf of papers into Rue's hands. He strode across the jetty to the open warehouse door. "Masters? You empty-bellied seaslug, these casks are as rotten as the water they hold. You've sold me shite!"

He stormed inside, took a flight of stairs three at a time and hurtled into the small office. Jonathan Masters, owner and merchant trader, sprang to his feet while fumbling at the desk drawer for a pistol. Jesamiah was faster. His own pistol was cocked and levelled straight between the merchant's eyes.

"You've been trying to cheat me, Masters. You've sold me scum water. And what state's the flour and pork in I wonder? Rancid and riddled with weevils and maggots? Let's go see, shall we?"

Roughly, Jesamiah grasped the man's coat collar and hauling him to the door kicked him, slithering and half falling down the stairs, deaf to Masters' cries of outraged protest.

"No cockroach merchant bilks me, savvy?" Manhandling him outside, Jesamiah thrust the spluttering man against the sea wall and holding him there, one hand gripped into his collar, the other digging the pistol between his ribs, called down to the men in the longboat.

"Jansy, Jasper; break open a couple of those casks. Mr Masters 'ere is insisting on inspectin' the quality of the contents. Wants t'make sure we're takin' fresh produce aboard."

A pause, a splintering of wood, then growls of outrage.

"Meat could practically walk into the 'old of its own accord, Cap'n," young Jasper, self-appointed cabin boy to Captain Acorne, announced with a snarl.

"Flour's rank too," the older man, Mr Janson, echoed. "I've seen better vittles dished out to slaves."

Kicking Masters in the back of his left knee, Jesamiah forced him down to the grubby cobbles. "The stores you showed me were in fine fettle; decided to switch good for bad, did you? Well I suggest you change things around again pronto, or for these last few minutes of your miserable life you'll be regrettin' crossin' me."

Letting go of him, Jesamiah marched back into the warehouse. Masters stood, brushed the grime off his breeches, and straightened his wig. He was a short, weedy little man with eyes like a weasel's. "You threaten me, Captain Acorne, and I'll have the militia on you! I don't stand no truck from you pirates! These are the barrels you approved, these are the barrels you'll be getting!"

From a few yards away, leaning against the trunk of a shading palm tree, Rue sniffed loudly. Exaggerating his French accent, Jesamiah's second-in-command tutted and shook his head. "It is not good to be annoying *le capitaine, Monsieur*. 'E does not threaten, 'e promises. And *le capitaine's* promises 'e always keeps."

Moments later Jesamiah reappeared at the doorway, backing out, unravelling a line of fuse. He laid it on the ground, stood with his pistol raised in one hand, the fingers of his other fiddling with the three blue ribbons threaded into his hair.

"You start shifting shipworthy provisions this instant, Masters, or you'll be 'avin' bugger all to ship in about two minutes." With a smile, Jesamiah tipped his three corner hat to the back of his head and shrugged. "Bugger all except smouldering timber and a pile of ash and rubble."

He squatted beside the fuse, clicked the hammer of his pistol and checked there was a resulting spark in the pan. "Not a good idea to store gunpowder along with other supplies, Mr Masters. Not a good idea at all."

"You, you scumbag! You bastard miscreant! You—"

Nathan Crocker – Nat – and the African, Isiah Roberts appeared on either side of Masters, linked arms with his. Nat, first mate, an ex-Royal Navy Lieutenant, lifted the money pouch from the merchant's coat pocket and tossed it, with a satisfying chink of coin, to Rue. Isiah felt into the man's inner pocket, removed the banker's draft.

"We'll be having this back, I reckon," Nat drawled while Isiah rested a dagger blade against Masters' throat.

Jesamiah held the end of the fuse to the spark. It sputtered and as he gently blew on the slight glow the fuse began to fizz. He set it on the ground, stepped backwards a pace and watched the hissing plume of smoke and array of sparks disappear slowly into the dim interior of the warehouse.

"I suggest all you slaves inside there get out now," Jesamiah called after it, "or start preparin' t'meet your maker."

They ran, shrieking and frightened: black men, women and children; a sprinkling of white convicts.

Masters squirmed but all he could do was watch in horror as Jesamiah Acorne stood, ambled a few paces, shoved his pistol through his belt and turning away from the now deserted warehouse, put his fingers in his ears.

Nat was counting. "Forty-four. Forty-five. Forty-six …"

"All right! All right! I agree! Put it out! Put it out!"

Nat continued counting. "Forty-eight…"

"Eh? Pardon? I didn't hear." Jesamiah cupped a hand around his ear.

"I said I agree. For God's sake put the fuse out, this warehouse and its contents is all I have! My entire wealth, my entire life! Please, put the fuse out!"

"I have your word you'll provision us with best quality at your own expense?"

"Forty-nine. Fifty."

"What? No! No, no I cannot afford to give my stock away!"

"Oh well then," Jesamiah put his fingers in his ears again.

"Fifty-three. Fifty-four."

"All right, I'll not charge you one whole quarter of our agreed price!"

"Half."

"Fifty-six."

"Half then. Please – the fuse!"

As if he was on a Sunday stroll, Jesamiah sauntered into the gloom of the warehouse.

"Fifty-seven. Fifty-eight, fifty-nine…" Nothing happened.

"Judged the fuse wrong, I reckon," Jansy muttered from where he was leaning on the gunwale of the longboat, then sent chewed tobacco spittle into the sea. "Never was a good judge of fuse length."

Jesamiah reappeared at the door, grinning. He walked up to Masters, shoving his face close to his, said, "Bang!"

Masters visibly jumped, then scuttled inside, not trusting that the burning fuse had been put out and removed.

Laughing, Jesamiah turned to his men, "The stuff I bought is at the back, lads. Take what's ours and get a move on. We've missed one bloody tide already."

He whistled to the slaves, beckoned them from where they were cowering behind walls and bales of hemp, sail, wool and cotton. "I promised them a shilling each for their co-operation and help with loadin'. Pay 'em when you've finished, will you, Isiah? Any wishin' t'sail with us will be welcome."

Jonathan Masters stood inside the door fists on hips, puzzled. The trail of burnt fuse covered about twenty feet and ended abruptly where Jesamiah had stamped on the flame. Beyond another two feet of unburnt fuse there was no more tarred cordage. No line of fuse snaked across the concrete floor towards the store of gunpowder, fifty feet away. Just the twenty feet of burnt fuse and the two more that were untouched. Twenty-two feet. Only twenty-two miserable feet. The bastard had never intended to blow the gunpowder! The bloody bastard!

Coming up behind him Rue laughed, slapped Masters hard between the shoulders. "Ah *Monsieur, Capitaine* Acorne 'e is not stupid, and 'e is good at the deception, *non*?"

Nat, organising a chain-line of slaves, added his laughter, "You don't think he would be so daft as to walk into a warehouse where barrels of gunpowder have a lit fuse attached to them, do you?" He broke off, shouted, "Aye – those barrels there, yes, those mate, they are the ones we should have." He leaned close to Masters. "Played you like a fiddle, eh?"

The laughter spread. Even the slaves grinned.

Jesamiah, clambering down the rusted and slime-slippery rungs of the iron ladder into a second, smaller boat, gave orders to cast off. He was not looking forward to this voyage, and with things already going wrong he had nagging misgivings lumping in the pit of his belly. Maybe the sooner they were out of Nassau the better.

"Cut the cackle up there!" he grumbled before he took his captain's place in the stern. "Put your energy into getting us loaded and under way."

Only later, after several fortifying glasses of brandy to calm his nerves, and after watching the *Sea Witch* haul her anchor and drop sail, did Masters realise that Acorne had not returned any of the money those degenerate knaves had removed from his pockets. They had not paid a penny-farthing piece for best provisions! Not a penny-farthing piece!

It was too late to make a fuss, the *Sea Witch* was slipping towards the sand bar. "You'll be back, Acorne," he cursed. "And when you are, by God I'll see you hang for this!"

Eight

Sunday 6th October – North Atlantic Ocean

The wind was freshening, blowing off the Carolina coast, and although the sun shone bright, a few lingering patches of early morning sea mist clung obstinately to the distant horizon.

Once clear of Nassau Jesamiah had spread as much canvas as he dared: courses, tops'ls, t'gallants and sprit'sl, all trimmed and set with the efficiency and speed he expected from his crew. Though they were running northward with the Gulf Stream current, the wind had been annoyingly capricious. They would have to wear ship again soon. Jesamiah eased the helm a point, watched with approval as the men met her and made the necessary adjustments to the sails.

Sea Witch felt alive beneath his firm, nursing hands, bucking and tossing as she skipped over the lively sea. The Atlantic rollers were breaking in quick succession against her bow, sending arcs of spray frothing over the bowsprit and foredeck. A trail of white, as straight as a cannon's bore, creamed behind. She was responding to his caresses like a mistress beneath a lover's touch, his skill as a seaman keeping her at the right edge of her best, gentling, coaxing her to perform like the duchess she was.

This was living. This made Jesamiah the man *he* was. The feel, sound and smell of the sea; the shrill of the wind as it whined through the rigging and bullied the sails into groaning billows; as it buffeted his face, tugged at his hair and blue ribbons. The exhilaration of his ship. The lift and roll and dip beneath his wide-planted feet as she sang to him, every fibre of her oak keel, every inch of her cordage and acre of canvas. Every single thing about her shouted a vibrancy of joy and life. And freedom. For this was freedom; to be at the helm of your own vessel with no man to give command or comment. To go where you pleased, how you pleased, at the mercy of nothing but the natural forces of wind and tide. That was freedom, total, euphoric, freedom.

His good mood faded the instant Alicia Mereno appeared on deck. She looked somewhat green about the gills as she lurched tentatively up the narrow companion way and stepped onto the quarterdeck. Clinging to the rail she made her way to where Jesamiah stood, apparently oblivious to her approach.

"Can't you stop this awful pitching? Slow down or something?"

Jesamiah continued to ignore her as she turned to face the sea and leaned over the side, retching. Nothing came up. After three days of seasickness, lying in Jesamiah's own bed convinced she was about to die, there was nothing left in her stomach to bring up.

Before they left harbour she had insisted on making use of his cabin. If she'd hoped he was going to share it with her she had soon been disappointed. Jesamiah had promptly ordered Finch to remove his personal belongings into Rue's cabin. Where Finch had put Rue's effects, Jesamiah did not much care. But then, Rue often spent more time below deck with the crew, unless he had a favourite woman in tow and required the extra pleasure of privacy. Despite the resulting grumbles, Jesamiah had also left Finch to see to Alicia's needs.

"You there, sailor. What be your name, boy?"

"Alexander Banks, Sir." The young lad who had finished swabbing the quarterdeck over to leeward touched his forelock in formal salute, "But I'm more generally called Sandy, on account of m'hair colour, Sir."

Jesamiah laughed. "Sandy Banks?"

Banks scowled. "Men seem t'think it be funny."

"Could've been worse." Jesamiah laughed again; "Sandy Bottom, Balls, Cock. There's half a dozen names more embarrassing."

There were several new crew, half a dozen from Masters' warehouse, two white Irish convicts transported to the Caribbean for the crime of poaching, and four black slaves. Taking their chance at sea had appealed more than the miserable life they were enduring as slaves. There were several women ensconced below deck too, but, as always, Jesamiah turned a blind eye and deaf ear to their presence, and to the cherub-faced molly boy who was prettier than all the whores put together. Sodomy was illegal, a hanging offence in the eyes of the law. Jesamiah had no respect for the hypocrisy of pious laws. The lad was of age and had come aboard of his own will. Which of the men were poking him was their business, not Jesamiah's.

As long as there were no disputes he was tolerant of what went on during leisure hours below deck, and made no censure about off-watch entertainments. The only rules were no excessive drunkenness, fighting or rowdy behaviour, and no gambling for money. The crew were to keep their weapons clean and ready for action and there was no smoking of pipes or cheroots on the lower decks. The whores – female or male – received their fair share of food, rum and ale, and were paid a set fee at the end of the voyage. In return, they earned their keep without bickering or squabbling.

A dozen other men had volunteered as crew, some were ex-pirates bored by sitting around with nothing to do; a few, like Nat Crocker and Alexander Banks, judging by his formal responses, were deserters from the Navy.

"Well then Sandy, I suggest you put the mop and bucket away and then coil down those lines correctly. I disapprove of a slovenly muddle on my quarterdeck. And stop calling me Sir. Cap'n'll do. I'm Captain because this is my ship, what I say goes; beyond that you are a free man. We divide any profit we make should we come across a Spaniard or Frenchie, and we pull our weight with the work. Savvy?"

"Aye Sir." The boy grinned, "I mean Cap'n." He set to with a will, although not until taking another lascivious look at Alicia who was now leaning against the mizzen stay, her eyes closed, one arm flung dramatically across her forehead.

Noticing, Jesamiah said nothing. When the boy stared again, commented, "Take the helm, Nat, will you? Another five minutes or so and we'll wear."

Nat Crocker also touched his forehead in acknowledgement. Old habits died hard.

Slipping off his coat, Jesamiah walked easily across the swaying deck and placed the garment around Alicia's shoulders.

She tried a wan smile. "So you do care about me?"

"Nope. But I do care about the effect you are having on my crew. I'll thank you to cover those apple dumplings more discreetly when coming on deck, if you please, Ma'am. Show your wares ashore as much as you like, but don't display them aboard my ship. Not unless you want to join the women below."

Affronted, she drew the coat closer. Her bosoms were her main asset. What was it the Bible said? Do not hide your light under a bushel?

"You've never objected before," she grumbled. "Not in bed, anyway."

About to answer that bed was somewhat different to his quarterdeck, Jesamiah's words were halted by a shout from the masthead.

"On deck. Sail ho!"

He tipped his head back, cupped his hands around his mouth, "Where away?"

"Three points, larb'd bow!"

Hurrying to the larboard rail, Jesamiah squinted over. Could see nothing except a blue sky with patchy clouds, a sea as blue, and the bright sun.

"I think it's 'er, Cap'n," Joseph Meadows' ethereal voice called again from aloft. "Sure looks like 'er set o' sail."

"How far? I can't see a bloody thing from down here."

Standing beside Jesamiah, Alicia was bemused. "Who? Who does he think she is?" Craning her neck she squinted up the hundred and fifty feet or so at the figure silhouetted against the sky.

Placing his hands on Alicia's shoulders, Jesamiah moved her firmly aside and strode to the binnacle box beside the wheel. He glanced at the compass bearing as he took up the telescope – the bring it close – and opening it to full length, returned to the rail. Cursing under his breath he scanned the ocean ahead; where was she? Ah! There! He had her!

"Aye, it's her," he announced. "Crammin' enough sail on, ain't they? Why're they in such a hurry?"

"Who? Tell me. What are you talking about?"

Staring steadfast through the glass, Jesamiah was studying the vessel miles ahead. Did not even hear Alicia. Frowned as he saw the ship's sails haul round. "She's veering towards the coast. Whatever for? We're well past Charleston."

"Who?" Alicia persisted, impatience riddling her tone. "What ship?"

Witheringly Jesamiah stared at her. "What d'you bloody think? The *Fortune of Virginia* of course. I'm tryin' t'catch up with my woman."

Alicia's face fell. She had not bargained on this. "But we are heading direct for Virginia, are we not? The Chesapeake?"

"Not yet we ain't. We catch up with the *Fortune* first, see my Tiola safely delivered to Bath Town, and then we go to Virginia." He chuckled, "Delivered for a delivery." He nudged her ribs, "Get it?"

Her answering smile was none too sweet; it took a great effort not to stamp her foot in obdurate frustration.

"On deck! There's another sail! Coming out that patch of mist!"

Jesamiah raised the telescope again, could see nothing.

"Wait…aye Cap'n, thought so. There's two of 'em runnin' in consort."

Not liking the sound of that, Jesamiah slammed the glass shut, thrust it through his belt and jumping down the ladder into the waist, grabbed hold of the mainmast shrouds and began to climb, aware his crew were watching him critically. The jests about the easy life of a captain had not escaped his attention; here was a chance to prove he was as fit and agile as any one of the swabs.

Refraining from taking the easy route through the lubbers' hole, he made the more difficult outward climb up the futtock shrouds, even though he was breathing hard. There were bound to be several wagers being laid on how far he would get without stopping. The men thought nothing of clambering from the lowest depth of the hold to the height of the main truck without pause.

Panting heavily he reached the masthead and settled himself to point the telescope at the blue sweep of the ocean.

"Not one word, Skylark," he growled when he had caught his breath. "I'm as fit as any of you."

Joseph Meadows had moved aside to allow his captain room, was sitting five feet away astride the yard. They called him 'Skylark' on account of his fine singing voice, his liking of spending hours alone on lookout, and his surname.

"M'lips are sealed, Cap'n."

"See you keep them that way."

The motion of the mast was swinging them in a corkscrew circle, forward, sideways and down; it took a while for Jesamiah to focus the glass, to find what he was looking for.

There was the *Fortune of Virginia*, and there about four miles to windward of her, well clear of the mist now, a sloop running with a smaller companion giving Chase. Jesamiah swore colourfully. He had been a pirate for ten years, had been in enough Chases to recognise the early stages of an attack. And the larger sloop was instantly recognisable. As distinctive as the oak leaf and acorn tattoo Jesamiah sported on the left side of his chest.

"The bugger!" he said with feeling, "The fokken bloody bugger!"

Hand over hand he slid quickly down the backstay, before his boots touched the deck was bellowing orders. "All hands! All hands on deck! Clear for action!"

Marching past Alicia, Jesamiah took control of the helm. "Sandy, stop your ditherin' with the running gear and escort the lady below. Give 'er to Finch and tell 'im to stow 'er somewhere safe."

Furious, Alicia shook the boy away as he took her arm. "I am not a keg of cargo to be manhandled. I am going nowhere unless you tell me what is going on here!"

"We're clearing for action, Ma'am." Polite, Sandy Banks gestured towards the ladder steps. "You'll be safer tucked down in the hold with the Cap'n's belongings when we start firing."

"Firing?" Alicia squeaked, turning back towards Jesamiah. "We are to fight?"

"Not if I can 'elp it," Jesamiah answered. "But I can't guarantee what that bugger Edward Teach, old Blackbeard 'imself, will do once 'e spots us."

She squeaked again, a sound nearer a scream, "But we could be killed!"

Jesamiah sniffed, wiped his nose with the cuff of his coat. Repeated, "Again, not if I can help it." He paused, added bluntly, "You'd best fetch her a pistol, Sandy. See it's loaded and primed."

"I will need no such thing. If you think I will be aiding you to fight in an act of piracy, think again Jesamiah Acorne!"

Jesamiah barely glanced at her, dispassionate. "It ain't for our benefit, Madam. If Teach gets the better of us you'll be wanting a quick death. As you said yourself, he ain't known for his nice treatment of the ladies. See the whores have weapons for the same purpose, Sandy. Even they don't deserve Blackbeard's brutality."

Banks nodded, proffered his arm again. "Ma'am? If you would care to accompany me?"

Men were spilling onto the deck from below, more than a few buttoning breeches or the loose-legged, knee length striped trousers most sailors preferred. Every man had his place: at the masts ready to haul the great sails or beside the guns, loosening the securing tackle on the wooden trucks; fetching shot, loading. Making ready. *Sea Witch* carried twenty-four cannon – Jesamiah had taken the opportunity these few idle weeks to increase her firepower, using as an excuse the fact that he had recently had a severe disagreement with the Spanish, with whom England had been embroiled in a short tit-for-tat war. Being half Spanish Jesamiah had briefly considered fighting on their side – as had several pirates, the English not being relied upon to keep a given word regarding amnesties and governor-granted pardons. In the end he had decided that the Spanish were even less reliable, and anyway, the disagreement had lasted for only the blink of an eye.

Eight guns a side on the lower gun deck, six on the open waist, three each to larb'd and starb'd; two seated in Jesamiah's cabin as stern chasers. And to complete the armoury, several swivel guns were placed fore and aft, the weaponry complemented by pistols, muskets and a quantity of grenados. The four boys, lads of between eleven and thirteen, were scurrying with buckets of sand to spread around the wheels of the gun trucks. There would be blood, there always was. Sand gave a foothold when the decks became slippery.

Sand, too, spread in a cramped area of the forward hold, safe below the water line where Mr Janson was setting out his surgical implements beside the table. He had served as loblolly boy for more years than he remembered, the title a traditional one for the surgeon's mate, even though he was mature in years. And even though they had no surgeon aboard. Not that it had made a difference when there had been. Jackson had always been too drunk to wield anything more than a bottle. Jansy had taken over as surgeon the day Jackson had been about to amputate the wrong leg from some poor wretch. A pity Miss Tiola was not here; her healing skills and dextrous hands would have been appreciated if the worst came to the worst. Still, Jansy did not quite hold with her insistence on cleanliness. What was the point of scrubbing instruments when they were going to get all bloody again? Though he had to admit she lost fewer wounded, but then, she had a woman's touch so that could be expected.

Throughout the ship echoed a general bustle of expectant but orderly noise, the thudding of running feet, energetic hammering accompanied by mild cursing. Jesamiah's great cabin had been altered in a matter of minutes; the bulkhead screens unbolted and removed, the stern windows folded up overhead, the glass panels of the skylight removed, to be stored in the hold along with the furniture, china plate and silverware.

Sea Witch, transformed from the elegant and immaculate mistress of the seas to a professional fighting ship. Deadly and accurate. The lark become the hawk.

On deck, awaiting orders, the hands at their stations beside masts and guns looked towards the quarterdeck, to Jesamiah. This was always the worst part, the catching up. And the waiting.

Nine

Port Royal – 1683

Watching his son and waiting for the Witch Woman to come again; to come and help him put right that which he had done wrong, Charles St Croix remembered…

He closed his telescope with a sharp 'clack' and leant on the starboard rail staring at the several ships resting at anchor in Port Royal Harbour. He had expected a warm welcome, had received a notable rebuttal. 'Come ashore and you will be arrested and hanged.' A fine welcome indeed!

The place was so different now to what it had been ten years past. The fortress rebuilt, the town doubled in size. The narrow streets appeared to be as filthy and stinking as ever, but they were busy with trade. Much of it legal, for all that most were inclined towards the vices of gambling, drink and women. The harbour was full – but not one of the ships that Charles St Croix had studied through his telescope, the bring it close, was a pirate vessel.

The various wars and sparring matches with Spain and France and Holland had ended. There was no more privateering, and no more piracy, at least not here in Jamaica under Captain Henry Morgan's administration.

St Croix spat disdainfully over the rail into the ebb tide gurgling past the hull of the ship. "Henry Morgan – beg pardon, Sir Henry Morgan, I forgot the King had knighted the rum-sodden old sot – was ever one to feather his own nest. He sits over there lording it as Lieutenant Governor, his fat rump planted on a gilded chair, while his drunken brain forgets the days when he sailed these waters as a pirate with his comrades."

"Do not permit him to hear you say that, my friend. Morgan insists he was a legal privateer. He sailed with the King's permission and did naught without it." The speaker, Carlos Mereno, also spat over the side. He was shorter in stature than his good friend St Croix, broader around the waist and across the shoulders, but where Mereno was dark-eyed and dark-haired, St Croix had inherited his mother's colouring. A tall, gaunt woman, long-nosed and olive-skinned, but her hair, the rich tone of spun honey and her eyes amber, like a cat's, had for all her plainness drawn men to her.

"Despite my breeding," Carlos Mereno smiled, "I have no love for Spain, yet the atrocities that man committed against my countrymen and women are beyond contempt."

St Croix shook his head. "Privateer? Pah! He is a pirate to the core, always has been." He had served with Morgan; had committed some of those atrocities. But then, the Spanish, or the French, or the Dutch, had been the cause of just as many.

Shrugging his shoulders Mereno sighed, a sound of resignation and regret. "Yet any man who steps ashore and makes mention of how he came about the gold in his pocket, or boasts of triumphs at sea, is named pirate and hanged."

"Aye, even when he learned all he knew from Morgan's own orders. It is a sad day when a great man, even if he be a fat-bellied, fart-arsed drunkard, forgets those of us who served with him for England's sake."

Mereno disagreed. "No, mi amigo, Morgan cared naught for England; he fought to gain for himself a fortune and to assure his name is remembered when he is nothing but worm fodder. He had not the same honour as do you and I."

Footsteps on the planking of the deck. Slow and measured, for the man making them, though still a youth, was heavy in build. The kudos of becoming Second Lieutenant had added weight to his bearing. Lieutenant Teach was now an officer and a man of importance, and he ensured all knew it.

"Be we t'go ashore?" he asked gruffly, the burr of his accent making him seem slow and ponderous, though St Croix knew him to have a sharp, quick intelligence. "Cap'n Morgan be a man of m'own heart an' thinkin', or so I b'lieve tell."

Charles St Croix did not look round. He regretted giving Teach the extra authority, for he was using it with malice and cruelty. The hope that perhaps a position of command would tame the fellow had been misplaced. He revelled in inflicting fear and pain on those who could not fight back.

"Aye, you are much like Morgan," Charles observed. "You care not who stumbles into your path. If someone – male, female, adult or child – stands in your way you crush them beneath your boot with no thought or compassion. Morgan would break a man's back to ensure a fast passage, and break a ship too, if it suited him. As will you."

Teach folded his arms, squinted into the evening sun, its blood-red reflection blazing upon the water. "There be always more crew, always another ship; bain't often a chance at treasure. Tha' way worked fer Morgan, it'd work fer me an' all."

Not looking at his second officer, St Croix remained staring across the harbour at Port Royal, said, "Morgan took what he wanted with pistol and blade. He thought nothing of starving a man to death or slicing open the belly of a woman, though she be great with child. 'Spanish turds,' he would say, 'they deserve to die.'" He looked at the darkening hills of Jamaica, the lights beginning to glimmer along the shore, in the town and from the ships. "I was a boy when first I sailed with Morgan. I once thought him a fine man."

"He still be a gurt man," Teach protested, "Looken where he be now! Knighted by tha King. No un'll forget his name I'd wager; 'til Trumpets sound he'll be 'membered. As'll I if'n it please God or tha Devil. As'll I."

The sun sank into the sea and the sky darkened.

"Who'll 'member thee, Cap'n St Croix?" Teach asked quietly into the night. "Who'll be carin' t' r'member thee?"

Aye, Morgan had been remembered. He had died with his body diseased with dropsy and his great belly bulging so far that his coat would not fasten around it. The rum he insisted on continuing to drink had drowned his innards and his sense. So desperate had he been for his name to pass forward, his will had made clear that his sole male kin, his nephew on his wife's side, could inherit only if he took the name of Morgan.

And where was he now, the legendary Captain Henry Morgan? He was beneath the sea, his grave gone, lost, and forgotten. There had come a great quake in Port Royal, the earth had split and crumbled, and the sea had swallowed much of the town whole. The destruction so complete they had rebuilt as Kingston, Jamaica, on the far side of the bay. Port Royal had become nothing more than a naval base. The sea goddess, Tethys, had claimed her own and Morgan was nothing more than a name from the past.

Charles St Croix sat alone beside the River, remembering.

What of Teach? Ah, even then, Teach had spoken as one who had traded his soul with the Devil.

Ten

Jesamiah's plan was to give chase, get in as close as he could, then send the two pirate ships scurrying for their lives. Simple. Except nothing concerning Edward Teach was ever simple.

Every pirate traded on a formidable conduct. To be feared was to be successful, it made sense to cultivate a strong reputation. Why fight if you could convince your victim to surrender with a minimum of resistance? Teach had adopted a fearsome identity, even down to his terrifying appearance and usage of the name Blackbeard. Despite his far from young age, in a fight he remained an awesome sight; tall, with a physique of limitless strength and endurance. He had no fear of death and thought himself invincible. There were few who doubted he had made a pact with the Devil.

Sea Witch had to tack twice, but she was a fast ship and whenever the variable wind shifted in her favour she ate up the sea miles as if she were a dolphin leaping through the white-capped surf.

"We'll tack again, Rue," Jesamiah said, "then one more should bring us in on a suitable course to intercept them."

Rue nodded, peering at the expanse of sail. He was not particularly happy with this venture. Blackbeard's reputation was feared by every man who sailed the Caribbean and American coast. A few minutes later, when the yards had been trundled round, the braces hauled and *Sea Witch* had settled comfortably on her new tack, he said, "You once told me you 'ad fought alongside Blackbeard. I did not know whether to believe you."

"Am I so poor to convince then?" Jesamiah chuckled, watching Nathan Crocker's final round of gun inspection; frowned as his first mate reprimanded the number four gun captain for not having his slow match made ready. There was a brief exchange of harsh words, Jesamiah waited, would intervene if necessary, but Nat had been a lieutenant aboard a Navy frigate. He knew his job, and was good at it. The gunner backed down, ambling away to fetch a match from the below deck store. It would be a while yet before the fight, but once engaged on a Chase Jesamiah never took chances.

"If you'd rather be demoted to deckhand, Crawford, I'm sure it can be arranged!" Nat shouted at the man. Crawford scowled, picked up his pace to a jogtrot. Jesamiah made a mental note to keep a weather eye on him. This was not the first time he had shown a lack of enthusiasm.

"I spent a week aboard a ship with Teach," Jesamiah confessed to Rue. "I was a few months off eighteen, m'head filled with pride at being made foretopman aboard the *Mermaid* under Captain Malachias Taylor. He was a good man, good sailor; what he didn't know about ships and the sea was not worth knowing. England was at war – another bickering waste of time squabble that fat Queen Anne had initiated with the damned Frenchies. I've no idea what it was about. We never asked the whys and wherefores of things in those days."

"As we still do not, *mon ami*," Rue chortled. "I'eard it that *les anglais* put the fracas down to a disagreement about the Spanish line of succession, *non*? Though the Colonies see it different and call it 'Queen Anne's War'. They say it was fought over who governed which territory and 'eld which fort. I'eard *les français* fought admirably against you English for what they considered their land."

Realising that he had been derogatory about the French, Jesamiah waved his hand dismissively. "Pah, you're Breton, Rue. I don't count you as a Frog."

"I am pleased to 'ear it."

"Since when have you been keen to hoist your colours for the French anyway?"

Rue adjusted the helm slightly, shifted his weight more squarely onto his widespread feet. Grinned. "I 'oist them for myself, *mon ami*. For myself and my comrades."

With his keen sight, Jesamiah measured the closing distance between the *Sea Witch* and the two rapidly nearing pirate vessels. "Talking of colours; Sandy, hoist mine if you will."

From the rail the African second mate, Isiah Roberts, rubbed at his nose. "You think that wise Captain? The *Fortune* will be mighty worried at seeing three of us in her wake."

"It's Teach I want to fool, Isiah. We need to get in close to show him the error of his ways. Have you any other suggestions for trying to convince him we are on his side?"

Isiah said nothing more, Sandy sent the black flag with the white leering skull and crossed bones to the top of the mizzenmast where it streamed, whipping and cracking, in arrogant menace.

"You were saying about Teach?"

"What? Oh aye." Jesamiah had been watching the bend of the sails and the distance the *Sea Witch* had travelled these last ten minutes, had forgotten Rue's question. "We teamed up with Benjamin Hornigold to prey on the French. Technically, we were all privateers then of course, all legal with Letters of Marque and the Queen's praises for her loyal subjects ringing in our ears. Changed her mind about us once we were of no more use. Teach was Hornigold's quartermaster. They'd lost several men in a skirmish so Malachias sent me over to help out. Said I'd learn a lot being under the command of a different captain and with a different crew. Teach was Navy once, did you know that? First Lieutenant."

Rue snorted disdain. "So, what did you learn?"

Jesamiah answered softly, confirming Rue's suspicion that his captain was also none too keen on what they were about to attempt. "For one thing, I learnt that Teach is insane."

"Even then?"

"Even then." Jesamiah took a deep breath, chased away the feeling of dread that was hanging like an undigested lump of stale bread in his belly. "To tell the truth I don't recall him having that great bush of a beard then. The notion of twining burning fuses into it came about after he captured that French slaver and renamed her *Queen Anne's Revenge*. He was a bloody fool to wreck her."

Rue and Isiah laughed outright. "If I recall," Rue said through the burbling chuckles reverberating round the quarterdeck, "that misfortune was directly down to you!"

Jesamiah fashioned a look of innocence. "Me?"

"*Oui. Vous.*"

Indignant, Jesamiah snorted and elbowed Rue away from the helm, taking the spokes himself in his strong hands. He could make *Sea Witch* sing like a siren and turn within her own length; could make her run faster than the wind, swoop like a bird of prey. Eager, like a lover willing to please she instantly obeyed his every whim.

"I didn't force him to chase us across those sandbars. Weren't my fault he didn't know the depth of the *Queen Anne's* keel were it?"

"You snatched an entire cargo of tobacco from under 'is nose then caused 'im to wreck 'is ship. 'E will never forgive you. You made a public fool of 'im."

The freshening wind caught the forecourse and sent *Sea Witch* momentarily skittering. Jesamiah's hands gentled her back to compliance and he rubbed surreptitiously at his sore ribs. Of the truth of Rue's statement he was only too aware. Gibbens and Red Rufus had very effectively jolted his memory.

He grinned. "So let's get on with this and convince him we are about to make amends for our misdemeanour, shall we?"

The waiting was over.

"Clew up! Clew up to fighting sail if you please gentlemen! Clew up!"

Eleven

Blackbeard's tactics would be to fire a couple of warning shots first, hoping the Chase would surrender without a fight. Usually they did. If not, he and his consort would disable the ship by firing chain shot, grape and langrage at the sails, masts and rigging, then, with the victim in disarray, swoop alongside and board. No anti-boarding nettings, half-hearted firing of pistols or muskets would keep out a shipload of pirates crazed with lust for the anticipation of specie, rum and women.

There would perhaps be a short, bloody, fight as Blackbeard's barbarians went aboard, but the capture would be over quickly and the captain and officers would pay dearly for their resistance. Passengers would be beaten, the women repeatedly raped. And some of the men. The pirates would lay alongside for as long as it took to transfer the acquired plunder, then be gone. Sometimes that took several days. If the passengers and any living crew were lucky – or unlucky depending on the devastation caused – they would be able to limp to the nearest port. Usually, Edward Teach preferred to set a trail of gunpowder and destroy everything. But then, most of his victims had no desire to stay alive anyway, not after providing the sort of entertainment Blackbeard and his crew enjoyed.

Jesamiah brought *Sea Witch* onto a course that would run her up between the two sloops. A mile away, assuming there were now three sea wolves on her stern, the *Fortune of Virginia* was panicking, her crew clumsily hauling the sails and almost missing stays. She was losing way and the pirates, intending to come up on either side of her, were rapidly gaining. Enough for Teach, ahead of his consort companion, to fire two warning shots from his bow chasers. Skilfully, Jesamiah overhauled the smaller, less efficient sloop, taking all her wind as he surged past to leave her floundering with sails aback, draped and dangling like wet laundry. She was a waterlogged, worm-riddled old tub, not even fit for firewood.

Most of her men, Jesamiah accurately assessed, were drunk. It would take them a while to sort themselves out again.

Spinning the wheel and shouting orders, Jesamiah sent *Sea Witch* leaping after Teach's *Adventure*. Several musket shots puffed from the *Fortune*. A foolish waste of powder and bullets, there could be no damage done at this distance. Why did they not defend themselves properly? Surely they had cannon? Surely?

~ *Tiola*? ~ Knowing it would be useless, Jesamiah tried calling her.

He had asked Isiah to take a good look with the telescope; no woman stood there. At least he had that to be thankful for. Like Alicia, Tiola should be safe in the hold.

Teach, hollering abuse, fired his larboard cannon at *Sea Witch* but he was too late and not accurate, for Jesamiah was cutting in across his bow, running in at a right angle. *Sea Witch* opened fire and raked a rolling broadside, hurling carnage straight along the *Adventure*'s deck from bow to stern as she swept past, leaving a wake of destruction to masts, sails and men.

The *Adventure* shuddered, almost paused, but bravely ran on, Teach swearing and cursing as his bowsprit barely missed *Sea Witch*'s stern. Only a few of his retaliatory shots slammed into her rails sending up shards of splinters, cleaving holes in the sails, causing rigging and shrouds to ping and snap. Most of the balls fell harmlessly into the sea.

Grinning wickedly, ignoring the noise and damage, Jesamiah removed his hat and gave an insolent salute. So close were the two vessels as Teach surged forward and past, Jesamiah could see the glare in the furious pirate's bulging eyes. Imagined he felt the ensuing projected spittle on his cheek. Jesamiah wiped it away. Sea spray. Only natural spindrift.

He had no need to load again. His first broadside had been from the starboard battery. His larboard guns were primed and ready, and he had no intention of giving Teach time to do anything except die. Teach had the same idea, but with a semi-drunken crew he was slow to reload and had lost valuable seconds deciding whether to go on after his original Prize or alter course and rid himself of this irritating flea biting at him. He decided to abandon the *Fortune of Virginia* and swat at the flea. He tacked, raggedly, his bellows cursing his slovenly crew with every crudity imaginable.

"Get this ship moving!" he roared. "Get after that whoreson bastard!"

Sea Witch was already fifty yards away, every delay aboard the *Adventure* taking her a further distance.

Had Teach also not been on the wrong side of sober, perhaps he might have wondered why Acorne was not yelling for all sail to be set, why the lowest sails were still clewed up, not tumbling in a roar and crack of canvas from the yards. Why *Sea Witch* was not running for her life. But he was not sober, was not sane, and unlike Jesamiah, did not have a disciplined, efficient crew.

"Hands to braces! Stand by headsail sheets!" As Jesamiah shouted, calm, in control, he put the helm down – hard, and the ship's bow fell away from the wind.

"I has 'im!" Teach's crow of victory sounded across the water as the *Adventure*'s yards eventually creaked around and she settled to run up on a parallel course."Tha bugger's done fer!"

Jesamiah grinned. Just as he had expected Teach to do."Back the fores'ls. Heave to!"

The men were anticipating the orders, Jesamiah had personally ensured each one knew what was intended and what to do. Within moments *Sea Witch* had come to a halt. Teach had not been expecting it. Had not considered that an adversary would stop suddenly and sit there waiting for him. But it was too late to wonder at the tactics for the *Adventure* was running up alongside with not more than twenty yards between the two vessels.

And Jesamiah was waiting. Waiting for the right moment. Not yet, not quite yet…

Teach was raging at his crew to reload, the guns had been fired. The *Sea Witch's* larboard battery was fresh, and ready.

Nearly…

"Nat!" Jesamiah shouted, "Get rid of his colours! Shoot his bloody ensign down!" He pointed at Blackbeard's flag, the gruesome skeleton of a devil spearing a heart."Make ready! On the up roll …Fire!"

Sea Witch's gunports belched a single broadside, all guns firing together. The *Adventure* shook visibly as each shot found a mark: railings shattered into deadly lengths of splintered wood, some one or two feet in length. The skeleton ensign was torn and shredded. The mast hung a moment, suspended, clinging by the quivering tendons of its stays and shrouds, then with a creaking groan and rigging popping like musket shots, it toppled in slow motion to wedge at a distorted angle, the dirty grey of the canvas falling like covering blankets over the decks and into the sea. Acting as an anchor it dragged the ship askew. Smoke loitered in a heavy, stinking pall. Too busy cheering, not a single man aboard the *Sea Witch* noticed their choking throats, stinging eyes and ringing ears.

Crippled, Teach's sloop slewed to a halt with not even a chance to fire another shot. Already the *Sea Witch* was under way again, manoeuvring, her captain intent on finishing off the second sloop.

The *Fortune of Virginia*, Jesamiah was glad to see, had taken full advantage of the distraction and was making her escape at a gallop. He well realised that unless he could think of a good excuse he would be a dead man if ever he and Teach were to come face to face. He ought to finish him off here and now, but not with that second sloop behind them. She would have to be dealt with first.

"Bring her round, Rue."

"*Allez!*" Rue paused to allow the men to scrabble into position; "Man the braces! Tops'l sheets! Tops'l clew lines! *Allez, allez; vite, vite*! We are not on some damned pleasure sail! Let go and'aul – another man on the mainbrace there!"

As the shadows of the mighty sails passed across the deck and the bustle below, Jesamiah put the helm down. Protesting, the rigging and canvas clattered, screeched and mithered.

"Meet her! Steady…let her fall off a point. *Oui*! Secure!"

At the helm, Jesamiah exchanged a grin of pleasure with his quartermaster. By Tethys, could *Sea Witch* turn!

The men were a good, loyal crew. They were comrades, family; brothers. Jesamiah shifted position slightly, glanced at the compass in the binnacle to check their course; his right hand was on a lower spoke of the wheel, the left cradling an upper one. Beneath his caress, *Sea Witch* was alive, her minute jerks and vibrations directly communicating to him as clearly as if she were talking, and he talked back through his coaxing fingers and palms, feeling her respond to his touch.

Now all they had to do was chase after that second sloop and finish it off – for the cowards had realised the superiority of Jesamiah's ship and ability and were scuttling away. For a moment, Jesamiah wondered whether to let her go, to stay here and see to Teach, but he had no doubt if he took his attention away the sloop would change her mind and come back. No, she had to be dealt with.

"Let go and haul!" Jesamiah called. "Set the lowers! We'll finish her and come back for Teach. He ain't goin' nowhere for a while yet!" And the clewed up mizzen, main and fore course sails tumbled from their yards, no longer needed to be kept out of the way to give a clear view along the deck, or be safe from the threat of spreading fire. Required, now, to take full advantage of the following wind and give speed and agility.

As the canvas tumbled, cracking and thundering, billowing outward like live beasts, *Sea Witch* leapt forward as if she was a hound unleashed from the slip, eager to be on the scent and racing after her quarry.

Twelve

Half aware there had been cannons fired, Tiola stirred in her sleep. She had taken laudanum – a single drop, for too much was almost as a poison to her. She wished only to sleep, to quell the churning that flared in her belly, not sink into a senseless stupor.

Who had been firing at them? Who had caused the panic among the men of the *Fortune of Virginia*? For there had been panic, even through the disorientating, muddled haze of her semi-consciousness she had registered that the crew were frightened. Pirates? She wondered as she battled to open her blurred eyes and willed her heavy body to lift itself, at least as far as a sitting position.

Jesamiah? The thought crawled into her sluggish mind. Was he close? She reached out with her hand as if feeling for the near proximity of the *Sea Witch*, but the nausea rose into her throat and she groped for the bucket beside her bed.

She lay back, her eyes closed, her head reeling around and around like a rushing whirlpool. Why, in the name of all sanity, would Jesamiah be attacking the *Fortune of Virginia*? The thought was ridiculous.

Seasickness? Being seasick was just as ridiculous. She did not get seasick. She could not get seasick. So why was she feeling nauseous? Why this distinct lack of equilibrium?

Tiola lay on her bed attempting to relax, and then tried to centre herself, to focus on her sense of balance, not only within herself but as a part of the Universe, as an Immortal of Light. After a while she gave up. She just did not have the energy to bother. Could that be it – the tidal pull of the sea was opposing her energy of Craft; as the moon pulls on the tides, so her Balance was being shifted? She needed to be on land to recharge her inner energy. In which case there was nothing she could do about it at this precise moment.

She willed the comfort of sleep to shroud her. With deliberation, set aside the more absurd notions that she could not explain.

Only her sleep was not comforting. She dreamt of Jesamiah. Jesamiah sprawled on a deck, blood-soaked. Jesamiah, dead.

Thirteen

Jesamiah kept his attention sharp on the sails as he listened to *Sea Witch* singing, aware of the rush and quivering undulations of water rolling beneath her keel, and pressing against the rudder.

"Cowards, making a run for it," Rue observed, tipping his chin in a pointing motion towards the sloop. "They are scum, fit only for the 'angman."

Even among pirates, there was no love for those who followed no code of honour. Who preferred to flee rather than fight.

"We'll catch 'em," Jesamiah answered. "Can't fail in our duty can we? I carry a Letter of Marque. It states I must clear the sea lanes of ne'er-do-wells, Frenchies and Spanish Dons." Carefully watching the inconsistencies of a wilful wind, of the fluttering along the edge of the main course, he adjusted the helm, brought it up a couple of spokes; the fluttering eased, disappeared.

Blackbeard's fleeing consort did not stand a chance against the *Sea Witch*, but the fools still led her a merry dance. She bowled along behind them for ten miles, Jesamiah deliberately holding back, herding them like a sheepdog drives the flock. Lulling them into hoping they could escape. Then suddenly he'd had enough of the game and swooping forward, overhauled them. They had to heave to and surrender. Sullen, awaiting their fate.

Going aboard, stepping down from the greater height of the *Sea Witch*'s varnished rails, Jesamiah made a cursory inspection of the smaller boat, but there was little of value to be plundered; a few kegs of rum, some salt pork. A pile of decent canvas hoarded in the sail locker, no doubt recently stolen from some poor wretch. Sea slugs such as these did not attack the French or Spanish, or ships with guns and weaponry. They went for coastal traders, small fry. And accumulated little of value to show for their trouble. Blackbeard himself attacked bigger fish, but as with all sharks, there were always the scavengers idling along behind.

There was also a pile of quality timber stacked aboard, suitable for replacing broken spars. Jesamiah ordered everything of value to be swung aboard *Sea Witch*.

If a vessel surrendered it was usual for the crew and passengers – beyond being lightened of their valuables – to be left alone, but Jesamiah had no intention of being soft-hearted with these scumbag miscreants.

He stood them in the waist while he mounted the narrow ladder to the quarterdeck. They huddled together, some too drunk to notice what was going on around them, others afraid, the majority grim-faced and resentful. He took his time to inspect the compass, which was poor quality, and to rummage through the stern locker where various flags and ensigns were crammed in jumbled disarray. His own were always neatly folded. Several, on close examination, were little more than moth-eaten rags, but a few would prove useful. A new English Jack, two Spanish colours and one French. He tossed them to Rue. Nothing else aboard was worth bothering with, for it was too dirty, valueless, broken or worn.

As if he had all the time in the world, he walked to the quarterdeck rail, leant his arms on it, scratched at his nose and tipped his hat to the back of his head. Surveyed the sour faces below him.

"Not much point in us boardin' you," he finally said using a sailor's lazy drawl. "All you're haulin' is a pile o' shite. Bit of a pathetic excuse fer pirates, ain't'ee?"

The pirates shuffled from foot to foot, glowering at the men of the *Sea Witch* and the barrels of primed and cocked pistols and muskets pointing directly at them.

"Can any one of you give me a fokken good reason why I shouldn't just sink this tub o' lard right'ere an' now? Send you all down to Jones's locker?"

More shuffling, a few coughs, some muttering. Several crude comments about Jesamiah shoving himself up a dark place.

"No?" He stood up straight, scratched at his right buttock, then his crotch, and ambled to the lee rail where *Sea Witch* dozed alongside. "Might as well put you all out o' yer misery then, eh?" He stepped up to the rail, grasped a halyard and prepared to swing himself to his own deck.

A voice cried out, desperate. "Sir! Cap'n Acorne Sir! I've a wife and bairns. Och, I did na' have nay wish t'be aboard a pirate. I beg thee, fer pity's sake t' grant a Scotsman mercy."

Pausing, Jesamiah studied his mainmast. That t'gallant shroud looked in need of attention. "How much are ye willin' t' pay me fer y'life then, Jock?"

The man fumbled eagerly inside his shirt. "I've a pouch of silver." Pushing his way through grumbling shipmates he held it towards Jesamiah. "I'll pay fer me life, Captain. I'll pay. Take me aboard y'fine ship an' I'll be o' service however thee may wish."

Slowly Jesamiah stepped down from the rail and descended the ladder into the waist. Walking towards the man he looked him up and down then held out his hand for the pouch, which he pocketed. "Any one else 'oldin' back on me with the specie?"

A hostile silence so thick it was solid.

Pushing his way through the crowd of ragged seamen, Jesamiah inspected each one closely, touched the occasional shoulder or nodded; "You. You. Aye an' you. You." Those chosen were shoved or kicked by his men to line up along the windward rail. Twelve in all.

"The rest of you, lower those boats and bugger off. The coast is that way." He jabbed a finger westward. With a generalscurrying, anxious-to-be-gone rush, the gig and longboat were swung out and lowered, men scrabbling down the hull cleats even before the vessels were secured.

"What about me?" the Scotsman protested, refusing to move. "You said you would have me as crew."

"I said nothing of the sort. You go in the boats."

"But —"

"But?" Jesamiah shoved his hands in his pockets, raised a single eyebrow.

Lamely the Scotsman indicated the selected men, "But you are taking those murderers and rapists, yet leavin' me t'm fate?"

Very slowly Jesamiah strolled up to him. Leant forward and whispered in his ear. The Scotsman blanched and scuttled after the others into the boats.

Isiah came up from below with Nat Crocker. Gave a single nod. "All set Captain."

"Very well. Let's get on with this and be gone."

Some of the men at the rail were grinning and nudging each other, tossing lewd gestures at their erstwhile companions as oars were shipped and they began to pull away. The coast was a long haul for those small boats; with no water, no food, only luck and skill would get them safe ashore. And this rabble possessed little of either. But they had the chance to survive, which was more than they usually gave their own victims who had failed to surrender.

The swaggering on deck came to an abrupt halt as Jesamiah's men produced twelve lengths of rope, each one fashioned with a noose at one end.

"What the —?"

Jesamiah smiled benignly. "As the man said, murderers and rapists. I know you, John Chatham, and you Horace Skelton. Tunny. Ralf White, Bones Bradford. Oséas da Silva. I know you all and what you've done. How many innocent lasses have you raped Cyril Munk? And you, Dan Pikesley, how many children, how many little boys, how many terrified, screaming little girls who hadn't even budded their tits did you bugger before slitting their bellies open?"

Pikesley returned the stare, eye to eye. "Enough t'satisfy m'need. Y'want t'try it Acorne. It's better'n swivin' a poxed harlot."

"You're filth. You are not even worth pissing on." Jesamiah turned away, disgusted, and stepped aboard the cleanliness of his beloved *Sea Witch*.

"Hang them," was all he said.

The twelve, with bound hands, kicked and struggled as the nooses tightened into the slow strangling death, their bodies evacuating piss, semen and faeces.

Those aboard the *Sea Witch* saw none of it, for they cast off and made way as soon as the twelfth man had been strung up.

In the solitude of his cabin, still cleared for action, Jesamiah sat on the wooden locker beneath the stern windows. There were no red velvet cushions and the paned windows were bolted up beneath the beams. It was cold with the wind streaming in. He gathered his coat tighter, called for Finch.

"We got any rum handy?"

"Aye. You be wantin' some then?"

"No. I was just enquiring. 'Course I do, you old faggot."

Any sour reply Finch was about to make was cut short by a sudden commotion a quarter of a mile behind. Fire and black smoke mushroomed against the blue sky as the fuses set and lit aboard the sloop ignited barrels of gunpowder.

Sipping at the tankard of rum that Finch brought him, Jesamiah wondered whether any of the twelve had still been alive when she blew. He disliked hanging people, it was a slow, evil death. But then, all of those bastards had been evil. Not one of them deserved to live, and he'd had no intention of allowing the ones cast adrift a chance to return to their vessel and sail after him. Not that they had the wits or savvy to do so. Their captain was the only one who could navigate, and he, Dan Pikesley, had danced a jig at the end of a rope. Jesamiah hoped there was a Hell, for Pikesley deserved to rot there for what he had done to innocent children

"What'll I do about 'er?" Finch asked. Jesamiah looked blank.

"'Er in the 'old. Mrs Mereno. She's screamin' blue murder down there. Do I let 'er out?"

Another sip of the rum. "Screamin' y'say?" Jesamiah scratched at his scalp. "Nah, maybe leave 'er there a while."

"Cap'n?" Nat Crocker ducked into the cabin, he was taller than Jesamiah, a good six feet two inches in height. "We're taking on water. One of those shots Blackbeard hit us with was lucky for him. Chippy wants to see you, urgent."

The pumps were going, Jesamiah could hear the steady thump, thump. He stood quite still for a moment his head cocked on one side, listening to and feeling *Sea Witch* move. She was sluggish, reluctant. Almost – almost – he could hear her whimper, like a wounded animal crawling away, wanting to find the solace of darkness to lick her wounds.

"How much water?" he asked, finishing the rum in one gulp.

"Couple of feet."

"Sod it, this puts paid to us hurrying back to finish Teach off. Stand the men down. We'll have to sort him out another day."

Going below to the hold Jesamiah stopped halfway down the ladder; raising his lantern he could see water slopping about. In the distance, where the hull curved inward towards the bow, the faint glow of a lantern glimmered. Voices.

"I reckon you'd best send someone to let Mrs Mereno out, Nat, 'else she's likely t'be swimmin." Grimacing, Jesamiah stepped into the black, cold water, the movement sending a drowned rat bobbing away.

He made his way along the carpenter's walk, the narrow space between the side of the ship and the tiers of stacked casks and barrels. He hated it, the darkness and the confined space. Several times he stopped, put his hand on the smooth wood of the inner hull, the unease of his ship giving him courage to move on, not turn back and run for the open space of the deck and the natural light of day. The life-rhythm movement beneath his sweating palm told him all he needed to know. *Sea Witch* was holed, she was wounded. If she were not helped, she would fill with water and sink. Would die. Every man, woman and boy aboard with her.

Near the bow the carpenter greeted him with a nod upwards that indicated the stream of water trickling down. "Damage to the hull just on the water line; each time we roll or a bigger wave hits us we ship more." As he spoke, *Sea Witch* rolled, and water gushed in. "I can patch it easy enough, but I'm concerned, look 'ere," he pointed with his knife then poked it into the wood – the blade sinking in for over an inch. He withdrew the knife and more water seeped into the dent to run in a single line downwards and disappear into the foul water slopping around their legs.

Jesamiah took the knife, probed again. "D'you reckon something's split? Backlash from the strike?"

"I reckon so. I'll be needin' a proper look. We're due a careen anyways."

Jesamiah grunted as he poked and pricked to either side of the seepage. Sound as a bell. They could not lay her up on a beach, empty her, send down the topmasts and give her a thorough overhaul just yet. For that, they had to be safe. Very safe. Careening within Blackbeard's territory was about as unsafe as you could get. Especially now that they had poked the hornets' nest with a very large stick.

"Would a few hours anchored in a river at low tide suit you?"

Chippy took the knife back, stored it safely in one of his leather apron's capacious pockets. "Possibly. For a temporary measure."

"Enough to get us to Virginia? My father's plantation has a graving dock, he insisted on maintaining his own vessels."

Chippy broke into a broad grin, "Couldn't be better Cap'n. Couldn't be better. But we'll be havin' t'do sommut about that hole and this crack first."

"Fother a sail?"

"Aye, I reckon. It'll get us to this 'ere river of yours, if 'n we sail steady an' don't meet no storms or stop another ruddy ball."

Curtly nodding, Jesamiah made his way back to the deck, calling for hands as he did so. "We're fothering – get a heavy sail thrummed and over the side."

The crew worked willingly and quickly, expertly pummelling coarse wool and hempen yarn into a mat-like surface then greasing and tarring it onto a spare sail. It took a while to heave the canvas over the side and pass it under the keel, to manoeuvre it into place and make all secure. If the water pressure did not force the tarred oakum into the openings and seal the leak, they would have to do it all over again with a second sail, and maybe a third. But the first held like a patched bandage. Would hold until they could make the quieter waters of the Pamlico River.

Sea Witch had been returned to normality; the removable bulkheads of Jesamiah's cabin bolted back into place, the square of carpet laid over the scratched wooden deck, his mahogany table set straight and laid with silver cutlery and china plate ready for dinner. The comfortable chairs were set in position, cushions plumped. In the galley, Finch had re-lit the cooking stove and the aroma of the captain's dinner, frying mutton chops and roasting potatoes, was wafting through the ship.

Tired, with dusk approaching, all Jesamiah wanted to do was seek the solitude of his cabin, have another rum, enjoy his meal and roll into bed. He had completely forgotten about Alicia.

"If you dare, if you just dare shut me in that filth and stink again, so help me Jesamiah Acorne, I'll geld you! There were rats down there. Rats running over my shoes, up my legs. Look at my stocking!" She hauled up her petticoats, showing a ruined pink stocking, "They locked me in, your bloody men locked me in with those rats –"

It had been a long day. Jesamiah walked to the cupboard where he kept the drink, selected two bottles of finest brandy, and with one in each hand headed out of the cabin. He would find somewhere quiet to sleep. If it had to be the hold, or up the mast, then so be it.

"I'll leave you on deck next time then," he snapped. "You can be the pleasure of a different sort of rat."

Fourteen

Monday 7th October – North Carolina

Tiola stepped ashore exhausted. Once the birthing was over she would have to find a way to deal with this debilitating problem of hers. A life at sea with Jesamiah while harbouring an inability to cross an ocean without losing her energy, awareness and concentration was ridiculous. Only in fairy tales were witches unable to cross water, and much of that belief was derived from the Christian Church's hideous witch trials. A woman, the poor souls were usually women, was accused of witchcraft and put on trial, often after various tortures to confess her crime. Water was the proof of guilt. If she floated she was a witch and was hanged or burnt. If she did not float, then she was no witch. But she was dead anyway. Drowned.

The fresh air, the solid ground, was reviving Tiola a little. She closed her eyes, attempted to centre her balance and equilibrium into the healing Earth. To shut her mind to the screams of the dead from the past.

The stupidity of the bigoted! The fear those men had harboured! Fear for their position, their wealth and status. Fear for their immortal souls because of a woman's touch or glance in case she might corrupt them more than they already were. Fears sown by the malevolence of the Dark.

Was there an element of truth in the superstition of witches and water, she wondered? Had she overlooked a small and insignificant morsel of her inherited knowledge? Was there something she had missed?

Oh what nonsense! This problem of crossing seas had not been so dire before she had known Jesamiah – had not bothered her for the countless thousands of years that her spirit had been in existence, dwelling in one body form or another. She stood on the jetty gazing down into the deep water of Bath Town Creek that ran into the larger Pamlico River, at the debris and scum that collected against the supporting pillars of the wooden landing stage. Gazed into the depth of water, her Sight wandering over the riverbed, the scatter of rocks and stones, the mud and sand, the creatures that lived there. The pull of the current, the influence of the distant sea fifty miles away.

At the edge of the jetty, Tiola felt herself being drawn in, coaxed down towards the murky depths, the twilight darkness of the water. Drawn, down, down...

"Mistress van Overstratten!" A hand grabbed her arm, pulled her from the edge, and Tiola gasped in alarm, surprise and relief.

"You were about to fall, Madam. Do you feel faint? My, but you are as white as a lily. Come, let me help you to the carriage. You must be hungry and exhausted."

"Why, yes, I –"

"Permit me to introduce myself – Nicholas Page, husband to Elizabeth-Anne, Governor Eden's niece. The lady you have come to tend. I cannot express how grateful we are for your agreeing to help us."

He was tall, about as tall as Jesamiah, but not as athletic and carried more flesh on his face and midriff. He was dressed well, with a white wig on his head beneath a jauntily feathered three-corner hat. Gloves, walking cane. A well-to-do family man in, Tiola judged, his late thirties.

She smiled into his eyes, received a genuine smile in return. She liked this Nicholas Page, who had sent all the way to Nassau for a midwife who, he had heard, had a special gift for the birthing of babies.

"I am well," she answered, realising the headache had lifted, and that the life-force strength of the Earth had returned into her. "I was but momentarily giddy. The adjustment from spending several days at sea to being once again on land."

Master Page offered his arm, directed her towards a waiting carriage. "In faith, I spew m'guts up stepping across a puddle. Why sailors profess to liking the ocean is beyond my comprehension." He settled her comfortable, spreading a blanket over her knees, pushing a cushion behind her back.

"I will see to your baggage." He turned to do so, swung around again, his clean-shaven face anxious. "Mistress van Overstratten. You will be able to help m'wife, will thee not? This is the fifth child she is to bear. She had some bad times. Two were dead before they took a living breath."

He broke off, hesitating to say more, then said all in a gabble, "The last was such a tiny, frail little thing. She survived but one hour; I held her so close and loved her so dearly for that one, short moment." The emotion choked his throat. "Girls, they have all been girls. We do so need a son. My wife insisted we try again, but I am so afeared that I may lose her. We have been told she carries a son. A peddler-woman read Elizabeth-Anne's palm. Do you believe in such things? Superstitious nonsense of course, but if it is a son, if it is..."

He looked at Tiola, appealing for her to understand. "Why is God so cruel? Why does He put a woman through so much and give only death at the end of it?"

What could Tiola answer when there was no answer to such a question?

"We do not know the why of these things, Master Page. Why do the rains not come or why does it flood? Why can the wind blow a ship safe to harbour or wreck it upon the rocks? Why does one child live, another die? It is the way of things and all we can do is keep love in our hearts and trust that we, in return, are loved."

He nodded, "Yes, yes of course you are right. Of course you are."

Tiola placed her hand over his. "Until I see your wife I will not know how fares mother and child, but you have my word I will do my best for both of them."

His smile broadened, spread again into the shine of his blue eyes. "And that is all I ask of you, Mistress van Overstratten."

"Please, use my midwifery name. As a baby-catcher I prefer to be called Mistress Oldstagh."

He nodded, trotted off to ensure her luggage was safely brought ashore.

Tiola stared out of the carriage window as a golden moon rose beyond the river, large and dominant against the rapidly darkening sky. An October moon. The Hunter's Moon.

But who, she wondered, suddenly fearful, were the hunters? And who the prey?

Fifteen

Wednesday 9th October

It took the *Sea Witch* a couple of days to reach Pamlico Sound, another half a day to wait for the tide to flood and take them safely across the sand bars and then longer than Jesamiah would have wished to sail the fifty miles up river. A wise man would have summoned a pilot to aid them; Jesamiah was wise, but not stupid. Edward Teach had influence, and for all Jesamiah knew the river pilots could be living in his gold-lined pocket. Or even if not, pilots had tongues that clacked as much as any idle housewife's. Weighing the risk of gossip against navigating the river, Jesamiah chose the river. He had been here before anyway, with Malachias Taylor and with his father. He could remember the shallows, the turgid currents. He never forgot a place he had sailed, and he had a sixth sense for those he had not.

The mouth of the Pamlico River was five miles wide, but even with the benefit of the incoming tide, the wind was, as ever, not in their favour so they had to tack and tack again, each change of direction and hauling of sails adding time to the voyage and strain to the seeping leak. And the shortening of Jesamiah's temper.

Sea Witch was not a small ship, but she was not designed to help a busy captain avoid an irritating passenger. In the end Jesamiah took his meals with the men, slept in a hammock alongside them and developed a fancy for the solitude of the maintop. At least there he could sit cross-legged, his back against the mast and read the fine poem Alexander Pope had written. *The Rape of the Lock*. He was enjoying it. Enjoying as much the excuse to be alone.

The height of the maintop also had the advantage of a good view.

Somewhere along here was a partially hidden creek where, when Jesamiah had been a boy, his father had anchored his sloop, *Acorn*.

Acorn. A noble and spirited little vessel that had turned in her own length and slid over shallows and sand bars as if she had no depth to her keel. *Acorn*. Promised to Jesamiah. Phillipe had set her ablaze the day they had buried their father. For that, for her destruction, Jesamiah had finally lost the suppressed temper and latent fear and had turned on Phillipe, beating him almost to a pulp. Fearing that he had killed him, Jesamiah had fled, found Taylor and become a pirate. He had taken his name from that sloop. Acorn; adding an 'e' for unique distinction.

But now secure the painted Vessel glides.
The sunbeams trembling on the floating Tydes,
While melting Musick steals upon the Sky
And soften'd Sounds along the Waters die.
Smooth flow the Waves the Zephyrs gently play
Belinda smil'd, and all the World was gay.

Jesamiah glanced down at the deck. Old Toby Turner's fiddle had lost a string and, out of tune, the sounds he was coaxing from it were more like a cat being strangled than music melting upon the sky.

Alicia – Belinda – taking a turn along the deck was probably not smiling, the wind was not gently playing, at least not from the right direction, and the world was not gay.

"Heigh-ho for the drama of poetry," he said, and stared again at the gloriously coloured mass of autumn trees edging the north bank of the river. He recognised the bend ahead. Was fairly certain the secluded tributary he wanted was not far beyond.

Father. His father.

It had been summer when they had come here. A long, hot summer of blissful days with endless blue skies. They had come, or so his father, Charles Mereno, had insisted, to make a courtesy visit to someone he knew in Bath Town. For the life of him, Jesamiah could not remember who that someone had been: a merchant was all he could recall, and one of wealth, for the house inside had been quite grand, the cook in the kitchen fat, jolly and happy to supply him with fresh-baked pie. The memories of a thirteen-year-old boy: the feeding of his stomach! Even had he been left to starve while Papa completed his secretive business, the trip would have been utter heaven. Phillipe had not accompanied them because he hated the sea and brought his guts up within the first mile. After trying it twice Papa had refused to take him again, for the boy had whined and moaned and bellyached. Jesamiah always paid a heavy price afterwards for the bliss and freedom, Phillipe taking his revenge on a brother several years his junior. But it had always been a price worth paying.

Surely Father had known? Surely he had been aware of the beatings, the tortures and degradations Jesamiah had endured at the hands of that bastard? Had he known and turned a blind eye? Why? Why? Jesamiah shut the book, leant his head back and closed his eyes.

Phillipe had always been sly and careful, the hurts had never been made in places that showed. Never to the face, always to belly, back and legs. Or inwardly, to the mind and the soul. And Jesamiah had never complained to his father or mother, for Father despised those who spilt tears, who whimpered and bleated. 'Be a man!' he had shouted at Phillipe as he had spewed over the side of the boat. 'Be a man; hide your discomfort! I cannot abide snivelling brats – perhaps I should toss you over the side now and be done with you!'

If only he had! Jesamiah had done it instead, all these years later. Resting his elbows on his knees, Jesamiah steepled his fingers and propped them against his bearded chin. The only comfort had been that Father had also despised Phillipe. That had puzzled Jesamiah as a boy. Hah, it puzzled him as much now! If he had so disliked Phillipe why had Papa tolerated him – why bring him into the house, treat him as a son – allow everyone to assume he was his son? In preference to his own real son.

~ *I had to, boy. I had no choice. It was a matter of honour.* ~

The words drifted into his brain. Where did they come from? Another thought. One that made Jesamiah bite his lip and frown deeper. What if he wasn't Charles Mereno's son either? There were so many lies here, so many tales to hide the truth. And no way of learning which was lie and which was not. Charles was his father, surely? He had disliked Phillipe; had rarely paid him much attention, always spoke gruffly, with impatience. Not that it had been of much help to Jesamiah. Mother, when once he had asked why Papa so hated Phillipe, had laughed and said he was talking nonsense. 'Your Papa loved Phillipe's Mama. Loved her dearly.'

His mother, aye. But not Phillipe. And not himself, not Jesamiah. One did not abandon a loved child to torture.

"Why did you not help me?" Jesamiah said aloud. "Why did you leave me to suffer?"

He cocked his head to one side, listening to the wind, the sound of the rigging, the creak of the ship. Heard nothing else.

Yet, now that he thought about it, Papa had paid attention to his younger son. He had employed governesses and tutors, for one thing. Had ensured Jesamiah had received a copious education – history, geography, literature; Latin, mathematics and even the sciences. And Jesamiah remembered that his father had personally taught him to sail, to tie knots, read a compass, navigate a course. To hold a sword, how to load and fire a pistol. To speak French. Oh aye, Malachias Taylor had taught him much more when he had gone aboard the *Mermaid*, but it had been Papa who had shown him the basic lessons. He must have shown Phillipe too, but if he had, Jesamiah had no recollection of it. For certain his half-brother had rarely attended the lessons in the sunlit schoolroom in the converted attic at the top of the house. Maybe that was why he had enjoyed them so; those Phillipe-free hours of pleasure.

Rue calling an order broke into his thoughts. The men ran to trim the sails. Jesamiah watched them, approving.

The men on that trip here to Bath Town all those years ago had been good too; quietly removing the *Acorn*'s illicit cargo under the light of a full moon and storing it, Jesamiah knew not where. All he had known was that by the next morning the *Acorn* lay somewhat lighter than when they had slipped silently into that narrow, hidden creek.

What had they smuggled? Jesamiah wondered as he studied the treeline.

~ Brandy. We smuggled best French brandy. ~

Jesamiah peered downward, expecting someone to be climbing up the rigging or creeping through the lubber's hole. No one. His frown increased. He was hearing voices now! Or were they just echoes of his own thoughts?

Was this other voice in his head something to do with Tiola? How could it be? This was a man's voice, a voice very much like his father's. Jesamiah shied away from thinking any deeper and concentrated on where he was sailing his ship.

There was the creek! An excellent place to hide *Sea Witch* and make stealthy repairs while her Captain paid a visiting call to Bath Town, five or so miles up river.

Slipping the book into his pocket Jesamiah took the quick way to the deck, down the backstay. Gave his orders, pleased with how his crew abandoned their apparent ease of lethargy and hopped to it.

Instead of dwelling on memories of the dead, of a father who had never much cared about him, he ought to be applying his mind to a very much alive black-bearded pirate. And a woman who had hair as black, but who was a damned sight prettier.

Sixteen

Tired, Tiola took early to her bed. She had been given a quiet, comfortable room at the side of the house overlooking the extensive gardens at Archbell Point. This was Governor Eden's grand house, the focal axis of his four-hundred acre plantation on the west side of Bath Creek. The gardens, like the house, were beautiful, clad in their russet, red and gold autumn finery. The owner, a proud peacock who placed little value on human life beyond how useful a man or woman could be. The place was maintained by black slaves and white household staff. From gardener to cook, to footman, to scullery maid all had their uses – and Governor Eden ensured all of them adequately earned their keep.

With no capital town yet established and no official buildings, Archbell Point served as the necessary administrative centre. The ground floor was devoted to offices, and a cramped council meeting chamber doubled as a court when necessary. North Carolina's neighbour, Virginia, was doing nicely for itself as a colony, but then, Williamsburg had not been attacked by rampaging natives three years ago, nor was its surrounding countryside a ruin of uncleared land that was wholly unsuitable for farming or settling. Governor Eden was determined to pull Bath Town and North Carolina from the mire, however, and he did not particularly care how he did it.

As with the previous two days, dinner in the dining room, which had a water stain on the ceiling and several serving dishes that were cracked, had been a gruelling affair. The Governor, Tiola had discovered, invited guests every evening. It amazed her that he managed to find so many obnoxious people, but then, as the only town in North Carolina, Bath Town attracted the sort of visitors who eventually made their way to Archbell Point.

This evening the women had been scornful and patronising towards her, while the men were overtly interested in the cut of her bodice and what lay beneath – which had contributed nothing to ease the mistrust of the women. Eden had been his usual pompous and dictatorial self. Tiola felt sorry for him. A man in his early forties trying to maintain an appearance of being in control while the walls of reality were crumbling into ruins around him.

He was a widower with no children of his own, and so he forged the resemblance of a united family by keeping his nephews, nieces and stepchildren under a rule of uncompromising authority. Only one among them would be inheriting the estate and one day soon, not soon enough for some of his family, he would have no further use of it beyond a burial plot in the churchyard.

With the exception of three of the family, Tiola cared not a rotten apple for any of them. Nicholas Page and his wife Elizabeth-Anne were pleasant people, though Nicholas fretted about the future and Elizabeth-Anne worried about everything. The stepdaughter, seventeen-year-old Perdita Galland, was a sweet girl.

"We need a son," Elizabeth-Anne had said with a sob in her throat as Tiola's gentle hands had explored the great swell of her heavily pregnant belly. "My uncle has stated over and again that he has no patience with girls, that if I am not fit enough to produce a son then I am not fit to live in this house." And the held-in tears had fallen down her flushed, hollowed cheeks. A sorrowful first meeting that had appalled Tiola and destroyed any chance of her developing respect for Governor Eden.

Tiola had not expressed her thoughts, but held her anger at the callousness of a bitter man firmly in check. She had merely smiled and assured her patient that the babe was kicking and healthy, and would be born when it was ready to be born.

"I so need to know I have a son! My dear husband frets over where we will go, what we will do if this is not a boy."

Drawing the curtains back and opening the windows to allow in the waft of the damp night air, Tiola reflected on the answer she had made. She never gave a woman cause to wonder that she might be somewhat different to other healers and midwives. Her technique – her insistence on cleanliness, her ability to take away some of the pain, she passed off as skills she had learnt in India and the Far East – in itself not an untruth, she just failed to mention that her knowledge had been gained over several incarnations through many centuries of time.

For Elizabeth-Anne Page she had made an exception. "You have a boy. A fine, healthy boy, and between us, when he is ready, we will bring him into the world."

Elizabeth-Anne Page had not asked how she knew it was so, all she had wanted to know was when that would be.

Tiola had smiled reassurance and answered; "Not yet, my dear. Not yet."

Breathing deep, Tiola filled all her senses with the heady night fragrances. Closed her eyes to savour the richness of the different smells. Wet grass and damp earth, a hint of frost in the air from the direction of the mountains. The trees, the river; the distant sea. A faint aroma of horses from the stables and the odour of humans, the slaves in their huts. Tomorrow she would go down there, see what she could do for the pregnant black women and for the men who needed the discreet intervention of her healing Craft. She did not like slavery, but it had always existed. Always would – another uncompassionate trait of the Dark Power that had infected the greed of human nature.

She wrapped her arms around herself, looked at the wide smile of the moon riding high in the black sky; could hear the giddy chatter of the stars as they swept by in their gay dance. Heard the whisper of the Universe, and the gentle rhythm of life itself, drumming its steady pulse-beat through the entirety of Existence. It was good to be alive. To be in love.

She moved away from the window, turned the lamp low so that it cast a dim, shadowed light and stood in the centre of the room, waiting.

He did not take long to climb the ivy, to wriggle over the balcony railings and step inside her bedroom.

"Brought you these," Jesamiah said, handing her a bedraggled bunch of wilting flowers. "I picked 'em some while ago. 'Ad t'wait fer the 'ouse 'old to settle didn't I?"

"I doubt water will revive the poor things," she said taking the peace offering and placing them in the jug on the washing stand, "but I suppose I should accept them graciously."

Pulling his boots off, not wanting to get mud on the floor, Jesamiah stood in stockinged feet on the square of expensive carpet. He spread his arms, inviting her towards him. "Sweetheart, I'm so sorry."

Making him wait a little longer, Tiola remained by the washstand, prodding the drooping blooms into some sort of tasteful arrangement.

"Did you make love to her again? Aboard the *Sea Witch*? In our bed?" She kept her back to him, not wanting to see his face, read his expression. She would know if he lied. Always knew when he lied.

"No," he answered, "and the thought of doing so never crossed my mind."

"I am glad to hear it."

"Though she spent all her hours scheming on how she could accomplish it."

Tiola turned, gazed at him standing there, his arms still spread, head cocked to one side.

"I spent most of the voyage up the main mast, reading Pope." He lowered his arms, unsure what to do next, anxious that she might not forgive him.

Spotting some bottles on a table he walked over to investigate; Spanish sherry, a cordial. Ah, brandy!

"When you were not firing your guns at the *Fortune of Virginia*, you mean."

He swivelled on his heel, bottle in hand, "Eh? We did not attack her. We were seeing Teach off!"

"That is not the way Captain Lofts saw it. He was a dinner guest, he informed Governor Eden, in front of us all, that the *Sea Witch* is a pirate in breach of amnesty. He wanted the Governor to send the Carolina guardship after you, but Eden was reluctant to do so."

Jesamiah laughed, "That's because a more notorious pirate than I controls the guardship, this entire river and the North Carolina coastline. Without Teach's say-so Eden does not even fart. And anyway, I think you'll find the guardship has a ruddy great hole in her keel. Eden has never bothered to ensure she was kept in good shape, but he would never let on to someone like Lofts that she's not seaworthy."

Shaking his head in dismissal, Jesamiah prised the cork from the bottle and drank deeply. "It's a simple misunderstanding. I'll sort it out when I reach Virginia." He grinned lasciviously. "When I've sorted out this other little matter of a misunderstanding?"

He put the bottle down, removed his hat, coat, cutlass, pistol and belts. Began to unbutton his waistcoat, untie the lacing of his shirt.

"I have a penance t'do I b'lieve."

Leaning against the wall, Tiola folded her arms. "And what makes you so sure I do not wish you to clean out pig pens or dance naked along Bath Town's main street as punishment?"

He grinned, moved towards her and pressing her body against the wall, encircled one arm around her waist and with the other began undoing the lacing of her bodice. "Because," he said as he kissed her, "I have a hard feeling you want me as much as I want you."

It was impossible for Tiola to stay angry with Jesamiah for she did so dearly love him. She threaded her arms around his neck, her slender body moulding into his strength, eager to kiss him back. Wanting him.

"Ma'am? Ma'am. Mrs Page wishes to ask you something. Will you come?" The knocking on the door was hesitant, but grew bolder. "Ma'am?"

"Don't answer," Jesamiah whispered into Tiola's ear. Gathering her tighter, more possessive, he brushed her cheek with his lips and nibbled at her neck below the curve of her jaw. "Pretend you are asleep."

She sighed, shook her head and pushed him away. "I cannot."

She re-laced her bodice, fetched up a wrap, called, "One moment! I am coming."

Disappointment flooded Jesamiah's face. He felt his erection subside, the twist of pain at her dismissal. "You always go to them," he said, dejected "You always put them before me."

At the door, her hand on the latch, Tiola paused to look at him. "Would you remain with me if you knew the *Sea Witch* was foundering or struggling to survive a gale? Would you not leave me in our bed and run to the helm to do what you could? And when the danger was passed, would you not return, knowing I would be there, waiting?"

He closed his eyes, defeated. Nodded.

Quickly she ran across the room and kissed his lips, a lingering, loving kiss. "Then wait in our bed, for I will not be long. The lady I have come to tend is not ready to birth her babe yet, this is a mere worry on her part. It is nothing. I promise you, I will not be long."

She whisked away, was gone.

When she returned twenty minutes later she found him sprawled naked across the bed, face down, asleep. He had such a beautiful body. His buttocks and thighs white against the brown skin of his torso, his arms and neck tanned a darker shade. His hair flopped forward to cover his face, one arm cuddling a pillow as if it were his lover.

Only his back marred the beauty, for it was crossed with the stripes of barely-healed scars. A flogging he had taken to protect her. One, near his shoulder, still had the faint yellow hue of bruising.

There was other bruising too, black and angry along his ribs. He was a rough man living a rough life. She wished he did not, but then, if he was different he would not be Jesamiah.

She removed her clothes, leaving them rumpled on the floor where they fell, and straddled his legs, her hands sliding gently up his spine and over his shoulders.

He murmured, made to move, then lay still. "Do that again, that was nice."

She complied, pressing harder with her fingers, moving down his back, over his buttocks, across his thighs.

"You going to stay here long enough for me to make love to you?" he said, into the pillow.

"I am."

Silence as she eased her fingers to the inside of his thighs and worked upwards.

"Good. I'd have to go find a serving maid to accommodate me if not."

"I be all the maid thee need, *zur*."

Jesamiah laughed, rolled over onto his back and caught Tiola in his arms, wrapped his legs around her, exhilarating in the delicious feel of her cool, smooth skin pressing against his.

"Then sit yourself astride me, wench, and do what you will to pleasure me."

Seventeen

Thursday 10th October

There was a distinct chill in the air in the quiet hour before dawn. Jesamiah stood under the trees, his hands tucked beneath his armpits, staring across the dew-wet lawn at the balcony and window from where he had just climbed, leaving Tiola asleep, her body curled, contented, hair tousled. A smile on her face. He had not woken her but had dressed quietly, placed one of the less wilted flowers in the dent of the pillow where his head had been, and left her.

"I'll come for you when you are ready," he had said as he had felt the shudders of ecstasy coursing through him, and had grinned as she had cheekily answered, "I am ready now, and you are about to come."

"That's not what I meant," he had repeated later, after she had crept down to the kitchens and stolen him some food; after they had sat in bed, naked, together, devouring the spoils and leaving crumbs on the sheets. "When you are finished here I'll fetch you." And had added, suddenly doubtful; "If you want me to?"

He smiled up at the blank darkness of the glazed window. "Of course I do," she had assured him.

"I want to know about my father," was the other thing he had said. "I want to know why he did nothing to stop Phillipe. Why he allowed a boy – a man, he was all those years older than me – to do what he did. I thought Phillipe was my elder half-brother, and I thought he did those things because being the elder somehow gave him the right. But he had no right. He was not my brother. He was not my father's son."

"Leave it,"Tiola had urged him, her palm on his chest. "They are gone, it is done. Leave it."

He puffed air through his cheeks, his breath visible in the coldness. If only he could. If only he could!

He was fiddling with his right earlobe, realised suddenly that the hoop of his gold earring was loose, that the attached acorn charm was not there. He cursed as he fastened the hoop, hoped the acorn had fallen off in Tiola's bed. That she would find it, keep it safe.

Lost in thought, he did not hear the whispered breath at his back until it was too late.

"Move a muscle an' thee be dead, bastard."

Jesamiah froze, willed himself to keep still as the pistol barrel pressed into his right temple. He forgot all about his earring as he heard the double click of the hammer. Prayed that his voice would not betray the fear thudding through him as he responded as nonchalantly as he could; "Hello Teach; you really have to learn how to move quieter if you want to creep up on people."

It was a lie, he had not heard a sound, but Edward Teach, Blackbeard, would not be knowing that.

"What be thee doin"ere, Acorne, skulkin' aroun'? Gotten thy eye on tha Guv'nor's silver, hast thee?"

Slowly Jesamiah lowered his hands to his waist and felt surreptitiously for the slender blade concealed inside the facing of his coat. "I would wager I've been doing the same as you. Taking my pleasure with one of the ladies of the house."

"Tha Guv'nor bain't be pleased to be hearing tha'."

"The Governor ain't goin' t'be 'earin' of it, is 'e?"

"No"til 'er belly swells."

"When that happens, Teach, I'll be long gone. Or I could put the blame on your nocturnal activities."

The bigger, older man snorted, pushed the pistol harder against Jesamiah's head. "Thee tried t'kill me. Thee crippled my sloop an' made a gurt fool out o' me in fron' of my men. Give me a reason why I shoul'nay shoot thee 'ere an' now. An' make it quick, I'm in no mood fer parlour games."

With his left hand, Jesamiah eased the weapon aside. "You fire that an' you'll wake the entire household. You'll probably think of an excuse to explain why you're standing over a dead body, but saying why you are here, in the dark, an hour before dawn will be more difficult. Add to that, you owe me. Seeing as how you reckon I owe you, that makes us quits."

Teach snorted again, but he uncocked the pistol, lowered it. "An' just how doos thee fathom tha'n? Thee lost me my ship. She were'n a fine vessel, tha *Queen Anne's Revenge*."

"I didn't lose her. You were pissed out of your skull and you sailed her over a sandbar. You wrecked her, not me."

A snarl began to pucker Teach's lips. "An' what of my sloop? *Adventure*? Thee nigh on scuppered 'er an' all, thee bastard."

Slipping the knife into his sleeve, from where he could retrieve it in a hurry should he need to do so, Jesamiah tipped his hat back slightly. "Actually, for some fokken stupid reason I saved your life, mate."

"Fuckin' tripe, thee bilge rat!" Raising the pistol Teach reversed it suddenly and brought the butt down hard into the curve where Jesamiah's neck met his right shoulder. Jesamiah cried out and slumped to his knees.

Willpower and gritted teeth made him ignore the agony shooting down his arm and stabbing up into his brain. He held his breath to ride it out.

A couple of deeper breaths and he forced himself to his feet. Halfway up he moved quickly. Stepping forward he thrust the blade up and under Teach's waistcoat, pushed it against the lower ribs.

"You even think of blinking and it'll be in to the hilt."

"Thee casn't kill me Acorne, nay un can. I'as made a pact with tha Devil."

"I'm willin' t'put that claim to the test." Jesamiah was very close to Teach, his face almost in his; the smell of bad breath and body odour was nauseating, even with the general stench of uncleanliness a familiarity. Through the concealing bush of his beard ulcerous sores were spotted around Teach's mouth and nose, a few blackened teeth were loose in his gums.

"I could kill you," Jesamiah said, taking half a step backwards, but not removing the dagger. "Send you to the Devil to find out if he lied. Or are you goin' t'throw the pistol into that flower bed over there and talk to me like a civilised gentleman?"

"Thee bain't got tha guts t'kill me, worm."

"Ah, but I have. Only, the price on your 'ead ain't 'igh enough yet. Give it another month an' you'll be worth killin'. Now, do you want to know why I stopped you attacking the *Fortune of Virginia* or not?"

Teach growled, tossed the pistol away.

Jesamiah removed the dagger, but kept it in plain sight. "She sailed from Nassau, where she had been commissioned by Woodes Rogers who, as you know, is a bosom pal of Virginia's Governor. The pair of 'em 'ave got bees buzzing in their bonnets about pirates who ain't sworn an oath of amnesty. Are you listenin' to me, Teach? They've got it into their 'eads t'be rid of scummers like you."

"I be list'nin'."

"You were going to attack the *Fortune of Virginia* – you see, Blackbeard me old mate, you're too fokken greedy. What had you assumed? That she was laden with rum; molasses; passengers? Slaves maybe?" Jesamiah shook his head, tried to ignore the throbbing ache in his shoulder. "You'd got it wrong. She was packed to the gunnels with armed militia. Her orders were t'draw you in, wait fer you to board. Then finish you off. Savvy?"

"An' thee," Teach sneered, "out o' tha goodness of thy putrid heart decided t'save me? Pull tha other leg, it has a bell tied to it!"

"I decided to warn you 'cause I figured if I did you a favour you'd stop sendin' your bloody men to spoil me pleasant evenings with a bottle and a blonde." Jesamiah slipped the dagger into his pocket, spread his hands. "I ain't got no quarrel with you, Teach, and I don't p'ticlarly like the way these bastard governors are tryin' to run us out of the Caribbean. This is our patch. Let 'em bugger off if they don't like the way we do things." He folded his arms. "I came here specifically to warn you, but if you don't want to listen,

I'll not waste m'breath."

Blackbeard grunted, nodded, fell for it. Every untruthful word. He put his arm around Jesamiah's shoulder and steered him away from the house, heading through the boundary trees to walk up-creek along a gravel path of crushed ballast that crunched beneath their feet. Began boasting how he had made the girl he'd been poking scream with delirious pleasure. "Left she crumpled in a heap sobbin' an' wantin' more. She'm nait been drubbed like that afore. Takes a man to show as how it be done prop'ly."

"Indeed it does," Jesamiah responded, wondering who the unfortunate victim was, then wondering if it was true. He could not see any woman willingly bedding with this odious man. And Teach could not have been ashore long. They must have taken a good while to limp home, and there was fresh tar on Teach's hand, Jesamiah noticed, while his boots were mud-caked. Come to see Governor Eden perhaps? To arrange the secret offloading of cargo?

Stopping at the bank beside a wooden jetty, Teach indicated a bumboat, four men were huddled together in the stern, snoring.

"I be goin' home to me bade, Acorne. I live'n o'er to there," he pointed in a vague direction across the creek, "at Plum Point. I be wantin' thee to row back tha way thee came, an return to thy little ship an' get off m'river. If 'n I catch thee here again I'll string thee up from thy own yardarm by thy balls. Be thee understan'in' me?"

Jesamiah touched his hat, turned on his heel. "Aye Cap'n." He walked away, heard the sound of a hand slapping against faces to wake up sleeping men. Heard grunts and grumbles and then the splash of oars.

Sweat trickled down his spine. That had been close. Thank God for his ability to think quickly and lie convincingly!

Peering over his shoulder, Jesamiah saw Teach's men rowing across the creek, Teach standing in the stern, one arm outstretched. Saw a flash, heard a loud bang and remembered belatedly that Teach always carried more than one pistol.

Felt the impact of a lead ball slam into his right shoulder. As he crumpled to the ground, heard a man laugh, then shout. "Nay'un tries t'better me Acorne! Nay'un!"

Eighteen

When had it all gone bad? The apple turned sour, the meat rancid? Charles St Croix, sitting beside the River of Eternity with only the stars to hear his troubled thoughts, set his chin on his indrawn knees.

War was always a bloody and brutal business, but there was profit in it, the gain of a prize and its reward for a privateer – piracy made legal. But they had not been privateers, nor pirates. They had become legal merchantmen, he and Carlos Mereno. Well, legal in part. They purchased goods at a low rate and then smuggled their cargo into those places where to declare it would accrue taxes in excess of any profit.

The tobacco and cotton they took to England, the brandy, lace, tea, went back to the Colonies. English, French, Dutch or Spanish, it made no difference which. The rate of pay was the deciding factor.

Until Carlos fell in love.

St Croix tossed a round, smooth white pebble into the blackness of the water, watched as it plopped from sight and the ripples spread slowly, so very slowly, outward.

The danger that went with the Chase had always kept the blood-rush heated to a fever pitch of excitement, and smuggling had proven to be as adventurous. They were rich, all of them, for as a privateer St Croix had been lucky; he had a nose for the scent of gold, and as a smuggler his luck had not left him. Smuggling had brought more wealth, its own dangers, and her: a Spanish beauty.

They had all loved her…No, that was not the truth. This was a place where the concealed truth was weighed against the told lies and deceits. In truth, they had lusted for her. Only Carlos had loved her. And she had loved only him.

St Croix covered his face with his hands and in despair wept bitter tears of grief.

When Carlos Mereno had fallen in love with the twin sister of a Spanish Don, jealousy had wormed its way into their minds, and their breeches.

*

The shot alerted him. Its sound distant, far, far away in another place, another world. Nothing to do with him.

But then, through the breach between the two worlds, came the laugh. That cold, familiar laugh that had nothing of amusement or gaiety to it. St Croix stood, walked to the edge of the black waters of the River. He peered at his pale image and at the pinprick reflections of light that were the many, many stars. He could not see into the water for it was so black. As black as the night. As black as that accursed soul's heart.

He knelt, leaned out as far as he could and slowly immersed his arm into the ice-black water.

"When you are ready," the Witch Woman, Tiola, had said. "When you are ready you will be able to reach from this place into that. And the wrong will, perhaps, begin to be put aright. I will come to help you when I can, but recognising the truth may give you some of the strength you need to help yourself."

A star fell. A single bright star that streaked down through the black skies, its tail ablaze. It fell into the River, shattering the still surface, and carried onward, down and down to tear, with its passing, a rift through the boundary of Eternity.

And eager, his spirit went with it.

Nineteen

Jesamiah lay on his back in the long grass, staring up at the starlit sky. Blood was pooling beneath him. He knew he ought to get up, seek assistance, but the stars were so bright against the blackness. He saw one fall, a streaked trail of gleaming silver.

Wish upon a star, he thought, then, *has it fallen to mark a birth or a death?* He laughed; coughed. My death? Has it come to keep me company while I die, or come to fetch me because I am already dead?

~ *Get up. You cannot die there. Not like this. I will not permit it.* ~

"Ain't much you can soddin' do about it, is there, mate?" Jesamiah murmured to himself.

A man's vaguely familiar face swam into his vision. It was blurred, distorted, as if it were a reflection in a river that was wreathed in a smoking mist. Again the man spoke, but his lips did not move. The voice was in Jesamiah's head. Insistent. Commanding.

~ *Get up!* ~

"Oh, bugger it!" Jesamiah rolled to his knees, stayed there a while, his forehead resting on the ground as the world receded. He passed out again. When he opened his eyes the dawn was rimming the horizon, sending rays of golden light into the purpling sky. The man's blurred face was still there, and the voice still spoke in his head.

~ *Get up. Get up. Do as I say, boy.* ~

"Stop bloody nagging. I'm trying."

On his knees Jesamiah managed to get his torso upright. He clamped his hand over the hole in his shoulder, felt the blood oozing stickily through his fingers. Closed his eyes. Knew he should try to stand. Couldn't be bothered.

The sky was turning a pale blue, the sun rose, sedately, golden and beautiful.

"Captain? Jesus Christ…Captain, Sir!" Young Jasper.

"Cap'n! Cap'n?" Joseph Meadows. Skylark.

"All right. I'm getting' up. Don't start nagging again."

"Who did this to you?" Sandy Banks.

"That fokken bastard, Blackbeard." Never before had Jesamiah been so relieved to see his men.

Skylark was on his knees examining the wound as best he could. Judging by the hole and amount of blood at the back and front, the bullet had gone straight through.

Jasper drew his pistol from his belt, angrily waved it towards the creek. He idolised Jesamiah who had rescued him from near starvation and the miserable life of a street urchin. He had been twelve years old and had attempted to pick Jesamiah's pocket. His victim's hand clamping around his bony wrist along with the accompanying growl of: "You don't want t'be doing that lad," had changed Jasper's life.

"I'll kill him. I'll bloody kill him! How dare he shoot my Captain!"

Grasping Jasper's arm, Jesamiah hauled himself to his feet. "You'll do no such thing, young man. I forbid it."

"But –"

"I forbid it, y'hear?"

Joe Meadows nodded at the fifteen-year-old. "Put it away, lad, there's no one to shoot." He slipped his arm around Jesamiah's waist, helped him along the path. "When you weren't back at the boat we thought we'd best come looking for you. We'll be off by dawn you said, last night." He glanced up at the sky, the sun bursting from behind a cotton-fluff wisp of cloud. "Dawn's been an' gone; sun's well up."

"Even though I told you to stay put?"

Sandy chuckled as he told Jasper to jump down into the boat and steady her while they got the Captain aboard. "Never was one to obey orders, Sir."

Grunting with the discomfort, Jesamiah half eased, half fell onto the bench beside the tiller. "I want one of you to stay here. Keep a discreet eye on Miss Tiola." Grimacing, he felt for the coin pouch in his pocket.

"I'll stay," Skylark offered. "Don't think no one round here knows I'm with your crew."

Jesamiah tossed him the pouch. "And if you see the man who helped me, thank him."

The pouch chinked satisfyingly as Skylark caught it. "What man?" he asked, frowning and peering up and down the river path.

Sandy and Jasper were already out in the middle of the creek, the rush of the current taking them swiftly, the oars dipping, leaving a trail of ripples and showers of sun-sparkling water.

He cupped a hand against his mouth, intending to call out, "We didn't see nobody," but changed his mind. The boat was already a way off and the morning was calm and quiet, why disturb it for something the Captain had imagined?

Twenty

Bath Town had two streets. One, long and straight, formed the main thoroughfare; the other wandered to the harbour and crossed the slatted wooden bridge spanning the creek. A busy little town that was rapidly expanding – already it held almost two hundred residents dwelling in private houses, taverns, and a variety of shops and businesses. The town also boasted a shipyard and the Colony's first public library. Farms and plantations dominated the surrounding land growing corn, cotton and tobacco. Now that the trouble with the natives had finally been sorted the place was rapidly prospering. The war with the red-skinned Americans had been brief and bloody, but the white man's superior weaponry, in conjunction with his imported diseases, had soon beaten the Tuscarora Indians from the coast, sending them into the forests to the west.

The walk into town from Archbell Point was pleasant, for the sun was shining and the road was dry, although the ruts from recent rainstorms had hardened solid. Tiola had persuaded Elizabeth-Anne to take some exercise, for the mother-to-be had been sitting about and her ankles were swelling.

"The fresh air will do us both good," Tiola had stated, "and I would so enjoy doing some shopping."

In the end, Nicholas had suggested a compromise that had won his wife round. "What if we walk in, and I arrange for the carriage to meet us and bring us home?"

Perdita decided to join them and it was, therefore, a merry party that eventually strolled into Main Street; the second shop, a milliner's, drawing the attention of the three ladies.

"Oh look at those bonnets!" Perdita pressed her nose against the distorted square panes of the glass window. "Look, Tiola, is the pink one not handsome?"

"It is indeed," Tiola, answered looking at the one next to it, a fancy array of straw and bows and ribbons. Blue ribbons, Jesamiah blue ribbons. How he would smile if she were to wear it. She rarely had the chance to shop, and she had not bought a new bonnet since, well, she could not remember when.

"The one with the yellow roses is prettier," declared Elizabeth-Anne.

Perdita patted her hair. "But I look dreadful in yellow, it makes my skin look sallow. I am going to buy the pink. It will go pleasingly with my new gown."

"To impress your sweetheart?" Nicholas jested good-natured. Perdita blushed.

"Oh Nicholas," his wife admonished, "how you do tease the girl. You know she has no such person."

Tiola retained her silence, but by the hastily hidden look of askance on Perdita's face she surmised there was indeed a lover, and no one knew of him. Tiola smiled to herself; she too had a lover of whom no one here knew. It may be fun to share a similar secret.

"Yes she has!" Nicholas rejoined, "The tailor's son, they are always smiling at each other."

"Oh you men do talk such nonsense." Elizabeth-Anne sniffed haughtily and drew her husband away. "He is naught but a pumpkin. He is trade, not of our class. How could he possibly be Perdita's sweetheart?"

Class; the wealthy who owned the land and did not need to work, and the poor who worked for them and owned nothing except their pride. Tiola wondered how the family would react if she were to divulge the nature of her lover. A pirate. But then, last night at dinner they had all appeared to be impressed by Edward Teach, talking of him as if he were some sort of hero. Indeed, he brought wealth to Bath Town by means of supplying goods for the merchants, which they bought cheap and sold at a profit. An even higher profit going to Teach who acquired the cargo for nothing more than the inconvenience of a Chase, although no one seemed aware of that fact, or at least, was not prepared to admit to it. His presence also brought people; visitors who came to see for themselves the larger-than-life infamous rogue who had, so he claimed, been reformed of his ways and was now a respectable citizen of North Carolina. Visitors spent money in the stores and taverns. Therefore, visitors were welcome, and so, it seemed, was Edward Teach.

Tiola threaded her arm through Perdita's, gave it a squeeze. "I would like the blue bonnet," she announced with conviction, "but I would value your opinion as to whether it will suit me?"

With a laugh, Nicholas steered his wife to the popular coffee shop across the street. "Do not buy the whole store," he teased over his shoulder, "you can only wear one bonnet at a time!"

The blue suited Tiola perfectly and the pink was flattering against Perdita's fair ringlets, matching the rose-blush of her cheeks.

"Let me purchase it for you," Tiola offered as a whim, "then none can say you were being extravagant. Was Mr Page right? Is it to impress a young man?"

Perdita's eyes brightened, a smile lighting her entire face. "Yes." She hesitated, blushed, "Miss Tiola? Can I trust you?"

Tiola nodded and Perdita experienced an overwhelming sense that indeed, she could trust this young woman. A shy, quiet girl, Perdita was the same age as Tiola, and eagerly embraced the joy of life that glowed within her, delighting in what promised to be a mutual friendship.

"His name is Jonathan Gabriel," she confided. "His father is the gentleman's tailor along the street. Step-papa says between them they make clothes that surpass those worn by the King himself, yet he would never permit me to walk out with Jonathan. I would never have the courage to suggest it. My step-papa would rather see me dead than shame him so outrageously." She put the bonnet on, tied the bow beneath her chin and added, "But oh, Tiola, I do so adore him. He is the kindest, gentlest, most endearing man I have ever met."

Refraining from saying that at her tender age she could not have met many to compare, Tiola thought of her own circumstances. Love was love and there was no denying when the spirit recognised a kindred soul. Who would have thought that after all her years of existence, all her many incarnations, she would fall for a rogue like Jesamiah?

Stepping from the store, proudly wearing their new bonnets having given orders for the discarded ones to be packaged and returned to Archbell Point, the two young ladies strolled together, arm in arm.

"We will walk to the jetty first," Perdita announced, "then take the lane between the *Horse and Groom* and the *Sailor's Fiddle*. We will be well seen along that route."

"And what makes you think I wish to be seen?" Tiola chided, as they set off in the planned direction.

"With a new bonnet? Why would you not?"

"Mayhap I have no regard to being appraised by the many young men who, assuredly, will be supping ale in the gardens of the aforesaid *Horse and Groom* and *Sailor's Fiddle*. Not to mention those swarming along the jetty loading or unloading cargo into or out of boats, or doing all the other one-hundred-and-one things that sailors are in demand to do."

Horrified, Perdita stopped walking, her expression woeful. "Oh. Do you think so? Do you think there will be many young men?"

Tiola re-tied the bow beneath her chin and patted a ringlet of her hair, then again slipped her arm through Perdita's, and giggled. "I do hope so! Why else did we purchase such beautiful bonnets?"

They passed a draper's, a chandler's store that smelt of hemp, canvas, tar and tobacco, and an apothecary, Tiola noting that she would visit it soon to replenish some of her dwindling medicinal necessities.

There were several vessels moored beside the jetty, none of them as large as *Sea Witch*, or as fine kept. These were coastal traders and fishing boats. A fair-haired man was seated on a stool absorbed in painting the view across the creek. Although not wishing to approach close and disturb him, Tiola studied his painting with interest. His brushwork was good and he had captured the sunlight playing on the water with an exceptional skill.

He must have felt her scrutiny for he turned, smiled, and raised his hat. Perdita giggled. Tiola bobbed him a curtsey.

Walking slowly, stopping now and then to peep into shop windows, twice to acknowledge a greeting to people Perdita knew, they eventually reached the furthest end of Main Street. The last store, *J. Gabriel and Son, Gentleman's Tailor* was situated opposite a row of moderate-sized houses and a stand of autumn-tinted trees. Tiola had noted how Perdita's step had lengthened and her breathing and excitement had increased, for her cheeks glowed pink with anticipation. So, was this, the tailor's, the reason for the new bonnet?

Within moments of seeing them the son came bounding through the door, as breathless and flushed as Perdita. Young hearts, young love.

Tiola's heart ached for them as they bowed and curtsied a formal greeting, each of them so wanting to touch but unable to do so because there were people in the street, and to do so would be the quickest way to ensure they never had the chance to meet again.

What hope was there for them? Would Perdita be willing to forgo the wealth and luxury of her accustomed lifestyle in order to live above a tailor's shop? To cook, clean, sew, bring up the children without the aid of servants? It was a hard choice for a young woman to make, although it was unlikely she would be permitted even the opportunity to decide. He was of the wrong social class, their attachment would be forcibly destroyed were it to develop into anything more than shy smiles and covert glances.

Two men emerged from the dark interior of the shop, one, tall with a black, bushed beard, the other clean-shaven, shorter and about ten years younger. Tiola knew him, Tobias Knight, the Governor's right-hand man, Secretary to the Colony. He had been at dinner last evening, her table companion. An officious bore full of his own self-importance; but then, many men in the Colonies held the same opinion of themselves.

The other man was, by his tanned, leathery skin and his rolling gait, a seaman. Tiola had never met him, never seen him, but knew exactly who this was. Edward Teach. Blackbeard himself.

Noticing Perdita talking to Jonathan Gabriel he guffawed loudly, the sound booming and bouncing down the street. "Why if 'n it bain't tha pretty Mistress Perdita! Good day t'thee, Ma'am!" He swept off his hat and bowed, Knight at his side following suit, although his attention lingered on Perdita a fraction longer than manners did perhaps dictate.

Etiquette demanded a response; Perdita was already politely curtseying and Tiola bobbed a demure greeting. Teach was studying her with interest.

"Ho, so we has a newcomer in our midst?" He strode towards them, a fiercesome sight. Fifty years of age, weatherworn and rugged, more than six feet in height, broad shoulders, stout of girth; built like an ox. His hair was tied in a queue, and the great bush of his beard, for which he was named, was neat and combed, but hung from his chin to garland his chest as if it were a grand chain of authority. Everything about him was immense, his body, his stance, his opinion, manner and voice. Tiola, a healer, also noticed the sores and scabs, the decayed teeth and receding gums. He was not a well man, but the symptoms could be caused by any number of diseases. Most notably among sailors, scurvy or syphilis.

Knight introduced Tiola as Mistress Oldstagh, and again Teach swept a gallant bow. But there, all etiquette ended. He reached out to pinch Tiola's cheek between his tar-blackened fingers, as if she were a child. His touch was brief, but a force of energy surged into her as if a bolt of lightning had seared through her skin. She felt as if the sun and all warmth, all love, care and compassion had instantly been erased from the world. A saturating darkness was surrounding her, seeping into her flesh, bones and mind; black, icy tendrils were twining around her body, her arms, her legs, her throat, as if they were choking weeds gone wildly rampant. The malevolence of the Dark Power!

Instinctively, she threw up a circle of protecting Light around herself. Immediately, the enveloping Darkness retreated with a shrieked howl of rage that no human could have heard. She stepped away from Teach, putting space between them, her gaze holding his, not blinking, not wavering from his returned snake-like stare. And realised that by using her Craft she had made a grave mistake.

The Dark had him! Its sinister presence surrounded, bound and permeated Edward Teach as if it were a shroud wrapped around a mouldering corpse. She was aware of a rustle of deprived annoyance as the Malevolents, the spirits serving the Dark, quested to locate what creature had scalded them with the sensation of the Light; from where, and how it had been raised.

There were only two things that the Dark feared; the strength of the Circle of Light and the power of those who wielded it, the Old Ones of Wisdom, the White Witches of Craft. Feared them enough to destroy them when the rare opportunities to do so arose.

Tiola hurled aside her encircling shield and erased all scent and identity of what she was. Let fear widen her eyes and sweat dampen her skin, for she dare not draw attention to the fact that she was not human. There was only one thing those of the Light feared. The potential strength of the Dark.

With no protection she was vulnerable, but she had a job to do here in Bath Town, a baby to bring to healthy life and a birthing was no place for the greed, hatred and narrow-minded evils of the Dark Powers to linger searching for prey.

Teach spread his hands, smiled, his mouth showing toothless gaps. "Thee bain't afeared o'me, be thee, wummun? I have a gurt respec'fer those who be acquainted with Guv'nor Eden's house'old. As long'n they doos respec' me in return." His accent bore traces of the West Country, though it was heavily tinted with a sailor's slang.

He was unaware of the ethereal clash of entities of the Dark and the Light, as every human was, unless the respective Powers elected to show themselves. But how clever of the parasitic Malevolents to choose this man to manipulate to their will! Madness oozed from him as boldly as his bad breath. For how long had he been possessed? How much of his soul was congealed and saturated by greed and lust? The Dark had entered him, and was devouring him like a cancer. That one touch had told Tiola there was very little of the man, the human soul and the rational mind, left intact.

Tiola's answer was polite, quiet, no hint of defiance. "Indeed, Sir, I am somewhat overwhelmed, you are a large man to confront a small woman."

He tipped his head back and guffawed. "By, but that put me in m'place eh, Knight? Thee has a tacker tongue in thy mouth, Mistress Oldstagh, an' I stan'here suitably ashamed by thy lecture." He did not appear to be in the least ashamed, but Tiola acknowledged his feigned remorse with another, small, curtsey.

"Mistress Oldstagh is here to attend Mrs Page's confinement," Knight informed his companion. "She has a reputation of skill, I believe."

Teach again chortled, "I bain't interested in birthin', only begettin'. Know of that then, doos thee?"

Her head tilted to one side, her eyes bright like a bird watching for its next meal. Her retort was succinct, her Cornish accent filtering to the fore. "*Ais*; an' ah knows a cock be only as good as 'is crow."

Amused, Teach saluted the retort by removing his hat and waving it in his nether regions, said, "I'll be pleased t' crow fer thee any time thee be wantin', missee."

Gesturing to Knight that he wished to move on, he paused, frowned. There was something odd about this young woman. Something he could not quite put his finger on. Had he seen her before? He truly did not think so, he would have remembered, and she was a beauty. For some reason the memory of Acorne suddenly came into his mind.

Outright, he asked; "A young lass like thee'd be wantin' a man in'er bed. Be it thee Acorne were swivin'las'nigh'?"

Wary, Tiola chose her answer carefully, instinct warning her to keep silent about Jesamiah. She hushed her accent, spoke with a genteel manner. "I am here alone, Sir, a recent widow." Neatly done, neatly said. Not untrue, but the full truth not told.

"Ah, but thee bain't wearin' widder's weeds, is thee?"

"I do not need to drape myself in black to remember my husband."

Whether it was because Teach realised he was making no impression, or because she was no longer frightened of him, he turned his attention to Perdita Galland.

"Mebbe it were thee he were thrummin'?"

The tailor's son, young Gabriel, bristled red with outrage and clenching his fists in a semi-upright position, set himself between Teach and the woman he adored. An ant squared against a giant.

"I will have you take that remark back, Captain Teach. You insult the lady."

Blackbeard merely cuffed the boy aside and glanced up and down the street. "Do I be hearin' a piddle of a pup yappin' somewhere?"

As often he did, he lost interest in the taunting. He slapped his arm around Knight's shoulders and steered him in the direction of the jetty. "Come Master Knight, thee be havin' a ship t'board an' business t'be 'tendin', I b'lieve? Mark as how thee were t'be obtainin' those financials thee promised me. I'll no' be patient with more of 'n thy excuses."

"As I said, Captain, I have been trying my best to secure payment, but there are those who owe me, and getting their money is like squeezing blood from a stone."

"Squeeze tha balls then. Or their necks." Teach stopped walking swivelled on his heel and regarded Tiola through narrowed eyes.

"Thy've nay need t' fret fer Acorne, Missee. I tooken care of him. He be dead. I shot him."

Tiola's face drained pale, her heartbeat lurched and the sound of a torrent rushed through her ears as the world tumbled, crashed and fell. She staggered, Jonathan Gabriel was at her side, his arm supporting her. His voice, asking if she was all right sounding distant and muffled.

No! Jesamiah! The scream was in her head, she managed to control herself enough to stop it reaching her mouth.

~ Jesamiah! Jesamiah! ~ She shouted his name, attempting to connect her mind with his. Met a wall of solid blackness, and instantly the Dark sent a wraith of shadow striking towards her. She slammed her mind shut. Quickly recovered her poise.

How she managed to answer Teach with such an air of indifference she did not know. "You have already quizzed me on the subject, Captain Teach and I have answered you. I find your boasting offensive."

Teach shrugged, resumed his conversation with Knight as they strode away. He did glance back once at the slight, very pretty woman. Felt an itch beginning to want to be scratched. She knew something of Acorne – by the way she had reacted he was certain of it. She would be telling him: in his own time he would discover what she knew of the whelp. Or if she insisted on this pretence of secretiveness, would regret it. As would Acorne, if fortune had aided him to survive that bullet.

"Horrid, hateful man," Perdita hissed. "He is crude and spiteful. Why so many think he has charm and is entertaining I will never understand."

"They flirt with him because he is a man of wealth, my dear," Jonathan answered gloomily. "My father thinks the sun shines from his backside because he has requested his entire wedding attire to be fashioned by us. Teach says he will pay us when the work is completed, but I full expect him to renege on the agreement. He never pays anyone else in this town! For my part I would have told him to walk from the shop and keep walking."

Brave words. He would have done no such thing. No one gainsaid Edward Teach.

~ *Jesamiah? Please answer me?* ~ With Teach now out of sight, Tiola tried again to reach Jesamiah, her senses alert for danger. ~ *Jesamiah?* ~

He was not dead. She would know if he were, for her soul would have ripped in two with his passing, and an empty, aching void set in its hollow place.

~ *Jesamiah?* ~

~ *Mmm? Tiola? Tiola sweetheart?* ~

The words were slurred, groggy and etched with pain, but they were his words and his voice in her head.

~ *Are you all right? Do you need me?* ~

~ *I just want t'sleep.* ~

~ *Then sleep. Sleep well.* ~ She withdrew hastily, aching to send her healing to him, but daring not for there was something slithering along the lane, an odourless smell, an intangible feeling, an invisible hand stretching out, fingers clawing and writhing searching for something: something it desperately wanted to find. Her.

"Wedding attire?" she queried, reluctantly forcing her attention away from Jesamiah and concealing her Craft from the presence of Malevolence. "He is invited to a wedding?" She could think of no worse guest than Captain Edward Teach.

"Not invited, no. He goes to his own ceremony. He is to wed Mary Ormond, daughter of John Ormond, a plantation owner of great means. She will be turned sixteen on her wedding day, and as his only heir…" Jonathan Gabriel cynically let the implication drift.

Tiola was appalled. "He cannot marry! The idea is abhorrent, what is this John Ormond thinking of?"

The tailor's son shrugged. He despised Teach but many in Bath Town did not. People came to gawp, fascinated by him, and those same people spent money which the town desperately required. Teach's presence brought wealth.

With regret Jonathan Gabriel took his leave, his gaze lingering on Perdita with the longing for some hope that somehow they may be together. If only this was his wedding coat that he had to sew. But it would never be. He was a humble tailor's son, and she was the stepdaughter of a royal-appointed Lieutenant Governor.

Perdita waved to the others who were walking sedately towards them,

Elizabeth-Anne leaning on her husband's arm, her face lined with the onset of tiredness. "In return for his daughter's hand Ormond gets the assurance of a safe passage for his cotton and tobacco cargoes," she explained. "With Captain Teach as son-in-law and heir apparent, no pirate would dare attack a single one of the Ormond fleet."

Would they not? Tiola thought as Nicholas handed the ladies into the waiting carriage. *I can think of one who would.*

Twenty One

Friday 11th October

A fever attacked Jesamiah and intruded into his dreams, stabbing ferociously at his mind. The pain coursing down his arm surged relentlessly through his fitful sleep and the intermittent bouts of agitated consciousness. He was unaware, most of the time, which was the reality of awake and which was not. Hushed whispers permeated through the searing redness; the touch of a cool hand on his skin, the feel of a wet cloth on his sweating body. Finch's surly grunt. Mr Janson's smell of tobacco and his gruff but soothing voice; "Lie still, lad; lie still."

Or was it Jansy? Sometimes the tone was deeper, familiar yet undetermined.

~ *Be still, lad.* ~

The same dream kept coming back. Each time it started he desperately tried to wake, tried to run, tried to help – to do something, anything, but each time he failed and the dream faded into screams and laughter. And tears. His tears. His failure.

Night. He was outside under a stand of trees. The wind was rustling through the leaves and he could see the stars and a thin crescent moon high, high above, bright against the tar-black, star-pocked sky. There was other light somewhere, behind and to the left. The pale glow of lamplight seeping into the garden from an open door. And there were sounds. A man's low voice, a woman's murmured response.

He could smell the sea. The pleasant fragrance of exotic flowers, the scent of the earth cooling after the heat of the day. The aroma of tobacco and the strong sweetness of rum.

That part of the dream was all right. He lay there, looking at the stars, aware he ought to get up. Ought to go to the house and close that door. Lock it. But it was pleasant here beneath the trees. And then the screaming started and the manic laughter of a madman. The blood. Blood was everywhere. Spattered on the flowers and the grass; on the floor, on the walls, on the bed. The sheets. On the woman. She was covered in blood. Hers and the man's. He could see her, hear her screaming.

Hear a man laughing. But he could not get up, could not move from where he lay, staring up at the stars and the moon, which had also turned red and was weeping tears of blood.

With a gasp Jesamiah awoke. His shoulder was throbbing, his throat was dry. He lay a while, the breath shuddering from his open mouth, his heart drumming. He had failed again. Had not been able to get up, had not been able to stop the killing, to help her.

Vaguely he was aware he was in a bed for there was a pillow beneath his head, a blanket covering him and the ceiling was moving, swaying. It was daylight, gold and silver patterns glittered and rippled on the woodwork.

That same dream. That same, damned dream! A tear of despair eased from the corner of his eye. It was only a dream, but he had not been able to help her, whoever she was, and the fear and guilt lingered in his consciousness.

Low voices. Mumbling. A man and a woman. Tiola? He turned his head, realised he was in his own bed in the small quarter cabin situated to the starboard side of his great cabin, aboard *Sea Witch*. She was under way; that was the movement, the patterns were the reflection of water and sunlight.

He recognised Rue's French-accented voice from somewhere above shouting at the crew to look lively. Felt a slight shift – watched the patterns skim and skitter across the overhead beams. Heard the grumbling, predominant sound of the rudder head; no slap and gurgle of water against the hull, no crack of canvas, no chatter of rigging. There was little wind then, yet from the shift of sunlight and shadow clearly they were moving. A duck quacked raucously, and very distant a dog barked. They were near land then. A river? Were they drifting downriver? Why were they not at sea?

He lifted his head, recognised Finch standing beside the table. A woman had her back to him, her head bent over her lap. Sewing?

"Tiola?" he croaked. "Sweet'eart?"

The woman rose, put her sewing down on the table, gathered her silk skirt in one hand and came swiftly to his side. Her mouth smiling, her blonde ringlets bobbing against her neck.

Alicia.

She saw the disappointment flood through his face, to her credit, retained the smile. "Now you just lay quiet, Jesamiah Acorne; you've been pretty poorly these last few days."

"Where's...?" Jesamiah was going to say Tiola. He saw the slight frown crease across Alicia's brow, saw her lips press together, changed to, "Where's Rue? What course are we on?"

Fussily busying herself, Alicia straightened the blanket, patted at the bandaging around Jesamiah's shoulder and chest. "Now don't you go thinking about that. Finch assures me Rue is perfectly capable of handling this boat without you poking your nose in. All you have to do is get strong and well again."

"Ship," Jesamiah muttered, "she's a ship." He suffered about a minute of administration, then throwing the blanket aside, swung his legs from the bed. Realising he was naked he grunted, pushed Alicia aside and lurched towards the clothes chest. "I need m'shirt and breeches."

Alicia got there before him and sat on its lid. "You need no such thing. You get back into that bed this instant!"

Finch was in the doorway, hand raised, finger pointing. "You'm do as she says. You're not fit t'be…"

Jesamiah cut him short. "I can arrange for you to be on heads duty if you so please. Where are my clothes?"

Folding his arms, Finch stuck his chin in the air.

Shove Finch or Alicia aside? Jesamiah doubted he had the strength to push a flea out of the way.

"Bugger the both of you." He stepped past his steward and marched across the cabin, determinedly telling himself that his head was not spinning, he did not feel sick and he was not going to pass out. The door was open. He ducked beneath the low lintel, stumbled along the short, narrow corridor and was out in the sunshine, standing below the quarterdeck in the waist. A quick glance to each side confirmed his assumption. They were gliding downriver. The Pamlico. Judging by the width, were only a couple of miles from the sea.

Sense made him think twice about attempting the ladder, so he strode a few paces and shading his eyes, shouted up at Rue.

"Why the fokken hell are we still on this river? We should bloody be at la Sorenta by now!"

Rue appeared at the rail, a look of puzzled concern changing almost immediately to a broad grin. "Maybe just as well we are not, *mon capitaine*," he nodded at Jesamiah's state of undress.

A few tittered giggles rose to a sudden chorus of full laughter. Jesamiah turned abruptly, clenched his fingers into fists, resisting the instinct to cover his genitals with his hands. The entire company of the ship's whores were draped around the deck, some sitting, a few leaning over the rail. Several had wet hair, drying in the hot sun. Some were sewing, more than a few held bottles in their hands. One had a baby at her breast. Most were showing more flesh than was considered decent.

"I like a man ready prepared," the nearest, a large-breasted redhead tossed at him.

"Ooh Sir, may I join you in a duet?"

Jesamiah glared at the molly boy who was mincing across the deck. "Rue!" he bellowed. "My cabin. Now!" He stormed back into the privacy of his own quarters.

"Seems our Captain's on the mend then, least, one bit of him looks in fine fettle," another of the whores chuckled.

"You mind your manners, Lily Makepiece," Rue chided as he stepped down into the waist.

"I'll be happy to mind the Captain's!" More hilarious laughter.

Rue schooled the grin from his face as he forced a glowering reprimand, "*Prenez garde*, Master Paget, there is only so much I will tolerate from a molly boy." All the same, he smiled when he turned his back.

Ducking into the cabin Rue offered a rare formal salute, his face remaining straight as Jesamiah struggled, one-handed, into a pair of breeches, both Finch and Alicia refusing to be of help.

"*Vous desirez, Monsieur?*"

"Stow it. I ain't finding this amusing."

"*Non, mon patron.*"

Jesamiah swore, glowered and, finally managing his breeches, pointed to the view beyond the stern windows. "Why are we still on the river? Why aren't we out on the Chesapeake, or sailin' up the Rappahannock?"

"Well, Cap'n –"

"I gave orders to set sail, Rue. I weren't unconscious when they brought me aboard."

"No, you were awake and swearing, but…"

"I distinctly remember giving orders to sail!" Jesamiah's voice was rising, getting angrier.

Rue too became angry. "*Merde*! If you would let me finish!"

Opening his mouth to protest, Jesamiah shut it again. Sat down in his comfortable chair.

Taking a breath, Rue continued more calmly, "We 'ave not been able to sail. The split in the side was deeper and longer than Chippy thought. We 'ave 'ad a job to fix it. We need to bring 'er out the water, strip 'er down and mend 'er properly." When Jesamiah said nothing, Rue added, "We are damned lucky to be sailing at all. If our carpenter was not as good as 'e is, we would 'ave been in big trouble."

Alicia had been rummaging for some linen, fashioning a sling, and ignoring his protest she slid Jesamiah's arm into its fold, knotting the ends behind his neck.

He fiddled with it, mumbling beneath his breath until he had it comfortable. "What were all them women doin' on deck? You know I don't permit them to be about when I'm around."

"You were not around, were you?" Alicia retorted before Rue could say a word. "I told them to come into the fresh air two days ago. The hold stinks and so do they. I made them all bathe in the river before we weighed anchor."

"Well you can damn tell 'em to get their arses down below again. I'll not have women or pretty-boys prancing all over my deck and drying their underwear on my rigging."

Leaning forward Alicia re-tweaked the sling to where it ought to be. "My God, you can be a miserable bastard at times, Acorne!"

"'E can be a miserable bastard most the time, Ma'am,"Finch contradicted, handing Jesamiah a glass of rum. He gave a second glass to Rue, whispered, "The women've got a few'ours yet. Cap'n'll be sleepin'like a babbie soon."

Rue frowned, not understanding.

"Don't do t'ave the Cap'n awake when'e's got'oles in'im. Right proper misery'e is. A couple drops o'laudanum added to'is rum does wonders, so it does."

Twenty Two

July – 1685

More memories. More gut-wrenching haunting from the past. More seeing the truth through the lies. Lies he had believed and the lies he had told.

Full of joy and celebration, the woman waited alone save for two trusted servants, alone in the house that her mother had bequeathed her. The house where she had been born and raised; her house where she would soon welcome her new husband and begin her life as his wife.

Two days past, the priest had met them secretly in the little chapel halfway up the hill and married them: Carlos Mereno and the woman he adored. Their love had burned as bright as the candles, their eager vows murmured and exchanged through the blessing of their God. The ring, passed to Carlos by his friend, Charles St Croix, sliding onto her finger as if it had always belonged there. Encircling and eternal.

They had waited the two days for her brother to be gone to the far side of the island of Hispaniola, leaving them safe to come together as a man and his wife should. Her brother was possessive and jealous; he would permit no man to take his twin sister from him. But Carlos loved her, and she him, and so it had all been done in secret.

When Carlos came, as afternoon drifted into evening, their laughter and their love filled the house. It would be safe here for this one night, and then tomorrow the ship would come and take them away forever. Love eternal, love enduring, love, so, so, easy!

Charles stood, raised his glass and proposed a toast; drank to happiness and love, and laughing, Carlos Mereno scooped his bride into his arms and whisked her away to the privacy of upstairs.

Wishing them well, Charles took the bottle – and another in his other hand – and stumbled, the worse for drink, out into the heady scent of the warm night air. He raised the bottle to the watching stars and cried aloud his blessing for the future of his two friends, and for the consummation of their love. It was good to see Carlos happy, though he did admit to himself, out here in the dark where the cicadas chirruped, that he regretted it was not he undressing in that bedchamber.

He tossed the emptied bottle away, opened the second one. Brandy. Best brandy. He looked towards the house. The two servants had cleared away the dinner things, had extinguished the lights and gone to bed somewhere around the back. Only a few lights glowed, the one from the open door and the hallway beyond; through the window halfway up the stairs, the one on the upper landing and the large double window to the left, overlooking the sea – the bedchamber where a husband was making love for the first time to his virgin wife.

Drink-sodden, Charles sat – half fell – beneath the stand of trees to the far side of the lawn, near where the steps zig-zagged down to where the creek formed a secluded anchorage. The crew would be bringing his sloop in soon, gliding in with the tide, using the darkness to hide her. They had brought her in many times, her cargo of contraband ready to be swung ashore with the minimum of fuss or noise. The vessel gone again by first light. It was a perfect place to smuggle goods under Spanish noses. To the house of the Don's own sister, who hated his arrogant domination.

Charles swigged the brandy. This night the smuggling was to be different. No cargo to bring in, but one more precious to take out. The new Mrs Mereno. If her brother was to learn of the plan, if he were to know…Ah, but the secret had been kept, and all was well.

Slumped against a tree, grinning inanely at the upstairs window, he sat in the pale light of the moon shimmering through the wind-tousled leaves, rippling them into silver shadows. He drank again, lay down, looked up at the stars whirling and the two moons flickering. He could smell the sea and the flowers; the scent of the baked earth cooling after the heat of the day and the satisfying aroma of tobacco and the strong sweetness of brandy. The sounds were soporific. The swish of the sea as it ran against the shore, the insects in the grass; the rustle of the wind through the canopy of leaves. He closed his eyes. He was drunk. Very drunk.

Was that the crack of a canvas sail? The squeak of cordage and tackle? The soft call of a command, the crunch of boots on the gravel path? He did not know, for the drink had claimed him. He lay on his back with the empty bottle clutched in his hand, his mouth open, snoring. Unaware that a ship had come and men were stealing ashore. That they were not his men.

The path of yellow lamplight seeped into the garden from the open door, gleaming like a lighted beacon. Voices, laughter.

And then the screaming.

On and on, an unending scream that tore the night into pieces, shattered the stars and chased away the moon.

Men. Men were everywhere; everywhere with the bobbing lantern light and the flickering shadows behind the windows that stared blindly out into the darkness of the garden and reflected the blood and the fear, and the woman's screams that would not stop.

He tried to rise, to get up, but he could not move. His legs would not work, the world swam and his stomach heaved. He was drunk, too drunk to get up, too drunk to help, too drunk to do anything to stop that incessant, high-pitched screaming that pierced through his brain as if someone were stabbing him with a knife. He crawled, dragging himself over the coarse grass, his breath held in his lungs as he clawed at the earth and willed the throbbing and spinning in his head and stomach to go away; as he implored his body to do what he asked of it.

The drink had consumed his senses. All he could do was lie there and give in to the sodden sleep of inebriation.

Lights swinging back down the path roused him. He ought to get up. Get to the house. The moon had gone, the patterns of the stars had changed – an hour had passed? Two? He half raised himself, supported on one crooked arm, his head down, nausea regurgitating into his throat. The screaming had stopped. Thank God, he thought. Thank God. It has stopped.

More laughter, chattering, excited male voices coming nearer, passing him by. From the creek, orders were called. Indistinct words a befuddled haze in his muddled head. They were making ready to leave.

St Croix raised his head. The path was ten, twelve yards away. He was in the darkness, no one could see him, but he could see them. Spanish sailors, going back to their ship.

Another man. Not a sailor, for he was too elegantly attired and those in his way parted with respect to let him pass. Charles St Croix saw him, recognised him, and all thought of getting to his feet, getting to the house, vanished. The nausea had gone, the blinding spinning, the confused inebriation went. Suddenly, he was iron sober as realisation hit him as hard as a hammer blow.

Don Damian del Gardo. Her brother. Her twin brother had come. And the screaming had stopped.

As quietly as he could, ashamed at his cowardice, Charles St Croix dropped to his belly and wriggled backwards into the darker, deeper shadows where it was safe.

Sounds from the creek of a sloop about to set sail. No more lights, no more footsteps. No more screaming. He risked raising his head, and there, not five yards from him stood Edward Teach pissing against a tree. Ending his stream of urine he buttoned his breeches.

"We left thee tha whore t'do with as thee please," he said over his shoulder, his back to St Croix. "After he had done with 'er tha Don shared 'er with us, his friends. I 'ads 'er twice. She were good."

He turned, looked straight at where St Croix huddled. "Many a year back I killed 'er what birthed me, fer she were a whore an' a witch, an' the Devil said as 'ow he'd see me right' if'n I choose t'serve 'im. An' he 'as. He 'as an' 'e always will."

*

Sitting there beside the River the memories he had no wish to recall flooded into his mind and mocked his weakness. Charles St Croix covered his face with his hands. The tears of shame were streaking his cheeks. He was supposed to have guarded the house, kept his friend and his wife safe. But he had got mindlessly drunk, then cowered there and lost his honour beneath the trees, while Carlos had lost his life, and the woman her sanity.

He had gone inside where the blood was everywhere. It ran down the stairs and pooled on the black and white tiles of the hall. Was daubed on the walls and stair-rail and on a picture of a sister and her evil brother.

Carlos was on the landing at the top of the stairs. What was left of him. He had been castrated, disembowelled and dismembered.

More blood. On the floor, on the sheets, on the bed. On her. The wife, the widow.

She lay there, naked, staring up at the torn curtaining of the bed canopy above her. She had been used and abused over and over, again and again. By her brother first, and then the men who followed him.

And by Teach, who had betrayed his own.

Charles St Croix had crumpled beside the bed and sobbed for what had been done.

And for what he had failed to do.

Twenty Three

Tuesday 15th October – Virginia

Sailing into the Chesapeake and then negotiating the lower reaches of the Rappahannock had been one of the worst voyages Jesamiah had ever made. If he'd had the use of both arms he may well have picked Alicia up and tossed her overboard. On several occasions the only thing to prevent him from attempting to do so had been the necessity to keep his attention on a safe course – and the knowledge that such a strenuous application of muscles would hurt his healing shoulder.

A good part of his irritation was the nervousness of returning home. Home? It had never been home. Home had been bewilderment and fear, nothing more. His agitation had climaxed as they had rounded the last point and there, ahead, was la Sorenta in all its opulent autumn glory. His mind and body had congealed into a solid lump of self-doubt and for maybe the first time in his sailing life his mind went blank and he could not remember the orders to bring *Sea Witch* into her mooring.

"All hands! Stand by!" For his sanity he could not recall what came next! This was stupid – it was like forgetting how to walk or use knife and spoon to eat!

As a crew they had nursed her through the heavy swells and strengthening winds of the Atlantic, were grateful for the comparatively calmer waters of the Chesapeake Bay. Yet despite the temporary repairs and the pump being manned continuously, the water in the bilge had risen. Once into the Rappahannock, with the wind and tide in their favour, the last few miles had been plainer sailing. To make a mess of things now, as they were approaching his father's plantation, his childhood home, mortified Jesamiah.

~ Haul taut, Son. Shorten sail. ~

Jesamiah exhaled, breathed in again. It was enough to steady his nerve and revive his concentration. "Haul taut. Shorten sail. Man t'gallant clewlines, fore, main, clewgarnets; buntlines." With the first words remembered, it all come back to him. He smiled, relieved, watched the men as they eagerly and efficiently carried out his orders. Not that they needed them, they knew perfectly well what to do without him standing here shouting, but it was his ship, his responsibility to bring her safely in. And leaving things uncoordinated could result in a haphazard shambles.

"Haul taut. In t'gallants. Up fores'l, mains'l. Furl t'gallants."

With short, hasty jerks, the great sails were gathered in, the men strung out along the yards fisting the canvas with all the ease and skill of their years at sea.

"Helm a-lee…Man tops'l clewlines, buntlines…haul taut; let go tops'l sheets. Top bowlines. Clew up."

Sea Witch glided as stately as a swan towards the jetty, bumped slightly and men leapt ashore to secure her to the wooden bollards. "Very good. Settle away. Take over if you please, Rue."

With a malicious vengeance all the fears and inner turmoil returned like a flood tide into Jesamiah's mind and stomach. He wanted to be sick, dare not let anyone notice his discomfort. By walking to the taffrail, gripping it so tightly that his knuckles whitened, and peering steadfastly astern he was able to counterfeit that he was studying the plantation; the state of the house, the fields, the slave quarters. The house was immaculate, not so the rest of it. Phillipe had permitted neglect. A sloop was moored at the far end of the jetty. The *Jane*. She appeared seaworthy enough, although his experienced eye could tell she had not sailed for quite a while. He would have to take a closer inspection later, she probably needed attention to her keel, toredo worm was always a scourge to wooden-hulled boats. The distraction gave him time to calm himself. To summon the courage he would be needing to go ashore.

As Rue ran out a gangplank, Alicia gathered her skirts and hurried across, masking her slight chill of fear at its steepness and the drop beneath her. Thankfully, she stepped on to dry land.

News ran like wildfire along the Rappahannock when there was something worth telling, and laboriously tacking *Sea Witch* had given word plenty of time to spread. Seven people, two of them gentlemen, were waiting on the wide porch. Three elegant carriages, the horses sweating in the humid air, waited on the sweep of the drive. Nearby, a third man held the reins of a lathered mount, impatiently tapping his boot with a riding cane. He stepped forward to meet Alicia, walking several yards to be out of hearing of those waiting in the cool shade of the wide porch.

From the way he was gesturing, and Alicia was answering by emphatically shaking her head, the pair appeared to be in disagreement. She raised her hand as if to strike him, but he caught her wrist, put his face close to hers and said something more.

She broke away, looked across the gardens at another rider waving his riding crop and coming at a smart trot along the track following up-river. Seeing him, the man with Alicia glowered, mounted, and adding another curt remark, spurred his horse down the drive. Beneath its hooves, gravel scattered in a wide-flung spray.

Unaware of the altercation, the newcomer removed his hat and waved it in a circle above his head then swung away from the river and jumping over a hedge, cantered across the green sward of lawn. He reined to a skidding halt, kicked his feet from the stirrups and slid from the saddle. Alicia smiled as he kissed her hand.

In thoughtful interest, Jesamiah tilted his head slightly, narrowed his eyes. A friend? A lover? From his appearance, he seemed no more than a wet-behind-the-ears youth. Folding his arms and leaning on the rail, Jesamiah wondered whether to charge an account for the repairs that would be needed to the grass. The rider was well dressed and mounted on a quality horse of good breeding. There were several plantations along these lower reaches of the Rappahannock, all with wealthy owners, most of whom boasted various broods of sons. Jesamiah barely remembered any of them.

The youth looked towards the *Sea Witch* and leaving Alicia to join those visitors awaiting her on the porch, led his horse towards the jetty. "Captain Acorne? Welcome home, Sir!" he called across to Jesamiah. "Did you have a good voyage?"

"Thank you, aye."

The lad noticed the sling around Jesamiah's neck. "Are you hurt, Sir? Do you require a doctor?" He half turned as if making preparation to mount. "I can fetch him straight-way if you so wish."

"No, no, it is nothing serious. Please, go join the others, I will come ashore directly." Jesamiah tipped his chin upwards towards the drive. "Who was that fellow? Do you know him?"

Frowning, the young man gazed at the dispersing cloud of dust. "Sorry, I have no idea. I do not recognise the horse either. Shall I enquire for you?"

"Nay, 'tis not important. Mrs Mereno's business is her own, not mine."

Jesamiah watched Alicia disappear into the house with one of the gentlemen, her arm linked through his. She would not find it difficult to acquire another husband. In Jesamiah's opinion Alicia had a knack for making friends, she could chatter to anyone, discover a life story within fifteen minutes and be an inseparable companion in another ten.

"I'll be going in then, will meet with you again shortly?"

Jesamiah nodded, saw the young man walk halfway to the house, falter, and return to the jetty, his face downturned in disappointment.

"You do not remember me, do you, Captain?"

Jesamiah lied. "Of course I do." He had a vaguely familiar face, but a name refused to come to mind.

"I am Kennick Trent's youngest son."

Trent. Jesamiah remembered the family, but he'd had very little interest in the estates or their owners as a boy. Always, for him, it had been the river and the shipping that had drawn his attention, not the people or the plantations.

The river! Of course! Samuel, the scrawny stick of a boy who'd always had tear streaks on his dirty face and bruises on his legs and ugly-tempered brothers.

"Now why would I be forgetting young Sam?" Jesamiah said, smiling, easily masking his lapse in memory. "We had a lot in common, you and I, as I recall."

"That we did," Samuel answered, his grin almost splitting his face in two. "We'll talk inside then? Yes?"

"I reckon."

Coming up beside him Nathan Crocker watched with Jesamiah as Trent tethered his horse, went into the house. Nat spoke quietly, keeping his voice and stance discreet.

"Captain, I think you ought to know, some of the men are a little disgruntled to discover that the nearest town is more than ten miles away."

"Are they now. They're too bloody lazy to row down river then?"

"It's the rowing back, I believe, Cap'n."

Jesamiah adjusted his sling, settled his hat more comfortable. "No one goes anywhere until this ship is laid up and Chippy figures what men he needs." He pointed to a suitable place beneath some trees where they could set up camp, then to an artificial, gated, side channel of water dug into the bank.

"My father built that graving dock when he had a disagreement with a shipwright down near Jamestown; something along the lines of him being a thieving scoundrel who put more holes in a hull than worms did."

Leaning his elbows against the top rail on Jesamiah's other side, Rue sniffed loudly. "*Quel age?* It does not look, 'ow you say? In Bristol ship-shape fashion?"

Scowling, Jesamiah scratched at three days' worth of beard growth. Noticed one horizontal panel on the open gates was missing, the others were covered in lichen and slime. Near the ground the bottom panels could not be seen because of choking weeds – the wood was more than likely rotten. Quite probably the entire basin was weed-choked. They would have to wait for low tide to conduct a careful inspection.

"Aye well, there'll be a few days hard work first; clear the weeds, build new gates. But it'll serve our purpose. Once fixed up all we need do is warp 'er in at high tide, wait for the water to drop, shut the gates and we're laughing." He turned his head slightly to look at Nat. "Then, and only then, and assuming these po-faced neighbours of mine ain't pulled the place down, the men can 'op along to the tavern a couple of miles that way." He pointed northward beyond the trees.

Nat frowned. "Decent place, is it?"

"Nope. Full of spit, piss, puke and ladies with no clothes on."

Nat shook his head, grinned. "Not suitable for our lads then."

"Doubt it."

Rue nodded at the flooded box-shaped basin. "That's going to take some manpower to clean up, *mon ami*."

Jesamiah half turned and pointed to the rag-tag shanty village of huts about eight hundred yards down river. "Plenty of labour. This is a tobacco plantation, mate." He did not particularly hold with slavery but until – if – he was running this place his way, the labour was here and it might as well be used. "I'll have no roughness though, savvy? They are to be fed the same as our men and treated with the same respect. If men are handled well, have food in their bellies and can take pride in what they do, they work with a will, longer and harder." He nodded towards the crew who were setting the ship fair. "The freedom of piracy has taught us that."

Twenty Four

To go ashore among such fine company, Finch demanded his Captain should wash, shave, and dress smartly. Jesamiah insisted he would do no such thing.

"I don't care for fuss and finery."

"An' I don't care fer 'avin me name tarnished as being poor at me job. Aside, what would y'ma say if'n she saw thee all dirt mussed and crumpled?"

"My mother's dead. As well you know."

"That's as maybe, but'er spirit'll be 'ere, won't it? An' she'll be a watchin' you. Mark m'words she will."

Finch got his way, not least because it occurred to Jesamiah that to change his clothes would also delay going ashore by another half hour or so. He washed and shaved slowly; took his time to dress, tie laces, pull on boots, adjust a clean linen sling. Could not put off the inevitable any longer.

If sailing with Alicia had been bad, his welcome to la Sorenta was worse. In the eyes of these plantation people Jesamiah was a pirate who had once murdered and thieved, and they made it quite plain that pirates, even those with a government-given pardon, were not welcome along the Rappahannock. The fact that Jesamiah had been driven to piracy by the insufferable cruelties of his brother was not part of their equation. But then, to be fair, they had no idea of the foul barbarities Phillipe had performed, or the real reason why Jesamiah had fled. How were they to know what had happened beside Charles Mereno's grave on the very evening he had been buried? And Jesamiah had no intention of enlightening them.

"You must not mind these people, they know nothing of the world beyond the boundaries of their estates." Samuel Trent offered to refill Jesamiah's wine glass. He was older than Jesamiah had first thought, although the line of fair hair on his upper lip was little more than a fuzz of down. How long ago was it? He'd now be eighteen? Nineteen? The nervous boy Jesamiah remembered had matured into a pleasant young man, even if he was a menace to front lawns!

"They have come here to be tantalised by outrageous gossip," Trent explained congenially. "Gossip which will provide for several months' worth of entertainment. They care not a maple leaf for who you are, only for why you are here." He indicated Jesamiah's sling. "And regardless of their disapproval, to hear first-hand the lurid stories of your past."

"I have none to tell. This was nothing more than a run-in with a black-hearted bugger of a pirate. But what about you, Mr Trent? Or may I call you Sam? Are you here for the same reason? To gather gossip?"

"Yes, Sam, please. I come for two simple reasons." At Jesamiah's raised eyebrow, elaborated, "To welcome you and Mrs Mereno home, and to beg employment here on your estate."

Making no comment, Jesamiah sipped the wine. Good stuff. He would have to investigate the wine cellar most thoroughly.

"When Father dies there will be nothing for me. My brothers will not share. Even in adulthood we do not get on."

Raising his glass as if offering a toast, Jesamiah said, "I have every sympathy."

Trent looked down at his feet, his face tingeing pink with embarrassment. "I desire to seek employment, make my own way, Captain Acorne." He looked up again, said, bolder, "If I had the wherewithal I would purchase la Sorenta from you, show them I am not the lack-brained mule they take me to be. But," he shrugged, "I have very little money. However, I do have knowledge and experience. Your last manager here at la Sorenta, name of Hawkins, died three months ago. He was drunk more often than sober; a brute and a bully. No one will miss him – he was useless at his job and your estate is in a sorry mess. You still have a shed full of tobacco that was not shipped with the last convoy. It was processed and packed well, for the slaves here know what they are doing, and I…" he broke off coloured red again, then summoned the courage to speak out boldly; "and because Hawkins was too drunk and your brother too lazy, I took the liberty of supervising it."

Jesamiah cocked his head on one side. "Now why would you do that?" Admitted, he knew little of running a plantation, but he did know what was involved with planting, picking, drying and storing the tobacco crop. He also knew its value. The fresh, first crops to reach London – or Paris, Cadiz or Lisbon – were the most valued. This lot of old stuff could be hard to shift.

Trent shrugged, apparently lost for a reason, unable to admit that he had enjoyed himself at la Sorenta, and that Hawkins' predecessor, Halyard Calpin, had been both friend and mentor. "I was friends with your friend, Mr Calpin," he said at last, a little sheepishly. "He made me welcome here after you had gone. I spent most of my time with him, trotting at his heels. He taught me much of what he knew. Your estate has not been what it was since he passed away."

Jesamiah did not need telling. He could see it with his own eyes. "Yes, he was a good man, but you have not answered my question."

Taking another deep breath – this was it, this was the culmination of a dream for Samuel Trent, he said, all in a rush; "I want to be your manager. Let me run la Sorenta for you."

"I may not need a manager. I may decide to sell."

Trent had expected that answer, he had a prompt reply. "You would be better to sell with the estate turning a profit. You will not make much on it as it stands, will you? We have just harvested, the tobacco is drying in the sheds – but the crop was poor. It was poor all over Virginia. Too much rain, not enough sun. But it will be better come the next planting. Hawkins did not clear fresh land – tobacco makes the earth stale, but then you must know that. I will clear new acreage, plant well. Take care of the seedlings. Next year we will make a profit. Give me three years and I will transform la Sorenta into the best plantation along the Rappahannock. And even if you do decide to sell now, the new owner will still be wanting a manager, will he not? Give me the position and the chances are that I will retain it."

That made sense. Jesamiah was impressed, and if old Halyard Calpin had indeed trained the boy, then there would not be anyone to better him.

"And there is one other consideration." Trent had stepped into his stride now, was gaining confidence. "If you sell, where will Mrs Mereno go? She is distraught that you may throw her out." He paused, then added in a lower voice, for he was aware it was not for him to make comment, "I am not blaming you; it was wrong of your brother to not make arrangements for his wife. To cheat her of what is rightfully hers."

Jesamiah's retort was indignant, "To cheat her? What about me? Have I not also been dealt a raw deal?"

"You left. Did you not forfeit all rights when you turned to piracy?" Trent retorted hotly, the accusatory words leaving his lips before he could stop them.

"You know nothing of it. Nothing of it at all. Kindly keep your nose out of my affairs!"

How often must I swallow the truth? Jesamiah thought. *Why not come straight out with it? Phillipe Mereno was rotten to the core, the result of incestuous rape, the bastard son of an even bigger Spanish bastard.*

Why? He knew very well why. Because until he knew the real answers he did not want others asking the questions.

Stung, Trent cleared his throat. Now that he had spoken, probably ruined his chances, decided to say it all. "I was a boy when you were declared outlaw, Captain Acorne, but I clearly remember the to-do. The whole of Urbanna was talking of how you had attempted to murder your brother. But Mr Calpin, he refused to believe it. He wept for your going, and he wept for the mistakes your father had made. As you say, he was a good man, was Calpin, he insisted you were a good man too. And do you know what?" Samuel Trent lifted his head, tilted his chin, defiant, "I agreed with him. I knew you were not the bastard your brother made you out to be, but now I say to you, to your very face, that perhaps I was wrong."

So, the boy had guts. Jesamiah well realised it had taken a lot of courage to say all that.

"I have not said I will throw Mrs Mereno out on her backside, have I?"

Trent swallowed down the rest of the tirade that had been welling in his mouth. He stared at Jesamiah then bowed his head, appalled at his outburst.

"As it happens, I am well aware that Alicia is as much a victim of my brother as I was. But I do not wish her to know my intentions too soon. Certainly not before I have taken full inventory of what is now mine, and not before I have sorted the legal muddle that appears to have been left me."

Trent nodded, apologised. "Forgive me, I spoke out of turn. I understand your father's lawyer holds a letter for you? A letter that mysteriously did not come to light at the time of his death. Why is that, I wonder? Because your brother wished it to be hidden?"

Jesamiah was changing his mind about the boy. Here stood someone with guts and astute intelligence. The initial impression that Samuel Trent was nothing more than a frustrated young man with something to prove to his unloved father and brothers began to disappear. Jesamiah nodded. "Go on."

"I would wager Phillipe Mereno discovered something not to his liking when your father died. This letter? It would not have been difficult for him to bribe the lawyer to keep silent on its existence, would it? But now Phillipe is dead, I perceive that worms are crawling from the woodwork."

Worms indeed; and all manner of other slimy creepy-crawlies. Jesamiah snorted cynically, how much had Phillipe paid to secure discretion? Apparently not sufficient to ensure a permanent silence. He drained his glass of wine, rubbed at where the razor had scratched a sore on his cheek. "Well we shall have to curb our curiosity, won't we? I ain't got the time to traipse to Williamsburg to fetch the thing at the moment. Until my ship is repaired this estate takes second place in the matter of my attention."

"It distresses me to see Mrs Mereno vexed, Captain," Trent persisted.

"Alicia? Vexed?" Jesamiah guffawed outright. "She came to Nassau to twist me round her little finger." A thought returned to him: had she arranged that alleyway attack and subsequent convenient rescue? Blunt, he asked, "Do you wish to marry her in order to unequivocally get your hands on the estate? Is that what this is all about?"

Trent answered with equal directness. "No Sir. I do not."

"Just as well, you ain't rich enough for her, mate, she'd turn you down flat. And as I said, at this precise moment I don't give a damn about her."

"Then, to safeguard her security, I will have to challenge you to a duel. It will be a pity, for I was beginning to like you."

"I might be a better duellist than you, boy."

Trent grinned; "Not from the looks of that sling."

"Well, you would have to wait for my wound to heal."

"What? And spoil my advantage?"

Jesamiah chuckled. He liked this young fellow. *Would he change his mind if I told him Alicia was once a Port Royal harlot?* he thought. *That I slept with her in Nassau? Would he still champion her cause?* Jesamiah decided against telling, had a feeling Samuel Trent already knew, or at least guessed. And that he did not care.

Desperate, Trent had one final go at achieving his ambition. "Captain Acorne, please, will you at least consider my proposal of becoming your manager? Unless my father suddenly becomes benevolent, or my brothers all meet with unexpected bad ends, I am faced with a depressing future."

"A pity they are not all like you, harbouring a tendency for pointless duels. You could pick 'em off, one by one."

Encouraged that at least Acorne had not sent him off with a flea in his ear, Trent acknowledged the jest with a smile. "From what Mrs Mereno has said, you know little of tobacco, except, perhaps, how to chew or smoke it?"

"Don't even do that," Jesamiah admitted. "Can't abide the stuff, 'though I ain't never 'ad no objections t'stealin' it." For emphasis of his meaning he slipped into the familiar clipped sailor's accent.

Sam answered with earnest passion, "I will work well for you, Captain. You have my word."

It was a tempting suggestion and Jesamiah was close to agreeing but he was not going to be pushed into anything. There was, as he had said, a lot of sorting out to do. And too many questions needed answering.

Across the room, Alicia was laughing. She was a beautiful woman and she had indeed made the house into a comfortable home, though Phillipe's ideas of improvement did not sit well with Jesamiah. He had removed an interior wall, making these two, already fair-sized rooms, into a single large one. The decoration and furnishing in the latest London fashion would have eaten the money like a hen devours corn. No wonder there was nothing left. The windows overlooking the terrace and gardens were bathed in early afternoon sunlight, catching the browns and golds of the surrounding oaks and the flame reds of the maples. Virginia was stunning this time of year. A pity some of her inhabitants were not equally as pleasant.

"I ain't decided what to do, Sam, but I will grant you the courtesy of lettin' you be the first t'know when I 'ave. Now, if you would excuse me, I 'ave m'ship to see to."

It was an excuse, rather a lame one, but the only one that came to mind. Despite the size of the room, the stretch of the windows, the light airiness, Jesamiah had felt increasingly confined. He had no liking for being indoors nor for meaningless small talk, and these neighbours were becoming tedious. If they wished to snub him then that was their prerogative, but not here in his own house.

He walked to the door then changed his mind and swivelled slowly on his heel, suddenly not caring how rude and uncharming he appeared. "Alicia, you may have been in the habit of inviting people to this house when you were its mistress, but it is now my property and I have no wish to be insulted by clacketting paint-cheeked old besoms in m'own living room. I'm goin't'see to m'ship and m'crew and I want this rabble gone by the time I return."

He stamped out, banging the door behind him.

Samuel Trent watched him walk away. Had his proposal gone well? Mayhap it had not. It was his only chance of freedom, he could not run away and become a pirate, the army or navy did not appeal as he had no appetite for fighting and killing, and he had not enough belief in God to follow the path of a clergyman. There were very few options left for a nigh-on penniless youth.

He glanced across at Alicia. They had been friends since she first came here, he liked her. But marry her? He shook his head. As Captain Acorne had implied, the moon would turn blue before Mrs Alicia Mereno would contemplate such an outrageous absurdity.

Twenty Five

Friday 18th October

Sprawling along the shore of the lower reaches of the Rappahannock, Urbanna was one of Virginia's oldest towns. In the last century twenty fifty-acre port towns had been established, at a cost of ten thousand pounds weight of tobacco, each. Through these, all trade was to take place: a guaranteed income for the entrepreneurial inhabitants. Originally, Urbanna had been no more than a small part of the first Ralph Wormeley's estate of Rosegil, but 1705 found the rapidly expanding town renamed as the 'City of Anne' for the honour of the English Queen.

At the riverside warehouse, planters exchanged tobacco for immediate cash or credit to exchange for imported goods. Aside it, the harbourmaster's house. Opposite, the Customs House, while up the hill the Court House stood, half complete.

The architecture and official buildings held no interest for Alicia. She was stepping delicately through the rutted mud of the main street with the sole intention of visiting Agatha Chalmondy, the draper and seamstress. At her last visit, Alicia had noticed some black French lace, in hindsight, was sorry at not purchasing it.

Tomorrow, the Wormeleys were holding a ball in honour of Virginia's Governor Spotswood, who was about to depart the area and return to the Virginia capital of Williamsburg. Everyone of note was invited and Alicia, this bright early morning, was determined to replace the drab lace of her best gown. Black would look impressive against the red silk.

Had Jesamiah been more generous she would have coaxed an entirely new gown from him, but he was too absorbed in his wretched ship, and she did not want to admit that her funds were too low to meet buying the necessary yards of fabric. To freshen an old gown would have to suffice.

She paused, her hand on the gate latch as someone called her name. Turned, regretted the hesitation as a man hauled his mount to a halt.

"We were unable to talk the other day, Ma'am, and I have but little time today for my ship is about to sail."

Alicia offered a graceful curtsey. "There is nothing further to say that

I did not impart before, Sir."

He dismounted, grimaced as his boot sank into a pile of horse dung. "But I think there is. Your husband owed me a great deal of money. You are his widow, you therefore carry his debt."

From her days as a whore Alicia had been acquainted with men who regarded women as items to be used at will. Phillipe had been one of the same breed of bastards. She would be eternally grateful to Jesamiah for freeing her of him. Yet here was another conceited pop-cock who regarded her with less respect than he would a sow.

"And as I have already told you, the estate passes to Captain Acorne. See him about debts, not me."

He never would, of course. This beast chose easy prey, the weak, the vulnerable, those who could not fight back. Were he to confront a man like Jesamiah he would be run through before he could repeat his demands – and after he had pissed his breeches.

The man grasped her arm twisting it painfully. He was a brute. "I have debts to settle of my own. I want my money, woman." He shook her, "So pay me or I will be forced to let slip your history to all these here in Urbanna – and aye, everyone in Virginia and North Carolina. That would be a great shame, would it not, Arabella Appleyard? Would it not be unfortunate for folk to learn your real name? That you were transported to the Colonies from London, convicted for thieving? That you became a gutter slut? Where will you be, my fine lady, once I make it all public?"

She wrenched her arm free. "I have told you. Until Acorne settles the matter of the estate, I have no money."

"Then persuade him to get on with it."

"Acorne is not an easy man to persuade."

He snorted derision," Hah, I would wager you can easily persuade him into your bed." When she made no answer he laughed scornfully. "Once a whore, always a whore. Next time I am here in Virginia I will show you what a *real* man can do, shall I?"

Finding the courage to retaliate she sneered direct into his face; "You are going to watch Jesamiah bed me then, are you? He is the only *real* man I know."

He slapped her, once, hard, across the cheek. "You will pay what you owe. I do not care how high you have to lift your skirts to do so, or who pokes beneath, but pay me you will." He spun on his heel and mounted the horse, jabbing it fiercely in the mouth as he picked up the reins, forcing its head to toss, ears back, eyes rolling.

"My business will see me in Virginia again come early November, Madam. You have until then." He kicked the horse into a trot, rode towards the jetty where a ship was awaiting the tide.

For a long while Alicia stood there blinking aside tears, trembling. Why did these vile whoresons have to ruin her life? Why of all the men she had served in Port Royal, had he been the one Phillipe owed money to? He was a spiteful little man, full of his own importance, and had made his fortune on the misfortunes of others. He would do as he said, for he did not believe in the word compassion, and she would lose all she had – the little she had left. All hope of achieving her dream of a respectable life would be taken from her. Would she have to return to the sordid existence of a prostitute? Alicia brushed at an escaped tear travelling slowly down her cheek. No, that she would not do. She would rather kill herself.

If nothing else, Alicia Mereno – the one-time London street urchin Arabella Appleyard – was resourceful. Something would happen. Something would turn up. Somehow she would persuade Jesamiah to give her what was rightfully hers, either the estate or sufficient remuneration. Meanwhile, she had a ball to prepare for and some black lace to haggle over with Agatha Chalmondy.

Returning to the carriage less than half of an hour later, a wrapped package of lace in her hand and a smirk of a bargained triumph on her face, Alicia settled herself in her seat. Told the driver to return home.

She took a long look at the river, at the forest of masts spearing the blue autumn sky. The smile as she tucked the travel blanket over her lap was one of deep satisfaction. She was no expert at identifying ships, but Agatha Chalmondy had pointed out one in particular. The woman had been in high dudgeon, her mind barely on the matter of making a sale, for her brother had returned home in a blistering temper intent on ensuring Governor Spotswood did something about the damnable pirates, for he had come close to losing his ship and his life.

Captain Lofts, a merchant trader, was often here in Urbanna and he had been chased once too often by pirates. Mrs Chalmondy was his widowed sister, her three daughters his family. Apart from his ship, the Chalmondy house above the draper's shop was his only home.

Cooing and tutting in sympathy, Alicia had let the silly woman prattle on, her mind galloping. She needed leverage to make Jesamiah give in to her. Something to blackmail him with. The idea of suggesting she was to bear him a child had been a spur of the moment, and one that would take a few months yet to be proven true or false. But this, this she could set into action right now!

The carriage jerked forwards, the driver encouraging the pair of bays into a smart trot. All she need do was send the good Captain Lofts a letter. Written discreetly and in an anonymous hand, naturally. Her problem would be solved. She smiled to herself. Her tormentor was not the only one who could stoop to coercion. Blackmail had never been beyond Alicia's capabilities before, and nor was it now.

Twenty Six

"I have been seeing the past."

"The place where you are is a place for reflection," the Witch Woman said, as if he should already have known that.

Charles sighed with tired despair. "Are you never afeared of what has already been, Mistress Oldstagh?"

"Of what has been? No. What is done has been done, you cannot fear the past, only learn from it." She fell silent, considering, then admitted; "But I do fear what is to come. The future. I fear for the one I love. I am afraid that I will not be there for him when he needs me the most."

Charles St Croix watched as a red-gold autumn leaf fell from the tree and landing in the River, swirled around and around before the current floated it away up the gentle incline, as if it were a little boat.

He wondered what the witch, Tiola, looked like; he had only heard her voice and seen a faint, ghost-like outline. He had the impression of hair as black as a raven's wing, of eyes as dark, set in a pretty face. She was not tall, not much more than an inch or two above five feet in height, and she was slender. That was all he knew. His son was a lucky man to be having her to love him.

He made his own admission. "The past haunts me."

"That is because you must lay the past to rest, forgive others, and then forgive yourself. You must close the door on what was, and open the one to what will be."

He felt her hand on his arm, a comforting feeling of her nearness as the despair saturated him.

"It will be hard to do, Witch Woman."

Sadness touched her. "Perhaps if you can find a way for Jesamiah to forgive you, then you will be able to forgive yourself?"

"If only it were that simple! If only it were that simple."

"Important things are rarely easy to do, that is why they are important."

"I made mistakes. I am afraid I will make yet another and never find the peace I crave."

"We all make mistakes," she said. "A mistake made the once can be forgiven. It is the lesson that is not learnt and the mistake that is deliberately made over again *that is more difficult to forgive."*

Do I not know that? *he thought.* Ah, do I not know that!

She breathed a light kiss to his cheek. "On the night when all here is reversed. When west becomes east, when what flows up, flows down and when the River of Death freezes with the memory of Life. On that night, I will come and help you to return to the world of the living. There, you can, perhaps, put right what is wrong."

He sat for a long while. Sat alone, and as silent, as the River that was impassable to any living soul as it flowed uphill on its eternal journey, separating one level of existence from the other.

Things here were wrong, small things that went unnoticed at first; water flowing up hill, coldness when the sun shone, heat when there was ice. It was a lonely, solitary, place, neither one nor the other. Not Heaven, not Hell. Not alive, not dead. He hated it here.

"I have been watching my son," Charles said to the rippling water. "But he is so full of bitterness. Because of me, because I abandoned him, and left him to fend for himself."

His eyes reflected the tears that sobbed in his heart. "I am so afraid," he admitted to the River. "I am haunted by what I have and have not done. Haunted by the future, for what I must do. That which I started I must end. It is the only way for me to find peace. But the way is hard. If only I could explain! Make my son listen!"

He brought his clenched hand up to his mouth, bit the knuckles to stifle the rise of panic and fear. The tears falling, wet, down his face.

"I am so tired," he whispered. "So tired of carrying this burden of guilt. I so want to rest and be forgiven."

He looked out across the River at another dawn rising in the west.

He wept, for he knew what he had to do to gain what he so craved. To put things right, to pay the penance of the guilt he carried, he had to erase what he had created.

Twenty Seven

Saturday 19th October

As Rue had predicted, the graving dock had been hard work. With the overgrowth of weeds and debris cleared, the man-made channel was re-exposed. Dug lower than the river's high tide level, its gravel floor had a slight curve echoing the shape of a ship's bottom and sloped towards the open sluice gates – which Chippy had more or less rebuilt with thickly tarred timber.

With the rising tide they had warped *Sea Witch* into her dry dock and when the tide fell again they had partially chocked her up with spars and blocks of wood, and heaving the gates shut had pumped the last of the water out. The ground would remain wet and muddy; some water inevitably seeped under the gates, but it did not take long to place a few upright timbers and lay a basic walkway.

With all the upper masts unstepped, her rigging gone, and stripped of all that was removable – including her cannons, she looked sad and forlorn. No longer an elegant beauty but naked and vulnerable. The open gunports stared empty, like blind eyes, worm had bored into the woodwork and barnacles clung everywhere. Her thin plating of copper along the keel had partially protected her, though it was worn and dented in several places. The men wasted no time and set to work breeming her with torches, burning off all the weed and barnacles.

The split in her side was quite clear and several other weak points were also noticeable now she was out of the water and was rolled partially to her side.

His neck craning backwards, Jesamiah looked up at the spaces where the great cabin windows should be; it was odd to squint through the funnelled hole that was the seat-of-ease, his personal 'necessary' situated in the larboard quarter cabin. The chute could do with a good clean, he noticed. No wonder it stank.

He wandered on, walked all the way round, his boots squelching in the wetness beneath his feet, stopping every so often to inspect any damage that attracted his attention.

Beneath where the spar of the bowsprit and jib-boom would point forward once they were re-rigged, he peered up at the lonely-looking figurehead leaning outward above the cut-water, the foremost part of the prow. A semi-naked woman, her ample wares well displayed, she was suspended there, her arm pointing the way ahead. A finger was damaged and her face was worn and scraped; some of her hair was splintered and the nipple of her left breast was broken off. She looked so neglected.

"You'll be beautiful again when we've finished with you, darlin'," Jesamiah said, patting the stem where the bow planks met at the very front.

He felt a murmur from the ship herself as his hand rested against the damp wood. He frowned, head cocked on one side, listening intently. They were not words audible by ear, were more of a feeling, a presence, similar to what he shared with Tiola, but fainter. He was always aware of Tiola, he could not see or touch her, but she was there, within him – like his heart, there, inside him. And now this second presence, an awareness of wood and cordage, canvas and tar. Of the sound and smell of the sea, the ripple of river water and the lift of an ocean roller. And more distant, a faint whispered echo, of what she had been before; a living tree. An oak, growing in the greenwood, branches reaching to the sky, roots spreading down and down into the good earth. The living spirit of the *Sea Witch* touching his soul.

She was lost and frightened, aware of her vulnerability, of her enforced helplessness. Jesamiah rested his head against the stem, closed his eyes and pictured her in his mind under full sail, heeling slightly, the wind pressing against her spread of canvas, foam churning at her bow. Spindrift surging over her fo'c'sle. She was alive and he loved her.

All his affection and reassurance poured into her; "You'll be all right, sweetheart. You're safe here, I won't let anyone harm you."

"Talking to yourself now, Captain?" Nat Crocker said from behind him. "They say as how that's a bad sign."

Jesamiah swung around, his free hand going to the dagger sheathed in the small of his back. He took a breath to calm the rapid beat of his heart, the sudden beading of sweat on his skin. He hated people coming up behind him. Another legacy from his damned brother.

"Bad for crew members who come sneaking up," he grumbled. "Aside I was talking to my ship."

Nat sniffed, reached forward to pat the wooden planking. Grinned. "Guess I'll only start worrying when she answers you back then."

Turning away, Jesamiah sniffed disdainfully, wiped his tarred hands on the seat of his breeches and walked away. After a few yards, tossed over his shoulder, "Better start worryin' then."

Apart from supervising, there was not much he could do. He had been avoiding Alicia and the house by insisting he had to see to his ship, but now that *Sea Witch* was laid up and the men were ready to start work on her, he was running out of excuses. And tonight he had to attend a ball.

The last thing he wanted was to prance around like a London fop, but to satisfy Alicia he had agreed to escort her. When he had made the promise, two days ago, his intention had been to keep her quiet about discussing the future of the plantation. Today, with both Finch and her wittering on about best clothes, baths and society manners, he was regretting the rash agreement.

On the other hand, maybe some of the residents of these parts could divulge something interesting about his father's past? Maybe it would be worth going, worth putting on an air of pleasant charm. Maybe tonight he could uncover a few of the answers he was searching for?

There was one thing he had to do first. Something else that he had been deliberately putting off since stepping ashore.

A little way up the hill, overlooking the river, the first of the tobacco fields and the formal gardens, was the cemetery plot. As a child there had been only one grave in the especially cleared space set within the boundary of a neat, white-painted picket fence. The final resting place of Phillipe's mother: Carlos Mereno's widow; Charles Mereno's first wife. On the night Jesamiah had left, after he had almost beaten Phillipe to a pulp, there had been two more graves. His own mother's and the fresh-dug, fresh filled grave of his father. He knew all trace of his mother had been obliterated, Phillipe had seen to that. Jesamiah walked across the short grass to where it should have been, to the left of his father. No headstone, no marker, not even an undulation or a shadow in the ground; the mound had been flattened, grass had grown over every sign of it ever being there. He had learnt, a few years ago now, that Phillipe had disinterred her and thrown her corpse into the cesspit behind the house. He did not know if it was true. Had Phillipe despised her enough to risk eternal damnation?

Impulsively Jesamiah decided to fetch a spade and find out. He turned back with a shake of his head. Leave it. Let her rest, wherever she was. She needed no grave or marker to be remembered, and a body corrupted whether it was placed to rot in a buried coffin or a debris-filled cesspit. She was dead, her soul had no need of the shell that had been her body. Tiola had taught him that.

To the far side was a stone marking the grave of his father's right-hand man, Halyard Calpin. He had been Jesamiah's only friend; had been his father's quartermaster upon the privateer they had both sailed in. Privateer? That's what Father had liked people to believe; that he had sailed with the authority of the Government with a Letter of Marque safe in the drawer of his Captain's desk. Hah! Once the wars were ended, Father had been as much a pirate as had Jesamiah!

Three much smaller graves were laid alongside the fence. Alicia's two boys and the daughter who had died a few days after birth. His daughter, Alicia had said. Was it the truth or was she just being spiteful? He never knew with Alicia; her lies tripped so easily off her tongue. He doubted she could recognise what was truth and what was not.

He walked over to the grave, the hand not thrust through the sling deep in his coat pocket. A plain wooden crucifix marker announced a single name, Charlotte.

He would like a daughter. A little girl to hug and fuss, to preen over and spoil. To buy fancy dresses for and expensive jewellery. To worry over when it came time for young men to come a-courting. He smiled. He'd see most of them off with his pistol. There would never be anyone good enough for a daughter of his!

Was Alicia expecting his child? She had said she was – what, almost three weeks ago now, but how had she known so quickly? How soon would the signs be showing? He tried to think, to picture her figure, tried to recall other women who were with child. All he could visualise was the large belly of an obvious pregnancy.

Why was Tiola not carrying? The thoughts swirled in his head as he stood staring down at the tiny grave. They did not use the lamb's intestine sheaths Tiola insisted on giving to all the men, and it was certainly not anything to do with lack of opportunity or technique. Jesamiah always fulfilled his exertions of passion when making love to her. And yet, only Alicia had claimed he'd sired a child. No other woman had demanded he acknowledge his planted seed. Was he infertile? Was this, perhaps, a punishment from God for all the wicked things he had done in the past? And the ones he was, no doubt, going to do in the future?

Yet Tiola had said there was no one judgmental God, that the rituals of religion only smudged the edges of unanswerable questions. There seemed to be a lot of those of late. Unanswerable questions.

Standing there in the quiet of the cemetery with only the wind for company Jesamiah recalled the rest of the conversation. A discussion that would have had them burnt at the stake as heretics were anyone to have overheard. They had made love and were lying together in their small bed aboard the *Sea Witch*, curled within each other, the sweat drying on their naked bodies, the throb of pleasure gradually fading. He had no idea, now, what had started it; some remark he had made. But he remembered her answer. Word for word.

"Existence began when the first spark of energy destroyed the void of Nothingness. At the Dawn of Time," she had said, "the power of that energy was so great that after a while and a while many, many life forms came to be, in this world and in others. Some thrived, most did not. A few developed the ability to think and remember, some, humans for instance, expanded the process of instinctive thinking into speech and a conscience; the ability to reason, to plan ahead and to know right from wrong."

"Though some have different ideas of what is right and what is wrong," Jesamiah had interrupted.

She had agreed. "Not all Life is what you perceive it to be. There are the

Immortals of Light – the Old Ones of Wisdom with our various gifts of Craft, and the Elementals of the trees, of the wind, air, earth, fire and water – the rain and the rivers, and in the seas where Tethys rules. She is benign for the most part, but has her rages, tempers and cruelties. Then there are the Other Folk, the Spirits who keep themselves hidden for they are shy and peaceful; and angels and daemons who either quietly protect or feed on hatred for their own miserable purpose. There are those of the night who are not bad or good, but merely predators who drink blood to exist."

He had interrupted her again, nibbling at her neck with his teeth, had teased, "Vampires!"

"Of a sort," she had laughed, batting him away. "Though they would take offence at that derogatory term. They are no more evil than is a tiger or a wolf. Many life forms feed on the kill, but it is the reason of the killing that dictates the quality of the life. To kill to survive or for defence is one thing. To kill with hatred, to destroy for no purpose, is another."

Jesamiah squatted beside his father's grave. He killed. He took life without a thought, although usually it was only when someone was threatening his life. But then, if he had not initiated the attack in the first place…A curious thing, this game of life and death.

He had said, "And you are a witch?"

"Witches – Earth Witch, House Witch, Hedge, White, Green – we are all the same. We are called 'witch' from the Old Language. *Wicca*, means wise. We have our gifts of Craft, our special abilities, but many in the past, and probably into the future, were persecuted by the human bigots who feared them."

Removing his hat, Jesamiah bowed his head a moment as he recalled her tears. She had lain in his arms, quietly weeping for those who had died horribly, accused of serving the Devil, though not one who called herself witch would knowingly cause harm, she had said.

"What of Black Witches then?" he had asked.

"Witches are not devil worshippers, Jesamiah. Outside the religions of Abraham the Devil does not exist. He is a creation of mankind, used to terrorise the innocent into believing what they are told. No true witch will cause harm, for what is sent out in anger or spite returns three-fold."

She had shown what she meant. Had pointed her finger at the window and as she pointed, tipped her hand slightly so he could see. "One finger pointing outward, three pointing back."

He tried it again, pointed at his father's grave. One out. Three back. It was a moral worth remembering. What she had said next, though, had been worrying.

"But there is a Dark Power, a negative energy of malevolence. A void of hopeless despair that gorges on emotions such as lust, greed and hatred, and destroys everything its presence touches. The Dark can turn a witch as well as a human. To counter the Dark Power, the Old Ones of Wisdom, with our knowledge of Craft, surrounded ourselves with the protection of the Light and became the Guardians of Earth. For the good of all, with harm to none."

Jesamiah knew there was more she had not said, a lot, lot more. More that she would never say, but she had partially answered one question that humans were not supposed to know, beyond their own limiting beliefs.

"What of ghosts? Is there another life beyond this? When I die will we still be together? Is there a Heaven, Tiola? A Hell?"

"The soul is eternal, it is only the shell it inhabits, the body, that dies. Some spirits move on, others remain behind or find a way to return," she had said. "If they have reason to do so."

And for the rest, she had stayed silent.

With a sigh, Jesamiah pushed himself to his feet. He remembered every word but understood little of it. He turned his attention to his father's carefully tended grave. At its head, a white marble stone giving name and dates:

Cpt. Charles Mereno
1643 – 1707

Nothing else. No mention that he had been a father, grandfather, husband. Idly, Jesamiah traced the lettering with his fingers. He had been four and sixty years of age. Not a young man, but what age was that to die? Old Toby Turner was in his sixties, or so he said, though Jesamiah often thought it a gross exaggeration. His joints creaked, he had lost most of his teeth and could not hear too well – but then none of them could. It was the guns, being so close to the cannon when they fired, that impaired a seaman's hearing. Were he still alive Charles Mereno would be five and seventy now.

Charles Mereno. Only that had not been his real name. His real name had been St Croix. Charles St Croix. So much deception, so many untruths. Lies.

"Why?" he cried aloud with bitterness. "Why did you not tell me he was not my brother? Why did I have to believe he was your eldest son? I thought I had no choice, I had to do as he said because I was the youngest. And because no one believed my mother was your legal wife. For all those years I thought I was the by-blow brat. And I suffered for it. I so suffered for it."

"Maybe your father also regrets the lie."

Jesamiah spun around at the voice behind him, cuffing with his sling at the frustrated tears that had started to trickle down his cheeks, his dagger coming into his other hand, the blade glinting in the late afternoon sunlight.

Embarrassment made him snap the words sharper than he intended. "Who the fok are you?" He had not realised he had been speaking aloud. Was shamed by his public display of raw emotion.

"I watched you sail in the other day. Recognised the ship. *Sea Witch*. She is a credit to you; a fine vessel." The man stood a few yards beyond the far side of the fence, his face in shadow for the sun was directly behind him and his felt hat, sporting a blue feather, was pulled low.

Squinting against the dazzle, Jesamiah could not see him clearly. He caught the impression of grey hair, a trimmed beard and moustache, wrinkled skin and gnarled hands. The clothing was well cut and of good quality, not the garments of a man in want. There was something familiar about him: something that did not sit quite right.

"Do I know you? Are you a neighbour?"

"I know your father…"

Jesamiah swore, interrupted; "Knew him well enough to be saying what he may or may not have regretted, did you?"

"No, you do not understand. I am…" The man hesitated, as if he were about to say something else; let it pass.

Sheathing the dagger, Jesamiah placed his fingers on the butt of the pistol thrust through his waist belt. "I can shoot with either hand, do not let this sling fool you. Who are you?"

The man raised his hands to show he was unarmed. "Your father."

Jesamiah jumped in, misunderstanding for a second time. "I don't want to know about my father. I asked for your name!" He aimed the pistol, his thumb on the hammer. "Come forward so I can see your face. Now."

From the corner of his eye he saw one of the black houseboys running up the hill. A summons. The ball.

"I loathed my father," Jesamiah snapped. "If you intend to try and change my mind on that, forget it. If he was here I'd spit on him for the misery he brought me." To prove his point he spat on the grave.

"He loved you."

"No. He did not. He abandoned me."

"He wanted you to learn how to defend yourself. How to survive."

"He had no time for me."

"Yet he sailed with you to places along the coast and to the Caribbean. He taught you to shoot. Ensured you could read and write, speak different languages. Taught you to navigate, and about ships and the sea."

"And how would you be knowing that?"

"I know it. As I also know how proud he was of you. And still…"

"Proud?" Jesamiah's fists clenched. "What was he proud of? The fact that I could endure misery and torture without a whimper?"

The boy was hopping from one bare foot to the other behind him. "Please Sir, Master, Mr Finch says you come. Says bath ready."

"Tell him to go pleasure himself."

The boy bit his lip, flinched away at the sharp retort.

Closing his eyes, Jesamiah stood, head tilted backwards, breathing in the warm air, staring at the cloudless blue sky. The smell of the river filled his senses, the sun-heated earth, the pervading aroma of tobacco. He put the pistol away, removed his hat and ran a hand through his hair.

"All right, boy, I ain't Master Mereno, I don't hit boys, slaves or women. Well, not unless they deserve it. Run along and tell Finch I will be there in a minute." He turned to speak to the man. "You ain't told me your name."

But he had gone. No one was there. No one stood on the far side of the fence.

No one was in sight.

Twenty Eight

"If thee were t'ask my opinion I'd say thee were a madman. What? Give all this up for a creakin' leakin' hulk of a boat?"

"Just pour the water, Finch, I've got soap in my eyes." Mad? Of course he was mad. Hearing voices that were not Tiola, seeing men who were not there? He was turning bloody madder than those poor sods in Bedlam!

"I mean all these rooms – a copper-lined bathtub. What we got aboard ship, eh? The deck and pumped sea water."

"You know damned well I've a tin bath aboard the *Sea Witch*. And she don't leak. Not normally." Jesamiah shut his eyes as Finch poured a jug of hot water over his head, washing away most of the soap. A second jug soon followed.

"An' linen sheets. Real beds. A kitchen that don't 'ave a stove that goes up and bloody down all the soddin' time."

"I get the idea Finch. You prefer it here. If you want to stay and be Mrs Mereno's houseboy that's fine by me. I'll find someone else to moan at me aboard *Sea Witch* shall I?"

Finch held out a towel, sniffed grumpily as Jesamiah stepped from the water.

"All I'm tryin' t'say is you're intendin' t'take Miss Tiola as wife. Where you goin' t'expect 'er t'live then, eh? Aboard a ship? In that cabin o' yours? An' what about when the bairns come along? Shipboard ain't no place for littl'ns. Whereas this great big 'ouse…"

"Yes, yes, I take your point. Can we drop the subject please?" Irritably, Jesamiah snatched the towel and began to dry himself.

"That one downstairs, she ain't got no right to this place. Nor 'as that cock-proud fop of 'ers. You want t'watch that Samuel Trent. From what I 'ear 'e's always 'ere. An" e don't go 'ome at night neither." Finch tapped the side of his nose, indicating he was revealing a great secret.

Jesamiah did not believe a word of it. All the same, he said, "Good. That means she won't be expecting me to pleasure her."

Walking into the bedroom, he eyed the clothes Finch had laid out on the bed; stockings, white breeches, fine linen shirt and an exquisitely embroidered waistcoat. "If you think I'm stepping into Phillipe's garments you can think again. I want them burnt."

"They ain't 'is. These were yer father's. Mrs Mereno told me to 'elp m'self; everythin's still there in 'is room. Ain't been touched. Put away proper they were, folded nice and strewn with the right 'erbs t'keep the moth out." He lifted the coat, brushed at some fluff, said proudly, "Come up right 'andsome they 'ave."

Hesitating, Jesamiah eyed the clothes. He had thought the waistcoat looked familiar. He remembered his mother embroidering it. Tentative, he peered closer, studied the intricate pattern. A swirl of oak leaves on a dark green background interspersed with tiny gold-thread acorns. Stupidly, a lump cluttered his throat. She had made it for Papa to wear on a special occasion; he could not remember what it was, but he clearly recalled watching them both leave the house and climb into the waiting carriage. Mama had been wearing a matching gown in the same contrasting shades of green. It had rustled as she walked across the wide hallway and out the front door, her heeled shoes tapping on the tiles. Papa had opened the door for her and bowed low. Jesamiah, peeking from the stairs, had heard him say how beautiful she looked. Where had Phillipe been? He could not remember that either, although he did remember running for one of the old oak trees and climbing up high into the canopy to watch the carriage rumble away down the drive. He had sat in that tree all night awaiting their return. And Phillipe, trying to find him, had shouted angrily. The idiot had taken several years to discover Jesamiah's secret refuge in that old oak, a hiding place like the king had used to elude his enemies. Papa had told him that story. Told of how Charles II had eventually escaped to France – or Spain, Holland, or wherever it had been. That part of the tale he could not recall, only the bit where a king had hidden in the sheltering foliage of an oak tree.

Jesamiah's fingers went to where his acorn earring should have been; he toyed with the plain gold hoop instead. Mama had always said that oak trees and acorns were important to Papa. He had never discovered why.

Who was that man he had met by the grave? The voice had been so familiar. The build, the stance. He could think of only one person who looked, sounded, like that.

No! That was nonsense! Silly nonsense!

Stroking the exquisite embroidery, Jesamiah had another thought. His grandfather had been a Cavalier – a Royalist, fighting in the West Country of England against Cromwell's Parliamentarians. That much Jesamiah knew. Nothing more. Was it possible that Papa had also served a Royalist cause as one of Charles II's men? He had sailed with Henry Morgan, a King's Man, so why not?

Handing the waistcoat back to Finch, Jesamiah began to dress.

Grandfather? He had never considered his grandfather before. He knew of Mama's father because she had sometimes spoken of him; on those wistful days when the rain fell or the river mist lingered. Her father had disowned her, had declared her dead for marrying a sea-rogue. She must have loved her husband very much to defy her father – her entire family. She had younger sisters, an elder brother. Papa had never spoken of his parentage, beyond saying his mother had been French and once, when he had been overly drunk, that he had well-to-do connections in Devonshire, England. Where Grandfather had fought? Papa had been base-born, that much Jesamiah knew. Charles had not known the man who had sired him until he was almost a man grown. That, also, Jesamiah knew, but not much more. He started speculating, idle, random thoughts wandering through his mind. Was that why Papa had not been a good father? Because he had no memory of his own childhood pleasures to draw upon? But no, there had been a stepfather, St Croix, who had given Charles his name. Jesamiah let that trail of thought go, only to have another drift in.

Who was that stranger by the grave? Had he been conjuring images; hallucinating? Or had the man really been there? And what of that previous time? Beside Bath Town Creek. The man who had made him get up? He shook his head, baffled. Perhaps he was going mad. He had to be, to put up with this latest nonsense Finch was insisting on.

"If you think I'm wearing that wig, Finch, think again. I'm content with my own hair."

The article in question was a full-bottomed, white-powdered affair with a centre parting and masses of curls which would cascade to the shoulders when worn.

"An' show us all up? Every gentleman wears a peruke, an' this'n is human hair. Very expensive." Lovingly Finch held it up, riffled his fingers through the curls. A moth flew out and powder showered onto the floor.

"I do not care if it cost a king's ransom and is human, horse, goat, cow, calf or a fox's brush, I ain't wearin' it. It's old-fashioned. I'll tie my own hair back."

Finch made a rude noise through his lips, helped Jesamiah into the coat that perfectly matched the waistcoat for style and colour – an elegant, dark green velvet. Normally, Jesamiah did not incline towards green, he would not have it aboard ship, but this was a pleasing, rich, colour. He quite liked it. And anyway, he was not aboard ship

Impassive, he wondered why his father's clothes had remained in the house, but then, clothes were often kept and re-sewn to fit the latest fashion, and these were costly fabrics. Even though they smelt of must and stale cedarwood.

Tempted to wear his own familiar cutlass, Jesamiah put it down at Finch's tutting, buckled on a thinner rapier. That too had been his father's, he assumed. It had a silver hilt and a family crest engraved into the scabbard, but it was rubbed and worn, he could not clearly make out the design. A handsome weapon but utterly useless for fighting. Still, he would not be doing any fighting. Not at a ball.

He finished the ensemble with a silk scarf that Finch fashioned into a sling. Frowned profusely as the man set the wig on his head.

"I feel like a molly boy dressed to tout for business," he grumbled as he descended the stairs, pausing at the bottom to remove one of the buckled patent shoes. "These are too tight; they're pinching."

"You look most splendid!" Alicia's exclamation was genuine. "I do declare, I will be the envy of every lady!"

"Well they must be hard for choice then. I ain't comfortable in these clothes." Jesamiah petulantly squeezed the shoe back on and growled as Alicia hurried forward to adjust the frothed lace of his cravat.

"Cease this fussing, woman. You and Finch between you are turning me into a poppet doll!"

"And very nice you look too," Finch said to himself from the doorway, a satisfied grin curling his usually dour mouth as he watched Jesamiah hand Alicia into the carriage. He walked back into the house taking a long, languid, look around the entrance hall. The elegant curve of the stairs, the paintings on the walls, the expense; the luxury. "I as reckon we could do very nicely 'ere." He nodded to himself. "Very nicely indeed."

Twenty Nine

Charles cursed himself. What a fool. What a fool! What had made him think Jesamiah would be pleased to see him? That his son would welcome him? He was dead, He was gone. To the living he was a ghost!

She had said, the Witch Woman, that it would be difficult putting right the wrongs of the past – huh! Why had he not listened? Angrily he stood up and marched along the bank of the River. The scenery was all the same, an expanse of nothing. Grey and bleak. No rushes or water reeds, plants, shrubs or trees. Nothing but emptiness.

All he had wanted to do, for now, was say he was sorry to his son, to Jesamiah! Yet again he had made a stupid, stupid, mistake. Take it slowly. Gain the lad's confidence – give him time to think. That is what he should have done.

Soon, the Witch Woman would fulfil her promise and help him cross the River and, when the time was right, he would do what he had to do. Until then, his grave anchored him. Near where his bones bound him he could appear in bodily form at will, albeit briefly. Anywhere else, as long as he was near the counterpart of an earthly river, he could project his voice or face – or a shadow of himself. Nothing solid, nothing even remotely real or alive. But come the Night of the Dead, all would be different…

Oh what good was any of it if his son did not want to acknowledge him? Charles groaned with remorse. How dull-witted could he be? His grave, the one place where he could appear as he had been in life, and he had been stupid and frightened the lad into aggressive defence! What in bugger's name had he been thinking of?

Stupid! Stupid!

Thirty

Saturday 19th October – North Carolina

The river was coloured as if it were running with molten gold, the setting sun dazzling on its surface, the occasional waft of a breeze creating diamond-bright sparkles on the flurried wavelets. Tiola loved the peace of evenings, the calm serenity as birds, beasts and the day itself began to settle for the night. Venus was shining low in the sky and Tiola bobbed a respectful greeting to her serene beauty, then sat on the grassy bank contentedly day-dreaming and listening to the sounds, breathing in the scents. Her fingers twiddled the golden acorn that hung from a chain at her neck. The maid had found it in the bed, had assumed it was Tiola's.

Stupidly she had felt unease when the maid had put it into her hand. A sudden feeling of disquiet. Jesamiah did not have his acorn charm – there was nothing to keep him safe. Beyond knowing where he was and that he was alive and recovering from being shot, she had no idea how he was, for she dared not communicate with him too often. She brought the charm to her lips, kissed it. Her doubts, these feelings of unease, were probably nothing. Jesamiah could look after himself, and what could happen in Urbanna? It was hardly the Spanish Main where at any moment he could be attacked by an opposing ship – another pirate, or the Navy. He was on his estate, repairing his ship. Nothing could happen there. Could it?

She set the silly thoughts aside. Tomorrow she would come here again, bring the artist's box she had found on the top shelf of the closet in her room. It was long while since she had taken pleasure in drawing. She was not very talented, but painting and sketching were relaxing pastimes. And despite the pleasure of the river and nature, she did ache for the time to pass quickly, had no desire to spend overmuch of it within the bickering and squabbling that permeated the household. Drawing was a respectable thing for young ladies to do, and conveniently, one that could be accomplished quite innocently in solitude. The young artist she had noticed on her walk with Perdita would perhaps be willing to advise her on the several mistakes she commonly made? How not to make the nose too big in a portrait; to give depth and dimension to a landscape.

But would he want paying? Her funds were running low. Nicholas Page would undoubtedly advance some of her fee were she to ask, but she was receiving board and lodging and did not want to appear in need.

With the sky turning to a darker purple, she closed her eyes and murmured a litany passed down by her ancestors, an ancient prayer of peace.

Light enclose the Circle,
All to fill the Air;
Warming through the deep Earth,
Within the Fire flare.
Light upon the Water
The river and the Sea.
Spirit become the Circle
Protect and bless thou me.

"Muttering to yourself, Mistress Oldstagh, will bring you a bad reputation. You may even be accused of witchcraft!"

Tiola gasped and half scrambled to her feet, the words of protection springing to her lips, which she hastily subdued.

"Forgive me, I did not mean to startle you." Jonathan Gabriel climbed over a semi-concealed fence and stood before her, hastily removing his hat and offering her a bow of greeting.

"You did somewhat surprise me," she confessed, re-seating herself. She indicated the undergrowth encroaching over the narrow track, "I assumed few people came along here."

"Most folk who want the river go to the jetty; there are not many in these parts who appreciate things for beauty alone. And there is nothing to bring them along here, for this path leads only to the Governor's private gardens."

Tiola smiled to herself. Yes, she knew that. She permitted the smile to play along her lips, to reach her eyes as she squinted up at him, his face shadowed by the last rays of the sun setting behind him. "You would not happen to be walking this secretive path for a specific reason?"

"Of course not!" His answer was too quick and loud. Too guilty.

Raising an eyebrow Tiola patted the grass next to her. "You are welcome to sit a while. It would not be advisable to go near the house at the moment. They are all in uproar concerning our near neighbour, Captain Teach. It seems he is among the guests to dine with us tonight. Mistress Page and Perdita do not welcome the prospect and the Governor is therefore affronted."

He sat, his eyes lit with a sparkle of joy at mention of Perdita, his long, lanky arms hugging his bent knees. He might have known this quiet, enigmatic young lady would guess the reason for his being here. This path led discreetly to the shrubs and trees that bordered the rear of the house, and in particular, where Perdita Galland's bedchamber was situated. "We do not meet often," he admitted. "Some evenings such as this I wait for nightfall, creep into the garden and gaze at her window." He glanced sharply at Tiola. "Is that so very wrong of me?"

Tiola squeezed his hand. He had long, slender fingers, those of his right hand callused where the sewing needles had rubbed the skin hard. "No my dear, it is not wrong. Love that comes from the heart and fills the soul is never wrong. Although Governor Eden may well not agree with me."

Frustrated, Jonathan plucked a stalk of feathered grass, began systematically shredding it. "I so love her, Mistress Oldstagh, but what am I to do? I am a tailor's son. Eden will never permit me to court her. Never. Yet he lets that sodding pirate romp through the house – begging pardon for m'language."

Tiola almost burst out with the fact that she was well used to bad language, being affianced to a man who was still in heart, body, and soul, despite his papers of amnesty, a pirate.

"All I can do is find a way to make my fortune. That is the only thing respected round here. Money. Look at Teach, he is admired because he scatters gold like," he tossed the grass into the water, "like grass seed."

There was little Tiola could say to console him. "It is a pity that men – fathers – put such store on wealth, for a husband who is skilled at a trade is a fine prospect."

"Not in my case. I would be better off were I to become a pirate." Jonathan's words were bitter as he stood, his face crunched into despair. "Thieves, murderers and rapists seem to be admired in this wretched town. Honest men who respect women count for naught." He tipped his hat, turned on his heel and walked away, unable to say more for the rage swelling in his throat.

A soothing charm of hope and calm would have been of benefit to him but Tiola dared not send one. Teach's influence had spread like a canker through Bath Town, his presence drifted on the wind as a foul odour. The man was consumed by the malevolence of the Dark Power, which sought the Craft of an Old One of Wisdom like a fox attracted to the hen house. And until that babe kicking so forcefully inside Elizabeth-Anne's belly decided to be born, Tiola could not risk slipping the bolt and luring the predator in to face his doom.

Thirty One

Virginia

The shoes were too small and the wig was itching. Jesamiah had already found two fleas in it. A few young ladies had fluttered their fans and eyelashes at him, but his scowl had soon sent them scurrying in search of more sociable company.

Ralph Wormeley's Rosegil was a splendid house set in a grand estate, with more than two miles of river frontage – twice that of la Sorenta. The Wormeleys, too, were a grand family, Virginia's answer to English nobility. The man himself acknowledged Jesamiah with a passing nod of greeting when first he had arrived with Alicia on his arm, but the family kept themselves apart from the general mêlée of guests. Once or twice the daughters had danced and the sons appeared to be enjoying themselves at the gaming tables. Jesamiah wondered whether his status would change were he to take over la Sorenta officially. As a landowner, would his face become acceptable?

By the look of her, Alicia was having the time of her life; two hours into the evening she had partaken of every dance and openly flirted with every young man present. Only one of the dances so far, Jesamiah noted, had been with Samuel Trent. He was busy talking to various men of wealth and connection. Attempting to raise money in order to buy la Sorenta, Jesamiah assumed. Good luck to him. Maybe if there was a decent figure offered he might consider the proposal. Four thousand pounds sterling would be about right. And it would have to be cash, not the tobacco barter based on what was available or the value of next year's tobacco crop. Hard, solid cash. It would not be easy for Trent to raise it. Only wealthy men had access to that sort of financial resource. And pirates.

That was another thing rankling him; Governor Spotswood's regulations against piracy. He'd had to ride into Urbanna to register his presence with the Constable. He hated riding, his legs were made for the sea not for sitting astride a fat-rumped cob. He'd had to sign his name and swear to God, with one hand on the Bible, that he had accepted amnesty and committed no offence of theft or murder on the High Seas or waterways below the low tide mark after the month of July. Both the signing and the ride had been a humiliating experience.

There was no sign of that other man, the rider who had cantered off on the day of their arrival. Jesamiah had not learnt his name or anything about him. But then, he had not asked. He was not interested. Who Alicia chose to squabble with was her concern, not his.

Jesamiah sipped the champagne, wondered whether he could ask for a tot of rum or brandy. Who was he fooling? He had no intention of remaining in Virginia. What did he want with a tobacco plantation – that tobacco plantation? Why not sell it to Trent at the price he could afford and be done with it? Yet curmudgeonly old Finch had been right; Tiola would not want to be spending the rest of her life at sea. Not if the bairns did start coming along.

He glanced at Alicia, poised and elegant as she joined hands with her present partner to lead out and turn single. What was this dance? Something like, *Swinny Was Tall* the musicians had said. No, that was the previous one, a new dance apparently. There had been a lot of laughter and a few stumbling feet from those unfamiliar with the steps. Alicia had known it perfectly. How did she learn these dances? Who had taught her? The questions were piling into Jesamiah's head. If she was with child, his child, how soon before she showed? Her belly was as flat as a dead-calm sea.

She looked exquisite in a scarlet silk gown edged with black lace. Knowing her as intimately as he did, Jesamiah guessed the colours matched all the way down to her skin. With her honey-coloured hair piled in an elaborate creation of curls and ringlets, and rubies dripping from ears, throat and fingers, she was the most stunning woman present. But then, most of the others were either over forty or giggling girls who had never been kissed.

He removed another glass of champagne from a servant's tray. "Who the heck was Swinny?" he asked. "And is he tall?"

The black servant shook her head, bewildered, not understanding for he had got the title wrong. Jesamiah shrugged, emptied the glass, exchanged it for another full one.

The dancing and hubbub of chatter slithered to a ragged halt, the orchestra's enraptured violinist screeching a few notes alone until he realised his colleagues had ceased playing.

"Well," Jesamiah mumbled into the sudden silence, resisting the urge to spit on the polished ballroom floor. "Alexander Spotswood himself. Lieutenant Governor of Virginia has graced us with his presence."

Opinion was divided regarding the Governor's popularity and the uncomfortable pause while he stood a yard inside the entrance removing his hat, cloak and gloves, was noticeable. Spotswood was not known for tact, conviviality or equanimity towards civic and church officials, while military men, richer plantation owners and those with an excitement for adventure approved of him wholeheartedly. The Governor, depending on whether you needed his favour or not, was either admired or detested.

Being at the head of the dance and near the entrance, Alicia was the first to sink into an elegant curtsey, her reminder of etiquette rippling through the crowded room like the crest of a rolling wave. As Spotswood walked further in, nodding a greeting here and there, several men failed to acknowledge him, a few clergymen and Virginia burgesses going so far as to turn their backs. Unperturbed, Spotswood disappeared into a side room where the gentlemen were playing cards or billiards and the underlying atmosphere in the ballroom almost immediately lost its chilled air of tension. Dancers and spectators began to smile and chat again; the orchestra resumed their lively tune and soon the room was vibrating with tapping feet and clapping hands.

"Are thee not dancin', Sir?" A middle-aged woman with three daughters in tow had to repeat her question twice before Jesamiah realised she was talking to him. "There are more men than girls here; always so of course. 'Tis a pity the young ladies must sit out and not be permitted to show their figures to best advantage. Do thee not agree?"

The young ladies she spoke of were reasonably pretty and Jesamiah should have answered politely, but his mood had been rapidly blackening with every tedious minute – and was not the sling around his neck an obvious reason why he did not dance?

"In my experience, Ma'am, the only way a girl's figure can be seen to best advantage is when she is stripped naked and moaning in ecstasy beneath me."

As a method of halting a conversation it worked most efficiently. Outraged, Agatha Chalmondy tilted her head in the air and took herself and her daughters off to the far side of the room where she began telling everyone, word for word, what Jesamiah had said, pointing at him to ensure her listeners correctly identified the disgusting scoundrel.

"What have you done to so offend people?" Alicia asked twenty minutes later during a pause in the dancing. "The gossip about you is somewhat ferocious." She flopped down into a seat beside him, fanning herself furiously, cheeks flushed with breathlessness and the heat of so many bodies and candles. "The ladies appear quite scandalised and the men are reaching for their rapiers. I believe three are considering calling you out. Honestly Jesamiah, can I not leave you alone for five minutes without you stirring trouble?"

"Then let me go home. I don't fit comfortable in these surroundings. Nor these shoes."

"Certainly not. If you leave I will be expected to go with you, and we have not even had supper yet."

Samuel Trent joined Jesamiah soon after Alicia was whisked away by a uniformed marine for another lively dance, one that involved a lot of skirt twirling, the risqué exposure of a well-turned ankle and the occasional raucous shout. With Trent, a navy officer: Lieutenant Robert Maynard.

"You are a seaman I hear?" Maynard enquired affably after the formal courtesy of introduction. "Was that your ship we saw heading in a few days ago? Blue-hulled; square-rigged?"

"It was. *Sea Witch*."

"A sight for sore eyes, I can tell you. Made a change to see a vessel trimmed as she should be and looking as pretty as any of the young fillies here present."

Jesamiah remained silent. The English Royal Navy had a selection of imbeciles for admirals and most of the captains were as bad. Men who had bought their positions or inherited them from prestigious fathers and uncles; few could sail a ship efficiently across a garden pond let alone an ocean. Too much emphasis had gone on the Spanish and French wars, too many captains had only patrolled up and down from Biscay to the Med, or maintained a blockade on French and Spanish ports. King George and his naval officers regarded the American Colonies and the Caribbean as unimportant. Several thousand miles of distance made for complacency. The vessels sent to patrol the seas and coasts, and ostensibly to hunt pirates, were poorly crewed and in poorer condition. Pirates could provision and careen when and where they liked, Navy ships were not permitted to use anywhere except official docks. In the Caribbean that meant places like Antigua, Port Royal and Nassau, or the scattered forts of the American coast. Uncareened ships did not sail well. They were sluggish, full of worm and soon rotted. Poorly fed men fell sick and died.

And most of the captains were easy to bribe or had fingers firmly dipped into various profitable but illegal pies. Was it any wonder not one single pirate had been caught and hanged in more than three years? That men like Blackbeard could piss in the face of the Admiralty?

Jesamiah decided on a tactful answer. "I thank you for the compliment. What vessel are you with?"

"The *Pearl* under Captain George Gordon. We are here to escort the Governor back to Williamsburg tomorrow. He has been surveying the land upriver this last month. He wants to encourage more settlers, I believe."

The *Pearl*? Jesamiah remembered seeing her.

"What line of business are you in?" Maynard asked. "I take it you are not in the tobacco trade?"

"As a matter of fact I am. I own la Sorenta."

Maynard seemed suitably impressed, if somewhat confused. "But I thought Mrs Mereno…"

Here we go again, Jesamiah thought. "My father owned it prior to her husband's occupation of the premises."

Still not quite understanding, Maynard let the matter go. He was young, in his early twenties, and had not been stationed in Virginia long, had, as he explained, only recently been appointed First Lieutenant and was anxious to prove himself worthy of the promotion. "It was a sad business, Mr Mereno's death."

"Not from where I stood. I killed him before he managed to kill me." As another conversation stopper, it was again blunt.

Samuel laughed. "I told you, Rob, our friend here is not one of our more conventional landowners. His heart remains aboard his ship and he'd rather have his seaman's boots on his feet than those ballroom shoes. Ain't that right, Jesamiah?"

Unexpectedly disgruntled at being addressed with such familiarity, Jesamiah bridled. The young man dared presume too much. "Captain Acorne to you, boy."

Trent collected himself and apologised, "Forgive me, Captain, I did not intend to offend. A surfeit of wine has loosened my tongue."

The moment the words had left his mouth Jesamiah regretted it. The boy was not to blame for this itching wig and the pinching shoes. He was, though, becoming a little too much of a close shadow. He had been at the plantation every day, offering to help where he could with getting the *Sea Witch* as she should be; had proved himself capable with saw and chisel – Chippy had been most impressed by his talent and eagerness. As indeed was Jesamiah, but it was becoming a little embarrassing to find him always there, somewhere close by. Trying to impress, of course, to show he was keen and reliable. Ah, the slip was not the lad's fault.

"Apology accepted, lad, though you have an advantage over me. I notice my glass is empty and I have not partaken of nearly enough wine to loosen anything. Perhaps as penance you would go in search of an unclaimed bottle or two?"

Trent took the hint and trotted off. He was mortified to have shown the Captain up in front of Robert Maynard. That was why Acorne had been sharp with him – a breach of etiquette to be so familiar while in the company of another officer. He had enjoyed himself these past days being with the men, working hard and honestly with those who genuinely appreciated his efforts. He did not want to lose the enjoyment.

Maynard skirted the exchange with dexterity. "I agree with you, Captain; give me a heaving deck in a hurricane wind with all sails blown out and the likelihood of sinking any moment over the fal-de-roll of a ball!"

A few months ago, in a similar circumstance, Jesamiah would have been rapidly thinking of ways to be gone as quickly and silently as possible. Piracy and the Royal Navy, for all their ineptitudes and granting of amnesties, did not mix. But he did have his pardon and he had signed that wretched declaration. He was no longer a pirate, could speak to a naval officer on equal terms if he so chose. And he did choose. He liked this fellow Maynard.

"Tell me, Captain," Maynard asked a moment later, "how would you go about making sure the next shipment of tobacco remains safe? I have been given the unenviable task of escorting the next tobacco convoy to London."

"Forget it, mate. The crop was poor and with Blackbeard not far away you'll not get out the Chesapeake."

Indignantly, Maynard drew himself up to his full height of almost six feet. "Neither Blackbeard, nor any pirate, frightens me. I have been offered this commission and I will succeed. As much as I respect and admire Captain Gordon, I would wish the title of Captain for myself. Aside, I hear Teach has been issued a pardon. He has surrendered the illicit life of piracy."

Jesamiah guffawed outright. "It was Teach who shot me, man! If he remains committed to a pardon for more than a moon month, then I am a butterball of a Dutchman. And if you do not fear Blackbeard, then you are a fool."

"I am a naval officer, Sir! I fear no one."

About to make a scathing retort, Jesamiah was interrupted by a booming, authoritative voice.

"Then you should. Teach is a madman, and mad men are dangerous." The speaker stepped away from the group he had been talking to, transferred his glass of wine to his left hand and held out his right. "Governor Alexander Spotswood. I understand you to be Jesamiah Acorne?"

Noticing the discourteous lack of his title, Jesamiah took a moment to decide whether to accept the handshake or not. His head tipped slightly to one side he scrutinised the man; mid-forties, well built with the encroaching signs of a paunch belly, a straight nose and direct eyes that matched his razor-sharp attitude. He was dressed elegantly but not expensively. A man who preferred to get things done rather than prance around in gold-buckled shoes. Brandishing his sling, Jesamiah gave a token bow and offered his left hand. "M'shoulder's barely healed. I ain't supposed to move it more than necessary."

"I believe you are here to take over la Sorenta? It is a fine property, though aside from the house and stabling, somewhat neglected. We cannot afford to waste land here along the Rappahannock. I am encouraging farmers to settle, to push westward, don't ye know? There's some fine ground further in, all it needs is for the forest to be cleared and crops to be planted. Wheat, to plant wheat, that's what we need."

Indicating two vacant chairs the Governor seated himself inviting Jesamiah to join him and chivvying Maynard away.

"Forgive me for saying so, but who is going to grow wheat when there is money in tobacco?" Jesamiah wondered how the Governor knew so much about him and why he was bothering to answer. He really did not care one way or the other for Virginia, or Governor Spotswood's idealistic plans. As he expected, the answer was direct.

"Tobacco brings in a profit when the harvest inclines to be good and when only the best is exported. I am dealing with that issue by the initiation of various inspection schemes." Spotswood laughed, "Though not everyone likes my reforms."

The laugh faded and he scowled at a group of men near the entrance who glowered as ferociously back. "Those who have a brain between their ears see the sense of what I am doing. No tobacco is to leave Virginia without an assurance of quality. Like most of them along the Rappahannock here, you grow Sweetscented, I assume?"

"Aye, though when I get m'bearings I reckon I'll change to Oronoco. It's a better crop for making money."

Spotswood tapped snuff from a small gold box on to his hand, noisily sniffed it up his nostrils, dismissive. "No, no, far too strong for the Englishman's taste."

"I'd not sell to the English."

The Governor frowned, his forehead wrinkling and eyes narrowing. "Aside from such an idea being against English trade laws, ye would entertain the damned Spanish and French markets? I think not, my lad, I think not!"

Leaning back in his chair – drawing in his feet as a pair of exuberant dancers whirled too close – Jesamiah smiled lazily. "I ain't a farmer, I'm a sailor and a trader. I'd take m'crop m'self, sell it where I can get the highest price, so why not Oronoco to sell to the Dons and Frenchies? We are not at war any more; last month's spat blew over in a few weeks." He chuckled humourlessly. "Must have been one of the shortest wars known. Lasted all of twelve days, or so we heard in Nassau."

Spotswood hrrumphed at being gainsaid, argued, "Mark my word, we will be at war again with one or other of 'em soon – an' even they don't like trash tobacco. Poor stuff mixed with floor sweeping and dust might sell once, the buyer will never come back for more. Which is why I am bringing in my inspection reforms. Quality Virginia Tobacco. Guaranteed."

Inspections would be impossible to oversee. "Out of interest, Sir," Jesamiah asked, "just how are you planning on enforcing your reform? There is nothing you could do to stop me loading my hogsheads of tobacco onto my ship and sailing away with it."

"Give me time, Acorne and my ideas will be accepted. Without a signed and sealed inspection pass, traders will not accept a cargo. You'll see. You'll see."

The dance was ending. Slapping his free hand on his knee, Jesamiah joined in the applause. He had to admit to himself that Alicia was most alluring. He watched Trent go up to her, say something which made her laugh. Should he let the fellow run the plantation? Or did he want to be rid of it?

"To sell tobacco you have to grow it," he said. "The last harvest has been bad and pirates roam the Chesapeake and Atlantic coast. One or other will shred the profits to nothing."

Spotswood sucked his cheeks a moment, then conceded the point, though Jesamiah had the idea that he had been about to say something entirely different. "Poor harvests will cripple us much as they did for those first settlers in 1607. Do you know y'history, Acorne?" Spotswood gave Jesamiah no opportunity to answer yea or nay, but launched onward without a pause for breath.

"One hundred and forty-three men and women under the command of Captain Newport almost starved to death. They sailed the *Sarah Constant*, *Godspeed* and *Discovery* thirty miles up the river they named the James in honour of the King, tied the ships to trees and set about building the first English settlement in the Americas. All the land not in the hands of the Spanish or the French they claimed as a colony for England and called it Virginia in honour of Elizabeth the Virgin Queen." He smiled ironically, "We tend to name a lot of places after our monarchs."

Jesamiah nodded. He'd noticed.

Spotswood pointed at the window indicating the dark night beyond the lights and movement reflected in the glass. "Take Urbanna here and Annapolis, both named for Queen Anne. Then we have Williamsburg as our capital town – and Maryland. I fought for Anne, you know. Served with Marlborough at Blenheim. God is my life but that was a battle I am both proud to remember and afeared to recollect! The damage to men and horses was horrendous. Horrendous."

"Don't see anyone falling over their feet to stamp our King George's name on anything," Jesamiah responded. "The House of Hanover ain't being glorified much, is it?"

The Governor cleared his throat tactfully. He was a king's man – he had to be, but he also disliked the German King, George. He also possessed a sense of humour. "Give it time, someone will find a turnip field for him. Though I'd rather the man would at least learn English before we started regaling him." Taking a glass from a servant's tray the Governor handed it to Jesamiah and took one for himself.

The champagne was one of the best vintages Jesamiah had tasted, and wearing these ridiculous clothes he reasoned he may as well behave the part of a landed gentleman to the hilt. He raised the glass. "To the King. May he soon be suitably landed."

Raising his own glass, Spotswood chuckled a response; "To the King. May his American rivers be long, his soil fertile – and may he stay as far away from them as possible!"

They touched glasses, drank.

"Those first settlers, Acorne, saw that Virginia was green and the game was plentiful, but they had inept leaders ill suited to making hard decisions and attending even harder labour. They built their settlement on the marsh, which brought disease and famine. Within three years, more than half of them were dead, but God intervened and the colony survived. I tell you this little homily for a reason. We cannot survive on tobacco. We can grow it, we can sell it – to Englishmen, the French or the Spanish, to whoever will buy it in fact, but we cannot eat it. What is more, where tobacco grows the soil falls dead, nothing more will thrive in it. So we clear more forest and plant more tobacco and take the life from yet more ground. What do we do? Follow this example all the way to the mountains, then over the ridge and into whatever godforsaken wilderness lies beyond?"

It was a rhetorical question but Jesamiah answered anyway. "So we grow wheat as well?"

The Governor slapped his shoulder, the uninjured one. "You have it, my boy. You have it! We grow wheat as well."

Wheat. Real farming. Ploughing, irrigating, harvesting, threshing. Jesamiah had no intention of becoming a farmer. None at all. He decided to change the subject. "Tell me, Governor, do the mountains truly have a blue ridge?"

Eager, alighting enthusiastically on his favourite topic, Spotswood nodded. "Aye, they do; it's a haze of the light or so they tell me. Y'know I took an expedition across there a couple of years back? First white people to do so. Knights of the Golden Horseshoe we called ourselves." His fingers went to a lapel pin, a horseshoe fashioned in pure gold. "You should see the Big Valley, lad, the Shenandoah." He closed his eyes, shook his head, remembering. "By Gad, our Lord used all his love to fashion such absolute beauty. The native Indians call it the Daughter of the Stars." He snapped his eyes open. "We need to push westward. There is land out there for the taking, land for growing wheat and corn – and tobacco and cotton. It is there, it is all there. Waiting."

Tempted to say he had no interest in pushing westward, in the condition of the soil, clearing forests or growing and exporting tobacco, Jesamiah held his tongue but quipped instead; "Plenty of opportunity for King George yet then."

Thirty Two

North Carolina

While the women of Governor Eden's household had initially objected to the evening's dinner arrangements, his other guests, male and female, were thoroughly enjoying themselves. And Tiola had to admit, albeit reluctantly, when he put his mind to it Edward Teach could be charming. He knew how to flatter, how to tease just that little bit near the edge – then draw back before offence was given. Could tell a tale that had every man and woman at the table listening, mouth agape, the food before them forgotten. He had them all caught, like fishes to the line. No wonder Bath Town so welcomed him. He brought entertainment as well as money.

He was dressed well, smart; was clean, tidy, every inch the gentleman. And not unattractive at first glance. On arrival he had kissed the ladies' hands, then escorted Elizabeth-Anne, as the eldest and senior woman present, to table where he proceeded to enthral everyone with tales and anecdotes, his broad Bristolian accent more subdued and not so noticeable. Listening, keeping herself as unobtrusive as possible, Tiola marvelled at his vocal dexterity. He had every one of those present, even herself at one point, eating out of his hand as he regaled them with daring adventures and exploits of his life on the High Seas.

He recounted how he had begun his life at sea after running away from home to become a midshipmen at the age of twelve. He had heard of a privateer anchored in Bristol harbour, her captain was looking for crew.

"I had heard of him," he said, "my mother had spoken often of this p'tickler cap'n." He had winked and guffawed, and added, "And aye, I often wondered when she did, why she'd'ad a twinkle glistenin' in her old eye!"

They had laughed and he had gone on to say how and where he had fought and what great battles they had won.

"I was presented at Court to good Queen Anne," he boasted, after raising several toasts to her memory. "It was after the Battle of Gibraltar – I was there, my ship was nigh on blown to pieces." And he had described the battle, thrilling them all with exciting detail.

John Ormond in particular was impressed by the fact that his future son-in-law had personally spoken to the old Queen, and declared, after another toast, that his daughter was fortunate to be wedding such a distinguished man of the world. Mary Ormond, seated next to Teach, blushed and smiled proudly, her arm going occasionally to touch his arm shyly. In response he took her hand, kissed it, made a comment that soon her belly would be as large and round as was that of Mistress Page. Everyone laughed and nodded benignly, Mary blushed again, Tiola pretended to be busy with her plate.

Mary was not yet sixteen. Teach was fifty.

A servant entered discreetly, spoke quietly into Nicholas Page's ear. He excused himself, left the table, Elizabeth-Anne watching him go. She looked well, if somewhat large, and Tiola had been surprised that Teach had not made one comment beyond remarking that the lady's child would be a son to be proud of – though was she certain she was not carrying an entire ship's crew in there?

Several times Teach had attempted to draw Perdita into the conversation, but she had refused to meet his eye and had spoken barely a word. Tiola felt sorry for her, forced to endure company she had no interest in while her heart and mind were on a young man elsewhere. Tiola knew exactly how the girl felt. Her hand went to the acorn on the chain around her neck. It took great effort to force herself to not even think of contacting Jesamiah. Even then, even with this small thought of him, Teach regarded her across the table, his stare intense, suspicious, and she heard the faint rustling of the Malevolents, saw the shadows in one corner of the room grow denser, darker. She let go of Jesamiah's acorn, busied her mind on selecting food from the platters in the centre of the table – and was relieved when the same servant who had summoned Nicholas Page entered and spoke quietly into her ear.

"It seems my healing skills are required," she said. "Pray, do excuse me."

She felt Teach's gaze on her back as she left the room. She knew that if she turned around he would be smiling, playing the part of the charming gentleman. Not one of the others, not Governor Eden, John Ormond or his daughter, Mary, could see through his deception.

Thirty Three

"Mistress Oldstagh!" Nicholas Page's voice. Striding across the hall, his boots rapping on the floor tiles, his expression creased into concern. "I apologise for disturbing your meal, but Royal Sunlight is in need of expert assistance."

Tiola frowned, "I am sorry, I do not follow you?"

"My best brood mare. It looks like colic to me; sweating, restless, kicking at her belly, but our head groom is fifty miles away attending his sick mother and I have no idea how to deal with this. She has been bad a while, I think, those useless grooms noticed nothing untoward until half of an hour since. I wondered if you would assist me?" He twirled his hat in his hands, embarrassed. "Though if my asking offends you please say. I would not belittle your experience or capabilities, she is nothing more than a horse."

Reassuring him Tiola touched his arm, "If I can I will help any creature in distress, human or horse. I will be needing linseed oil and plenty of light, if you would organise those I will fetch what else I require from my room."

She touched his arm again and smiled. "And believe me, the interruption is most timely."

Ten minutes later, her fancy gown changed for something old and practical, and a valise containing a few useful items in her hand, she ran down the back servants' stairs. They led directly to the rear of the house and the stable yard, a quicker route than the main front stairs.

Halfway down she met a maid struggling upward with a basket of logs for the Master's chamber. The girl looked dismayed, fearing she would have to trudge downward to allow the young woman to pass, but Tiola shook her head and flattened herself against the wall.

"Come girl, you are stick thin, there is plenty of room."

With one flight to descend, Tiola heard a door open somewhere below, briefly caught the clack of voices and laughter before it shut again. The dining room. Had someone entered or exited?

The narrow hall at the bottom of the stairs was dark, lit by only one frugal lamp, but Tiola found her way to the kitchens with ease. The servants were a little startled to see her, but at her polite request eagerly put water to boil and provided her with a lantern to light her way.

Wasting no time with following the gravel pathway, she walked quickly and direct across the expanse of lawn, her boots scuffing the dew-wet grass, the hem of her gown soon heavy and sodden around her ankles. A stand of trees to the centre rustled in the night breeze; an owl called. She paused, head turning to one side, listening. Something was wrong.

Too late! Footsteps moving fast behind! An arm grabbing her around the waist, a hand clamping over her mouth.

"Hello wummun. I think thee and me need to talk."

Teach!

Thirty Four

Dropping both valise and lantern, Tiola squeaked in alarm and fear. The lantern rolled a few feet, the flame spearing weird shadows, then went out. Her natural instinct built a spell of protection, but as immediately she discarded the reflex action. She could not give her abilities away; had to react as would any ordinary woman.

She kicked and squirmed as best she could, her fingers clawing uselessly at the arm holding her tight about the waist and at the hand over her mouth.

"Now, now, missee, thee behave an' thee'll not be 'urt."

Tiola had control of every nerve and fibre of her being; she made her glands secrete sweat, raised her heartbeat and breathing level. Drenched her body with the reaction of fear. In her mind she was seething with fury. How dare this wretch assault her! How dare he! By the Word of Wrath, Jesamiah would have something to say about this if she told him! Except she would not tell. This, she would keep to herself.

Keeping his hand firmly over her mouth, Teach swivelled so that he was facing her, his body pressing into hers, the bulge of his erection hard against her. "I be goin' to remove m'hand from thy mouth, missee. But I be warnin' thee, one soun' an' thee'll regret it. Doos thee be understandin' me?"

Beyond widening her eyes and increasing the tremble of stark fear Tiola made no response.

Bruising and hurting, he pressed with his fingers, digging them into her cheek and jaw, shook her face beneath his grasp. "I said, be thee understandin'?"

She nodded.

He released her, his hand going instead to the chain at her neck. "An acorn. Doos thee know someone called Acorne?"

She shook her head.

"Know what, missee? I doesn't believe thee. I b'lieve thee know Acorne very well. Intimately well."

Instinct was screaming at her to keep that she was Jesamiah's woman, secret.

Teach guffawed. "Ah, 'tis no matter. If 'e still be alive when thee doos next see him, thee can tell 'im how much better I be at satisfying a wumman, eh?" He dipped his head and covered her mouth with his own.

Tiola gasped. The man had syphilis! Through her healing Craft she could taste it, smell it. That explained the sores, the foul odour, the insanity. Even without the sexual disease he tasted vile. That poor girl, Mary Ormond. He was rife with it, his wife would be infected the moment he entered her on their wedding night. Tiola whimpered as he probed with his tongue and felt his hand groping for her gown, edging it upwards. Mary Ormond, for now, must needs take care of herself, Tiola had her own problem. Edward Teach had every intention of raping her.

Had she been the quiet, shy person he thought her to be he would have succeeded. With her gift of Craft she had the ability to end his life here and now, but that was not an option. Even in situations of personal danger she had to take care to not reveal who and what she was – an Old One, a Witch Woman. With her use of Voice she could send an assailant stumbling off, his mind blank of what he had been intent on doing; or raise a shield of defence, an impenetrable barrier that would enclose and protect her. Where appropriate, she could transform herself to appear old and haggard, or even to blend with her environment, become one with her surroundings, invisible to the human eye – or any number of other things. But she dared not risk showing her Craft, for the Dark was vindictive and cruel. Not until the child was born safely would she risk drawing attention to herself. Not if there were alternatives.

She did what any backstreet whore would do. She let her body relax, seemingly resigning herself to his violation. He responded by pushing her against the solidity of a tree, holding her there by the force of his pressing body. Meeting no resistance his left hand went beneath her petticoats, eagerly groping upwards, his right unfastened his breeches. His breathing was fast, sweat gleaming on his forehead, his excitement building to its peak.

Tiola moved fast. She bit his lip and with her hand, grasped his ear and twisted it, hard. Simultaneously, she raised her knee and connected solidly with his testicles.

He bellowed pain and rage in a roar of surprised agony and crumpled to the grass, his hands clutching at himself. Tiola hitched her gown to above her knees and fled.

Hearing the outer stable door slam, Nicholas looked up from where he was squatting stroking the mare's sweat-soaked neck. She had been laying down these last five minutes, her eyes closed, groaning. He saw Tiola's dishevelled state, the anxiety on her face. He hurried to her, took her arm. "My dear, what has occurred? Are you ill? Are you harmed?"

Slowing her breath, Tiola shook her head and reassured him she was unhurt. "There was a man lurking in the trees; he frightened me."

"He attacked you?"

She decided to lie. To tell the truth would make a fuss, and she did not want that. She shook her head again. "No, I was alarmed, being ridiculous; my thoughts were on your mare and he startled me, that is all. He was only relieving himself, poor man." She forced a laugh. "I dropped my bag though, perhaps one of your grooms could retrieve it?"

One of the men sauntered out into the night, quickened his pace when Nicholas barked at him to shift himself.

"Where is this mare?" Tiola asked, heading for the open stable door, putting Teach's unpleasantness behind her. She went immediately to her knees, took the sweat-drenched bay's head into her lap and stroked the mare's face and cheeks; her wet, trembling neck.

It was colic. And Tiola had been called too late.

Thirty Five

Virginia

Trent watched Robert Maynard approach one of the young ladies and offer to dance. He was a brave soul; the girl in question was horse-faced, plump and as poor as a church mouse. No one else had paid her any heed all evening, unlike Alicia who, in Samuel's opinion, had enjoyed the benefit of too much attention.

Couples were beginning to drift towards the dining room where supper would soon be served. Where was Alicia? He could not see her – had she already gone to the tables? Surely not, she would have waited for her escort, Acorne, and he was engaged in conversation with the Governor. Trent smiled wryly to himself. Spotswood was full of good intentions but so easily alienated people with his outrageous ideas and sheer bloody-mindedness. He was also a pirate hater. Samuel wondered how Spotswood would react when he found out about Acorne's background, although it would not surprise him if the man already knew. Spotswood had a reputation for knowing everyone's personal business. It was said he was aware of every passed belch and fart, and who was illicitly sharing which lady's bed.

For his own part, for all his respect and liking for him, Samuel was unsure whether he condoned what Acorne had been or not. Pirates were murderers and thieves, thugs and bullies – yet that description fitted his brothers as aptly. If there was a choice between Jesamiah Acorne as a pirate and his brothers, aye, he knew all too clearly where his sympathy would be placed.

When their father died he, Samuel, would become a homeless pauper. His brothers had already made that as clear as day. His talent, his enjoyment, was for farming tobacco. He had started learning by trotting at heel to his father's various managers and overseers – initially because it had been a place to be safe from his brothers' bullying, but very soon he had taken an interest, started asking questions and rapidly digested the answers.

As estate manager to la Sorenta he could make a handsome living. He would more or less be his own boss, free to follow his own life. And the slight misgivings over those years of piracy notwithstanding, he would enjoy working for Captain Acorne. Enjoy it very much.

He looked across at the Captain deep in conversation with Spotswood. The Governor wanted able men to assist him in a variety of projects – more settlers to push further inland and to clear the forests, reclaim the fertile land for growing wheat. Men to explore westward; to finance the completion of his palace down in Williamsburg. Men to aid him in his war against piracy. Samuel wondered if he ought to have warned Jesamiah – Captain Acorne. Damn, he should force himself into the habit of retaining respect, but it was so difficult when, from a boy of tender years, he had always called him Jesamiah.

The fact that the Captain had not at first remembered him had stung a little, but then, on reflection Samuel took it as a blessing. Events that had happened here along the Rappahannock, for both of them, were perhaps best forgotten.

A late-comer hurried into the room, red-faced, wig askew, much to the annoyance of the busybodies who immediately began tutting about the bad manners of appearing as supper was about to be served. He stood in the doorway searching for someone in particular, then hurried towards the woman Jesamiah had insulted, his short, quick steps taking him across the dance floor as participants were lining up for the next caper. From the gestures and angry expressions Samuel guessed the ensuing conversation was a continuation of the indignity she had suffered. He shook his head, suppressed a smile. Captain Acorne should never have upset the lady; she was known in these parts as a righteous harridan and her brother as an intolerant oaf. What was it the Captain had said? The smile broadened. If the whispers were to be believed it had been most scandalously rude. Samuel wished he could find the guts to say something as delightfully spectacular!

Still smiling, he strolled through the open French doors and sauntered onto the terrace. He had enjoyed himself this evening – apart from that silly stumble he had made – and he had no wish to witness the shouting match which was probably about to be unleashed. Let others be so entertained. Although, he paused, considering. Would Captain Acorne be grateful for assistance? Huh, of what use would he, Samuel Trent, be? He was as useless with quick-witted rhetoric as he was with fist, sword and pistol.

Leaning on the balustrade he admired the extensive gardens illuminated by the flickering lights of dozens of lanterns and pitch torches. The coolness of the night air was refreshing after the heat and hubbub. The last of the wild roses, for which the house was named, sparkled jewel-like from the autumn dew. Some of the maple leaves had already fluttered to the lawn, the slaves would be out at first light to rake them away.

Alicia was sitting on a bench under one of the trees on the far side of the expanse of grass, a fur wrap pulled close about her shoulders, her head leaning back against the trunk, her eyes closed. Her gown was as red as the autumn leaves and for a moment, in the wavering, smoking, shadows he saw her breast as blood-soaked. He gasped. An omen? He wanted to rush over, persuade her to come inside, but she would only rebuff his concerns. She thought him a naïve fool, only tolerated his company because he amused her.

She was using him for her own purpose, of that he was aware, although what that purpose was he had no idea. He was like a little dog sitting at her feet gazing lovingly into her eyes, his curled puppy tail forever wagging, awaiting her indulgences. Throw a stick, tell him to fetch and he would run. To roll over and die? Was he indeed the fool she thought him? But he did so, so, want to be respected, to have a position of authority and honour. Would do anything to get it. Even be the dew-eyed lap dog if that was what it took.

He almost ran down the steps and across the lawn, but he controlled himself, walked quickly instead. Approaching her he felt as if he had two left feet, like a boy at his first ball, not a grown man with sense and refinement. God, but she was a beautiful woman! Petite and fragile; delicate, as if she were fashioned from that new and exquisite Meissen porcelain his father had purchased a month ago. And Alicia was as expensive. But was she to be used as an everyday object, or set away in a glass cabinet to be lifted out and admired on special occasions only?

"All on your own Alicia?" *What a pathetic thing to say*, he thought, embarrassed, as he slowed his pace. "I thought you were enjoying yourself within doors," he stated as he came to a halt. "It looked as if you were."

Alicia had watched him come out on to the terrace and cross the lawn. She had chosen this spot deliberately for it was secluded and private, while the house and ballroom remained clearly observed. No one would think twice about her sitting out here taking the air, and she suddenly resented not having a few more moments to enjoy the solitude. It was not that she did not like Samuel – on the contrary, he was a sweet boy who had been helpful and most kind to her – but he had no money and could not help her out of her predicament.

"Do you mind if I join you?" he said, offering a low bow.

"Why? Have I fallen apart?" It was an old, worn jest but she was feeling old and worn. It was not Samuel she wanted here with her, but Jesamiah. Ah, this was so utterly stupid! She *had* fallen apart, her sense, her pride – her heart – all of her had been dashed into a thousand pieces that first evening when she had seen Jesamiah in Nassau. No, before then. She had always loved him, had fallen for him all over again when he had turned up unexpectedly at Phillipe's party – the christening party for their son. How her heart had leapt when she had seen him across that room. Even though he was disguised she had known him instantly, had recognised his eyes and his smile. And his hands. Jesamiah; the only man to have ever treated her kindly. The only man she had ever truly loved. But he had another woman, would never want her instead. And for that she hated him and had no qualm about setting in motion what was soon to be happening inside the house. Or so she told herself.

Nassau, she now realised, had been a grave mistake. The moment those hired footpads of hers had set upon him in the alley she had regretted the plan she had hatched. Her concern, after conveniently arriving with the militia as his rescuer a few moments later, had been sincere. Her feelings had melted and all the love she had always felt had engulfed her totally. Going to bed with him had been a genuine desire, not just part of the intention to entrap him into giving her money.

Samuel knew none of it of course. Would never know. It was none of his business. She did not flinch away when he took her hand, nor when he delicately kissed it. It was all he would do. All he ever did. Kiss her hand. She was aware that the boy – she could not think of him as anything other than a boy – would ever dare kiss her mouth or touch her intimately, doubted he even knew how babies were made or where they came from.

With her permission, granted with the minimum of a nod, he sat beside her.

"Captain Acorne is in for a rough ride. Lofts has arrived. He will not be best pleased at the insult paid to his sister and nieces."

When she did not respond he sat back, studying her. "Alicia? Be there something amiss? You look most pale."

Her answer was too slow and spoken with too much of a catch of regret in her breath. "No, no there is nothing amiss." She sat for a moment watching the sway of dancers through the windows, saw them part in a flurry of disruption.

I could stop this, she thought. *I could get to my feet, go back to the ball and tell Captain Lofts I had made it all up. But if I do that I will be exposed for what I am, and this boy beside me will then despise me and I will have no one to call friend. Whereas, if I sit here and retain my countenance none shall be the wiser. And when it is all played out, Jesamiah will be forced into granting me la Sorenta or an adequate living and I shall be free to do as I will.*

But what if it all ran foul and went wrong? She shivered. "I did not tell the truth, Samuel. I am sorry, forgive me, I do indeed feel unwell. I think I have overtired myself. Please, would you be so kind as to escort me home?"

Thirty Six

Daniel Lofts was nearing fifty-five years of age, had a renowned poor temper, no wife, a demanding widowed sister, unattractive nieces and to cap it all, arthritis in his knees. He was also a merchant sea captain who had finally had a belly-full of Governor Spotswood's empty promises to make an end of piracy. Well, those promises were going to be fulfilled or he, Captain Daniel Lofts, would want to know why!

Listening to his sister's agitated complaints his anger was growing, and when she pointed out the scoundrel who had offended her, Lofts' enraged shout boiled across the ballroom. "That is him! By God, you rogue; you murdering, thieving, seadog! How dare you flaunt yourself here!" As he crossed the ballroom Lofts drew his sword; reaching Jesamiah, held its tip to his throat.

"I was informed this degenerate would be here, Governor – Gad, I almost ignored the letter as a prankster's jest! He is a pirate – Blackbeard's accomplice, no less. I demand you string him up. Here! Now!"

Keeping calm, Jesamiah attempted to push the blade gently aside, but Lofts flicked the weapon and drew a line of blood that dripped on to Jesamiah's cravat. Sensibly, he remained very still, made no attempt to drop his hand to his own weapon. It would be useless anyway; a rapier was not meant for serious fighting, it would shatter at the first contact of blade against blade.

"I assure you, Sir, you are mistaken. I do not sail with Teach." With supreme effort Jesamiah kept his temper, and his fingers from inching towards the blue ribbon restraining his black hair into a tethered queue beneath the wig.

Lofts flicked the blade again, another thin line of blood welled across Jesamiah's cheek. "You lie. You attacked my vessel, the *Fortune of Virginia*, forty miles south of the Pamlico estuary. I clearly saw your face through m'bring it close."

"I do not deny you saw me, but I was chasing Teach away. I never fired at you, never chased you, never attacked you."

"Lies! My first mate will verify what I say, aye and m'crew. Every one of us saw you come up with Teach."

"Then how do you account for Teach and his consort breaking off? For the fact that you were given an opportunity to run? Had I not distracted them you would be at the bottom of the sea, not standing here unjustly accusing me."

"Fancy words and scuttled lies! You've been caught out and are wriggling at the end of a hook. Lies come glib to scum such as you! I know full well what I saw. Am I to be held responsible for a falling out between thieves? Is it my concern that you and Teach were squabbling between yourselves? Naturally I took advantage of it."

Seeing he was getting nowhere with the imbecile, Jesamiah turned to Spotswood for support. "Governor, I do not deny I have been guilty of piracy in the past, but I have done nothing illegal since I signed Woodes Rogers' amnesty. I came to Virginia to see to my estate. I repeat, I did not attack the *Fortune of Virginia*. I was attacking Teach."

"And why would you be doing that?" Spotswood asked. "I can understand a captain coming to the aid of a fellow seaman, but taking Teach on single-handed? Even my brave naval captains would not be such simpletons."

The glib answer that naval captains were simpletons anyway hovered on Jesamiah's lips, but this was not the time for sarcasm. All he need say was that his intended wife had been aboard the *Fortune* – but what if Teach got to hear of it? He was not frightened for himself, he had stared death in the face too often to be scared of dying, it was only the manner of it that bothered him. A quick bullet was one thing, slow twenty-minute strangulation on the gallows, another. If Teach got to hear the truth it would be Tiola who suffered. And Jesamiah knew enough about Teach to know how he could make a woman suffer.

"I have my reasons for getting the better of Teach," was all he said as he rubbed his shoulder. "An' I'ave one more, now."

"Angry with you for buggering up a Prize, was he?" Lofts sneered. "Get him to prove under God's oath and at trial by judge and jury that he is not lying, Governor. Or are your promises to rid us of pirates nothing but piss and wind?"

The entertainment was more exciting than the dancing, or even the prospect of supper, and an audience was gathering, ranged in a semi-circle around the object of interest.

"Mrs Alicia Mereno can vouch for me," Jesamiah heard the desperation rising in his voice. "She was aboard the *Sea Witch*. She will testify in my favour."

Heads swivelled expecting to see her, the level of chatter rising higher as it became apparent that she was not in the ballroom. Robert Maynard suggested she be sought, his blushing face accompanying an attempt to convey that perhaps she was attending a call of necessity.

Five minutes passed. Ten. The search was widened. Another five minutes.

Governor Spotswood was more than a little taken aback by Captain Lofts' revelation, for he had started to like this fellow Acorne and was appalled that he had made an error of judgement. He regarded the impatient faces, sensed the rising hostility. Had indeed promised to do all he could to rid the sea lanes of pirates – and here he was befriending one? He could not make a fool of himself in front of so many people, many of whom already doubted his integrity. He was King George's representative here in the Colony of Virginia and he took his position of authority most seriously. But then, he was also a fair man who abided by the letter of the law and who would not condemn someone without a trial.

Governor Spotswood cleared his throat uneasily. "I remember well your past, Acorne, for I witnessed the way you stole a boat from beneath your own brother's nose – do not frown at me, Sir, I was there, I heard and saw with my own ears and eyes your despicable behaviour. I am therefore aware of your nature." Spotswood paused, glanced around the room. No sign of Mrs Mereno.

"Unfortunately the lady in question is temporarily absent. If you are indeed innocent of this charge then your name will be easily cleared, will it not? But piracy is a serious offence, one which we do most profoundly disapprove of in Virginia. With regret I must place you under arrest. You will have every opportunity to verify your story in Court. Surrender your sword, Sir, and any blade you may carry, if you please."

Jesamiah stared at him, not believing he was hearing this. Arrested for something he had not done? For saving the lives of an entire merchant crew? Someone moved forward, intent on taking his rapier; he growled, a low animal sound and the man hurriedly backed away. Unbuckling its strap himself he handed the weapon to Robert Maynard, along with a folded pocketknife. Less humbling to hand over his possessions voluntarily.

Shackles were produced, someone had been quick off the mark to run to the gaol and fetch them. His sling was torn away – he cried out at the stab of pain down his arm – and the iron chains were fastened to his wrists and ankles. Almost before he knew what was happening, gruff-faced and rough-handed men had grasped his arms and shoulders, were bundling him from the house, dragging him across the cobbled stable yard and through the gateway; along the rutted lane. The restraints caused him to stumble and trip. He was too stunned to attempt to fight back.

The door to Urbanna's small and primitive gaol was open and he was thrown into the confine of what was little more than a damp cellar. It stank of mould and rot, and once the door was closed and bolted it was without light. There was an iron-barred window in the door, but once the light was taken away everything was black. Jesamiah hated dark, enclosed spaces.

He had lost a shoe, his breeches were torn and beneath his hands the floor was damp and disgusting. It was difficult to move with the shackles. His hand touched human hair and he stifled a cry, realised it was his own wig that had fallen from his head. Trembling, he crawled to the nearest corner, sat with his back against the cold brickwork and rested his forehead on his indrawn knees, the chains at his wrists rattling and heavy and already chafing his skin.

~ *Tiola?* ~ He tried concentrating, putting all his thought and energy into picturing her face, filling his senses with her; imagining he could feel, smell, hear, her. ~ *Tiola? Sweetheart? I wish you were here with me. God's sweet love, I wish it!* ~

Thirty Seven

North Carolina

There was no moon and a low, sullen cloud covered the stars. Night did not usually concern Tiola, nor the cold. Often she would sleep with the windows open, listening to the variety of sounds that were so different during the night hours; comforted by the smells of scented flowers and damp earth. Not tonight. Tonight she had hurried to her room and bolted the door, had slammed the windows shut and pulled the curtains across the menace of leering darkness. And then she had lain face down on her bed and wept.

No animal deserved to die in pain, not through the stupidity of ignorant humans. The grooms, lazy and skimping their duty because the headman was away had left it too late and the animal had suffered. Tiola shed tears into the pillow, sobs shuddering through her defeated and weary body. Her fingers curled around the acorn charm on its chain.

Many horses contracted colic. Yards of intestines were folded up within the belly, a mass of gut crammed into a small space; a gut which so easily became blocked. Sometimes a bran mash worked, sometimes an enema or a linseed oil drench poured direct into the stomach. An energetic roll somewhere safe where the horse would not be injured or trap its legs – a paddock, well away from fencing – could do the trick. With the trapped wind passed and a chance to lie still and rest, the animal could be on its feet and contentedly grazing within the hour. If it was not merely blocked wind, they either got better, or died. That length of coiled intestine could rupture or twist, knotting like a dropped ball of twine. And nothing could be done except put a quick end to the suffering.

Nicholas himself had shot the mare with his pistol. Two imaginary lines from the base of the ear to above the temple; where the lines crossed he had placed the barrel, squeezed the trigger and fired. Tiola had sat there, the mare's head in her lap, soothing her, not moving aside until that last moment when all the pain would be gone for good. The shot had been loud in the brick-built stable, the smell of gunpowder and scorched hair acrid in the air, but there had been little blood, and death, with the bullet passing straight into the brain, had been instant.

All the same, Tiola wept for a life she had been unable to save, and for her own inadequacies of failure, loneliness and despair. She wanted to feel Jesamiah's strong, capable arms around her. Wanted his hands stroking her hair, her back. To rest her head on his chest and quietly cry, knowing he would wait, say nothing and expect no explanation until she was ready to tell him why she was weeping.

Wanted to tell him how filthy she felt from Teach's foul touch and smell; how frightened she was of the Malevolence that had invaded him and dwelt within as a domineering parasite; knew the bastard would try again if he had the opportunity. Wanted to tell Jesamiah everything but could tell him nothing, for he would go after Teach. And she was so scared that if he did, Jesamiah would be killed.

After all these uncountable years of her soul's reincarnations, why had she so totally fallen for Jesamiah? There had been relationships before – husbands and lovers, for the line of those who held the Craft had to continue, grandmother to granddaughter. Children had to be conceived and born, but in this incarnation, in this body, she had been virgin pure when Jesamiah had first made love to her, and never before had she so completely united her soul with another. Had never felt this unconditional bonding with a human male. She more than loved Jesamiah, he was everything: life, love, light – a part of her.

She lay in the bed, staring at the darkness of the overhead canopy and at the partially closed drapes to the side. A faint light spread briefly under the door as someone walked by with a candle. She listened to the footsteps retreating down the hall. A female, light step. Perdita, she thought. Had she slipped outside for another secret assignation with Jonathan Gabriel? Poor children, what hope was there for them?

What hope was there for herself? Getting so stupidly jealous of a past lover! She knew perfectly well that Jesamiah had no affection for Alicia, his only interest was the heat of sex. What had she been thinking?

~ *Tiola? Sweetheart?* ~

She sat up, scuffed the tears from her face. Jesamiah! He was unable to call her, the Craft did not work like that, but she must have been sending her own thoughts without realising. Relief flooded through her. Relief and joy and love, his spirit-presence filling all her senses, driving away that debilitating ache of fear and grief.

~ *Oh Jesamiah, Jesamiah! I so miss you tonight!* ~

~ *Is anything amiss? Your voice feels all wrong in my head.* ~

Hastily she shut out one reason for her misery. He must not learn that she was frightened, for he would insist on coming. Insist on facing Teach down. And that she did not want.

~ *No, no. A horse died, I could not save her.* ~

~ *It happens, sweetheart. Things have to die.* ~

~ *Ais, but it was because of lazy ignorance. It should not have been so.* ~

She felt the comfort of his presence. His understanding.

~ *Both of us are cold and lonely, eh?* ~

~ *Ais.* ~

~ *As soon as that babe is born safe, everything will be shipshape.* ~

~ *I do not want us to be parted again, luvver. I want us to be together.* ~

~ *This is the last time I make a stupid fool of myself, Sweet. I'm an idiot, I'm sorry. I'll not give you another cause to run away from me.* ~

Tears were trickling down Tiola's cheeks. She brushed them aside. ~ *Is that a promise?* ~

~ *It is.* ~

She had to laugh, an amused giggle. ~ *Oh Jesamiah! You have not kept a promise in your entire life!* ~

In her head she heard his responding laugh, deep, warm and loving. ~ *Well, I promise to keep this one.* ~ He chuckled, admitted, ~ *For at least a week, anyway.* ~

Tiola burrowed beneath the bed covers, remembering the delicious lovemaking she and Jesamiah had shared in this bed.

~ *Night, sweetheart. I love you.* ~

~ *I love you too, Jes. With my heart and my soul.* ~

And then she heard the giggle. Faint, distant, but unmistakably the malicious presence of the Dark.

~ *Goodnight, Jes.* ~ She shut the link, slammed it as if she were forcibly closing a door.

She should have been aware of Teach's presence out there beneath the trees. And she should have been aware that the Dark would be searching for her. She must take care! How foolish she had been! She must take care!

She relaxed her body, muscle by muscle, calming her breathing. This was not Craft but simple, everyday quietude. Safe, the seeping Malevolence excluded, she stilled her shivering and calmed the raggedy thump of her heartbeat. As she drifted towards sleep, a smile filtered on to her mouth. Jesamiah would never keep such a promise. He enjoyed the pleasures of the bedroom too much. What a pretty woman had to offer, especially in the bosom department, would always be too tempting a lure for him to resist. She snuggled deeper beneath the warm bed covers, did not mind. Truly did not mind. Those women were nothing more than a night of entertainment. He would not love any one of them, not as he loved her. So no, she would not deny him the passing pleasures of satisfying his natural lust.

As long he always came back to her. As long as he did not bed others when he could be bedding her. And as long as he continued to love her as much as she loved him.

Thirty Eight

Sunday 20th October – Virginia

"She is a fine ship."

Rue glanced up from prodding his knife into the *Sea Witch*'s keel in search of soft, wet spots, to see a gentleman standing atop the graving dock bank. His cocked hat adorned by an extravagant, blue-dyed ostrich feather was pulled low, hiding his face, though there was a glimpse of silver hair and a short, well-trimmed grey beard. The collar of his great coat was hitched up around his neck to stave off the cold wind that was blowing in from the river. Finely dressed, his boots were of good leather, his coat and breeches quality cloth. One of the neighbours? Certainly a man of means.

"*Oui*, that she is."

"English built? I watched you sail in, was curious about her rigging. Copper cladding is new to me too. I assume it must be of great benefit to stave off worm? The set of the jib sails is unfamiliar to me – and be that what they call a dolphin striker? I have heard of them being placed on the very newest ships, but never had the privilege to see one."

Closing the knife and slipping it into his pocket, Rue shielded his eyes against the sun to see all the better. He could not make out a face. Asked; "You are a seaman then?"

"Not now."

"She is a mere couple of years old, but our Captain had a few innovative ideas of his own, so made changes and had her re-rigged." Rue answered easily, suddenly aware they were conversing in French.

"She is fast?"

"Very. You are from France?" he queried.

The stranger inclined his head, added, "As was my mother, and the man who brought me up as his son."

A pause, neither knowing what to say next

As an offer of friendship, Rue gestured for the man to come on down, take a closer inspection. "We have almost finished our repairs. A few more days and she will be afloat again. As beautiful as ever."

The man shook his head. "Sadly, my friend, that may not be. I came to warn you, the Governor has arrested your Captain. The militia are on their way here to take the rest of you to gaol."

Rue cursed, "*Merde*! Why did you not bloody say? Standing here making petty chit chat…"

"You have plenty of time. They have not yet left Urbanna." The man pointed towards the woods that swept up the hillside. "Take shelter in there. I doubt they will search the trees, but if they do, there are plenty of places for you to hide for a day or two."

Calling his gratitude, Rue shouted for the men to stop what they were doing, to run to the woods. No one questioned him. Not on a ship where not so long ago they were sea-faring pirates. When Rue, Nathan, Isiah Roberts or Captain Acorne said run, they ran.

As Rue was pushing through the thick and unyielding undergrowth he realised he had no idea who the man was or why he had instantly believed what he had said. For that last though, he needed no confirmation. One of the lads had shinned up a tree, could see easily down the hillside.

Red-coated militia were swarming all over the estate.

Thirty Nine

This had been a wild goose chase. Maynard was frustrated: there was nothing of interest or value on board the *Sea Witch* – literally. She was stripped down and laid up for careening. Nor, in the warehouse, had he found anything among the piles of stuff that had come from the ship.

Mistress Mereno had been of no assistance, and those scoundrels who were lurking in the kitchens claiming they were household servants, were no better. If they were not of Acorne's crew then he was a brass monkey. Just how the rest of the crew had known to run for it he had no idea, but someone had tipped them the wink for tools lay where they had been dropped, tasks abandoned, jobs uncompleted.

This was a waste of time – he had known it would be, but orders were orders. Add to that, he was certain Acorne was innocent of the charge laid against him. Captain Lofts was a myopic old fool who blustered more than a dented blunderbuss. Of the two, in Maynard's opinion, Jesamiah Acorne's testimony would be the more reliable.

"Do we search the woods, Lieutenant?"

Maynard shook is head. "No point. They are all long gone – unless you fancy traipsing through thick forest, I suggest we agree that we have done our duty to the best of our ability."

"Aye, aye, Sir. Shall we return to Urbanna?"

"Aye."

Climbing back into the gig, giving orders to shove off, and idly watching the river pass by as the oarsmen rowed steadily but easily back downstream, Maynard considered the afternoon's strange experience. The Governor himself had issued orders to round up any lingering pirate crew. Maynard had not protested, but neither had he hurried. He was certain they were barking up the wrong tree. If Acorne did indeed carry a Letter of Marque, his arrest could prove most embarrassing. But there had been no letter. In fact, there had been nothing of value, nothing untoward whatsoever.

Except for the old man. He had been sitting on the bank up above the graving dock. Had watched the militia come, search everywhere, had not moved position, just sat there. They had left him alone for he was old, not, in Maynard's opinion, one of the *Sea Witch*'s crew.

Maynard had spoken to him; asked his name, what business he had to be sitting beside a known pirate ship. The answer had been most curious.

"I have more business than you to be keeping this vessel company. She is on my land. Nor is she, or her captain or her crew, a pirate. They carry an official Letter of Marque. I suggest you go back to whence you came, son, and tell your cock-proud Governor to get his priorities aright. It is Teach you want to be going after. Not Acorne. Acorne be on your side of the mast, Sir. He be on your side. You want Acorne to advise thee, not hang him. He knows Teach. Knows the waters Teach sails in. Do you?"

Maynard watched a pair of ducks take off into flight amid a flurry of quacking, wildly flapping wings and sprays of water. The man was right. Maynard had no doubt whatsoever that he was right. But the odd thing, when he had later asked Mrs Mereno she had said there was no old man on the estate, let alone one who owned it. The only person who may have fitted the description, she had said, was Captain Mereno.

And he had been dead these many long years.

Forty

The tolling of Urbanna's church bell calling to Sunday morning service awoke Jesamiah. He was cold, stiff, and the mood of feeling sorry for himself had depleted into one of indignant outrage. Getting to his knees then his feet, he shuffled awkwardly to the door and began hammering on the wood with his fist.

At least it was light now, sunshine streamed in through the window opening and seeped in through the ill-fitting gaps around the door.

"You cannot imprison me without trial! What about Habeas Corpus? The 1679 act, eh? My right, my body? Or whatever it sodding means." He muttered the last, aware his banging and shouting was having no effect on anyone outside – there were people around, for he could hear voices. He was about to try kicking at the door when the sound of bolts being scraped open stopped him. He overbalanced and fell backwards. Heaving himself to his knees again he looked up angrily into the face of a militia guard.

"I demand to see the Governor. This is all a bloody mistake."

"Guv'nor's at Church. God's more important than a raggedy-arsed pirate. An' if ye want t'be a corpse I'll gladly oblige with shootin' thee." Too late, Jesamiah saw the bucket of water being raised: he tried to scrabble away but most of it sluiced over him.

"Now keep yer noise down or I'll be dousing ye and yer lice again!" The door slammed. The bolts grated on rusting locks.

Cursing, Jesamiah crawled into the small patch of sunlight. Within fifteen minutes it had disappeared and he was shivering violently in the dank coldness. He wore nothing except thin, fancy clothes; missed his buckram long coat and canvas breeches that had been worn soft and comfortable through constant use. He only had one shoe. Angrily he kicked it off and sent it flying across to the far side of the cell.

"I want to speak to Spotswood!" he yelled again. Was not surprised when no response was forthcoming.

He stood up and walked around as best he could. Another half hour passed. He thought he could hear singing, a rousing God-fearing hymn, then shortly afterwards the drift of voices, horses' hooves and the rumble of carriage wheels. Church was over then.

"I'll talk to anyone!" he tried as an alternative plea. "I have money!" Awkwardly he attempted to feel into his waistcoat pocket, the wrist shackles inhibiting movement. No coin pouch. It must have dropped out. Damn!

A long hour ambled by, and then another, the time kept by the clang of the church bell. The wafting smell of food being cooked was unbearable; he had not eaten since yesterday afternoon.

The day dragged by as slowly as snow melts in winter, the small patch of sky beyond the grating turning to vivid golds and pinks as the sun began to set. Outside, there were no sounds except natural ones; a bird calling, a cat fight somewhere. The rustle of a wind getting up in the trees.

The tide will be turning soon, Jesamiah thought, *the wind always shifts with the ebb.*

"Cap'n! Cap'n Sir!"

Jesamiah was on his feet and craning his neck to see better through the bars of the small window.

"Jasper?"

A face appeared. "Cap'n? You all right?"

"No I bloody ain't! Send Rue here. I need to know what's happening. Have they found Mrs Mereno yet?"

Jasper was puzzled. "Found her? She ain't lost, she's at home. Came home last night with Mr Trent. Mr Finch were waiting up for you. Got right narked when you didn't appear, you know what he's like. An' I can't send Rue. He's gone."

"Gone? What the fok do you mean gone – gone where?"

"They've all gone save me, Mr Finch, Jansy and Toby Turner. I'ad t'run an' warn 'em. They was in the house y'see, sittin' in the kitchen, but Mr Finch says there were no need fer us to go, on account of Mrs Mereno would vouch as 'ow we were servants."

With extreme difficulty Jesamiah kept his patience, though his fingers were curling in a desire to throttle the boy. "Would you care explaining, or do I have to play this damned game of riddles?"

"I brought these for you, Cap'n." Grunting with effort, Jasper was squeezing various items of clothing through the gaps of the barred grating – shirt, breeches, woollen socks. "The militia came with the intention of arresting everyone – bloody said we was pirates! Only your friend Mr What's-'is-name had already tipped us the wink. The men scattered into the woods. Reckon they'll be laying low for a couple of days."

Jesamiah stared down at the clothes. *How the bugger am I going to get these on?* he thought. Said, "But did Mrs Mereno not try to stop the militia?"

"No, Cap'n. She said she hoped they'd find everyone, she weren't keen on having pirates on her property."

Jesamiah squatted on the floor, ran his hands despairingly through his hair, the chains clanking annoyingly. What in the name of all the oceans was happening here?

"They searched through the ship's accoutrements."

That news did not improve Jesamiah's bad mood. "Find anything?" he sneered.

"Took away your brandy barrels. I was right cross, we'd took special care to assure they were stored safe, but I couldn't do'owt."

If searching for contraband and stolen property, they would have been disappointed and found nothing. The brandy had been smuggled, but not by Jesamiah, and there was a legal bill of sale for it in his desk drawer. As there was for all the provisions, from salt pork to candles – though he had not, in fact, paid Masters a penny for any of it back there in Nassau. The merchant would have a hard job proving it though, since Jesamiah had the signed bill.

There had been nothing illegal aboard *Sea Witch*, at least nothing obvious or findable. It was either secure in a bank or safely stored in various warehouses. Jesamiah was not so stupid that he would sail with a hold full of stolen goods or contraband into a colony that disapproved of piracy and was governed by a stickler for the law. Nor was he so stupid as to leave what he did have where it could be found."They searched my desk?"

"Aye Cap'n. And a right job it was an' all. Darn thing was at the back of where we'd stored everything while careening. Them bloody soldiers made us muck in with the slaves to shift everything out. Toby's wrenched his back again and Jansy's cut his hand open. There were blood everywhere."

The relief outweighed Jesamiah's displeasure. While he resented anyone leafing through his personal papers, the desk was where he had stowed the Letter of Marque from Henry Jennings that Alicia had presented him with. It clearly stated he had Governor Roger's permission to go pirate hunting. And while that would possibly get back to Teach, who would then know he had been told a hold-full of lies, Jesamiah did not particularly care. Once freed from these shackles and an unjust confinement, and as soon as *Sea Witch* was seaworthy, he would be rounding up his crew and setting his stern to the American coast, the Caribbean and the entire Spanish Main. He'd had enough of it. Although where he was going to sail instead, he had no idea.

Then a thought hit him."If they've been at my desk how come I'm still in here? Did they not find my official papers?"

"They took nothing away except the brandy, as far as I could tell, Cap'n." Jasper's voice faltered, his bravado leaving him."Mr Finch says they're going to hang you. That ain't goin' to happen, is it, Sir?"

"No. This man who warned you, who…"

"You! Get away from there!"a voice bellowed.

Jasper glanced round, saw two militiamen with muskets pointing straight at him, and bolted.

Jesamiah cursed. All he could do was sit and wait. He was buggered if he would do so quietly, however.

The flare of pitch torches sent shadows leaping up the cellar walls. It had grown dark quickly once the sun had set, and despite Jesamiah's resolve to be a nuisance, he had fallen asleep.

The door opened. A guard came down the steps and kicked him awake. "Come on, let's get moving. Tide don't wait for degenerates who are going to hang."

Jesamiah stayed where he was. He did not understand any of this and refused to co-operate. "I ain't going nowhere; not until I see Governor Spotswood. An' you can't hang me without a trial."

That had been Jesamiah's only comfort. Being a stickler for the law worked both ways. Spotswood would not permit a lynching. And by law, all pirates had to be tried in the Colony's main courthouse, which meant Williamsburg. Until a few years ago it would have been London, Marshalsea Gaol and a hanging on the low tide-line at Wapping. The Admiralty had insisted that it was their duty to punish acts of piracy, and their responsibility to warn others of the consequences of crime upon the seas. Funny how they had changed their tune when the Navy had been unable to catch any pirates to take to trial.

The second guard, standing at the top of the steps casually raised his musket. "Suit yourself. We have orders to set you aboard the *Pearl*. No one said nothing about you having to be alive. If you insist, I can shoot you now and save everyone a lot of trouble."

Distracted, Jesamiah did not see the first man step behind him, felt only the blow from a pistol butt to the back of his skull. They dragged him from the gaol, hauled him onto a cart and headed for the river and the jetty. The street fell quiet. It was Sunday evening and only the militia, the Governor's staff and the crew of the *Pearl* were abroad and making ready to set sail. The wind whipped cold from the direction of the Chesapeake Bay, and most citizens of Urbanna were pleased to see the back of Governor Spotswood. Had no interest whatsoever in a reprobate of a pirate who would soon be swinging from a gibbet.

Forty One

Captain George Gordon glanced uneasily at Governor Spotswood sitting on the opposite side of the table. The *Pearl* rolled in the choppy waters where the Rappahannock met the Chesapeake, but the third man, standing a few feet inside the cabin, barely noticed, for Lieutenant Robert Maynard's natural balance swayed easily with the familiar movement. He was pleading his case with considerable passion. "Where can Acorne go, Governor? Captain? What can he do? He is most unlikely to swim for the shore and I do sincerely believe he is innocent of this charge."

"Are you calling Captain Lofts a liar, Lieutenant?"

Straightening his shoulders, Maynard indignantly lifted his chin, stood a little taller. "No Captain, I am not. I do believe he is mistaken, however." He turned slightly to look direct at the Governor. "Captain Lofts is a competent man but I know for certain his eyesight is not as clear as once it was and he is, when all is said and done, a merchantman. Unlike those of us serving the King in His Majesty's Royal Navy, Captain Lofts has had no experience in matters of warfare. To be blunt, Sir, he would not know the difference between shots fired in earnest or those fired as bluff. In my experience merchantmen are inclined to panic as soon as a pistol is waved."

Governor Spotswood partook of some snuff, offered the silver tin to Gordon who shook his head. What he wanted was a drink. Two or three drinks.

Stepping forward Maynard rested his hands on the edge of the table. "It is my watch tonight. I give my word I will keep my eye on Acorne, and I will vouch my honour for his temporary parole while we are at sea."

"I admire your compassion, Maynard, although I am not convinced of your wisdom. The rascal you speak of is notorious for deviousness and cunning. What if he were to take you hostage against his release?"

Maynard spread his hands and answered Spotswood with barely concealed amusement. "Unarmed? With a full complement of able crew manning this ship – and your own trusted men to assist them? Is that likely?"

"I do not want trouble," Captain Gordon growled. Already his stomach was starting to churn. Without a generous dose of medicinal brandy the seasickness always debilitated him.

"There will be none, Captain, I assure you. It is my judgement, despite his past background, that Captain Jesamiah Acorne is a man of honour."

Spotswood sneezed heartily into a kerchief. It had been a long day and he wanted his bed, although it was unlikely with cramped shipboard conditions that he would obtain much sleep.

Maynard sensed he was wavering. He could not understand the conviction he felt in this, but something inside, a gut feeling, was insisting that they were treating Acorne unjustly. Planting his palms flat on the table again, he gazed direct at Spotswood. "May I speak plain?"

The Governor concealed the wry smile that was threatening to twitch at the corners of his mouth. Maynard had been speaking plain this past half hour! He nodded. "You may."

"It is my opinion that before long we will have to take action against the pirate they call Blackbeard. Until he is dealt with the Chesapeake – and therefore all our shipping, all our tobacco, our very livelihood – will be in jeopardy. Captain Gordon here is a brave man, as are you, Sir, and myself – but we have two frigates. Two! What match are we against a man such as Teach who knows these waters three, four, times better than do we?"

Spotswood drummed his fingers on the table. All this was true, but he took no liking to being reminded of it. "Your point is, Lieutenant?"

"My point, Governor, is that Teach is not going to come to us, we must go after him. To do so, we need someone reliable who can send word when the bugger next sails – and believe me, he will before long. All this talk of him becoming a respectable, settled gentleman? My arse!"

Interested, Spotswood rubbed at his chin. "Go on."

"We then have a choice. We sit here waiting for him to attack or we attack him first." Maynard was warming to his subject. He had been thinking about it all day. "Governor, we must turn pirate ourselves."

The blustered response of outrage from the two gentlemen was predictable. Obstinately, Maynard ignored the indignant protestations and waded onward. "We turn pirate regarding tactics. We go out, meet the bugger and beat him at his own game. We find him, attack him. Destroy him."

Spotswood could see the logic in that. "Ah, now you are talking my language young man! But still I do not understand what this has to do with Acorne?"

Lieutenant Maynard smiled knowingly, "Do you not? As I said, we need someone who can get close to Teach. So close he will know when the devil needs to piss, how often he picks his nose – and when he intends to set sail. Rather than hanging him, we could make Acorne that man. In fact, he suits the task of spying on Teach most admirably."

Captain Gordon's laugh was derisive. "What utter nonsense! Let Acorne go? He will suck his thumb at us and join the pirate's bloody crew!"

"No, Captain. He will not."

"You sound pretty certain of that Maynard?"

"Aye, Governor, I am. First, I am convinced Acorne is innocent of the charge. What he says is the truth. Second, I have made enquiries – I am friends with that lad, Samuel Trent. He tells me Acorne has no liking for Teach. We may be able to persuade him to work with us."

Pursing his lips, Spotswood shook his head. "I will not manipulate justice, Lieutenant."

"I would not expect you to, Sir. If Acorne is innocent and we have shown him compassion, he may well aid us of his own volition. If he is guilty, then he can work with us or hang. Either way we get the result we want. Someone who can report back to us from Blackbeard's camp."

Gordon rose to his feet. "I am sorry, but I do not agree with this nonsense. Such talk is heading for trouble, and Acorne is trouble."

Quietly Maynard answered, "Acorne has been persistent with claiming his innocence, and to make trouble would go against him most assuredly. If we can think of some hold that we can have over him to ensure his loyalty, then Sirs, what have we to lose? We use his pirate knowledge to go against Blackbeard. If we succeed we win everything. If we lose..." Maynard paused. It slightly went against his honour to say the next, but say it he did. "If we lose, then we blame it on Acorne."

Captain Gordon remained unconvinced. He was not a great man for seeking out action, wanted only a fast, safe passage to Williamsburg. One where he would have little to do and even less to worry about. "I say no. 'Tis best to leave him fettered in the hold, then take him to trial and see him hang."

Any trouble aboard this ship would be caused because you are too lazy to get off your backside. Very nearly Maynard spoke his thoughts, bit them back. For all his liking of Jesamiah Acorne he had no intention of finding himself also clapped in irons for insubordination.

Spotswood saw the clenched jaw, however; read the thought only too well, for it was precisely his own. He had small regard or respect for Gordon. Like too many sea captains he had bought his position with family money and had not an ounce of sea sense when it came to anything beyond the ordinary.

He stood, offered his hand to Maynard. "I agree with you. I think it an excellent plan. We show compassion to the fellow while he is aboard ship, give him a fair trial, then use him as we see fit. He can do no harm if set free of those shackles while we are at sea. Were he foolish enough to jump overboard we would not be heaving-to, as he is probably well aware; and if he is not, well, it will save us a hanging."

Spotswood yawned expansively. "I give him into your care, Lieutenant. But mark this," he wagged a warning finger, "If I lose my prisoner, I will hang you instead."

Maynard nodded, saluted smartly and left before his superiors could change their minds.

Some minutes later, calling for the bo'sun, he hurried down through the for'ard scuttle into the darkened gloom of the below-deck world of the common sailors. Hoped he was not about to make the biggest mistake of his life.

Forty Two

Jesamiah was feeling wretched. He needed to urinate, had a head that was throbbing like all the drums of a massed battalion and felt nauseous because he had not eaten for over twenty-four hours. The shadows of a carried lantern bobbed and flared alternately as he heard footsteps approaching, but he did not look up. What would be the point? No one would have any sympathy for him; probably the opposite, he had already been kicked several times by jack tars as they had hurried past. His only pleasure, setting sail had not been as smooth and efficient as his own crew would have achieved. Either these men were lubberly raw recruits or the Captain was not respected. Maybe both.

"Acorne."

Looking up into the bo'sun's scowling, cragged face, Jesamiah made no answer. Was surprised to find the bosun's cane that he carried and used with malicious spite was tucked away beneath his armpit. That cane was normally in constant use rapping legs, arms, buttocks, backs and heads; 'starting' anyone who was slow to move or obey. Bo'suns were a sadistic lot who could make life aboard ship one of utter misery for their victims. The harsh, often undeserved, discipline they wielded could not be avoided for there was nowhere to hide aboard a ship. Jesamiah was more surprised when the man bent down to unlock the ankle and wrist shackles that tethered him in an uncomfortable sitting position to the deck.

"On your feet."

There was someone else standing behind him, but Jesamiah dared not look around, for that would be playing into this bastard's hands. He flexed his legs, suppressed a gasp as cramped muscles screamed a protest.

"I said get up!"The cane dropped into the man's hand.

"Easy, Bo'sun, I've told you before you are too handy with that cane. Captain Acorne is trying his best to comply."

Maynard. Robert Maynard. What was this? Were they to hang him now? Where no one would notice or give a damn?

A pair of sturdy hands slid beneath Jesamiah's arms and assisted him to rise, held him firm while the blood flowed back into his legs in an agony of needles and pins.

"I can manage from here, Bo'sun, thank you." Maynard's voice was pleasant, rich and deep, like a mug of steaming, velvet-smooth hot chocolate.

Grunting disapproval, the bo'sun marched away, his raised voice floating back a moment later as he reprimanded some unfortunate found lacking.

"I was unable to convince the Governor that you would appreciate a cabin, but you can at least get reasonable shelter to leeward beneath the Captain's gig. And I have ordered the galley cook to fetch up hot food and a tankard of something equally warming. I've had to pay him of course; I'll be expecting you to reimburse me at your earliest opportunity."

Bewildered, Jesamiah took a sideways look at Maynard as the Lieutenant attempted to support his waist and aid him to walk a step or two to get the circulation going.

"It would help," Maynard said, "if you were to put your arm around my shoulders and at least try to put one foot in front of the other."

Jesamiah draped his arm as directed, but stood still. "I don't understand. What the fok is going on?"

"I assume you have no objection to giving me your word that you will make no effort to escape, nor cause me embarrassment?"

Jesamiah looked blank.

"You have the title of Captain. Your rank, in my opinion, deserves courtesy. I have therefore secured your temporary parole – and I tell you this, if you let me down I will personally put the noose around your neck and kick you off a barrel."

Taking a few tentative steps, Jesamiah nodded his gratitude. "Where are we headed?"

"Williamsburg."

A few more steps and the cramp began to ease.

Maynard released his hold and fetched a bundle he had left at the foot of the ladder. He tossed it to Jesamiah, who caught it awkwardly. Then passed Jesamiah two old, worn, longboots. "Your boots and clothes. Your boy left them behind, I managed to retrieve them. They will be more suitable than what is left of that finery you have on."

Clutching the bundle to his chest, Jesamiah remained quite still, utterly perplexed. "Jasper said the militia came to arrest my crew."

"That they did."

"Was it you who warned them? Told them to run?"

Maynard shook his head. "I would not be that disloyal to my rank. Though I happen to believe you are telling the truth."

Jesamiah began to strip off the disgusting apparel he had on and to replace them with his old familiar clothes – equally dirty but far more comfortable. "Navy believing a pirate? Now I've 'eard everythin'."

"I also happen to admire your sailing skills. I think it stupid and a waste to hang someone who can handle a ship as well as you can."

Jesamiah laughed. "So you want to recruit me into the Service, do you? I hate to disappoint you, mate, but I'd rather hang." His wrists and ankles, he noticed in the faint lamplight, were chafed raw; the blood dried into a black mess. The sores would sting like mad later. He put the embroidered waistcoat back on, then his beloved long coat and rummaged in the pockets. No weapons, nothing, every pocket was empty.

"Our bo'sun gave it a thorough search," Maynard apologised. "I'm sorry. It was that or keep on what you wore previously."

Touching the gold hoop in his right earlobe, Jesamiah remembered his acorn was not there, then felt for the ragged ribbon tying his hair back. It was loose, he re-tied it, said; "No matter. I have all I need, should I need it."

With Maynard's occasional assistance Jesamiah found he could move reasonably well now the cramps had eased, even up the steep, narrow ladder to the open deck above. The night was cold and fresh, the blackness overhead studded with bright stars. He took a few deep breaths then made his way to the heads for'ard. He had been tempted to piss where he stood on the deck but some poor sod would only be punished for it, and it was not the crew's fault he was here.

Maynard was waiting in the waist. "You are not thinking of jumping, I trust?" he queried, as Jesamiah stood at the rail peering at the black solidity of the distant shoreline. "I would hate to admit to Governor Spotswood that I made a fool of myself."

Turning slowly, Jesamiah rested his elbows on the rail, leant back, "There are many things that I am, but stupid ain't one among 'em, Rob. There's a lot of cold water and strong currents between us and the shore, an' I ain't keen on swimming at the best of occasions." He paused, looked directly at the Lieutenant. "Mrs Mereno. She should have vouched for me."

Maynard shook his head. "I questioned her personally. She said she was sent below. Saw nothing except you chasing after the *Fortune of Virginia*, and heard cannon fire."

"And my Letter of Marque was in my desk drawer. I put it there myself before I sailed from Nassau."

"There was no letter, Captain Acorne."

The cook's boy delivered a bowl of stew. Most of it was weak stock and gristle, but sitting cross legged on the lift and dip of the deck and spooning it down, Jesamiah reckoned he had tasted worse. The tankard of rum which followed was well watered, but tasted as good as the elixir of the gods. Figuring this could well be his last drink for quite a while, he swallowed the lot down, then wrapping his coat tight about his body, went to sleep thinking, as he dozed, that his shoulder was healing remarkably quickly, considering.

There was only one reason why the letter had not been in that drawer. Alicia had removed it. Which left a new riddle to be answered.

Why?

Forty Three

Monday 21st October

Alicia had gone to church yesterday morning as she did every Sunday. She had no particular faith in God but she enjoyed singing the hymns, and sometimes the Reverend Gull's sermons were entertaining in their own, banal way. Besides, Sunday morning worship was a weekly chance to attract the eye of young gentlemen. There was always new blood in church, for Urbanna was a busy port.

Samuel Trent had been in church too, sitting frustrated in the family pew alongside his dowdy mother; his father and brothers cleaned and polished. Trent Senior was adamant about the Lord's Day, no one on his estate worked or played on a Sunday. God, he insisted, must be granted the respect of peace and dignity on the Sabbath. It was a pity, in Alicia's opinion, and she rather assumed, in Samuel's, that the miserable bugger did not pursue similar Christian values on the other six days of the week.

Peering closer into the mirror on her dressing table Alicia inspected a spot below her cheekbone. Rummaging through the array of jars bottles and phials she found a lead-based cream, dabbed it on the blemish and then coloured her cheeks with a Spanish Paper impregnated with cochineal.

For half a minute she considered whether to use red crayon on her lips, but it did so blur and smear. She bit her lips a few times. There, that had reddened them.

One final inspection in the mirror. She looked perfect. "Is the carriage ready?"

"Yes, Ma'am." The maid, perplexed at all this activity bobbed a quick curtsey. Unless it was a Sunday, it was rare for the mistress to be from bed before ten of a morning, let alone go out.

As the carriage swung at a smart trot down the drive and Alicia caught a glimpse of partially replaced masts, she wondered when the men would be returning to complete the repairs. Presumed they would reappear in a day or two the worse for wear, and drunk. The visit from Lieutenant Maynard and the militia had alarmed her yesterday. She had not expected soldiers, nor had she calculated that her scheming might affect the entire crew of the *Sea Witch*. She had no quarrel with them, but they had made themselves scarce, so no harm had come of it. She had been quite proud of her answers to Maynard's questioning. Her apparent indifference towards Jesamiah had convinced him that she was not compliant with having pirates inhabit the estate.

A pleasant journey into town; the day was sunny but not over-hot. All the same, Alicia raised her parasol to protect her skin. She was pleased and happy. Today was going to be the last day of her problems.

Urbanna seemed quiet for a Monday morning. Several ships, she noticed, had gone from port although she had no idea which ones. A slight frown of unease wrinkled her forehead as the footman handed her down from the carriage. The gaoler usually came eagerly running from his drab little house whenever someone called. More often than not shrugging on his coat and wiping food from his capacious mouth. Or buttoning his breeches. It was no surprise his wife was constantly pregnant. Mind, Alicia, along with half the town, was of the opinion that whenever any females occupied the second small cell, his wife had a chance to get off her back and put her legs together.

People paid to view the prisoners. A shilling, sometimes two, depending who was behind the bars. It was a welcome addition to the gaoler's modest income.

She walked to the back of the house, towards the larger cell. Stopped short, her mouth open, her heart beginning to thud.

The gaol door was open. Wide open. In a confused daze she moved forward, peered inside, down the steps and into the squalid interior. Empty. She ran to the next cell, the smaller one. Nothing. No one.

In a panic she dropped her parasol and lifting her gown, ran along the lane to the square of unkempt grass behind the church. She fell to her knees, her heart almost bursting with fear, tears of relief trailing down her face leaving ugly white streaks in the cochineal.

The gibbet was empty. Thank God. Thank God!

Forty Four

Tuesday 22nd October

Charles watched the men return from the forest. They had fared well enough among the trees, for these were men used to living rough – indeed, sleeping and living on the land was easy compared to the many hardships and squalors of shipboard life. Here, there was food in abundance, fresh water to hand, shelter from the rain and the warmth of a fire to keep away the cold. But to a sailor, it was not the same as the sea. The sounds were different, the smells. And once the food was caught and cooking on the fires, once the wood to keep the fires lit was gathered, what was there to do?

The boy, Jasper, had come up into the woods to find Rue and to say the Governor and his navy and militia soldiers were gone. That Jesamiah, too was gone.

And so it was that Charles St Croix Mereno watched the men come out from the forest with dragging feet, lowered heads and heavy hearts.

They built another fire beside the Rappahannock River, and sat around it – those men who had come back, for several were missing; those who had decided to give up a life at sea, who thought that hanging, even though they were supposed to be free men with a grant of amnesty, was too much of a risk. They had sweethearts and wives, families, so they had drifted away. A few, just a few had left for the opposite reason – they missed the life of reckless plunder, of giving chase and fighting. Amnesty was not for them, nor this skulking in the woods alert for the merest sound.

"So what do we do?" Nat Crocker asked, as he sat hunched and mournful.

"Can we find a way of setting the Captain free?"

"How? If we go to Williamsburg, then we too will be arrested."

Charles stood in the shadows and watched and listened. He felt so helpless! There was nothing he could do except damned watch! Oh yes, he could shout at them, tell them to get up, get working, finish setting the *Sea Witch* fair, but he could not make them *do* anything!

But then, as they said themselves, what could they do?

Forty Five

Thursday 24th October – North Carolina

The rain, pouring down as if the sky were a waterfall, provided an adequate excuse for Tiola to stay within doors. No one thought to query her decision, no one else had any intention of going out either. For the most part she stayed in her room, pretending a chill, admitting only the servants and Perdita, although as one dismal day drifted into another, even her presence was becoming a little difficult to endure. Tiola had to exercise extreme patience with the girl, who was moping and bored. Not an ideal combination to conduct congenial companionship.

"Damn." Tiola held the sketched drawing away from her, eyeing it critically.

From the window seat where she sat, knees tucked beneath her, sewing lying limp on her lap these past fifteen minutes, Perdita turned to look at her. "Is it not going right?"

Sighing, Tiola grimaced. "I cannot get the stern lantern as it should be. It is too flat. The base is not quite straight." Wrinkling her nose, she held it up.

Perdita scrutinised the drawing. A ship at anchor, viewed from the stern. One of the great cabin windows hinged open. The rigging was intricate, the clouds and the sea echoing the rainstorm that was lashing the horizon. The name was across the back, with a motif of oak leaves.

"*Sea Witch,*" Perdita said, "is she a boat you know?"

Tiola had another attempt at altering the lantern that would, on the real vessel, stand almost as high as a man's shoulders. It was a huge thing which the men crawled inside to clean. Her tongue poking between her lips in concentration she did not look up. "Mmm?"

"I said do you, then, know a boat called the *Sea Witch*?"

"Ship. She is a ship, she has three masts – a boat has only one or two – and *ais*, I know her."

Perdita set the sewing aside and uncurling her knees felt for her slippers, which she had discarded and left on the wooden floor. She put her hands on the window seat, leant forward eagerly. "And you know more than just this ship?"

Cocking her head on one side, Tiola added a little shading. Did that help? Not really.

"The Captain for instance? Do you know the Captain?"

Putting the drawing and her charcoal aside, Tiola smiled at the girl, admitted that she did.

Leaping to her feet, with her arms outstretched, Perdita did a few excited twirls, then brought her arms in to hug herself, her head tipping back, eyes closed. "A handsome sea captain sailing to distant and exotic lands of the eastern Indies. He is to bring back teas and spices, and silks and perfumes." She opened her eyes, carved the air with an imaginary sword. "With brave gallantry he will save his crew from cannibals and pirates." She clapped a hand to her shoulder, staggered a few paces. "Oh! He has been wounded." She fell into a chair, the back of her hand held against her forehead. "Oh, my poor captain!" She pretended to faint then planting a kiss to her fingers, threw it into the air. "Love will revive him! He dreams of his sweetheart, and her dear face gives him strength and hope!"

Tiola was amused at the girl's mummery. "Don't be so absurd. His ship is in the Chesapeake undergoing repairs."

Perdita ceased the dramatic pose, her expression that of disappointment. "No tea or spices?"

"No tea or spices."

"Silks and perfumes?"

Tiola shook her head. "No."

With an exaggerated sigh Perdita wandered back to the window and wiping the condensation from the glass with her hand, peered out into the grey gloom.

"He is at least handsome?"

Tiola wondered whether to hold her silence, then realised she desperately wanted to share her secret with someone. Needed so badly to talk of Jesamiah. Of her hopes and fears, of her love for him. But she could not. For all that she trusted this dear, sweet girl, she dared not risk the accidental spilling of a wrong word, for Jesamiah's safety – and her own.

"*Ais,*" was all she said, "Yes, I assure you he is at least, most extremely handsome."

Forty Six

Virginia

Publick Times were in full and boisterous swing. The gathering of men and women of Virginia – and beyond – for the purpose of the Quarterly Trial Sessions, conducting official business, selling exorbitantly priced wares on the market stalls and enjoying the wide range of entertainments. The latter included horse racing and the excitement of the court trials and subsequent hanging of convicted murderers, felons and pirates.

Jesamiah's grant of parole aboard ship had been short-lived, lasting only for the sea voyage from the Rappahannock to a safe anchorage at Jamestown. There, the shackles had been replaced, his freedom removed. The Williamsburg town gaoler and the miserable gaol he was dubiously in charge of had played host to Jesamiah for three days. He was not overly impressed by the poor hospitality, dreadful accommodation or mouldering victuals. The square, wooden-built cell that housed nine men was like a bake-oven during the day and an icehouse by night. The wind came straight in through the grid window, swirled around the floor then whipped out beneath the inch-high gap under the firm-bolted door. The only place where there was no draught was beneath the window, but that was directly next to the seat of ease. The hole was situated on the highest of three steps, several feet from the ground; natural gravitation took the effluence to a cesspit outside. There was a lid that covered the hole and it was an efficient utility – but it stank to high heaven.

With his back firmly wedged into a corner, Jesamiah was resting his head on the wall, trying to ignore the obnoxious surroundings. Trying to sleep. It was not easy. At the window stood a boy, no more than eight, who had alternately been snivelling or whining all day. At first Jesamiah had felt sorry for him, arrested for stealing a loaf of bread, but the constant belly-aching had soon made him want to call for a noose and hang the little grub himself. Four of the other men awaiting trial for theft and assault were bickering between themselves and arguing with two of the others. The eighth was a molly boy, arrested for sodomy. He sat in the opposite corner to Jesamiah locked in his own world of horror and terror. There would be no hope for him, he would hang.

A hatchway slit was drawn open revealing a rectangular hole large enough to pass a tin plate through. Food. The wrangling halted for a few seconds, then began again as the men barged and shoved to be the first and grab a plate. It was always first come first served, the first getting the food warm as opposed to stone cold. Jesamiah heaved himself to his feet, couldn't be bothered to elbow his way in. He waited until each man had dispersed then took the plate as it was thrust into the opening, his nose wrinkling. Corn mush. They had been served the same for yesterday's single daily meal. And the day before, and the day before that. Indian corn mush was quick to prepare, cheap to provide and just about kept a man alive.

He bent and put the plate on the floor, thrust his hand quickly into the opening. "Oi, John Redwood, you thief," he complained as the hatch began to slide shut, "we're one short. Hand it over or I'll make sure Spotswood hears you're a fokken swindler!"

It was the duty of the gaoler to keep his charges alive, to spread clean straw on the floor and provide decent food from the allowance per head that he was granted. John Redwood took his duties seriously, but he was paid only thirty pounds sterling per annum, which in his opinion was nowhere near adequate. If he could make extra he stayed a happy man. Hence the sparse diet and mouldy straw.

The last plate appeared accompanied by a curse, and the hatch snapped shut. With the prisoners fed in this way the main door was never opened except for the daily privilege of an hour's meagre exercise shambling around the high-walled courtyard, or someone was taken out or put in. And that door was double bolted and locked from the outside. Unless you were heading for the courthouse or the gallows there was no way out.

Jesamiah took the second plate to the molly boy, toed his leg then hunkered down next to him. Persuaded the boy to look up. He was fifteen maybe, hardly had the first fuzz of a beard.

"You got to eat, Dick, it could be a while yet before we get to be taken to trial."

The boy looked up, eyes hollow, face gaunt. "I'm not hungry."

"Aye well, this ain't exactly food, it's more like pig slop, an' I doubt it'll do much against hunger anyways, but you still got to eat."

"You fancyin' the arse-pricker, pirate? Want us t'look away while you try 'im fer size?"

Ignoring the crudities, Jesamiah put the plate in the boy's hand. At fifteen it was highly unlikely the lad had chosen to be used for sex. Whores, male or female, rarely had a choice. "Eat up," Jesamiah repeated as he picked up his own plate. The stuff looked revolting. He wandered back to his corner, trying to decide if he was hungry enough to eat this mess. The man who had been crude was sitting there, looking smug. Jesamiah stood in front of him. The man said nothing.

Tempted to empty his own meal over the whoreson's head, Jesamiah thought again. The food was lousy but it was better than nothing and he'd had worse. On the long Atlantic crossings the stored flour, meat and butter, went off and weevils moved in. Eating rancid food was nothing new.

He scooped the mush into his fingers, ate as he stood there. Finished, he wiped his hands on the seat of his breeches and took the plate to the hatch, left it there for Redwood to collect later. Wandered back to the corner.

"That's my place, mate."

"No it ain't. You decided you wanted the sodomite over there, go cuddle up with 'im."

Patient, Jesamiah repeated; "You are in my place. I sit there. Move."

The man grinned showing rotten teeth. "Make me."

He then made a mistake. He licked the plate, took his attention off Jesamiah – who moved fast. Kicking out, Jesamiah caught the bottom of the plate with his foot and rammed it, hard, onto the man's nose. Spluttering blood, the antagonist tried to get to his feet, but ignoring the twinge of protest from his healing shoulder, Jesamiah was already following up with three punches, one to the belly, one to the face and the third to the groin. He grabbed the man's hair and jerked him forward, sending him sprawling; kicked his backside for good measure.

"I said this is my place. I suggest you learn to listen."

The man lay groaning, blood frothing from his mouth and nose. Jesamiah lifted his ankles and dragged him, face down, to the centre of the cell.

From outside there came the sound of the militia marching past heading in the direction of the Governor's palace, the crowds cheering and applauding the rat-a-tat of their regiment's drums and piping of flutes and whistles. An entire world away from the sordid existence within Williamsburg's gaol. Sitting astride his victim, Jesamiah twisted an arm back savagely. The man screamed.

"Now, I've said this before an' I ain't goin' to say it again. You leave that lad alone; he ain't done nothin' to offend you, but you offend me." Jesamiah twisted the arm higher. "An' I get seriously mad with those who do that. Savvy?" Releasing him roughly, he went to his corner, intent on another attempt at sleeping.

The mollyboy forced a quivering smile. "Thank you, Captain," he whispered, then louder, in frail defiance; "My name is Henry, not Dick."

Not bothering to open his eyes, Jesamiah responded; "Dick's more appropriate though, don't y'think?"

Forty Seven

A raised voice aroused Alicia slightly. She lay a moment listening, then burrowed deeper beneath the bed covers, her head throbbing, her stomach threatening a renewed attack of the nausea that had plagued her since Monday morning.

"Sir. I insist. You cannot enter. My lady is unwell."

"All the more reason to permit me to see her. Let me pass or I will forcefully remove you from barring my way."

The maid must have moved, for Samuel Trent entered Alicia's bedchamber.

Momentarily disorientated by the gloom within, he stood inside the threshold – leaving the door open behind him for propriety's sake. The room was spacious, well furnished, but the windows that were on two sides of the room were shuttered and curtained. With the day being dull and inclined to a light drizzle, and although it was not far from noon, the room was quite darkened. Allowing his eyes to adjust, he went to the bed where he could see Alicia's form hunched beneath the covers.

"My dear! They said you had caught a chill. Has the physician been? Has he examined you?"

Muffled, Alicia begged him to leave her be. "Please Samuel, I thank you for your concern, but I will be well soon, I am sure."

"Can I do aught? Fetch you brandy, wine, something tempting to eat? A little chicken broth perhaps? Or coddled egg?"

"No. Please, just go away."

Was that a sob he heard in her voice?

"I would do anything to assist you if you are in trouble, Alicia. You know that."

"Yes. Please go."

What more could he do? Forcibly pull back those blankets and sheets? Bully her into telling him what was amiss? He could do neither such thing! He rose, returned to the door from where the maid was anxiously peering in at him. "If there is anything, anything at all that I can do…" He paused, chewed his lip. Should he say? Perhaps, aye, he should. "Has your malaise to do with Captain Acorne, Ma'am? He is taken to Williamsburg for trial. I am certain he will be acquitted after a fair hearing. Governor Spotswood is a man who well observes the law."

The sob that issued from the bed was like a child in pain. Fearful, Trent sprinted across the room, heaved back the covers and took Alicia into his arms, cradling her to him, her face buried into his shoulder as she wept great gasps of dread. He stroked her hair, patted her shoulder, unsure what to do.

"My dear, please, do not distress yourself so. Captain Acorne will be able to show that this is all a matter of a mistake. He had a Letter of Marque, after all, and..."

The sobs burst into a crescendo of anguished wails. "You do not understand! Oh you do not understand!"

All Samuel Trent could answer was the truth. That no, he did not understand. What was there to be understood?

The shout of rage a few moments later silenced the rest of the house. Trent's bellow of, "You did what? You stupid woman! In God's name, why? Why?" echoed from room to room, only silenced by the abrupt slamming of Alicia's bedchamber door to shut the listening servants out. Several moments passed before Samuel could calm his furious temper. He took a series of deep breaths, spoke deliberately; slow and measured.

"Tell me again. You took Captain Acorne's Letter of Marque and hid it. Why? For the sake of God, woman, when Maynard came searching for it, why did you not give it him?" The anger was rising again. He choked it down. Shouting would get them nowhere.

Hunched, miserable, her eyes red-rimmed, her cheeks blotched, Alicia buried her face in her hands, the tears trickling through her fingers. She had never heard Samuel shout before. Never seen him so very angry.

"I was being blackmailed," she hiccuped. "I needed to get some money to keep an odious little man quiet. I thought that if Jesamiah was arrested I could let him worry for a day or two, then offer him back his letter for the amount I needed."

"Which is how much?" Samuel spoke in almost a growl.

"Two hundred pounds," she whispered.

He did not hear. "How much?"

Her temper getting the better of her; embarrassment, confusion, distress, all of it combined made Alicia slam her hands to the bed covers and shout, "Two hundred bloody pounds! Where was I to get such money? What choice had I? What was I to do? Sell my jewellery? Have everyone know I need money?" She shuddered at such a detestable thought. "Were you in a similar position you would have done the same!" She drew breath, screeched on, "Do not tell me you have not thought of ways of getting money. Had you thought of it, had you had access to that letter, would you not have used it to your advantage?"

Samuel swung away, disgust gorging bile into his throat. He stood at a window – the curtain thrown wide and shutters opened now, for he had not been able to tolerate the close confinement. If he craned his neck slightly he could see the graving dock. The men had come back on Tuesday morning. From here he could see only *Sea Witch*'s masts and the tangle of half-completed rigging. Nothing of her decks or keel, but he had walked down there this morning and seen that she seemed, to his landlubber's eye, almost ready to return to the water. She was most certainly an exquisite vessel.

To his reflection in the glass, not daring to look around for fear the anger would boil to the surface again, he said, "I thought you were a lady. Ever since I first saw you I thought you a goddess. Why? Because you were arguing with your husband and he was getting the worst of your tongue. God's good truth, but I thought you the most wonderful woman in the world for that. I so despised Phillipe. Twice I had resolved to shoot him. Did you know that? Twice. But I did not have the stomach to do it."

Alicia blew her nose.

"How I rejoiced when I heard the rumour that his own half-brother, that Jesamiah himself, had finally done away with him." He turned around slowly, his fists clenched at his side, his expression like God's own wrath. "They condemned him, you know, those bigots in the town. Condemned Jesamiah for throwing that louse overboard. You should have heard my father! 'Like father, like son,' he kept saying. 'Mereno Senior was a fish-gut scavenger. So is his son. So is his son.' God's teeth, but the times he said it! Over and over, and each time I wanted to hit him. I wanted to pummel his face and shout that Jesamiah was a good man – that Phillipe was the fish-gut heap of offal!"

Blowing her nose a second time, Alicia had become curious. From the first day when she had arrived here as Phillipe's bride, she had been aware of the boy from the next plantation up-river. A skinny, shy, lonely lad, the youngest of a brood of sons. She had befriended him initially out of pity. He was a cuckoo in the nest if ever she saw one. Out of place among his brash, bold family; out of place anywhere, probably.

Trent hesitated and moved a step closer, "I was aware of what Phillipe did to his brother, how he tormented him. I used to hide in the bushes down by the river to escape my own brothers. They were as foul and evil as your dead husband."

Suddenly, he strode across the room, stood beside the bed, tall, straight, his arms folded. "Once, when I was eight years old, my brothers were swimming in the river. Phillipe was with them, having a grand game of throwing me in. I could not swim. They had a rope tied around my waist, thought it amusing to haul me out when I started to drown, drag me on to the jetty and throw me in again." His attention wandered to the window, to where the river lazed by outside, reliving the horror in his mind.

"I can still taste the choke of water in my mouth, my lungs bursting for air, the fear that writhed through me as they took hold of my arms and legs, one limb each, and swung me back and forth then tossed me in. Again and again." His voice faltered, the memory too vivid, too cruel. He pulled a chair forward, sat, wiped his sleeve across his eyes. "And then Jesamiah came along. Only a few years older than me, younger than those bastards – already afeared of his brother." He stared at Alicia. "And do you know what he did?"

Slowly she shook her head.

"He tried to defend me; shouted at them to leave me alone, but of course they only laughed and threw me in the water yet again, then pitched him in as well." Samuel Trent laughed, a short, sharp sound. "They were no brighter then than they are now, my brothers." Another laugh. "You see, Jesamiah could swim. He grabbed hold of me, cut the rope, towed me to a safe distance and took me to his mother. We told her I had fallen in. She dried my clothes and gave me honey cakes and lemonade. But it turned out she had seen what had happened and she promptly marched over to my father and gave him a piece of her mind. She was a lady, was Mrs Mereno. My brothers left me alone after that. But not Jesamiah. He suffered for intervening. So I did the only thing I could, I copied Mrs Mereno's example and stomped right up to Captain Mereno and told him what had happened. Told him everything. The Captain scared me witless more than all my brothers ranged together. But tell him I did. I was expecting him to do something. To stop Phillipe's abuses. But you know what he said?"

The tears had almost stopped as Alicia had listened. She dabbed again at her eyes, mumbled, "No. Tell me."

"He said Jesamiah was on his own. He had to learn to look after himself. And he said it would be better for me if I learnt to swim. Jesamiah said the same a few days later. Took the time to teach me, in that rocky inlet the other side of Urbanna." His voice trailed off. "I will always be grateful to him for that. Always."

Alicia was silent a while, digesting everything. She had known none of this but then, why should she? Phillipe had never spoken of Jesamiah, or the past here at la Sorenta. And then the way in which Samuel had said 'I will always be grateful to him for that', sank into her brain. And she suddenly realised something.

"My God," she said, her hand going to her breast, her mouth opening, astonished. "You love him. You are in love with Jesamiah. You are a sodomite – that is why you are different! My God!" She did not know whether to be shocked, outraged or disgusted: sodomy was illegal in the eyes of the Church and the law; but then, she had known many a molly boy in her days as a prostitute. Not one of them had been evil like her husband.

Slowly Samuel wandered towards the door. "Love is a strange thing,

Mrs Mereno. Jesamiah believes I love you – I do not. I never have, I never will. But I used to admire you. I used to think of you as my friend." He shook his head, lifted one hand, dropped it, defeated, to his side. "No longer. I have no interest in sluts who lie and would see a man hang for their own gain."

Stunned by his words, made all the more vehement by the dull, flat tone in which he spoke them, Alicia shoved the covers aside, swung her legs from the bed. "No! I only wanted him in gaol for a day or two, nothing more!"

She hurried to her dressing table, yanked a drawer open and rummaged through the froth of laced underwear. Retrieved the Letter of Marque with a modest flourish of triumph. "I have it here. I have the proof Jesamiah needs!"

In three strides Samuel was across the room. He snatched it from her, glanced quickly to ensure it was the correct document and shoving it into his coat pocket was back at the door.

"Where are you going?" she cried, running after him, suddenly afraid. He was halfway down the stairs. She leaned over the banister, her hands gripping white-knuckled on the mahogany rail. "Samuel! What are you going to do?"

He did not pause, did not look up. "Rescue Jesamiah. What do you think I am going to do?"

Alicia crumpled to the carpet runner on the landing, incongruously noted a stain across the red and blue of the pattern. It was a Wilton weave, purchased from the catalogue from England. The carpeting for the house had cost Phillipe a fortune. Except it had been her fortune and there was now none of it left.

Samuel's footsteps rapped smartly across the tiled hall, the door slammed as he went out. She rested her forehead on the turned wooden spindles, closed her eyes. He was going to sort this mess out. Jesamiah was not going to hang. "Oh thank God," she breathed, "thank God."

Only later, as her maid helped her back to bed, a fever on her cheeks and beading her brow, did Alicia pause to wonder what she was now going to do about that foul little man who knew so much about her past. She would have to sell some of her jewellery. She no longer had a choice.

Alicia turned on her side, buried her face in the pillow and sobbed.

Forty Eight

"But how long before she can sail?" Trent was almost dancing in frustration as he hopped from one foot to the other. "We need to sail. I need to get to Williamsburg. We need to get to Williamsburg."

Nat Crocker scratched at his unshaven chin, sniffed loudly, shook his head. "You see, it is like this. If any one of us goes within spitting distance of Williamsburg we will be arrested and hanged. So we stay here."

"And leave your Captain to hang? Good God, you spineless worms!"

Several of the men nearby stopped the work they were doing – finishing the paintwork of the hull – and glowered at him, offended. The *Sea Witch* was almost finished. They had worked hard cleaning, repairing, restoring her to her full beauty. All it needed was for the paint and varnish to dry, the rigging to be completed and the next high tide to float her clear of the graving dock. Then her cannon would be swung back aboard, her ballast replaced, food and water stores replenished, and she would be ready for sea.

"It is not a matter of leavin' our *Capitaine* to 'ang *Monsieur*. There is nothing we can do to stop it. 'E knows that. 'E is not a fool." Rue spread his hands, at a loss for what else to say. "Without a letter of authority, we are marked as pirates. And as pirates we shall 'ang."

Trent almost screamed with annoyance; "But is that not what I have been trying to tell you?" He fished in his pocket. "The Letter of Marque has been found. Somehow it was inadvertently put among Mrs Mereno's personal papers."

Forty Nine

Friday 25th October

The two-and-a-half storey brick built Capitol Building of Williamsburg, Virginia, was essentially in the shape of an H. It was actually two structures of seventy-feet by twenty-five, connected by a central arcade. Each wing on the southern side terminated in a semicircular apse, with the ground floor punctuated by three circular windows. The classical, corniced architecture was topped by a six-sided cupola crowning the ridge of the hipped and dormered roof. To most observers it was an impressive building, but Jesamiah, being marched and prodded across the road from the gaol to the rear entrance and the single small holding cell beneath the courtroom in the west wing, was not overly enamoured. The Capitol Building was only thirteen years old and this cell seemed to have accumulated every bit of dirt and muck from every one of them.

In a room no more than a few yards square, the unwashed and unshaven prisoners sat in near darkness along a bench, their shackles chafing at wrists and ankles from the short but uncomfortable walk.

Yesterday, some of Jesamiah's fellow prisoners had been taken to their doom. Immediately after trial and sentencing the eight-year-old boy had been given a severe thrashing to his backside and sent on his way. Two of the men had spent the rest of the day in the stocks being gleefully pelted by rotten vegetables, mud and dung – human and animal – and three had been branded on the cheek as thieves and set free. Were they to be caught again for the same crime they would hang without trial or deliberation.

This morning, three men had been hanged, one of them the whoreson Jesamiah had attacked. Another had been Henry. His trial was short, a foregone conclusion. He had been caught performing a sexual act of gross indecency with another man twice his age in a tavern's miserable back room down in Jamestown. The man had escaped leaving Henry to take the full wrath of Christian moralistic judgement. He had pleaded guilty and had walked with pride and dignity to the gallows. It had been the bully who had pleaded for mercy, broken down and wept as the noose had been laid around his neck. He had taken twenty minutes to die, slowly strangling, accompanied by the sound of hisses and boos. The crowds did not like a coward.

Jesamiah's invitation to join the proceedings was the last to be issued. He dared not say anything as the bailiff prodded him towards the door and the short flight of stairs beyond. What was there to say? This was all a lie, a misunderstanding? He had been saying that since his arrest, with only Maynard to speak up for him. But Maynard was not here in Williamsburg. He was at Jamestown with his ship, or at sea somewhere, it did not matter where.

It was difficult walking with the leg irons, twice Jesamiah stumbled up the steps, only to be punched in the back and grumbled at. He halted at the top, blinking in the brightness of the light and airy courtroom, the sun streaming in through the circular windows making his eyes water. The level of talk from the spectators – a gladiatorial audience – increased as he stood there, disorientated, his heart beginning to thump with apprehension. This was no jested prank, this was a courtroom where he could very well be sentenced to swing alongside poor Henry's corpse come tomorrow morning. The spectators were seated on wooden benches placed in rows as if they were pews in a church; those come to gawp who had no room to sit, stood along the back, the muttered words of pirate and murderer galloping around the room and soaring up to the ceiling many feet above as Jesamiah appeared.

The room was all polished wood and windows, dust motes swirling in the shafts of sunbeams. At the front, the clerks were poised with their ink and quills, all staring at him as if he were a horned, tailed devil hissing fire and brimstone from his mouth and arse.

Jesamiah was prodded again, chivvied to move forward. He was aware that he stank, his clothes were stained and torn and his matted hair, like his body, was filthy. He had not washed or shaved since the day of the ball. Proud, determined in his innocence, Jesamiah squared his shoulders and walked with as much dignity as he could, considering the restrictions of the irons, to the bench at the front which the bailiff was pointing at.

The muttering died a little as Jesamiah sat, his back straight, but the whispering continued. The staring, the pointing, the wrinkled noses of utter disgust at his appearance, at what he supposedly was.

Is Alicia here, Jesamiah wondered, *enjoying the entertainments of Williamsburg's Publick Times? Enjoying the mischief she's created?* He was certain, now, that she had procured his letter. Quite why he had not fathomed, but probably for some selfish, mean-spirited reason of her own.

"All rise!"

The voices stopped but the coughing and shuffling of feet was as loud. Governor Spotswood entered walking, as if in royal procession, down the centre aisle and took his place at his judge's bench, a throne-like chair raised on a dais. The clerks dipped their quills in the ink, bent their heads and began to write.

Spotswood was handed some papers. "The Court may be seated," he said, then began to read. He had not looked at Jesamiah.

More rustling and shuffling. Unable to keep silent, the whispers began, then grew louder as if a wind was getting up in distant trees.

"Bailiff," Spotswood stated without glancing up, "I remind you, this Government Court is in session. On several occasions this day I have found cause to remind you that I will have silence. If there is one more sound I will order the room cleared. Do you understand?"

The whispering ceased as if the little rise of wind was running off over the meadows.

The members of the Council who sat as jury were, to a man, merchants and traders. Each one strictly biased against piracy. The bailiff jerked Jesamiah's chains and he was brought to stand at the low wooden bar.

At last Spotswood raised his head, stared at him.

"You are Jesamiah Charles Mereno, better known as Jesamiah Acorne?"

"I am innocent of this charge, I…"

Spotswood slammed his gavel with a resounding crack down on the bench. "You will answer the question and speak only when spoken to. I repeat; you are Jesamiah Charles Mereno, better known as Jesamiah Acorne?"

Jesamiah took a steadying breath to control his rising temper and the sudden galloping fear. This was not going to be a fair trial. He nodded. "Aye, Sir."

The Secretary of the Court rose, began to drone the legal necessities.

Jesamiah listened to the first two words then stared at the nearest window, gazing out at the blue sky beyond. Had Rue rounded the lads up? Had they started on *Sea Witch* – finished? Would they have completed all the repairs in a week? They could usually careen in two or three days, and in the graving dock she would have been easier to get at – although there was a lot to do. Were the sails repaired? The rigging overhauled?

He sighed, listened to the secretary's boring voice for a few sentences. He had missed the nature of the charge brought against him, but he knew what that was anyway. Piracy with intent to commit theft, arson and murder upon the High Seas.

"How do you plead?"

They had to repeat the question.

Lifting his chin, standing as proud and straight as the manacles and leg irons would allow, Jesamiah stared direct into Governor Spotswood's eyes. "Not guilty." A ripple of conversation ran like an Atlantic roller around the room. Spotswood used his gavel again.

A few witnesses, men Jesamiah did not know, were called, men who, he discovered, were crew of the *Fortune of Virginia*. They all said the same thing, as did Captain Daniel Lofts, although his testimony was more elaborate and succinct in detail. Their combined testimonies and depositions were damning; the *Sea Witch*, captained by Mereno-Acorne, had boldly and blatantly attacked the *Fortune of Virginia* with intent to damage, rob, and murder.

Jesamiah was forced to listen to the drivel, not permitted to say a word in his own defence.

Governor Spotswood studied some of the papers again for a few minutes, then looked ponderously at Jesamiah. "Prisoner at the Bar. You have heard the words of these witnesses. Jesamiah Mereno, have you in turn any defence to make or witnesses to declare on your behalf?"

"I prefer to be called Acorne, my Lord, if it so please the Court. I have not used the name Mereno for many years."

Someone among the spectators called out, "Aye, not since you beat your brother to a pulp then ran away to a life of theft and debauchery!"

"And eventually to murder him!"

Spotswood banged his gavel for silence, then scratched his nose and considered a moment. He nodded, spoke to the clerks. "I will accept the name Acorne." He transferred his attention to Jesamiah, waiting for him to speak.

Jesamiah remained silent for a moment, considering his best option. Tiola would testify, but this Court would only see her as his mistress, would treat her words with scorn, and aside, there remained the problem of keeping her identity secret from Teach. For the same reason, would they listen to Alicia? On the other hand she was Phillipe Mereno's widow, how could the Court misinterpret anything she said as his witness?

"Mrs Alicia Mereno was aboard the *Sea Witch*," he said boldly, doubting as he said it that the words would be of the slightest use. "She will testify that I did not attack Captain Lofts."

Spotswood glowered at the faces in the Court. "Is the lady here present?"

The Secretary to the Court stood, "My Lord, I understand she was questioned by Lieutenant Maynard when he took the militia to search for this fellow's accomplices. His report is included in your papers."

The Governor shuffled through the papers and impatiently tossed them to his table. "You have a copy? Read me the relevant information."

Complying, the Secretary found what he was looking for, and cleared his throat; "Mrs Mereno was questioned as to her presence aboard the vessel *Sea Witch* during the interval of the offence of piracy. She answered that she knew nothing as she had been forcibly incarcerated below deck. She was abandoned there and possibly left to drown, for water was up to her waist before her screams secured her release."

The bitch, Jesamiah thought. "I sent her below because I had every intention of engaging Teach and drawing his fire from the *Fortune of Virginia*," he interrupted. "On deck during an engagement is no place for a woman."

"So you admit she was below?" Spotswood responded. "If that is so then how can she prove witness to what occurred?"

Captain Lofts jumped to his feet, dramatically pointing his finger at the Governor then at Jesamiah, "Do you seriously believe this rag's lies? That out of the goodness of his heart he was trying to save my ship from Teach's ravaging?"

Peering at him sternly Spotswood repeated that he would have silence in his Court, then added, "Your statement is noted, Captain, but as to the accuracy of it, are we not all assembled here to ascertain that fact?"

"My Lord Governor," Jesamiah said, aware that everything was tumbling down around him. It felt like the ceiling was caving in, the floor giving way and he was falling into an abyss of panic. He grabbed at the bar, the manacles grating against the wood. Fought down rising nausea and made one last plea. "Governor, I carried a Letter of Marque with a precise remit to aid the Admiralty in the clearing of undesirables from the oceans. To hunt pirates. That was why I attacked Teach and went to the defence of the *Fortune of Virginia*. I was doing what I was commissioned to do."

A stir of surprised incredulity rippled through the spectators and swelled in volume.

Teach'll come and finish the job of shooting me when he hears this, Jesamiah thought. *He'll have to 'urry; get in before they 'ang me.*

"Silence!" the bailiff cried.

"And where is this letter?" Spotswood enquired, leaning forward and patiently folding his hands together.

"In the drawer of my desk, aboard the *Sea Witch*."

"And why was this letter not produced?"

The Court Secretary glanced up from writing in his ledger. "Because no such document was found, my Lord. Lieutenant Maynard discovered nothing of use or value anywhere aboard the said vessel."

More chatter. To be heard, Jesamiah shouted above the noise. "I had one, my Lord! Ask Captain Henry Jennings, he it was who issued it! Send word to him!"

"Silence! Silence!" The gavel banged twice. "Jennings is in Nassau, this is Virginia. Enough of this time wasting. Council, how do you find?"

A moment of conferring, nodding heads. "Guilty, my Lord."

Alexander Spotswood passed his papers to the Secretary. "You are found guilty of an act of piracy against the vessel *Fortune of Virginia*. The sentence is that you shall be taken to a place of execution and there hanged by the neck until you be dead. And thereafter your body shall be bound in chains and left upon the gibbet as a deterrent to others."

The gavel banged down, a sharp sound of dreadful finality.

Jesamiah stared at Spotswood, his mind in turmoil, stomach churning, throat dry. Twice he opened his mouth to speak but no sound came out. He tried again; "Sir. I beg leave to appeal."

The hush fell over the noise that had been rustling through the courtroom, all faces turned towards the ragged pirate.

Jesamiah repeated himself, louder, more confident. "I beg leave to make appeal. I am entitled to a stay of execution for a period of three weeks from this date in order to present evidence. I am innocent of this charge and I ask the Court to write to Captain Jennings of Nassau in order that I may prove it so."

Spotswood considered for a few moments. Acorne was correct, he did have the right. The Governor was a fair man who respected and abided by the law; was it possible that Acorne could supply evidence of carrying a Letter of Marque? If that was so, and he did indeed have a commission to hunt pirates, then, as Maynard had once suggested, he could prove to be of great benefit to Virginia.

He nodded once, curt and abrupt. "So be it. Secretary to the Court, you will write to Captain Jennings and ascertain the truth."

The gavel banged down for a final time and Spotswood rose, swept from the courtroom where the bailiff pleaded unsuccessfully for silence. Above the uproar, he could not be heard.

Fifty

Monday 28th October

They did not hang people on Sundays and the horse racing had occupied attention on Saturday, so Jesamiah was left alone in the cell to await his potential date with the noose. So far, it was proving to be a long, lonely and anxious wait.

Not every governor or judge abided by the three-week adjournment. They were a corrupt lot, easily persuaded by necessity, and if a crowd grew ugly and demanded a hanging, it was likely the demand would be granted – and as this was the end of Publick Times it was quite possible they would want something memorable as a grand finale. The hanging of a notorious pirate would provide an attraction to round things off nicely.

It was still night outside, but Jesamiah was awake staring through the grill on the gaol door, waiting for the rectangle of darkness to start turning pale blue. He could see a small scatter of stars, they made him think of nights at sea, his ship ploughing through the Atlantic rollers, her bow lifting then plunging downward as the stern rose; the phosphorescence twirling and dancing around her masts and rigging, and the frothing glow of her wake. His hands loose but confidant on the spokes of the wheel, his balance subtly shifting, moving as one with her joyful, vibrant motion. Each individual sound of wind, sea and ship like a lover's secretive murmur in his ears. He had his hands around the bars of the door, closed his eyes; could feel *Sea Witch* beneath his feet. Could hear her voice.

~ *Jesamiah? Are you all right my luvver?* ~

Tiola! He sprung away from the door, guilty, as if he had been caught in a mistress's arms.

~ Missing my ship, ~ he admitted. ~ *If they do not hang me soon I will die of boredom. Otherwise, I'm fine, sweetheart. I smell a bit. Wouldn't say no to a bath. Especially a tub big enough for two.* ~

He felt her warmth infuse him. What would he have done without the comfort of Tiola's dear, sweet, voice in his mind? Or the feeling of her close presence? There were occasions when he awoke from a deep sleep certain she had been lying next to him. He had reached out, once, to touch the dank straw but it had been cold, no sign of any indentation. She had been with him in spirit only and he had not tried touching again for it was too disappointing to discover she was not physically there.

At the start of it all she had said, ~ *I will come; tell them the truth.* ~ But he had insisted no. Once Teach found out who she was, there would be no going back to Bath Town for her, and beside, she had been below on the *Fortune of Virginia* for the entire voyage, unaware of what was happening. What could she tell the Court that they did not already know?

~ *You cannot lie, Tiola,* ~ he had said, ~ *and the truth will damn me as much as I am already damned. We must trust in Jennings sending a replacement Letter of Marque. Though I would give much to discover what happened to the original.* ~

She spoke to him, was with him, on the rare occasions when Teach was gone from Bath Town to conduct his business. No one ever asked what that business was, where his sloop had been or from where he had obtained a cargo. No one ever asked questions of Edward Teach.

The minutes crawled by. Half hour. An hour. Two. A lively wind stirred the fallen leaves that lay scattered in the enclosed courtyard, swirling them into little eddies as if they were chasing each other around and around in an endless race. Above the wall between the gaol and the outside world he could see the sky, bright now with full daylight, and the tops of autumn-painted trees rapidly thinning of their coloured foliage. His entire world had shrunk from the exhilarating freedom of the open sea to this stark view of a brick wall. Jesamiah hated being shut in enclosed spaces, the darkness of the hold sometimes terrified him – another legacy from the cruelties of his damned brother. Even now, knowing it was a lie, he could still only think of Phillipe as his brother, damn him to hell and back. Jesamiah kicked the wall in frustration; if he had not been able to see the tops of the trees and the sky, he did not know what he would have done to retain his sanity. Occasionally, when the gateway was opened he would catch a glimpse of what lay beyond: a lane, more trees, people walking past. Yesterday, as the gaol keeper, John Redwood, had left by that route bound for church, Jesamiah had seen a small boy gazing at the gaol in fearful wonder. Redwood had said something and the boy's eyes had widened a moment before he had hared off as if all the Hounds of Hell were after him. They probably were. *That is where they put you before you be hanged.* It did not take much imagination to know what that heartless misery Redwood had said.

Beyond the rustling of leaves and a faint moan of the wind Jesamiah could hear the plod of hooves in the lane and the rumble of wheels. The noise stopped. Voices, but too muffled to follow precise words. The gate opened, John Redwood trotted through accompanied by four red-coated, musket-bearing militia guard.

This was it then. A dawn hanging. They were not prepared to wait for a reply from Jennings. The feeling in the pit of Jesamiah's stomach had been right: that had been his last night, this his last morning. Tomorrow he would be – God alone knew.

~ They are not going to hang you, Jesamiah ~ Tiola had said to him once, during the lonely hours of darkness. If only it were true.

"Well, here be a merry party," Jesamiah drawled, his hands draped through the bars as the soldiers halted in a ragged line a safe distance from the door, muskets raised.

Fumbling with the keys Redwood gestured for him to step back and then unlocked it, drew the bolts and swung it open with a heavy creak to the rusting hinges.

Making a low bow Jesamiah flourished an invisible cocked hat and with an elaborate gesture invited the men inside. "You are welcome to enter but I warn you, the chambermaid is a lazy bitch. Me room's in a bit of a mess. I reckon it needs a dustin', a touch of polish 'ere an' there an' a new carpet, mebbe?" The stench emanating from within and from Jesamiah himself was ripe. The youngest of the militia guard put his hand over his mouth and gagged.

Used to the smell, Redwood produced wrist shackles. "Enough of your fooling. It will be no bother to disable you with a musket ball to your knee."

With a sigh, Jesamiah retrieved his hat and settled it on his head, pulled on his coat and held out his arms. No point in making a fuss. Not with loaded muskets holding the balance of opinion over an argument. Mind, to be shot would be a quicker death than hanging – assuming they aimed straight. On second thoughts, hanging would perhaps be the better option; this lot barely knew which end of a musket was which.

Leg irons were fitted. Did they really expect him to run? It was a thought that occupied his attention as he was marched outside and bundled awkwardly into the cart. Would he run if given the opportunity? Or would he face death with dignity? He supposed it would depend on weighing the options: how far he was able to run – if he could run at all; how likely an escape would be. And if death was inevitable, would he have the strength to stay silent? He'd cut out his tongue before he'd beg for mercy. Or would he? There was no way of knowing until the moment came. But to be hanged for a crime he did not commit? The final irony.

It was early morning, admitted, but everywhere was strangely quiet. There were no spectators, no one jeering or cheering as the cart moved off, its wheels rumbling. The only sign of life, a she-cat heavily in kitten slinking beneath the shelter of a bush. The wind had a vicious chill in it, but it was an unlikely reason to keep people away. No one had been told. His hanging was to be secret then, that was the only explanation. Spotswood knew full well that to hang him before the respite of three weeks was up was illegal. Huh, he might have guessed, Virginia's Governor was no more honourable than the rest of them.

They went west along the undulating back lane of Nicholson Street, the bay cob plodding lazily between the shafts, Redwood, the driver, not hurrying the animal. Jesamiah was grateful for the fresh wind on his face, its touch caressing his grimed skin. He closed his eyes. The wind, unless it was in a temper, was always a friend to a sailor.

The cart turned north into England Street, passing the timber-framed skeleton of what would be a large house when finished and, further along, the mill, its sails turning sprightly, creaking and clanking and groaning. Then west again at the next junction. Ahead, at the far end, the Governor's grand palace. Jesamiah frowned; this was an odd route to be taking to the gallows, was it not?

A man of about forty years was mending a broken fence to the front of a newly built house; a one-and-a-half storey building clad with four-foot lengths of white-painted weatherboarding and a clapboard roof, not shingles. A typical design of the Williamsburg properties that were springing up like mushrooms. He banged in another nail, wiped his hands and leant on a sound section of the picket fence.

"You are up early, John Brush," Redwood observed as the cart drew level.

"My eldest daughter was daft enough to tether her pony here yesterday. Stupid beast pulled away and took the fence with it. I reckoned the Sabbath was a day of rest though, so left the fixing 'til today. He for hanging then?"

"None of your business," the eldest militiaman answered, suggestively cradling his musket across his chest. "You get on with that mending, else that pretty daughter of yourn may tell your Missus about you slacking."

The pretty daughter in question was pegging wet laundry to a length of stout rope strung between two trees, taking advantage of a fine drying day. The girl was staring wide-eyed at the sight of a real pirate no further than a few feet beyond the fence. Her father turned to glower at her and she hurriedly reached for the next item in the basket at her feet. Blushed scarlet when pulling it out, she realised it was a personal undergarment. Hastily, she stuffed it out of sight and glancing up, saw the pirate grinning at her.

"Ma'am," Jesamiah touched his hat and then ruined the polite effect by winking at her.

Reddening deeper she hid behind the screen of a flapping sheet.

"Bit strange you coming this way, Redwood, is it not?" Brush had no intention of returning to work when there was a chance to gossip. "Gallows was the other direction last time I noticed."

The same thought was in Jesamiah's mind; a twist of unease knotted in his stomach, one that had nothing to do with a noose going round his neck. What were they intending to do with him? Torture him perhaps? Make him tell all he knew of Teach? Well there would be no problem, he'd clack straight out as cheerfully as a hen announcing she'd laid!

John Redwood clicked his tongue at the cob in an effort to make her walk faster. The mare flicked her ears and swished her tail but did nothing more. "Like you were told, Master Brush; none of your business."

Directly ahead now, the Governor's palace. From the front it looked splendid; dormer windows for the third storey, a balustrade around the high cupola – but a network of scaffolding was erected at the rear and as they passed the stable yard it became clear that no one could use the side entrance, for builders' materials were piled in haphazard heaps right up to the walls. Spotswood's project to create a dwelling fit for a man of his rank was taking longer – and more money – than he had originally planned. Some of the cost he was now having to foot at his own expense, for Williamsburg refused to advance him any further financial assistance. But even incomplete, the building was probably the finest in British Colonial America.

Governor Spotswood had determined to create a palace and grounds of formal grandeur and symmetrical balance. It was to reflect the Colony's – his – dignity and status. Sited at the top of a broad green and a drive that swept up from Main Street towards the iron gates and brick walls enclosing the forecourt, the palace completed Williamsburg's primary north-south axis. Why he was being brought in this direction though, Jesamiah still had no idea. To prove a point? That Governor Spotswood was all-powerful and Jesamiah was a mere nothing about to hang?

To his surprise the cart turned in through the main gates with their supporting pillars, each adorned with a heraldic beast rampant atop, and halted. With elaborate waving of muskets he was ushered out of the cart, up the steps and in through the front door. Not easy to accomplish with dignity wearing leg irons and shackles.

"Goin' to 'ang me in style, are they?" Jesamiah quipped, baffled at what was going on. A prisoner about to hang being escorted through the front door of the Governor's palace? Why? Again his stomach churned. Why did they not just get on with it? Finish him?

If the intention of the entrance hall was to impress, then Jesamiah was suitably impressed. Was it octagonal in shape? Was an octagon eight-sided or ten? He could not remember, started counting, stopped. What the heck was he doing? Did it matter what bloody shape the entrance hall was? Did he care?

To one side a marble fireplace, doors leading off to left and right; ahead, the main doorway and beyond, the staircase to the private family residence. The elegant floor was black and white marble set as a vague flower petal pattern; the walls wood-panelled. And the walls were the reason he had been brought here, for they were adorned with a dazzling display of weaponry. Each panel formed an intricate pattern of blade overlapping blade, or gun barrel over gun barrel. Gleaming swords, immaculate polished pistols and muskets. The Brown Bess, weighing fifteen pounds with a ball three-quarters of an inch in diameter. Used in battle by rank upon rank of men – you knew about it when one of those got you. But individually? They were slow to load, inaccurate and unreliable. There was enough of an armoury displayed here to fight a small war, though. To attack Williamsburg was not a sensible option. Was that why he was here? To be shown resistance was futile?

That they were expected became apparent when the butler appeared and made no protest at having a degenerate standing in his entrance hall. He did, however, register his disapproval by sniffing loudly and curling his lip in distaste. Redwood and the militia were ushered outside, although John Redwood did try to get a word in to ask if the Governor had agreed the funding for his house yet?

"My lodgings are a mite inconvenient. Tell the Governor that if we could get on with building my house next to the gaol, there'd be less chance of any escapes and such." No one took any notice of him. For the past few months, Redwood's sole line of conversation had been the promised building of his house.

Jesamiah alone was shown through the right-hand door into the Governor's parlour. Two men awaited him. Governor Spotswood sat at his desk writing in a ledger book; seated in a chair, Samuel Trent. He rose, a smile of delight on his face. He took a couple of steps towards Jesamiah his hand outstretched – his nose wrinkling, thought better of it and sat down again.

On the desk were two documents. Jesamiah recognised Captain Henry Jennings' distinctive writing on the Letter of Marque he had issued, and beside it a sealed parchment bearing his own name. Jesamiah Charles Mereno. He said nothing, stood, wrists bound by the irons.

"You owe your life to Master Trent here," the Governor said returning his quill to its stand and dusting the wet ink with fine sand. He blew the excess off, closed the book, set it aside and finally looked up. "He has informed me that Mrs Alicia Mereno found your Letter of Marque. It seems it had inadvertently been placed among her own papers." The cadence of his voice conveyed that he did not believe a word, but no gentleman would openly call a lady a liar.

"So the lying bitch had hidden it? I thought so." Jesamiah knew Alicia was no lady and he had never claimed to be a gentleman.

"She was most distressed, Captain. I was present when she discovered it." Samuel gallantly attested. "I came straight'way to Williamsburg and have made a nuisance of myself to be granted an interview with the Governor." He had repeatedly been denied the request, but had been most persistent, had finally been rewarded with an interview an hour since.

"He stated the case for you most eloquently Captain Acorne, but you understand, this puts me in a damn difficult position."

"How so?" Jesamiah contradicted, shifting his weight to his right foot. His left ankle was sore and aching abominably from where the shackles had rubbed. "I am innocent of the charge. You knew that from the start."

The Governor cleared his throat. "I have made a promise to the people of Virginia to rid the Chesapeake of every conceivable element of piracy. It is my duty to abide by that pledge."

"An' a fine, 'onourable pledge it is. I whole hearted give my support and blessing for it, Governor, but I ain't no pirate, so what 'as it got to do with me?"

"The trouble is, Captain," Samuel said hesitantly, shy of speaking before the Governor, "too many people along the Rappahannock – and elsewhere – think you are."

"Yes, thank you Trent, I am dealing with this. Perhaps you would care to wait outside?"

Samuel did not care, but one did not argue with a Lieutenant Governor in his own palace. He collected his hat from a side table, glanced at Jesamiah, gave him a wan smile.

"I'll be all right, lad. It ain't likely the Governor is goin to 'ave me 'anged in 'ere." Jesamiah grinned confidently. Not wanting them to see the weakness of relief coursing through him, added, "He'd get piss and shite all over 'is floor for one thing."

When the door was shut and they were alone, Spotswood rubbed at his nose then linked his fingers over his stomach. "And there lies the rub," he said. "Unless we can think of a way to sufficiently counter public opinion, I am obliged to hang you."

Pointing to the Letter of Marque Jesamiah narrowed his eyes, "But that vindicates me!"

Staring him straight in the eye, not moving a muscle in his face, Spotswood stated; "It does not. Anyone can forge a document. I would wager you are proficient at it."

Jesamiah swore colourfully and called him a particularly dishonourable name.

Unabashed by the expletive, the Governor unfolded Henry Jennings' letter and re-read its contents, then studied the signature. He tossed it back to the desk. "I am certain this is genuine, but how do we convince the good citizens of Virginia?" He sat leaning forward, rested his elbows on the desktop. "I suggest that were you to be of service to the Colony in some way, there would be no problem. Would there?"

Not liking the sound of this, Jesamiah remained silent.

Spotswood crossed his legs, studied the fellow before him. Saw a man in desperate need of a shave and a bath, but a man who oozed astute confidence and competent ability. Just as his father before him had done.

He picked up the second letter. The paper was yellowed, a bit dog-eared at one corner and sealed with wax and a ribbon.

A blue ribbon, Jesamiah noted, though a paler blue than his own deep royal colour. ~ *You were not the first to wear blue ribbons, lad. From where do you think the idea came?* ~ Jesamiah frowned at the voice inside his head. Another of those intrusive thoughts that sounded so much like his father.

"This has been awaiting your collection for some years, I believe," the Governor was saying, unaware of Jesamiah's slight distraction. "I understand the rascal who served your father's legal requirements had been instructed to destroy it by your elder brother. It seems he was paid to do so, but he is not a totally honest fellow." Spotswood chuckled beneath his breath. "Ain't yet met a lawyer who is."

To save having to answer, Jesamiah poked at a loose molar tooth with his tongue.

"You were to have received this at the time of your father's death. I have no idea of the specific content, for as you see, the seal has not been tampered with, though I am led to believe it states information to your advantage."

The Governor held the letter towards Jesamiah who took it, the irons on his wrists chafing and rattling. He was annoyed to see that as his fingers closed around it, his hand was trembling. He held his wrists stretched out. "It would be more convenient to read it without these pretties adorning m'wrists like a set of lady's bangles."

Ignoring the request Spotswood sat forward, lifted his quill and opened the ledger. "I suggest, Acorne, before you indulge in whatever your father writ you, that you consider your situation. I can offer a way out of your predicament. The outcome could leave you well off and held in highest esteem. I can ensure all charges against you are dropped."

Obstinately, Jesamiah remained holding his arms out, even though the iron shackles were a heavy weight and the letter felt as if it was burning his fingers. He should have had it the day after they buried his father; instead he had been forced to run for his life and ended up at sea as a pirate. How different his life would probably have been! Suddenly not wanting to read it he flicked the letter on to the open ledger book. From the day he had stepped aboard the *Mermaid* under the command of Malachias Taylor he had been a free man, from that first weighing of anchor living a life he loved. Had he remained in Virginia he would never have seen what he had of the world, never have made a fortune – and would never have met Tiola. She had told him to let go of the past. She had been right.

"So what is it you want me to do?" he asked, finally withdrawing his arms.

Governor Spotswood pushed the letter aside and wrote some alarmingly high figures in the expenditure column of the palace accounts. He did not look up, merely stated, "In return for your unequivocal freedom, and the same for your crew, I want you to help us be rid of Blackbeard."

The bastard! So that's what this is all about. Jesamiah's tongue prodded at the loose tooth while he pretended to consider the offer. "That too, is probably a death sentence."

"Probably. But unlike hanging, not definitely."

Part Two

…And thus it ends.

Here, in this place of waiting, the Eternal River chained his soul as effectively as his bones tied him to his earthly grave. Charles Mereno could see his son and could communicate with Jesamiah in the same way as the Witch Woman – she had at least given him that ability. He could appear as he had been in life at the place where he had died and been buried, but he wanted more! Needed more!

He was impatient to put right that which he had done wrong, impatient because he was tired and wanted to rest, to sleep, in peace.

Soon though, the Witch Woman would help him again. On the Day of the Dead, she had said, his spirit could cross the River. The boundary that held him captive would be open, and he could walk among the living, stay for as long as necessary for him to appease his guilt.

Would he be able to do what he had to do? Could he do it, coward that he was?

He covered his face with his hands, despairing.

The price of paying for his wrongs was high and hard; and he was not certain he was strong enough to pay it.

One

Monday 28th October – North Carolina

Tiola sat and sketched pretty drawings beside the river. Some were fanciful – a swan skimming the night sky, Cygnus in flight; a mermaid sitting on a rock, combing her hair. Naturally, the ship in the background under full sail, white water creaming around her bows, was *Sea Witch*.

She also sketched Perdita and Jonathan strolling together, close but not touching, along the opposite bank. Perdita, in the drawing, had her head bent towards her beau, listening intently as he recited from the book of poetry that he held in his hand. The boughs of the trees drooped downward and two birds swooped above the couple's heads, as if nature, too, was listening as enraptured as the girl.

It was a charming picture but Tiola hid it away. She would not be offering it as a keepsake to either one of the two lovers, for despite the intimacy of the captured scene, the sadness was also unexpectedly there. An air of hopelessness permeated each bold or shaded line. All Perdita and Jonathan would ever be able to do was walk and talk, and share poetry.

"Ma'am?"

Tiola turned her head quickly to see a man hurrying along the river path. He removed his hat as he came nearer, offered her the briefest of bows. "Miss Oldstagh, Ma'am, I suggest you move on from here and maybe the same for them two over there."

Narrowing her eyes, Tiola stared at the stranger. Of average height and build, moderately dressed in clothing that was neither elaborate nor common, he had brown hair, brown eyes; a tanned and wind-weathered skin. She guessed mid-twenties in age.

"And why, pray Sir, should we be so considering? It is quiet and pleasant here beside the river, and I am enjoying my creativity, as lacking as my skill may be."

"There are others on the path, Ma'am. It would be best for you to leave." With impertinence the man bent and began gathering Tiola's drawing implements.

She batted him away, annoyed. "Leave me be. How dare you!"

He ignored her flailing hand, slid her drawing into the leather case and tucked it beneath his arm. Held out his hand in order to assist her to her feet. "Ma'am. The Governor and Teach are coming this way. I doubt it a sensible idea for the latter to find you here, or the former to see them." He nodded brusquely towards Perdita and Jonathan, some yards away now on the far bank.

For a moment longer Tiola hesitated. Curse her inability to use her Craft! Had she not forced it into quiescence she would have been aware for herself. Nor dare she awaken it now to sense whether this man spoke the truth or was up to mischief.

"Please Ma'am, I urge you to hurry, for them if not for yourself." He again pointed towards the young couple.

Accepting his sincerity Tiola nodded and started getting to her feet. He put his free hand under her elbow, both assisting and hurrying her. "I am Joseph Meadows, Miss. The Captain and the rest of them call me Skylark. Captain Acorne, that is."

"Jesamiah?" The revelation stimulated her sluggish perception. This man was in earnest! Dare she call out to those two across the river? Anyone on the path would hear, for sound did carry so near water, even with the close proximity of the sentinel trees. She shoved her belongings into Meadows' arms and setting aside all acceptable decorum, raced along the path. Coming level with Perdita and Jonathan she waved her arms, but they were too absorbed in each other to notice. She bent, selected a handful of stones and threw them, hurling the missiles as if they were Roman ballista bolts. They fell, plopping into the river, each one making its own disturbance of sound. The tailor looked up, sharp, annoyed, saw Tiola frantically signalling for them to hide.

She cupped her hands around her mouth, risked the small magick of sending her voice across the water. "The Governor comes!"

Perdita squeaked alarm, but Jonathan kept his head. Without a word he backed into the bushes, guiding Perdita after him. The branches and leaves parted, swinging back into place with a gentle rustle of movement to hide their passing. Perdita was wearing green with a brown cloak; her companion was also in sombre colours. They were gone, hidden.

Tiola glanced the way she had come. The man, Meadows, was strolling away in sedate calmness, her belongings tucked casually beneath his arm. She realised now where she had seen him: several times, in various places, seated at an easel industriously painting. An artist; a clever guise. No one queried where a man sat to capture the beauty of the landscape or the fine elegance of a house. No one questioned that mayhap he was there for another reason entirely. Even Tiola had not.

Eden and Teach had appeared around the bend of the path, some eighty yards away. As Tiola backed into the shelter of the trees she saw Skylark touch his hat in greeting as he stood aside to let them pass, distracting their attention enough for her to take several more steps and crouch beneath the spread of a bush. With her Craft it would have been no problem to have hidden herself. With ease she could have used illusion, blended her form with a tree trunk and become one with it. But not with Teach so near. Not with the Malevolence that inhabited his soul.

As it was, he stopped for a moment and stared into the undergrowth. Tiola looked downward, lest he may catch the gleam in her eyes, kept herself perfectly still.

"So, you think I ought to marry m'stepdaughter to Knight, do thee?" Eden said, walking on.

"I doos. Tha man'll turn coat agains' us if 'n thee do not. I seen it afore. A man like he, been widd'erd this twelvemonth, will be wantin' a wummun – an' be wantin' more from us 'til there be nay more t'give."

"Keep Knight close by, you reckon?"

"Yass, he'll not betray his own, not if 'n he be expectin' t'inherit. He hath ambition doos that one."

Holding her breath Tiola could smell his closeness, her Craft was burning inside her, wanting to be released. Or was it the Dark trying to flush her out? Ah, she was wise to that trick!

Teach was frowning, he could sense something...There was something he could not quite see...? He shook his head, walked after Eden, his long stride easily catching him up.

Tiola stood quiet. Prayed to the Spirit of Calm that the two lovers on the far side of the river had not overheard. How dare the Governor so callously discuss the girl's marriage as if she were a horse or a cow to be sold at market! And to discuss it with Teach of all people! Tiola turned away in disgust and hurried down the path in the opposite direction. She had to get back to Elizabeth-Anne to ask if she knew anything of these disagreeable arrangements; finding Meadows would need to wait a while. There were a few pertinent questions she intended to ask him. The first of which would be why one of Jesamiah's crew was here in Bath Town. And the second, assuming her guess at the answer to the first was correct – to protect her – where in the Seven Names of Peace had he been the other night when she had required protecting?

There was a third, but that one she would keep until she had established the credentials of the other two, and perhaps, for more affable times. Where had Meadows learnt to paint? He was, indeed, very good.

Two

Teach bade farewell to Eden where the path divided, one direction leading through a shrubbery into Archbell Point's substantial gardens, the other to the town. Teach had a fitting of his new clothes: his wedding apparel. He was not eager for the experience, for all this poking and prying and fal-da-rolling was becoming tedious. Why in the devil's several names could he not simply marry the wretched girl, bed her, impregnate her and be done with it? John Ormond wanted a pirate's services to protect his valuable cargo, well, there would not be much protecting being done while the *Adventure* lay at anchor, would there?

This whole performance ashore was becoming more of a nuisance with every passing day. Was it worth it? Was it worth all this bowing and scraping and pretending to be a gentleman? Aboard ship he could do as he pleased, whatever he commanded was instantly obeyed – by God he ensured it was so! Yet not here in this pockmarked pretentious town, where not a-one of them if stripped of their lace-edged finery and curled wigs were any better than he underneath. If you peered close enough they were all thieves and scoundrels: lying knaves and poxed whores; townsfolk turning a blind eye to the fact that he and his entire crew were wanted men and should be dancing a jig at the wrong end of a rope. Ormond was only interested in making money from the safe shipment of his cargo – the man cared not a frayed bowline for what his daughter thought. Mind, neither did Teach as he swaggered along Main Street tipping his hat left and right to person after person who feigned pleasure at seeing him. Mary Ormond was a ripe fruit ready for plucking and virgin maids were a rare treat for a sailor to sample. Eden and Knight, for all their official status, were another pair of mendacious rogues doing secretive deals with a pirate to swell the gold in their private coffers. They were nothing more than greedy thieves, using people for their own gain, and they were either fools or not the God-fearing men they pretended to be! How many times now had he brought them stolen goods? Tea, cocoa, sugar, brandy, rum. Timber, silver plate, furniture, silks, spices. Every bit of it delivered with the same yarn: he had found a vessel run aground and abandoned in the shallows of the Ocracoke, so he said. By the law of the sea, whoever found such a boat was entitled to whatever he could salvage. Just his luck that each one had a full and valuable cargo.

Teach was careful to give the larger portion of the spoils to Eden and Knight, who not once had murmured a single doubt about his claim of salvage. And naturally, Teach ensured any Chase he captured was blown to pieces and burnt, every soul aboard sent to a watery grave. There was never to be any evidence to gainsay his plausible stories.

The tailor's shop was ahead. Another obsequious buffoon. Did Master Gabriel seriously think he was going to be paid? Hah! Not by Teach he was not! Teach guffawed to himself as he stepped into the tailor's shop, his eyes taking a moment to focus in the shadowed interior.

"Good day to you, Sir, your garments are ready. If I may say, the coat is exceptionally exquisite. You made a superb choice of cloth and colour."

Almost retching at hearing his father's grovelling, Jonathan Gabriel remained in the rear of the shop; he knew he would be summoned to assist with the fitting. He was sweating from running and a little dishevelled, but if his father noticed anything amiss he could easily make some excuse. When his name was tetchily called with the order to fetch out the coat and waistcoat, Jonathan ran a hand through his hair to smooth it, calmed his nerves and stepped through the curtained doorway fixing a professional shopkeeper's servile smile to his face.

A smile which he managed to retain when a moment later Teach stated; "Been walkin''long tha river, have thee, lad? Thy boots be muddy. Were it thee in tha bushes tumblin' tha young Missee from tha house?"

Three

Tuesday 29th October – Virginia

According to his own written account, in 1610 Captain John Smith had ordered the demoralised and close to starving New World settlers to build a fort at the mouth of the James River. Although the land had not been officially named as 'Earl of Southampton Roadstead' until over half a century later, it had not taken long for the name to be colloquially shortened to 'Hampton Roads'.

Jesamiah had read the account as a child, and even then he had considered those early settlers to be either simple-minded or brain-mashed. They had argued with Smith, who in a fit of pique had gone off on his own expedition, only to return months later to find the colony barely surviving on a daily ration of one pint of wormy grain boiled in water.

Shoving the bowl of succulent lobster across his dining table – the wood newly polished and gleaming – Jesamiah urged Samuel Trent to eat.

"You may profess to not be hungry boy, but I have been treated to a diet of corn mush. I am taking advantage of something worth eating while I may." He selected a lobster claw and sucked out the meat. "Those early settlers had no idea these creatures, abundant in these waters, were suitable for eating. Can you imagine?"

Samuel made no answer. He was not hungry and he did not feel like talking.

Jesamiah was ignoring the sultry mood. Trent was not sailing with them to North Carolina and that was final.

"Not being a sea-fellow you may not realise that in maritime parlance, 'roads' means safe anchorage. Even without the lobster this would be one of the best harbours in the area. Williamsburg was found to be a better place to build and live, though – too marshy down here, too many mosquitoes and those years ago, not enough friendly natives." He tossed the claw away, selected another, "Mind, old Captain Smith found himself an Indian girl as a friend. According to popular myth they were lovers, though I always understood from Smith's writings that she was only thirteen. Did you know she went to England? She is buried at Gravesend along the Thames."

Gruff, shoulders hunched, mouth turned downward, Trent muttered, "I am sorry, I have no idea what or who you are talking about."

Jesamiah sighed. "Ain't you learned any history? I'm talking about Pocahontas."

Trent retained his blank expression. Jesamiah gave up with the small talk. "Look. You ain't coming. You are no use to me aboard ship and you will be no use to me once I get to Bath Town. Can you fight? Can you fire a pistol?"

"You know I can. I challenged you to a duel, remember?"

"Aye well, maybe you can shoot a gentleman's duelling piece when you have a fair chance to take your ten paces, turn and fire at your leisure. Could you do so when others are running rampage and are determined to shoot you first? And aside of that, have you ever actually killed a man?"

Belligerent, Trent folded his arms tighter, shook his head and pouted. "No."

"No. An' going against Blackbeard ain't the best of occasions t'start practising."

The great cabin door opened, Rue peered round it. "The water is aboard and stowed, *mon ami.*"

"Very good Rue. We will sail as soon as Mr Trent here gets himself ashore."

Rue approximated a rough version of a Navy salute which went only as far as his chin. "*Oui Capitaine.*"

Jesamiah stood, gestured towards the door, which Rue had left open. "I will not change my mind Samuel. I thank you for retrieving my Letter of Marque. I thank you for taking it direct to Governor Spotswood – and aye, I thank you for bringing my ship here to Hampton Roads, but I as much thank you to go ashore and return to Urbanna."

One last, desperate try. "But I have nothing to go back to. No reason to be there or stay there. I do have a reason to be here." He pointed at his feet.

"And what reason would that be?" Jesamiah answered with gentle patience. "To get yourself killed on my behalf? That ain't no reason."

With a drooping head and dragging feet Samuel allowed himself to be escorted along the short, dark corridor and out onto the open deck. A harbour boat was bobbing alongside and the men of the *Sea Witch* were waiting for it to be gone. Even though they had disguised her as a merchant ship, the *Sea Siren*, not one of them had felt easy idling here at Hampton under the suspicious eyes of the pirate-hating Virginians. They were ready to make sail; leaning on the shipped bars at the capstan, waiting to heave the anchor cable in; ready to run aloft. Braces, lifts, tacks, sheets were all coiled down clear and ready for running. The topsail halliards were of new rope and had been well stretched to prevent any kinks when first used. An awning that had been rigged was stowed away, as were the many other things that crept on deck when in harbour. In the tops, gear was coiled down and the lubber-holes left clear.

So many other things that to Trent went unnoticed but to Jesamiah's experienced eye told him both ship and crew were ready and waiting. The pumpwell would have been sounded, the flaps on the scuppers were of new leather. The splashboards were fitted and caulked around the gun ports, and tompions were in place to protect the bore against salt corrosion. The guns themselves run in and secured.

Jesamiah walked with Trent to the entry port; held out a hand. Despite his moroseness, Trent had a firm, solid handshake. He was a good lad, would become a good man. One to be trusted, no matter what. With genuine feeling Jesamiah said, "I sincerely thank you, Samuel, but you cannot come with me."

Nathan Crocker stepped forward, handed Samuel a canvas-wrapped package.

"This is for you," Jesamiah explained, "a token of my appreciation. There is a letter in there too, for Alicia."

There was another letter waiting on Jesamiah's desk. The one from his father, sealed, unopened, untouched. At the right moment Jesamiah would read it, but not here. Not now.

As Samuel settled himself in the stern thwarts, the package on his lap, he looked upward and Jesamiah caught the stark anguish in the young man's eyes; took it for acute disappointment. "Take care of Mrs Mereno for me," he called down. "I wish to deal with her myself when I am finished about my present business."

The bumboat began to pull away, Jesamiah saw Samuel mouthing some words but could not hear them, for the strengthening wind took them away and Nat was shouting at the men to stand ready to loose the headsails. Those at the capstan began to strain at the bars, pushing their weight against that of the anchor. The capstan jerked as the men began to stamp around and around, then cranked steadily bringing the dripping cable slowly inboard.

"Hands aloft! Loose tops'ls," Jesamiah shouted. The rigging and shrouds were suddenly alive with men running upward like agile monkeys.

The men at the capstan broke into song, a chanty to keep the rhythm steady and make the work less arduous. A single voice refrained the main line of the verse, everyone eagerly joining the chorus, their tones varying from deep tenor to light soprano.

We're bound for the wide sea, no more land now for me…
So heave ho, heave ho, heave ho m'lads.
The crew are me best mates, the rest are a right state…
So heave ho, heave ho, heave ho m'lads.
The bosun's a daisy we know he's half crazy…

Rue stepped up beside his captain and friend, leant his arms on the rail as Jesamiah was doing. "It took that lad a long while to persuade us to come 'ere, *mon ami*, but 'e is as persistent as a terrier down a rabbit 'ole. 'E is, I think, most fond of you?"

"He will be even fonder when he opens that package. I have written instructions that he is to manage la Sorenta until we return."

"And if we do not?"

"Then he will be managing it for a long time, won't he?"

They watched as Trent climbed the wooden ladder on to the jetty, the package clutched firmly in his hand.

"Alicia may change her mind about him now he has a position of authority." Jesamiah remarked as he raised an arm in farewell.

The pawls went *clack, clack, clack,* as the men pushed their weight against the capstan, the sound of their bare feet hollow on the wooden deck. The thick, heavy anchor cable coming in inch by slimed inch was fed down the hatch. Many a pirate ship let it pile up wet and stinking where it fell, leaving it to gradually rot, for they would simply replace it with a new one on the next Chase. But Jesamiah ran an efficient ship. He would not tolerate slovenliness. Men would be down in the cable tier wrestling with the tons of sodden rope to lay it neatly on the wooden slats that drained, dried and aired it. A horrible, filthy, disgusting job, but a job that had to be done.

Rue chuckled, pressed Jesamiah's arm. "Madam Mereno may, but my friend, 'e will not." He slapped Jesamiah's shoulder. "It is not only the ladies who adore you, *Capitaine*, over there is another who is smitten by your 'andsome *visage, non?*" He walked away, the chuckles becoming loud guffaws.

Jesamiah frowned after him, not understanding. It took him a full two minutes to comprehend what Rue had meant. He reddened, embarrassed, then realised what chanty the men were singing. Knew the next line:

"*The Captain's a bugger but his friend buggers better…So heave ho, heave ho, heave ho m'lads!*"

"Anchor's hove short!" Nat called, neatly halting Jesamiah from berating the men with the sharp side of his tongue. Grumpily he stomped up the ladder to his accustomed place to leeward of the helm on the quarterdeck and kept them all waiting for several seconds, aware that many of them were grinning. Why had he not seen the obvious about Trent? Everyone else had apparently, damn it. Damn it!

"Man the braces! Lively there, Crawford!" Annoyed by the jest at his expense, Jesamiah found the man's repeated slackness all the more irritating. "That man has one more chance, Nat," he said. "If he catches my attention again he's off this ship. Make sure he knows it."

The great topsails were billowing down, flapping and cracking in the wind like wild confused beasts set free from their cages, the seamen clinging on to the yards, taming them, chivvying the expanse of canvas to obey, to come to order.

"Aye Cap'n." Nat hid a grin; best to keep from Jesamiah that Crawford had not pulled his weight during the careen either. If ever there was an idler it was Bob Crawford.

Isiah Roberts was at the helm, his steadfast gaze watching the set of the canvas.

"Set course to take us out of here, Isiah. Or are you too busy chortling to steer straight?"

"Me Sir? Chortling Sir? No Sir. I wouldn't be chortling."

Rue, remaining down in the waist, doubled over with laughter, the tears drizzling down his cheeks. It was infectious, the entire crew joined in, the sound of hilarity rippling through the ship like the upsurge roll of a wave.

"When you have all quite finished," Jesamiah remarked sternly, "perhaps we can get under way?"

"Aye Sir; certainly Sir."

Jesamiah looked from Nat at the rail to Isiah, who stood legs planted apart, both hands on the spokes staring solidly at the widening expanse of canvas. "And cut the fokken piss-taking, the pair of you. If this were a Navy ship I'd be 'avin' the lot of you flogged round the fleet for insubordination."

"Don't you mean for insub-arse-ination, Cap'n?" Nat's quip was crude but it set everyone laughing again.

Rue joined Jesamiah on the quarterdeck, scrubbing at the laughter tears on his face. "Ah lad, lad, if this were a Navy ship, we would not be sharing the friendship of a *très bonne blague*, would we, eh?"

"A very good joke you call it, do you? I do not." Jesamiah shrugged, then conceded defeat. "All right, I admit it is funny. But I would prefer to retain some form of discipline aboard my ship – even if it is only to get under way with a glimmer of efficiency. Savvy?"

Rue nodded. Fair enough, the jest had served its purpose but was now outstaying its welcome. Time for the serious business.

"Anchor's aweigh!"

Sea Witch moved forward taken by tide and wind, set free of her restraints. *Clank, clank, clank,* the capstan continued to turn, the anchor swinging like a pendulum as it rose, dripping and weed slimed above the surface of the water.

"Lee braces! 'Eave away!" Rue called sharply. "Jump to it! Main and fore course!"

With a roar like thunder the sails filled and hardened to the steady thrust of the wind, no more confusion or lazy flapping. Isiah threw himself to the spokes of the helm to hold her steady.

Jesamiah felt the deck cant over in the sweetest possible way as the *Sea Witch* paid off into the wind and showed a faint gleam of the new-cleaned copper bottom. She was under way, sliding gracefully forward through the water, a beautiful, almost living thing, her sail pressure balanced against the rudder. His dull temper lifted as she spread her wings and flew; he tipped his head back and guffawed, at last seeing the jest for himself. "I hope that molly boy ain't no longer aboard, Nat," Jesamiah said against the roar of the wind, the rumble of canvas and the sound of the water rushing past the keel. "If he is, toss him overboard. One lover-boy is enough to be dealing with, thank you very much!"

The yards braced round to take maximum advantage of the wind and the anchor being hauled towards the cathead.

"Ain't seen any of those whores since we reached la Sorenta. They scarpered as soon as we moored. Reckon the lot of them made for the brothels in Urbanna," Rue said.

Jesamiah grinned back at him. "Thank God for that!"

Everything was creaking and banging. The wind whined through the rigging as if an orchestra of demented fiddlers were playing some god-forsaken devil's tune.

"She seems well," Jesamiah said a few minutes later, nodding his head at his ship. "You did a handsome job. I'm proud of you all." He stepped towards the mizzen stay, reached out and scratched it affectionately, felt *Sea Witch*'s deck ripple beneath his feet as she shifted balance. Could have sworn that he felt her smile.

When he looked back, Hampton Roads lay well aft, Virginia itself a blur of land, its intricate features indistinguishable.

"Let her run freely, Isiah. We may need to reef down if this wind gets stronger, but I want to make as fast a passage as possible. Old Edward Teach is going to be so surprised to see us." He paused, peered over the taffrail, added, "And get someone to put my ship's name right. We've no more need for a false identity." He crossed the deck, put his hand on the backstay, whispered, "Have we sweetheart?"

Four

Wednesday 30th October

Now they had left the shelter of the Chesapeake and were out in the Atlantic, the wind was blowing up, spray pluming over the fore rail each time the bow dipped into the next trough, the stern tossing skyward. It caused an odd sensation in the stomach, but Jesamiah was used to it, paid no heed. The weather was nothing Rue could not handle. For Jesamiah, the wildness was oddly comforting; he knew his ship and crew could cope with this. After the long days of sedentary confinement it all felt and sounded so alive; the shout of the wind buffeting at him, the lift and dip of the deck and the boom and clamour of canvas overhead. There was nothing like the possibility of death by hanging to ensure the appreciation of living. But he was very tired. He left the quarterdeck to Rue and sought the solitude of the great cabin. Finch, grumbling at leaving the house and its comforts, had prepared a meal, but Jesamiah was not all that hungry. The accumulated deprivations of the past days were taking their toll. He had slept in gaol but it had been an uneasy, half alert sleep; he longed to curl up in his own bed for what was left of the night and shut out thought and worry, even if for only a few hours.

He finished the pork and with a hunk of bread mopped up the gravy that had not slopped over the edge of the dished plate, not really tasting any of it. He declined coffee but thanked Finch for his diligence and got the usual curmudgeonly answer. Finch would not be Finch if ever he was to discover that the muscles around his mouth could turn upward now and then.

Jesamiah dragged himself into his quarter cabin – his body ached, he was almost asleep already. He sat on the bed – a wooden, double-sized cot suspended from the overhead beams by ropes – and raised his leg for Finch to pull off the first boot. "I promise you, my friend, that once I have sorted all this and wed my Tiola we will find ourselves a nice house on solid land with as many rooms in it as you can imagine."

Finch grunted, removed the other boot. "I can imagine a fair few. Grand 'ouses don't come cheap. La Sorenta be a perfickly good 'ouse."

"So it may, but I have no intention of living there. The place harbours too many bad memories. Asides," Jesamiah broke off as he removed his shirt and breeches, "it is haunted."

Finch, his hand outstretched to take the discarded clothes, froze, horrified. "Haunted?"

Sliding into the bed, Jesamiah noticed it had been made up with fresh, clean sheets. He felt a twinge of remorse at bursting Finch's pleasure, but the old scoundrel did go on and on so.

"Aye. Haunted."

"Haunted? As in ghost haunted?"

"Mm hmm."

"You certain?"

"As certain as I'm here waiting for you to stop gabbin' so's I can get t'sleep."

"Ghost, you say?"

"Mm. Up by the cemetery plot. Seen 'im with m'own eyes."

"A ghost? As in dead ghost?"

Jesamiah wriggled beneath the sheets, pulled the blanket under his chin. "Don't know as there be such a thing as a live ghost. Blow the lamp out and bugger off. There's a good fellow."

Finch extinguished the lantern swinging from the central beam, shut the door behind him. "Don't be wantin' no ghosts. Ain't good, ghosts. Dead ought' stay dead says I. Ain't got no business comin' t'life again 'ave ghosts."

Jesamiah, hearing him muttering as he crossed the outer cabin, smiled. The outer door to the great cabin clicked shut and he lay in the dark listening to the familiar, comfortable sounds of his ship. Her creaking and groaning; the sea chuntering past her keel; the grumbling of the rudder. The thud of feet as hands ran to haul the yards to turn her. Rue would be taking in a reef if this wind got any livelier. He felt the motion as she settled to a different tack, pulled one of the pillows into his arms. The bed was so empty without Tiola.

He heard Finch up on the quarterdeck talking to Rue, his voice floating down through the slightly open skylight.

"You 'eard anything about a ghost?"

"A ghost? *Oui*, I saw it. A fearful boogieman with two 'eads."

Jesamiah chuckled. He could always rely on Rue to back up a good yarn.

Half an hour later, deeply asleep, Jesamiah was dreaming of sun-kissed beaches and making love to Tiola, but the noise woke him instantly. He knew every whisper, every mumble, every creak and sound that *Sea Witch* made. Even in his sleep he listened to her murmuring and knew exactly what she was saying to him. That the wind had risen and she did not like running in a gale…but this sound – a screech, a howl of discomfort – was different. Trouble! Something was wrong!

He was out of the bed, grabbed his shirt and pulled it over his head.

Barefoot, not needing light, he ran from his cabin to the open deck outside, hardly noticing the toss and pitch of the wild, wind-tormented sea. Other men were there standing, looking confused, some running towards the long boats, hauling at the tackles to launch them.

"Belay that!" Jesamiah roared, his shirt flapping against his naked buttocks and legs as he bounded through an open scuttle and slid down the ladder. Rue followed close behind, a lantern in his hand. *Sea Witch* rolled, gunwale under. Jesamiah grabbed at the ladder rail, steadied himself as she came up. There! That sound again in the after-hold, the sound of a rush of water.

Men were at the bottom of the ladder, pushing to climb upward, their faces chalk-pale, fear in their eyes. Jesamiah went down, shoving them aside.

"We've sprung, Sir! As sure as hens lay eggs, a butt's started. We're goin' down, Cap'n! We're goin' down!"

"Belay that talk, Crawford! We're doing no such thing!" Jesamiah pushed him out of the way, struck the face of another. "You! Unship that grating there, let me into the hold!"

Chippy, the carpenter, was there suddenly, with Nat Crocker and Isiah Roberts. Jesamiah laid his hands on the grating to help move it aside, was the first down into the darkness, his hand reaching up to take a lantern.

"We're all a'drownin'!" Crawford shouted, undecided whether to wait to see what the Captain found, or get to where he would have a chance to reach the boats before *Sea Witch* foundered.

Chippy followed Jesamiah down and the spot of light disappeared from view. *Sea Witch* rolled, and again that dreadful sound as if the entire ocean was flooding across her hold. Then laughter. Jesamiah's and the carpenter's deep guffaw.

The light bobbed back towards the open scuttle and Jesamiah's face appeared. "The head's been knocked out of a fokken barrel. A load of dried peas are rolling about down here!"

Again *Sea Witch* dipped to larboard. The sound of peas rolling with the movement was exactly like the gush of incoming water. Everyone stood for a moment staring at each other. Then Rue laughed and slapped Nat on the shoulder.

"*Dieu nous bénisse!*" he cried, "God bless us!"

"I'll second that," Chippy echoed.

Sheepish laughter erupted, spreading from man to man. Jests rippled with the hilarity, many of the men falsely claiming they'd known it was nothing serious all along.

After hearing from Rue that the gale, though strong, was nothing the night watch could not handle, Jesamiah returned to his cabin. He found Finch bundling up the silver into a tablecloth.

"Put it all back, it was nothing serious," he explained as he headed for his bed. "Shut the door when you're done, Finch," he called over his shoulder. "Wake me at dawn."

He lay for a while, his face buried in the blue shawl Tiola had left behind. It smelt of her; summer hay-meadows and sweet-scented flowers. The space beside him too empty without her. A shawl was a poor substitute. Gods, but he did so miss her.

Rain beat down, rattling on the stern windows and the skylight. He heard Rue shout orders, felt *Sea Witch*'s movements, guessed they had reefed. She was sailing well enough, aye they were pitching and tossing, but they had experienced worse. The lantern hanging from the beam was swinging wildly, the shadows rising and falling up and down the walls. He ought to get up, extinguish it, but was too tired to bother. Tired, but he could not sleep.

He had not read his father's letter. Did he want to read it? After all that had happened, did he care any more? Father was dead. Phillipe was dead. What was it Tiola had said once? *The past is done and cannot be undone. The future is yet to be done, so do it.*

He yawned, climbed out of bed and padded, naked, into the great cabin. There was just enough light from the lamp swinging behind him to see by. The letter was in the top drawer of the desk. He lifted it out, looked at it again. Whatever his father had to say to him now, it did not matter. If this was an apology, then it was too late for 'sorry'. If it was an explanation, then that, too, was of no use. How would knowing the whys heal the hurts and mend the wounds? They were already scabbed over, he did not want to pick at them and make them bleed again.

Suddenly, he did not want to know. He would rather shut the door on it and walk away. That was what Tiola had told him to do, and she was right. He had the future, why dwell on the past.

He went to the stern windows, stood looking out into the black night, the faint reflection of salt griming the glass panes, the foaming wake churning behind his ship, white against the darkness. He opened one window, was blasted by a shriek of the wind that howled into the cabin like a banshee.

He leaned out, held the letter up. And the raging wind grabbed it and took it away.

Five

North Carolina

It had rained hard during the night, with a wind that had driven it into crevices and through cracks in window frames and beneath doors. The servants had been kept busy at Archbell Point mopping the flood from the basement; as if they had not enough to do. When the dawn rushed in, it came with ragged clouds and a leaden sky that reflected in a scatter of sullen puddles. After checking Elizabeth-Anne and reassuring her, yet again, that the babe was doing well and would be born when he was ready to be born, Tiola pulled on her old boots and took her usual morning walk into Bath Town. As expected, the artist was there on the jetty, as he always was.

"Do you not grow tired of painting this view?" she asked him after admiring a few deft brush strokes.

"Folks seem eager to buy what I paint. For some reason this view be popular."

"Plum Point. Captain Teach's property?"

He nodded. "I find that when I add a man – just here," he indicated a significant space on the canvas, "and if I give him a cocked hat and a black bushy beard, then I can ask twice the price."

She watched him finish the colouring of some trees. "Is Captain Acorne aware you are an artist of talent?"

This had been the first chance to speak to him in private. Usually she was accompanied into town by someone from the house – most often, Perdita, but today the girl had an assignation with Jonathan Gabriel. Tiola was not supposed to know, but she had seen Perdita slipping from the house a while ago, her hood up, running for the shelter of the bushes on the far side of the gardens. To Tiola's knowledge, nothing had yet been said of the proposed marriage of Governor Eden's stepdaughter to Tobias Knight. The poor girl would probably be told when arrangements were made and a dowry agreed. Until then, no one in this predominantly selfish household would think it necessary to inform the bride.

Joseph Meadows continued his painting. "The Captain does not. But then he has not had cause to know."

"You do not deny that he sent you here to keep watch on me, then?"

Meadows sat back, eyed his work critically. It would do. It was not as good as one of the Grand Masters, but it would do. "Be there much point in me denying it?"

Tiola laid a hand on his shoulder. It was good of Jesamiah to think of sending him. Good of Skylark to be here.

"I paint this view," Meadows explained, "because I can observe the comings and goings from Teach's place. I first tried to watch Archbell Point, but I was moved on. I then noticed this artist's equipment for sale in Mr Quigley's store along Main Street, and thought it a good disguise. No one, so far," he touched the wood of his easel, "has challenged me sitting here hour after hour. No one queries if I change position to paint another view – of, say, the tavern."

"Where Teach is drinking."

Meadows grinned. "Coincidence of course, Ma'am; only coincidence that I always choose where that bugger – begging your pardon – happens to be."

"I thank you for your diligence, Mr Meadows, and appreciate it." Tiola did not add he had failed to protect her the other night, but that was not the poor man's fault, he would not have expected her to be attacked in the supposed safety of Archbell Point.

She began to walk away for she had some items to collect from the apothecary, but Meadows grasped her arm.

"I warn you though, Ma'am. I can see most of Plum Point from here, so I know when Teach comes across the creek, but there is a tunnel about half a mile downstream on this side. It runs direct into Eden's cellars. I understand it was built as a bolthole in case the Indians attacked, but it must also serve a good purpose for smuggling. If Teach were to use that route, I would have no knowledge of his whereabouts. Do you understand my meaning?"

Tiola nodded. She understood. Teach could attack her without warning. She again cursed her inability to use her Craft, for then he would not be able to get within a quarter of a mile of her without her being aware of his presence. But if she used it for even a moment, the evil that possessed the man would sense her.

Once that baby was born, once Elizabeth-Anne and her child were safe it would be a different matter. But there were at least two weeks to wait yet, unless he decided to birth early, but in her experience, babes, especially boys, usually lazed abed.

The apothecary, a widower and a lonely man outside of running his business, had become a friend during these long, idle days. A man who had knowledge of medicines and potions, he welcomed her wisdom in return. As always they sat together in the small living area behind the shop discussing the benefits of various herbs. It was therefore close on noon before Tiola retraced her steps homeward to the Governor's house. She would be expected to take luncheon at twelve-thirty with Elizabeth-Anne and pass the early afternoon with her. It was not a task Tiola objected to, for unlike several in this house, her charge was a pleasant woman and they enjoyed each other's company.

Undecided, Tiola hesitated at the end of Main Street. Would she continue on and take the shorter route, or turn aside and follow the river? She chose the river path.

The wind was still stirring the trees and rippling the water into ruffles and flurries. Cloud was building again, great banks of cumulus that heralded more rain. She hoped it would be fine tomorrow for Mary Ormond's sake. No young lady wanted a downpour on her wedding day. Her father had ordered the gardens to be decorated with bunting and garlands of flowers – had commandeered nigh on every servant in town, or so she heard tell. Everyone was a-chatter with the promised excitement; it was not often that such an entertaining celebration took place in Bath Town. Tiola had no intention of attending. She had been invited, but Elizabeth-Anne in her advanced condition was not to go and had begged her company, for the house would be lonely. It was an ideal excuse to stay away.

Governor Eden was to officiate, as Bath Town had no priest. The last one had over-indulged in a surfeit of seafood and had died of food poisoning a year previously. No other clergyman had considered the town worthy of Christian salvation.

Two ducks were paddling mid-stream, one dived, head under, tail up; Tiola wished him good fishing. There were a few birds still twittering in the trees, despite it being quite a way into the autumn now. All the trees were red, or gold or brown, although a lot of leaves were on the ground. Tiola kicked through a pile, delighting in the childish pleasure of the rustle they made beneath her boots. She thought Joe Meadows a gifted fellow for he managed to capture these hues exactly. Her own attempts always came out too vivid on the eye. She skirted a small patch of poison ivy, its group of three bright green leaves looking so deceptively pretty and innocent. The irritant would not usually bring her skin out in a rash, but she did not want to test whether her suppression of Craft would affect her immunity.

~ *Witch Woman! You are needed!* ~

Like a startled doe Tiola's head shot upwards; the man's voice speaking clearly into her mind was not Jesamiah's, although the deep, husky timbre was similar.

"Captain Mereno?"

~ *The girl. Along the river – hurry! I can do nothing.* ~

Tiola set down her basket of packages, trusting to their safety, and ran. The path was slippery from the night's rain and her boots splashed through puddles sending showers of spray and muddying her stockings and gown. She paid no heed, ran, for she could hear screaming now. Perdita!

Around the bend Tiola halted, uncertain what to do. Teach had Perdita on the ground, her skirt up around her waist, one hand and his knee pinning her down as he fumbled at his breeches. What could Tiola do? She could not use her Craft as much as it was bristling beneath the surface, as much as the urge to release the power tingling in her fingertips was building and building, she could not use it. But she could act as would any human; as any woman.

She bent, picked up a hefty branch that had fallen in last night's storm and tapped it against her palm to gauge its weight. Taking firm hold with both hands she walked forward, making no noise, coming up behind Teach who was too busy attending his base need to notice or sense her presence. The branch broke; splinters of wood and bark flew outward at the thwack of its impact on his skull, sounding like a pistol shot echoing across the river. He grunted and fell unconscious to one side. Immediately, Tiola gathered Perdita into her arms and held her tight, rocking her backwards and forwards as the girl clung to her, sobbing, shaking, terrified.

"Did he penetrate you?" Tiola had to ask – had to repeat her question several times, but at last Perdita heard, understood. Shook her head.

"Are you certain?"

Through her weeping the girl nodded, her teeth chattering as she spoke. "He did not violate me."

Tiola cradled her tighter, closer, shut her eyes and murmured her relief. "Thank the All Mighty Spirit of Light and Wisdom! Come, my dear let us leave here. Leave the rat to fend for himself." She ushered Perdita to her feet, saw at a glance the girl was otherwise unharmed, save for a muddied gown and a trembling that would not abate. Tiola began steering her away, but Perdita halted and stared with contempt at the prone body of Edward Teach. The anger was rising now she was safe: anger, hurt, indignation, fuelled by the shudder of fear coursing through her.

"Is he dead?"

Tiola bent close, rolled him onto his back and shook her head. Unhappily, no he was not. She was not permitted to kill. The laws of her Craft forbade it, yet in this instance she regretted the limitation, was tempted, so very tempted, to finish him here and now and save who knew how many souls from future suffering.

Perdita peered down at the unconscious face, the heavy jowls, the scabs and scars. He had a pistol tied by a ribbon to a crossbelt over his shoulder. She stretched her hand towards it…

Tiola stopped her "I know you have an urge to shoot him, but would that not make you as bad as he? A murderer?"

Ignoring her, Perdita had a compulsion to do something; to take some form of revenge. She detached the pistol and aimed it at his groin. Her hand was shaking. She brought the other up, tried to cock the heavy hammer, could not move it. She had never fired a pistol in her life.

"My dear, put it down. Please."

In disgust at herself and him, Perdita hurled the weapon into the river. She met Tiola's calm, unwavering gaze then walked away. "I trust you never regret making me do that, Mistress Oldstagh. I would rather be condemned to Hell for murdering that bastard than live knowing that, had I shot him, someone else would remain inviolate. Alive."

From where he watched, on his side of Eternity, Charles Mereno saw Teach's senses return, saw him crawl to his knees, his head thundering, a trickle of blood matting his hair. Saw his anger as he searched for his pistol and found its ribbon caught on a bush beside the water.

Heard his bellow of rage and shouted curse: "Thee shall regret displeasing me, girl! Thee shall regret it!"

Grief stirred in Charles' heart and mind. Monsters like Edward Teach should never have been born.

Six

Thursday 31st October – All Hallows' Eve

The house at Archbell Point was quiet. Almost everyone had gone to the wedding. With her keen eyesight Tiola had seen Jonathan Gabriel peering from the shrubs bordering the far side of the gardens. From the window she watched Perdita hurry across to him, her hood pulled forward, cloak gathered close against the squall of rain. Saw him draw her into the seclusion of the shrubs, hurry her away, probably towards their hiding place. Tiola was glad. Perdita needed his tender and loving company after the foulness of yesterday. The girl had pleaded illness as an excuse to be excused the celebrations. Tiola smiled; she had recovered quickly once the house had emptied.

"Oh!"

Frowning concern, Tiola turned her head quickly. Elizabeth-Anne sat beside the hearth – it was chill enough today for a fire to be lit – her sewing half dropped to the floor, one hand pressed against her swollen abdomen.

"Be you all right?" Tiola got up from the window seat, hurried across the room, hoped the birth would not come this night as she had other important things to do.

"Yes, yes I am fine. The baby kicks that is all, he took me by surprise."

Tiola smiled, retrieved the baby-gown Elizabeth-Anne was stitching and put her own hand on the woman's distended belly. She giggled at the hefty thump. "My, but he has some energy!"

"It is a pity he cannot use it to push himself out into the world."

Bending forward Tiola lightly kissed Elizabeth-Anne's cheek. "He is not ready, he is still wrong ways up and back to front." She laughed, "As with all men he cannot stir himself to hurry." She returned to the window seat. These afternoons spent as a companion to Elizabeth-Anne were not usually tedious, the opposite in fact, for her friend was a delight to talk to, but this was a difficult day and Tiola was full of foreboding.

"He will drop soon, will he not?" Elizabeth-Anne asked, anxiety wobbling into her voice.

Tiola answered with reassurance, "He has time yet to be as he should, but even if he is determined to do things in his own way it is no matter. I have delivered many a stubborn child backside first. It would perhaps be more worrying if this was your first birthing, but it is not. I am not concerned, so neither should you be."

It was not a lie, but nor was it the whole truth. These were the last few weeks and the child was growing its fastest. Elizabeth-Anne looked and felt ungainly and was suffering from low, dull backache, normal for any pregnancy but she harboured as much anxiety. There was time a-plenty for the foetus to turn around and present as he should; if he did not there could well be complications. However, Tiola was not going to admit any of it to Elizabeth-Anne, for what was the point in causing worries that may not occur? There were already enough to fill this day, the last in October, twice over.

Elizabeth-Anne stretched, groaning against the ache in her spine. "It pleases me to not bring my child into the world this day though. The Eve of All Hallows is not a suitable choice."

All Hallows' Eve, Hallowe'en, corrupted by the Christian Faith to be a night of menace, when hags and witches rode their brooms and the dead returned to haunt those left behind.

"Where I come from, in Cornwall, we call it *Samhain*," Tiola said. "It is the eve when winter begins and the days grow dark and cold. The unwanted cattle are slaughtered and butchered, for they are hard to feed when the snows come. The harvest is full-gathered and stored. We celebrate as a thank you for what has been given to help us through the days of darkness. All that grows is dead, but there will be re-birth come the spring. Samhain belongs to neither the past nor the present, nor this world nor the other."

"So–in?" Elizabeth-Anne stumbled over the unfamiliar word.

Tiola repeated 'Samhain' slowly, sounding it as *sow-in*. "It is an old word, from an old, old language, and we do not believe it to be evil. Your son would come to no harm."

There was the legend that spirits of mischief gathered on Samhain Eve and tainted any crops left unharvested, but that had a practical explanation. Crops left in the fields at the end of October were likely to be blackened by frost, wet, or mould. There was nothing supernatural about it.

"But do the dead not walk on Hallows' Eve?"

"*Ais*, the River between the realm of the dead and that of the living becomes frozen and ceases to flow, leaving a boundary that can be crossed between the two worlds. But why fear the spirits of family and friends? Is it not pleasant to welcome them to the hearth on this one night, to feast together and to remember them with love and affection?"

Elizabeth-Anne was confused, this went against all she had been taught and what she had read in her Bible. "But what of the Devil and evil spirits? Do they not come to create mischief?"

Tiola glanced out of the window. Perdita and Jonathan had gone, there was no sign of them. The sky was grey, louring towards a heavier rain. She hoped the pair of them would be sensible, find somewhere dry to make love. There was a hut she remembered seeing in a clearing where the trees ran denser beside the riverbank. Would they go there? She did not require her Craft to tell her they intended to commit themselves to each other. Why should they not? They were young and they were devoted. She intended to ask Jesamiah, when all was done here, to consider granting Jonathan the finances to start his own tailor's shop, perhaps in Williamsburg. Perdita would have to work hard, but she had a steady hand when it came to sewing. They would manage, if they had the provisions to make a start and if they truly wanted it. But what of the evil of All Hallows Eve?

"Evil fears love, Elizabeth-Anne, for love is the more powerful. Samhain is a time to say goodbye to the old and to welcome the new. Christians, though, have the belief they must pray for the weeping souls who wait in purgatory to be judged before entering the Kingdom of Heaven or the Pits of Hell. They fear the dead, for they fear their own mortality. I believe Samhain is not for fearing evil, but for remembering love."

"All the same," Elizabeth-Anne said, crossing herself, "I would rather not be birthing my child this night and I confess, I detested my mother-in-law, may God rest her soul. I have no wish to welcome *her* back."

With nothing more to say Tiola returned to her musing. Evening would be approaching soon and she would need to excuse herself from Elizabeth-Anne's company. She had things to do this eve, for *ais*, this was the night when the dead could cross the River. And one in particular needed her help.

On this one night she was safe, she could use her Craft as always she had. There would be too many voices from too many souls for her to be identified; too much Light and too much love for the Dark to find her.

Seven

It was close, the time was coming closer. Soon, all this would be over. At last! At last after all these years of guilt his torment was to be ended!

Charles St Croix Mereno sat beside the River, his hands clasped together in anticipation as its ponderous ripples began slowly to harden and then freeze. What he had begun would soon be ending. The watching and the waiting would be done with, and then he could enter Eternity and rest in peace.

He so wanted to end this lonely non-existence, so wanted to get away from this damned indifferent River. But at what cost?

Something caught his attention. A fold of paper caught beneath the surface of the solidifying water. He recognised the blurred writing. He leant forward, thrust his hand through the cold, cold ice and clutched his fingers around it. His letter to Jesamiah.

Eight

They were all weary. Beating down through the wind in a heavy swell and against the current of the Gulf Stream had taken its toll on the ship and her crew. Aside the broken barrel of peas, *Sea Witch* herself had suffered minor damage: a poorly sewn tops'l had blown into shreds, and some foremast rigging had snapped. One man had fallen overboard. The incident left a sour taste in Jesamiah's mouth, for they had not been able to save him with the wind and sea so strong. By the time they had manoeuvred he would have drowned or been swept away, his body impossible to find among the high rollers and deep troughs. It was the reason most sailors did not learn to swim. Better to drown quick than prolong the inevitable end.

Bath Town seemed quiet as Jesamiah stepped on to the jetty from the jolly boat. For prudence's sake he had anchored *Sea Witch*, as before, lower down the river. They had turned her and set her anchor cable on a spring. If they had to leave in a hurry she would be ready.

"Not many people around?" Sandy Banks observed.

"Tucked up safe behind barred doors, I reckon. It is All Hallows after all, and it is almost dark. These sort of folk are afraid of their own shadows, let alone wraiths and ghosts." Jesamiah would not admit to it but he would have preferred the security of his ship and his own cabin this night as well. Having seen what he was now certain was the ghost of his father he was not too keen to be meeting him again. On the other tack, Tiola was here in Bath Town. He doubted any ghost would have the audacity to get past her. Aside, confronting Teach was more daunting than meeting any apparition.

"Cap'n?"

"Skylark! Glad t'see you're still here."

Momentarily Joseph Meadows was affronted. He straightened his shoulders, lifted his chin. "I do not disobey orders, Captain Acorne."

"'Ceptin' for when you deserted the Navy?" Jesamiah chuckled, slapped his shoulder. "Nay, I'm jesting. I appreciate your loyalty. Is all well?"

Meadows gave a full, succinct report. Miss Tiola was at Archbell Point; Edward Teach, with most of the town's folk, was at his wedding.

That news astounded and amused Jesamiah by turn. "Well, well," he announced after considering a moment, "maybe if I were to call in and wish him felicitations he will grant me long enough to say my piece before cutting my throat."

He was not amused when the crew of the gig laid wagers on how long that granting would last.

Nine

Edward Teach changed his mind about the benefits of marriage during the course of the ceremony. The festivities were supposed to have been outdoors but the rain had persisted. With foresight John Ormond had ordered the great barn cleared and decorated so at least there was a dry area. The harvest had been crammed into every other available space and would have to be moved back into the barn afterwards, but that was work for slaves and therefore of no consequence. Had there not been so many guests – as Teach had wanted – the house would have been adequate.

He had underestimated the full implication of the social status of the occasion. It seemed the world and his wife had been invited to witness the union and partake of the wedding feast. Bad enough to stand up in front of their gawping eyes to exchange meaningless vows presided over by a brain-addled, mumbling Eden, but to have Miss Mary Ormond – Mrs Edward Teach – telling him to speak up and speak correctly, had been the turning point. She had said nothing about his languid West Country accent before; to do so in front of all these people, who had laughed at her impertinent chastisement, had been embarrassing. And Edward Teach was not agreeable to being embarrassed.

Another straw had snapped when Mary had insisted her husband dance with her. He had refused, saying he did not caper like a monkey. She had stamped her foot and danced with someone else instead. *What be it,* he thought, *that makes a wumman into a shrew tha moment she says 'er vows?*

Israel Hands, Teach's second in command and one of his few friends, persuaded him to sit, eat and drink. The feast was provided by Ormond, why waste it?

"She be makin' a fool of 'n me."

"She is young," Israel answered, "by the morrow she will be understanding the duties of a wife and there will be nay more of this nonsense." Hands winked and nudged Teach with his elbow, indicating his precise meaning.

Teach merely grunted and gulped another glass of brandy.

"Hello Teach."

Dancers were frolicking a lively jig, the hired musicians scraping enthusiastically on their fiddles, one a little out of tune and two beats behind the others. Laughter and merriment: guests on the far side of sober enjoying themselves. No one noticed the groom's brooding silence as he solemnly regarded the man standing before him.

"Don' recall askin' thee t' m'weddin', Jesamiah Acorne."

"Do you not?" Jesamiah patted his long coat pockets. "I am sure I have an invitation somewhere."

Israel Hands had got to his feet, his fingers sliding into a deep pocket where there was a pistol.

Teach made him sit down again. "Nay, nay I'll be listenin' t' wha' tha scummer has t' blather' afore thee doos finish him."

Jesamiah smiled irritatingly at Hands, pulled up a stool and sat down – after removing his hand from his own coat pocket and laying the pistol it contained on the table.

Hands scowled. Got the message.

"Says what thee have t'say, Acorne, an' be gone with thee, else I'll be shootin' thee a'tween thy eyes, not in tha shoulder."

Jesamiah reached across what had been a white linen tablecloth until a bottle of red wine had been spilt on it, took a glass and filled it with brandy. Raising it he nodded at Blackbeard and drank. It was all the toast for good fortune Teach would be getting from Jesamiah Acorne.

"I've come to apologise, Teach."

Edward Teach's head shot upwards, his brows narrowed. "Has somethin' happened t' m' hearin', Israel? I b'lieve I heard this squit say as he were apologisin'?"

Not rising to the bait, Jesamiah answered, "This squit has had enough of arse licking to the lying fokkers who prance around as Governors. They ain't nothing but stinking bastards who couldn't keep a word of a promise if their poxed lives depended on it."

A man seated next to Israel Hands sneered, "The saying 'pots and kettles' comes to mind."

Jesamiah glanced at him. His face was familiar but he could not place it.

"Havin' trouble, bist thee?" Teach chortled.

"You could say that. I was arrested for something I did not do."

Teach leant back in his chair, stretched his legs before him. The new breeches were tight around his belly after eating so much. He belched. "That nay be what I heard. I 'eard tell from Mr Knight here, thee lied t'me. Tha *Fortune o'Virginny* were no' carryin' militia were she? She were full laid wi' cargo worth tha takin'."

"If that is so, then Master Knight here knows better than me. I was told she was after you. Governor Rogers told me himself." Jesamiah leant forward, planting his folded arms on the table. "I was lied to. Stitched up like a corpse in a shroud. These Governors have no wanting of the likes of us. Amnesty? It ain't worth the paper it be signed on. They want to be rid of us, Teach; well I ain't fokken going without a fight." He paused, had another drink. "There's a fortune to be made in these waters and down in the Main. All it needs is someone with guts and determination to take it."

"These'n be my waters, Acorne. My coast."

Jesamiah's turn to stretch his legs out, cross them at the ankles. His boots were muddy he noticed. "And you are happy with avoiding the various naval frigates patrolling north of here, are you?"

Knight pitched in with a disparaging laugh. "Captain Brand of the *Lyme* is a pompous oaf who has not fought a single battle at sea and George Gordon of the *Pearl* is rarely sober. Is Captain Teach to be afeared of such lubbers?"

It had suddenly occurred to Jesamiah where he had seen Knight. No matter, there were more pressing matters in hand.

"Your squawking parrot, Teach, has been taught to sing the wrong tune. I would be careful of his information were I you. Knight's version ain't accurate."

Knight half rose, "Are you calling me a liar?"

Jesamiah lifted his pistol, examined it, his expression apparently surprised that it was loaded. He shifted the hammer to half cock. "Ask yourself this, Teach. Why has Master Knight not told you that Captain Rhett is patrolling near Charleston? Or that Vernon is in Jamaica? Or of the competent Lieutenant Robert Maynard?"

Teach glowered at Knight who shrugged and then shook his head, sat down again.

"I knows o' Rhett an' Vernon. I can handle they."

Seeing as Knight had backed down, Jesamiah uncocked his pistol, did not put it away though. Said, as if it were a minor matter, "Maynard is the First Lieutenant aboard the *Pearl*."

"I know that, Acorne," Knight hissed. "What of it?"

"Maynard is young but he is keen. He is also very, very good." Jesamiah pointed the pistol at Knight. "Why is it that you have neglected to inform Captain Teach that while at sea Gordon shuts himself in his cabin and Maynard takes command? Hm?" He put the pistol back down on the table, looked square at Teach. "I've come to talk with you, Teach, not your cabin boy." He smiled pleasantly at Knight. "This bottle is empty, perhaps you would be so kind as to fetch us another?"

Knight began to bluster, but Teach cut him short. "Make it two bottles if 'n thee please, Mister Knight, Israel 'ere will 'elp thee, will thee not Hands? I be needin' a private word with Cap'n Acorne 'ere."

With the men gone, Jesamiah spoke plainly. "Spotswood aims to rid the coast of you, Teach, but I aim to rid the coast of as much of value as my hold can carry. If we were to form a partnership, sail in consort, neither

Spotswood, Rogers in Nassau or all the enthusiasm Maynard may possess could stop us. Not if we were partners. None of 'em is clever enough to go against the both of us at once."

Rocking in his chair Teach threw back his head, his black beard– trimmed and combed for the formal occasion – rising and jerking on his broad chest as he guffawed. "Thee expec' me," he wiped tears from his eyes, "thee expec' me t' be thy partner?"

Wary, Jesamiah did not let a flicker of any expression touch his face. Bland, he answered, "No. I will be *your* partner. You are senior to me, but I would rather we conferred on what ships we chase and where, so we assure full agreement and work together, not against each other."

Letting the chair drop forward Teach stopped crowing, stared at Jesamiah. "I doos b'lieve thee bist serious?"

Jesamiah raised a single finger to touch his hat in a mild salute. He mimicked Teach's West Country accent perfectly. "Yass, I bis'n serious."

Resting an elbow on the table Teach massaged his cheeks and chin, ran his tar-stained fingers through his beard. He trusted Acorne no more than he would trust a polecat – but Acorne felt the same about him, and what he said of the Navy was true. Knight had mentioned nothing of Lieutenant Robert Maynard, but Teach already knew of him from other sources. In fact, Knight was as useless as a holed bucket, but as long as he was Bath Town's legal spokesman and ascertained that no one was breaking any laws, then Teach was content.

It would not last of course. Eden was already messing his breeches with fear. All it needed was an arrogant sod like Alexander Spotswood to insist North Carolina do something about the problem of piracy and this lucrative little caper would come to an abrupt end. Teach did not want that end to be a sudden stop by a length of rope. And to avoid the hangman he needed to use his wit and cunning – and a fast, quality ship. A ship like the *Sea Witch* would do very nicely. Tempted, he narrowed his eyes, pondering, considering. Planning. It would not be easy taking the *Sea Witch*, but it would be a damned sight easier if she was at least nearby, and if Acorne was lured off-guard. Once the idea had settled into Teach's mind that the *Sea Witch* could be his, he resolved to stop at nothing to get her.

Jesamiah had no doubt of what Teach was thinking; could see he was wavering. Was about to add another juicy carrot, when a girl, her hair festooned with ribbons, her gown of cream silk decorated with pink roses, pushed to Teach's side.

"Edward, this is no good. No good at all." Mrs Mary Teach stood beside the table, her hands on her hips. She noticed Jesamiah, had no idea who he was and was not best pleased at having yet another seafaring ruffian at her wedding.

"Sir," she said disparagingly, "you have tar grimed all over you. Do you not know the purpose of soap?" She reached for her husband's hand.

"I have relatives wishing to speak with you, Edward, but you sit here talking to these knaves. It will not do."

"Leav'n be, wummun. I bist busy."

"No, I will not. My Uncle William wishes to inspect the catch I have landed."

"Then thy uncle'll be dis'pointed will'n he? Be gone with thee." Mary flounced away. Jesamiah was inspecting his hand. There was a thick streak of ingrained tar across his knuckles, it would take him weeks to get it off, but he'd had to put it there to hide the tattoo of Tiola's name from Teach.

Moving with exaggerated slowness, Jesamiah spat on the palm of his right hand and held it out. "I would not sail with anyone who did not know what he was doing. We are equals you an' I. There ain't no one to match us. No one."

There were several other pirates he could think of who would dispute that, but Teach was vain and he would not disagree. He pushed his hand out further. "Do we 'ave an accord, Cap'n Teach?"

Teach's gaze did not waver from Jesamiah's. He noted there had been no mention that twice now Acorne had proved himself to be the better man. Teach had lost the *Queen Anne's Revenge* because of Acorne's quick thinking and seaman's skills, and he had nearly lost the *Adventure* for the same reason. As much as those facts annoyed him, Teach was astute enough to recognise Acorne's ability. Maybe it would be a good idea to run together as a pack. Acorne could fit well into his plans, at least for a while. Until the opportunity to take the *Sea Witch* for his own arose. And he would ensure that it did. Add to that, this how-nowing to these prancing people here in Bath Town was beginning to get wearisome. His fourteenth wife, for all that she was young and pretty, was already proving to be one wife too many. Ah well, he could always do as he had before – take his pleasure then sail away, only to return when it suited him. The trick with wives was to keep them apart by several hundred miles of ocean. Love them, then leave them.

Acorne's idea was a good one, but he was not going to make agreements too easily. He needed time to think it through. He ignored the outstretched hand. "I be enjoyin' m'weddin' feast. I'll think on it."

Retracting his hand, Jesamiah stood. "I have other business to attend. *Sea Witch* is moored down river. I sail tomorrow evening, take or leave my offer, Teach, I will not repeat it." He finished his brandy and nodding a farewell, left.

Teach beckoned over his second in command, Israel Hands. "Set some'un t'see where he doos go. Rufus'll do a good job, he's as slipp'ry as tha fox he be named fer."

"To follow him?"

"Nay, there bain't many places here. Gen'ral headin'll do."

Teach was curious. What else in Bath Town would attract a man like

Jesamiah Acorne? It had to be a woman. A woman at the Governor's house? Had to be.

Despite the scorn that Mary and her father were so keen to pour on him, Edward Teach was an educated, intelligent man. His West Country dialect was looked down upon by those in established society, but it was an old tongue, akin to the Saxon of Wessex and he saw no reason to change it just to suit their jumped-up snobbery. In Teach's opinion those who went clackety-clack and gabbled two dozen words a minute had nothing of value to say. His style was to take it slow and to ponder, which frequently made people underestimate his mental ability, giving him a clear advantage. And a quiet chance to ponder riddles. Riddles such as what Acorne was up to.

He was swiving the newcomer at Archbell Point. The midwife. Had to be. Yass, and what vessel had she arrived on? The *Fortune of Virginia*. So there was the answer to another riddle. That was why Acorne had stopped the attack.

Teach sat through another dance, thinking and watching his wife making a fool of herself with a young fop who had teeth like a horse and a laugh like a jackass. There would have to be a few harsh lessons in decorum if he decided to keep her.

Did he want to sail in consort with Acorne? Not especially, but nor did he want to stay here mouldering with these poultry-headed mummers. Another month of this and Spotswood would have no need to worry, he would be driven mad enough to hang himself. There again, was Acorne telling the truth? He was right about Knight. A useless worm if ever there was one.

Teach's thoughts returned to *Sea Witch*. Acorne had a good ship. She was fast – and seaworthy. He also had good taste. That little missy, the midwife, was a woman worth drubbing. There was something different about her. Something inexplicable that drew him like north draws the needle on the compass. Something she was hiding. He sat, stroking his beard. He would like to see that young woman again. He had unfinished business with her.

Israel Hands came back, bent low to talk quietly into Teach's ear. Teach nodded. "Along tha river path thee say? Why fore'n he be goin' there d' thee s'pose?"

Mary was allowing the fop to twirl her around and around, her mouth open in laughter, her skirts flying out to reveal too much of her ankles and lower leg. Making a public slut of herself. Teach had had enough.

"Israel, tidden good t' be blatherin' roun' here. Gather tha crew, I as reckon as we ought be makin' us'n way down river. Time us had us own fun of a frawze to do, eh?"

Delighted Israel agreed. Land life was boring for a sailor, and all these self-important bags of wind made it doubly so. He trotted off to round up the men and make ready as Teach stepped out into the twirl of dancers, earning himself several annoyed rebukes when he trod on toes or used his elbow to force a way through. Reaching his wife he clamped his fingers around her wrist and glowered at the orchestra until they scraped to a ragged silence.

"Tha party be over. Fetch'n thy things, wummun. We're goin' aboard my ship an' settin' sail."

She attempted to wrest her arm free; failed. "But we cannot. My guests – our room, it is all made ready."

"Then it'll need be made unready. Fetch'n thy things or come as thee be."

"Look here, Teach, Edward, I do not think –"

Teach cut his father-in-law short. "That'll be thy trouble, thee casn't think." He let go of Mary, turned to leave. "I'll send some'un to escort thee aboard."

"Where are you going?" she shrieked. "I demand to know."

Teach stopped at the open doors and scratched at his backside. "If'n tha must be knowin' m'business, I be 'eadin' fer a sits on the privy. What I doos after tha' be me own conc'rn."

Ten

On the Night of the Dead, he was aware of others crossing the frozen ice. Could sense their presence, hear their nervous laughter and anxious squeals as feet slid, or the ice shifted and creaked.

What fools they were! They were already dead, they could not die again! Yet no soul knew what would happen if one fell beneath the ice, or should fail to cross back over as dawn first touched the eastern skies and the River turned again to flowing, deep, dark water. Be condemned to walk forever, lost between the two worlds, he assumed. For him though, he would not be returning. The Witch Woman was to use her Craft to help him stay among the living for a while. If something went wrong, well, it was a risk he was prepared to take. Nothing could be worse than the condemnation he was already enduring, and would continue to endure for all eternity unless he set things right and paid for his guilt.

She, the Witch Woman, had said she would help him, so why did he sit here and listen to all those unseen forms make their way with gleeful chatter to the hearth-fires of their loved ones for this one night? Why, why did he just sit here?

He looked again at the sodden paper in his hand. At the unbroken seal. Why had the boy not opened it? Not read it?

He had retrieved the letter and sat here, holding it, though night had fallen and it was time to go. Sat here, grieving.

Some of the words he had written were not too blurred and could still be read, but he had not the heart to look at them. He had tried to explain, had tried to tell his son that he had loved him in life – as he loved him now, in death. He had been a fool. Such a bloody fool.

"Captain? Captain Mereno? I cannot hold the energy I need to do this for long. You must come now or come not at all."

The Witch Woman, Tiola. Jesamiah's lady was a good woman and Charles had a moment's doubt and guilt about deceiving her, for there was more to this than he had revealed.

He stood, dropped the letter. A wind flurried and blew it away as he set one foot upon the ice. He caught his breath as it crackled beneath his boot. He had scoffed at the others – he saw now why they had been so afraid!

He took one slow step, then another, and another. He had been told, when first he came to this place, that he had to pay a high price to relieve the burden of his guilt.

Where land becomes sea
And sea becomes land,
Where one is not the other
And all is not it seems;
Time stands and waits
For the life beat to cease.

He walked towards the Witch Woman, the midwife who brought life into the world, her arms outstretched towards him in welcome.
He hesitated. Did he want to do this? No, he did not, but he had to. To find peace, to rest, he had to pay penance.
He had to take the life of his son.

Eleven

It was cold beside the River, the touch of ice in the air turning Tiola's breath to mist. Everything was white with hoar frost and glistened under the careful watch of every star that lit the Universe. In any other place it would have been beautiful, but not here by the boundary between Life and Death, where souls crossed from one world to another. Where, on the Other Side, those who could passed into the Eternity of Peace; the Elysium Fields, Valhalla, Heaven. It had many names, and as many appearances. What was happiness and contentment to one, could be hell and suffering to another. The exact state of peace, joy, happiness, was the choice of each individual soul. Unless that soul was unable to choose because regrets obstructed the acceptance of what was, and what had been.

Tiola was unsure that she was doing the right thing. The fact that she had the ability to do something did not make it acceptable. But Charles St Croix Mereno had asked for her help, and so in an oblique way, had Jesamiah. The both of them had an entwined past that needed laying to rest, and sometimes choices were not always easy or comfortable when balanced against conscience.

"You must come now," she called, "while the energy does flow between this world and that, while the boundary is open and Life is Death and Death is Life."

As he came nearer she could see him more clearly. He was much like Jesamiah, except Jesamiah's black hair and dark eyes were from his mother. Charles had the same swagger, the same air of pretended confidence – a mask to hide the reality of stomach-twisting fear. She reached out her hand and took his. It was cold, ice cold. He stepped ashore, exhaled a breath that, unlike hers, did not puff a misted cloud. He was not a corpse; he was clothed, his flesh looked like flesh, his reddish hair was tied neatly at the nape of his neck with a ribbon. He looked human, looked alive, but he was not either and only those who had known him would be able to see him. And only if he wished it so.

"On this night alone," Tiola said as she welcomed him to her side of the

River, "I can work my Magick, for the opposition between the Light and the Dark becomes suspended. The balance is level and neither can influence the other. Nor can I be detected amongst the chatter of returning souls."

"A temporary cessation of the battle?"

"If you like. For this one night, between the setting and the rising of the sun, Death, in whatever its chosen guise, and the Bone Mother and the Soul Hunter do not have claim over the dead. While the River runs still and turns to ice, there is a flux of motion between the plains of existence. That is why I can bring you here."

They walked together a while, Charles wondering if he should tell her the full truth of why he had come, but about to speak, he stopped, pointed along the path. Someone was coming. A lantern, held high, was throwing a bobbing patch of light to the muddied ground, footsteps splashed in the puddles.

Tiola turned to Charles Mereno, but he had gone. She had played her part, now it was for him to sort his conscience and quieten his soul.

With a warm smile she waited to greet the man coming towards her. The one she loved. Jesamiah.

Twelve

"Tiola?" Jesamiah lifted the lantern higher, caught sight of his woman a few yards ahead. "What the fok are you doing in the dark by the river? What if you'd fallen, hurt yourself?"

"That is not likely, luvver, I can see perfectly where I set my feet."

"Without a lantern?" He was standing before her now, perversely cross because he had been concerned and had no need to be. And because he had unjustly shouted at Joe Meadows a few moments ago for letting her come along here on her own. It had not helped that Meadows had shouted back, or that Jesamiah knew full well he had not been in the right.

"I need no lantern, Jesamiah. I appreciate your anxiety but it is unwarranted."

"You were with someone. Who was it?"

"I have been about business this night."

Belligerently he studied her face in the flickering, yellow light, remembered belatedly what night it was and what she had probably meant. He looked sharply around, could see no phantom ghosts prowling in the darkness.

Her witchcraft worried him, not because he was afraid of it, although there was an element of that this particular night. Ingrained superstition was hard to ignore. His fear was for her safety. Not long ago they hanged or burned witches; there was no guarantee that, were she to be identified, the noose or the flame would not suddenly be resurrected.

He lowered the lantern. "I yelled at Skylark for not accompanying you."

"Then you had better apologise to him; I did not want to be accompanied. Only the dead could have walked with me to where I went."

Again Jesamiah's eyes flickered towards where he was certain a man had disappeared beneath the trees. If there had been someone he was no longer there. It did not occur to him to doubt her fidelity; her loyalty put his wanderings to shame. He puffed air through his cheeks, admitted the truth of his unease. "I'm sorry, sweetheart. Teach has got me on edge, and I have missed you more than I can say."

Tiola threaded her arm through his and continued down the path, heading for the Town. "It has been hard not sharing my thoughts with you these weeks. I am protected this night because there is a surfeit of Magick in the air, there are other spirits, there is much power, but once we have parted and the dawn comes, my protection will be gone and I will again not be able to speak with you in our private way. Not until the babe is safely born." She reached up and cupped his cheek with her palm. "But my silence will not be for long and I do so love you, Jesamiah."

He set the lantern down, took both her hands in his. She was cold, as if she had been touching ice. The proposal coming out of nowhere; he suddenly asked, "Will you marry me, Tiola? Now. Here, tonight?"

She nodded. "*Ais.* I will." She had been waiting a long while for him to say those words in a way that he meant them.

"I can get Governor Eden to officiate if I offer him a tempting payment. I…"

Reaching up she stopped his words by putting her finger on his lips. "No. There is an older, more binding way for us to follow."

She took the lantern and set it in the centre of the path and moving her fingers above it released a gentle *hie…asssh* sound. And the lantern had gone. Only the stub of the candle and its flame remained: a blue flame that flickered and wavered in the wind, but never faded and would not be blown out by earthly means.

Tiola began to sing; words that had no meaning, a lilt that ached the heart for it was so full of love. And as she sang, the candle became two candles, and then three – and the three flames were green in colour, the hue flickering to brown and then purple as the three candles became a circle of six.

Her song changed in pitch, the unheard words in the rippling cadence transforming the six purple flames to a glowing red, and as they then turned to orange the six candles became nine and the orange flared brighter and brighter until the flames burnt with a fervent yellow heat. Tiola's voice rose like the joyous song of the lark and lifted the candles until they danced in the air three feet from the ground in a perfect circle of bright white.

The Circle of Light, the Circle of Love.

She took Jesamiah's hands so that their arms formed around the candles in another unbroken circle, and she walked with him, around and around and around three times, as the circle of candles turned, and the stars circled above. The circle set within the circle, within the circle. Unbroken. Unending. Forever.

Her words were soft, but sure. "Three times, I honour thee with my words. Three times, I honour thee with my touch. Three times, I honour thee with my love."

And again they circled.

"Once, I walk the Circle to bind thee to my body. Twice, I walk the Circle to bind thee to my heart. Thrice, I walk the Circle to bind thee to my soul."

A third time. "Seven times the Three do I want thee. Eight times the Three do I worship thee. By Nine, the Power of Three by Three, do I wed thee and take thee as mine own."

Jesamiah repeated the words as Tiola spoke them. They stood, holding hands, and the candles and the watching stars became motionless.

She smiled directly into his eyes, and through them to his soul, knew that he was looking at her in the same way for she could feel his loving presence deep within her. She spoke in barely a whisper; the sealing of her vow was too great to be shouted, and too intimate. "I love thee. I love thee. I love thee. So may it be."

Jesamiah squeezed her hands, his throat felt tight with emotion, his heart full. "I love thee. I love thee. I love thee. So may it be."

Tiola reached for the acorn earring that she had on a chain around her neck and put it over Jesamiah's head. "When you can, wear it as it is meant to be. I have blessed it, the charm will protect you."

"I need no charm, sweetheart. I need only you." He pulled her close, kissed her. She was his wife and he, her husband, and he did love her so.

As he broke away, stepped back, the candles disappeared and the clouds covered the sky. Only the lantern burning with a single flame was on the path between them, as if nothing else had ever been there.

Thirteen

"Someone comes!"

Jesamiah looked up, startled. A man was there, not four yards away pointing along the path, his features in shadow. That same man, the one who had been beside the grave. His father. No! His father was dead, buried, gone!

"It is Teach!" Charles Mereno shouted. "Be gone, Tiola! Boy, extinguish the lantern."

Jesamiah was flummoxed, but his bewilderment was shoved aside by an inrush of anger. How dare this stranger give him orders! "I do not know who the fok you are, mister, and I don't p'tickly care. I will handle this my way. No one orders me about. Savvy?" Muttered, "Especially not some bloody dead ghost."

He glanced at where Tiola had silently stepped into the darkness beneath the trees. He thought he saw a movement of her gown, but when he stared harder there was nothing there. Coming nearer, the unmistakeable sound of footsteps treading heavily on the path, squelching in the occasional patch of mud. Mereno obstinately remained standing where he was.

Jesamiah ignored him. He lifted the lantern, held it high and stood, waiting for Teach to come nearer.

"What be thee doin' 'long here, Acorne?" Teach asked, his tone suspicious, craning his neck in an attempt to see past Jesamiah who was blocking the way.

"Unless we agree to be partners, Teach, my business remains my business."

"Tha's why I doos come t'find thee." Teach scowled again over Jesamiah's shoulder at the indistinct shape of a man leaning against a tree. "Who be this'n then?"

Charles Mereno stepped forward so that the feeble glimmer from the lantern would shine on his face. "I think you already know who I am, Edward."

Teach blanched and his hand dropped to the cutlass at his side. The words flew from him in a hoarse whisper of disbelief. "Nay! Thee be dead!"

"Am I? Mayhap you are not the only one to make pacts with the Devil?"

And he was gone. In the silence only the river could be heard gurgling past; the wind rustling in the trees. An owl called some way off; nearer, its mate answered.

Teach turned slowly, glowered at Jesamiah, the whites of his bulging eyes gleaming in the pale lamplight. "What thee be doin' consortin' with that bugger?"

Swinging the lantern Jesamiah peered up and down the empty path. "You are the only one who knows about buggers, Teach, and I see only you. I'm here to make an agreement. If you want to see things that are not here, then that is between you and your conscience; it ain't nothing to do with me. Perhaps you've had too much to drink?" He spat on his palm, held out his hand. "Now, do we have an accord or don't we?"

Teach glowered. Ghosts? Phantoms? What did he fear from either? No ghost was going to do Beelzebub's partner any harm. That apparition, Mereno, must've been some trick of Acorne's – and what was there to fear from this young pup?

"Too much t'drink? I'll see thee under tha table any day!" Teach spat on his own palm, slapped his hand into Jesamiah's. "Yass, we have accord."

For all his bravado, Teach, Blackbeard himself, was glad he had Jesamiah to walk with, and that the candle in the lantern lasted until they reached the jetty at Bath Town's apology for a wharf. Mereno's likeness, whether it was a trick or a ghost or his mind playing games, had unsettled him. He had forgotten all about Charles St Croix Mereno. He did not especially want to remember him, alive or dead.

He stood on the jetty, staring across the river in the general direction of his own property and at the patch of darkness where the *Adventure* was moored, her masts and rigging black against the night sky. He looked in the opposite direction, upriver, to where there was a blaze of lantern and torch light, the sound of music and voices and laughter. John Ormond's estate. The wedding carousal. Only it was not the sort of do that befitted a pirate. Genteel manners, dainty bites to eat that would not fill a gnat's belly. Wine and champagne that tasted like piss to his way of thinking, served in pretty glasses – not kegs of rum to fill tankards to the brim.

Teach set his back to the light and noise, spoke plain to Jesamiah. "I've had me fill o' they dullards. I be goin' aboard me ship. Will thee b'joinin' me?"

The last thing Jesamiah wanted was to spend a wedding night – his or Teach's – anywhere except in Tiola's bed, but what he wanted and what he was going to get seemed likely to be two different things. That Teach was after *Sea Witch* was all too evident, but he was going to be very disappointed, wasn't he?

"Why not?" Jesamiah said, shrugging one shoulder and forcing enthusiasm. "I'll just be tellin' the tavern I'll not be wantin' a room after all."

The excuse was a good one, creditable. Teach nodded, walked on across the bridge towards Plum Point, his footsteps rattling on the wooden planking. "Dint' thee be dallyin' long, Acorne. I weigh anchor within tha hour."

It took Jesamiah only a quarter of that to find Joe Meadows and tell him what to do. "Find Miss Tiola, tell her I'll be finishing what we started as soon as we have the chance. Then get yourself downstream to the *Sea Witch* and tell Rue to take her back to la Sorenta. I do not want her anywhere near here or that madman. Tell Rue to employ time usefully by stowing what tobacco there is. I have a mind to take it to London and sell it. If we can."

Finally, as the night neared its midway zenith, Jesamiah stood at the head of the path that led along the river. He did not have to go with Teach. He could find Tiola, make love to her; make her properly his wife. But then that would go against his reason for being here, would it not? He had to clear his name, no matter how much the doing stuck in his throat, and to do so, he had to find out what Teach was up to. He might as well get on with it.

And as for his father? Aye well, Tiola may have something different to say if he asked her, but in his book, ghosts did not exist.

Fourteen

A frawze, spoken in Teach's dialect as frawzee; a feast, a celebration. An excuse to get skimmished, drunk. Not that Teach or any of his ramshackle, degenerate crew needed an excuse.

Mary Teach wrinkled her nose and leant away from the red-haired man sitting on her left, Red Rufus they called him. His breath and body stank. She was not certain which was the worst offence, his stench or the fact that three times now she had slapped his hand away from her breast.

The only decent man was Captain Acorne, but he sat over the far side of her husband's great cabin, propped in a corner with a bottle of rum as a companion. By the looks of him he was asleep. She rather regretted being churlish with him earlier, about the tar on his hand. Compared to the disgusting state of these men, that was a minor offence.

There were about twenty-six men. Where the rest of the crew were she did not know or care, nor had she listened to the names of these ruffians, let alone remembered them: Morton; Gates; a Negro. Hands of course, she knew him. He spoke well, kept himself as clean as a sailor could and knew his manners – after a fashion, but he was on his back flat on the floor, dead drunk. Garrett Gibbens, the bo'sun, was continuously leering at her. She did not like him, was a little afraid of him. In fact, she was afraid of them all.

As a captain's cabin this was pitiful. Ten feet by twelve, shoddy, dirty, barely any furniture save what was essential. No curtaining to make the tiny compartment to one side, which was apparently her bedchamber, private.

Nor was there any privacy for the necessary. The only provision was what they called "the heads" – a hole up at the front of the boat which you positioned yourself over. How was she to manage that with her fine gown and array of petticoats? She wanted to relieve herself, but was not going to use that dreadful place. It stank of faeces and urine – most of which was on the deck, not evacuated down the hole. The mere thought made her gag. And nor was she going to lift her skirts with all these men watching. She would have to ask for a bucket, she assumed.

Where was she to hang her gowns? Set her hairbrushes, powders and perfumes? Where was she to dress? What was she to do during the day? What of tonight – what was left of it.

This was not what she had intended.

At her home, her father's house, the big bed had been made with fresh linen sheets and soft-woven blankets. Petals and perfume had been strewn about, sweet-smelling candles stood ready to be lit, a fire laid in the hearth with scented wood. A bottle of Papa's expensive wine, crystal glasses; sweetmeats on a silver dish. It had all looked so beautiful, and here she was in her wedding gown that was muddied at the hem and torn in two places, aboard a rat-infested ship! She blinked back tears, and pushed Gibbens away as he tried to kiss her.

Mary had expected to be mistress of Plum Point. Edward had talked of rebuilding it, of adding a wing and another storey; of buying slaves to tend the gardens. She realised now, now it was too late, that it had all been nothing more than talk. She had been bewitched by his false charm, the romantic allure of being singled out by a pirate – by a man of fame and fortune whom everyone courted and fawned over. Along with the rest of them in Bath Town she had failed to see the rotting hulk she was now shackled to. Not that she'd had a choice, but had her father – had any of them – known the reality behind this barbarian's gentlemanly façade, would she be here, drowning in this nightmare?

Perhaps, when he decided to set sail she could feign seasickness and persuade him to send her home? He had said he was going to sea, but they had only drifted a few miles down river and then dropped anchor again. Apparently it was too much bother to go any further.

Captain Acorne had been furious. His ship had gone. She was supposedly anchored where they were now, but there had not been a sign of her. He had stamped up and down the deck yelling obscenities into the darkness about ungrateful bastards stealing his ship; and then he had found the rum and stopped shouting.

She glanced across at the narrow, box-like bed. One grey, grubby sheet, a worn blanket. Was she expected to share that with Edward? Maybe there was somewhere else they would go to? She glanced at it again. She was so tired she doubted she would notice the fleas, lice and bed bugs. Most of the men were asleep. Surely it would not be long before her husband dozed off? Then she could go to the privy and get to bed. And in the morning? She had not the energy or inclination to think of the morning.

Gibbens again tried to kiss her. She slapped his face. "Do you not care who insults your wife?" she snapped.

Teach laughed and emptied the bottle he had in his hand, throwing it across the cabin, the glass shattering against the bulkhead. He belched and reached for another.

"Nought wrong with a kiss, wummun. Us shares what we 'as on this'n ship."

Fifteen

Jesamiah was not asleep. He felt uneasy at being aboard the Adventure, but the agreement was for him to keep an eye on Teach and report back to Spotswood when anything significant happened – if anything happened. Until then he would have to stay here. If the sum of their sailing was going to be all of five miles a day, his staying was going to be interminable.

Why in all the names of all the seas was he doing this? Why? Because otherwise he would be a corpse mouldering in an iron body-cage on the gibbet. Because his crew would be wanted men and because, at the time, there in Governor Spotswood's comfortable office, all this had seemed a good idea.

"Why did I agree?" he mumbled, his eyes closed, trying to distance himself from what was going on around him.

"Because you have a disagreement to settle? Teach shot you, I recall."

"I could do that without having to be aboard this shite-hole."

"Well then, it is because you are now an honest man and must prove your honesty?"

"I told you to leave me alone." Jesamiah put down the bottle he was clutching, opened his eyes and glowered. His father was standing there, leaning against the bulkhead. "I am here because I was backed into a corner, and I did not exactly have much of a selection as regards choice. Leave me alone. Go away. You are dead. You do not exist."

Charles Mereno walked over and sat down beside his son. "I am dead, but to those I wish to show myself to, I exist. The woman you have taken as your wife has made it so in order that I may settle things." When he received no answer he continued, "There is much that I have done wrong; much that I must put right. No, Phillipe was not your brother, but because of me he was born and I undertook responsibility for him and his mother."

Jesamiah staggered to his feet. He had drunk more than he realised. "I am not interested. Go save your corrupted soul elsewhere." Pointedly, with no intention of sharing and not considering that perhaps ghosts could not drink rum, he picked up the bottle and tottered to another corner near the stern windows. He stepped over the prone body of Red Rufus, on his back, mouth open and snoring loudly, stated irritably; "Not a lot of interest happens aboard this bloody ship, does it, Teach?"

"Tha' be because I bain't yet undertook m' marital dooties." Teach was very drunk; his slurred words were barely understandable but the crude gesture near his crotch was meaning enough. He belched again, removed his hat and flung it across the cabin. His coat and waistcoat followed.

Only five of his crew were awake to applaud. They were easily entertained Jesamiah assumed, for he saw nothing to get excited about. His father's ghost, he noted, had gone.

Impatiently, Teach gestured for Mary to stand up. Her face was pale, rings beginning to darken beneath her tired eyes. She glanced towards the wooden bed, dread swamping her, the implication of a loveless, ill-matched marriage hitting her with all its stark finality.

"What thee still wearin' this'n fer?" Her husband wound his fingers into the lace at the neck of her wedding gown and wrenching it, ripped the dress beyond repair. She cried out in dismay but he had a dagger at her throat – she backed away, whimpering. He crowed the louder and with a few deft strokes cut the lacing of her corset. Without giving her chance to protest he tore her undershift, exposing her breasts to the accompaniment of drunken cheering.

No romance, no love, no consideration, he dragged her to the bed and tossed her on to it. No matter that these men of his crew watched, no matter that they stamped their feet on the floor and banged their fists on the table in time to his thrusts into her. No matter that she begged him to stop for he was hurting. He slapped her face and heaved and pushed and grunted some more as he tried to maintain a failing erection.

These last months it always happened. Every time he took a woman his piece faded before he could relieve his need. He took his disappointment out on her. There were other ways of receiving gratification.

"As I said, we shares aboard this ship."

He twisted his hand into her hair at the nape of her neck and pulling her, screaming, from the bed threw her face down onto the table, scattering the bottles and tankards to the floor.

"Durn't any of thee say thy Cap'n bain't gen'rous. Those o' thee not so skimmished thee casn't find thy cock can have thy turn!"

He opened a new bottle of rum and sat on his captain's chair at the head of the table, one leg hooked over the arm, and watched indifferently as his wife was raped. The bo'sun, Gibbens, took his pleasure first, then the Negro, Caesar. Mary stopped screaming as the third man used her.

"Bain't thee takin' a turn, Acorne?"

Teach stood over Jesamiah, swaying, the half empty bottle in his hand.

How much drink does it take to knock him out? Jesamiah wondered, he feigned sleep, had tried not to hear the girl's screams. He had raped a girl once when he was seventeen. Had never done it again. The shame still turned his stomach. He took pride in his lovemaking, always ensured the women he slept with received as much pleasure as did he. This was not pleasure. This was sadistic brutality.

Teach kicked his shin.

Jesamiah waved his hand. "Too drunk."

"I said it be thy turn." The click of a pistol hammer. "Thee'll not insult me by turnin' down me gen'rous offer, would thee, Acorne?"

Jesamiah got unsteadily to his feet. He wanted no part of this, but Teach's mood was becoming ugly, and maybe he could do something to help the girl? He certainly would not be able to as a dead man.

"If 'n'e ain't one o' us," Gibbens snarled from behind Teach, "then what's 'e doin' 'ere?"

Mary lay on her back, rigid with fear, naked, spreadeagled across the table. Blood smeared her thighs, her face was bruised; her lip was cut. Marks of bites and scratches were on her throat and breasts. Her eyes were open, blank like a corpse, staring and staring at the overhead beams, seeing nothing while the scream went on and on in her head.

Teach prodded Jesamiah in the back with the pistol. "Get on with it."

Slowly Jesamiah crawled on top of her. She whimpered as his weight pressed down. What to do? What to do! She was just turned sixteen; a child for fok sake! He nuzzled her neck, kissed her; nibbled her ear. His hand fumbled between her legs then went as if to unbutton his breeches.

"Mary. Bite me," he whispered urgently. "As hard as you can. Do it girl! It is the only way I can save you!"

Terror had frozen her senses but she recognised this man as the one with nice eyes – such nice dark eyes.

"Bite me," he urged.

Instinct made her obey. She turned her head and sank her teeth into his ear. In genuine pain he roared his outrage.

"You bitch! You bloody whore!" He slapped her, making the blow look harder than it was, hauled her from the table and hoisted her over his shoulder. "Bite me, would you? I'll fokken learn you how to behave, Madam! So help me I will!"

The black mood had lifted, the men were laughing, following along behind as Jesamiah stamped up the ladder to the open deck, joining in his torrent of abusive language. Suggesting a few crude things he could do to her as punishment, all of which he paid no heed to.

He hefted her on to the rail, sat her there – she was screaming again, terrified of the drop behind her, clinging to his hair, his shirt, her poor battered face flooded with tears.

"Listen to me," he hissed, "the bank's only a few yards away. Get yourself ashore. Find Tiola." He shook her to get her attention, made it look as if he was shaking her out of anger. "If you can't swim, kick your legs, splash your arms. Get to shore and find the midwife at the Governor's. Go to her. Go to Tiola!"

He heard Teach coming up behind him, knew he had to get Mary away from here. It was her only chance of survival, Teach and his men would use her until she was dead beneath them. Aye, and even after then.

"You little cow!" Jesamiah shouted. "I'll fokken learn you your manners!" He tipped her over the side, swivelling her body in the direction of the shore. She gasped but did not scream. The fall was quick, there was a splash.

He stood at the rail waiting for sounds of her swimming or splashing about. Prayed she was all right. It was too dark to see, there was no sound beyond the normal night noises. Should he dive in? Help her? No, apart from distracting Teach to give her time to get away, he had done all he could. She was on her own now.

"That be my wumman thee've tossed o'er board."

His hands spread apologetically Jesamiah turned cautiously. "The bitch bit me. Done you a favour I reckon, what would you be wanting to keep a harridan like that for?"

Teach peered over the side and sniffed noisily; unbuttoned his breeches and pissed where he stood on the deck.

"Thee nay be so clever as thee make out, Acorne. Thee be stupid nay to 'ave drubbed 'er first."

Jesamiah peered over the side again, thumped his fist on the rail. "Shit, I never bloody thought of that."

Teach chortled, slapped his shoulder. "Nay mind lad, thee'll learn tha way o' things after a couple o' months aboard me vessel. M'lads an' me'll show thee 'ow t'use yer cock proper." He wobbled, almost fell, guffawed again.

"I think you're ready for your bed, eh?" Jesamiah said, settling Teach's arm around his shoulder and steering him below. Surely he was drunk enough to sleep now? Surely, poor Mary would have struggled to the bank?

Encouraging Teach to lie down, making crooning noises, Jesamiah covered him with a blanket and thanked every god he could think of when he was rewarded with a stentorian snore. Stood there, considering whether to kill him here and now. A pillow over his face would do it. Or one quick slash with a dagger across the throat.

"There's always one among us who thinks of murderin' the Captain," a voice grated from behind. "But then, there's always another to persuade a change of mind."

Jesamiah stiffened. He hated people coming up behind him. Looked around. Gibbens. "I could always kill you too."

"Oh aye?" Gibbens stubbed the barrel of his pistol against Jesamiah's spine. "Give me an excuse t'pull this trigger, Acorne."

Slowly, Jesamiah turned around, raising his hands, a lazy smile on his face. "Sorry Gibbens, I hate to disappoint you. I can leave you in charge of sleeping beauty then, can I?" He walked away, headed for the open deck.

As much as he wanted to kill Teach, he did not want the infamy of doing so. The bugger was disliked, but he was also admired by those who saw themselves as his equals. Charles Vane, Stede Bonnet, Howell Davies, Black Bart Roberts. It went against the Pirate Code to kill another of the brethren in cold blood, especially a captain. That's why marooning was favoured; when a man starved, died of thirst or shot himself, no individual could be held responsible. Not that Teach respected the Code, but there were plenty who did. Men who would use any excuse to hunt down a pirate who broke with honour – Jesamiah was not afraid for himself, but such feuds escalated. Tiola, Alicia, la Sorenta, his crew, his ship, everyone and everything he cared for could be destroyed. Aside, murder was not part of Spotswood's hard-driven bargain.

'I need an excuse, Acorne, I cannot touch Edward Teach while he languishes in North Carolina, but were he to threaten Virginia – ah, that would be a different matter.' That is what he had said, along with, 'I need an informant. Someone reliable to tell me where Teach is and what he intends to do. The moment we are alerted that he is a threat to us, the Navy will do the rest.' That was fine by Jesamiah. Let the bloody Navy do the dirty work.

The others were asleep, draped like poppet dolls abandoned at the end of a children's game. He went up on deck; stumbled on a ladder rung, his footsteps dragging with weariness. He peered again over the side. Was it worth getting the jolly boat out? Should he search for her?

"Mary? Mary lass?" He dared only call softly. "Mary!"

"She is dead."

"She may not be. She had a good chance of getting ashore."

Stepping from the shadows, Charles Mereno spoke with compassion. "Son, she is dead. Believe me, I know."

Laying his forehead against the rail, Jesamiah shut his eyes tight. A few hours ago he had been so deliriously happy to have made Tiola his wife – and now all he had was this! He had not meant Mary to drown. He had been trying to help her!

"Do you think she would have wanted to live after that, lad?"

Jesamiah did not answer his father. He did not speak to ghosts.

"The same happened to Phillipe's mother – Teach was among those who raped her." Charles hesitated. Did he tell his son everything? Should he be honest? "I have reason to believe that Teach was Phillipe's father, Jesamiah. Not the Spaniard."

Looking out into the darkness, at the trees black against a star-studded sky Jesamiah choked back a sob. "That explains a lot," he said miserably. "The pair of them, as mad as each other. As mad as I appear to be."

"Why are you denying my existence? All I want to do is explain. To talk to you."

Jesamiah spun around, would not accept what his eyes saw – his father.

Father was dead and ghosts did not exist. Or if they did, Jesamiah did not want to believe in them. He did not want to hear, speak to or see the man who had been his father. He'd had a belly full of the past, and the immediate future was not that promising either. Anger, at himself, at Teach – at not being able to be with Tiola – directed itself to the one man he really wanted to hurt. His father.

Stamping across the few feet between them, Jesamiah poked Charles Mereno in the chest. Was surprised to discover that he felt solid, real. It was an illusion. It had to be. "There were a lot of things I wanted to say to you not long ago, Father. A lot of things I wanted you to say to me. About my so-called brother, about why you abandoned me to his tortures. Why he got my home and I did not. But do you know something?" Jesamiah prodded his father harder. "All of a sudden I don't give a toss. For you, for Phillipe, for Teach, for none of it. It is done. Over. Finished. I've weighed anchor and left that wretched harbour behind. I have a wife, a ship and a chance to gain an unequivocal pardon for what I was – and with it, as soon as I take what information I can back to Spotswood, I get my freedom. On top of all that, I 'ave no intention of conversing with a bloody phantom that don't exist outside of my raving mind! So go away and let me live my life in peace."

Charles was at a loss of what more to say. How could he tell his son that no, it was not done, was not finished? That all he also wanted was the bliss of peace? That the only way for it to be granted was to pay the demanded price.

"You could not have killed Teach, Jesamiah. Those stories, the ones that say he has traded souls with the Devil? They are true."

Jesamiah laughed, swung back to the rail, peered over again hoping against hope to see Mary struggling ashore. "That's bloody nonsense. Tiola told me; there is no such being as the Devil."

"But there is the Dark. The Dark can possess and protect a man, and only a Witch Woman can defeat the Dark."

It was true, Jesamiah knew it was true. That was why Tiola had to protect herself now. The Dark would destroy her if it could. As, indirectly, it had destroyed an innocent young life here tonight.

Jesamiah took the chain with its gold charm from around his neck, dangled the acorn above his palm. The sailor's belief: he must have something to pay the ferryman to take him across the Eternal River to the Other Side. Did Mary have anything to pay her passage?

Riddled with guilt, her death had been his fault, he held the chain out, dropped it into the water. "Take this, darlin', I freely give it you, and wish you the chance to find peace." He rubbed his hand across his face, sighed. Was this reality or was he indeed mad?

"I don't want to know, Father. About you, about Phillipe, or bloody Teach. All I want to do is forget the past, get off this fokken miserable ship, report back to Spotswood, collect my woman and then sail away in my ship." He said a few more things, lashing out, his anger hurting, twisting like a knife inside him. Then he strode away, went aft to find himself somewhere to sleep. Tiola would speak to him in their special way as soon as she could and meanwhile he had a black-bearded devil to deal with.

And nothing, nothing at all, was going to make him believe that he had just told his father's ghost to fuck off.

Sixteen

Friday 1st November

As dawn approached, Tiola found herself busy. Not all spirits knew their way, they were often disorientated, some lost. As a midwife it was her duty to care for those coming into the world and those leaving it. With love she cleaned and swaddled the newborn child, and with as much kindness washed and laid out the dead. The circle of life, beginning to end, completed.

Soon, the sun would rise; the ice on the River melt, and the boundary between the plains of existence close for all but the new souls.

~ *Jesamiah?* ~ She had tried calling him several times, but had been aware, even through all the babbling confusion of the many excited voices of the dead that he had been close to Teach and so she had backed away. Something else had happened though. Something terrible.

~ *Jesamiah?* ~

~ *Sweetheart.* ~

He sounded beaten and defeated as if he had no more strength to carry on. Tiola caught her breath – it could happen! The seeping of energy between the plains sometimes drained a living form's life force so it became snared by the returning souls, unable to fight free! The ill, the old, the young were those who usually succumbed, Jesamiah was vulnerable, he was tired, and sounded so sad, so lonely.

~ *Let me come to you,* ~ she said. ~ *We can meet beneath the trees.* ~

His answer was sharp, frightened. ~ *No! Stay away!* ~

She heard him exhale, steady himself. Was aware that he was on the edge of losing control, was sweeping tears from his eyes.

~ *We shared something so beautiful this night, Tiola, and now it has been tainted by vile ugliness. When I make love to you as my wife I want nothing to come between us. Nothing to spoil it.* ~

~ *Jesamiah? Can you not tell me? What has happened?* ~

He merely responded with, ~ *Bad things.* ~ Then added, to change the subject, ~ *I keep seeing my father.* ~

~ *He wants to make amends, needs to cleanse himself of his guilt. Oh!* ~ Tiola broke off, cried out in distress. ~ *Mary? Mary Ormond? Why are you here?*

Jesamiah, what has happened? Mary, you poor, poor child! ~

He heard nothing more, but felt the pain of Tiola's grief. Shared every emotion with her, for he was drowning in the same sorrow.

All else forgotten, Tiola ran to the sad form that was the keening spirit of sixteen-year-old Mary. Tears glistened in the girl's dull eyes and shone against the marks of bruising and dried blood. Tiola wanted to ask how she had come to be in this state, but it was not her place to do so. Others on the far side would do that, and in the asking and the telling would comfort and heal. All she could do was walk beside Mary and guide her to the River, talking and reassuring, easing with tender love and respect the pains that wrecked the earth-bound spirit.

Mary hesitated on the riverbank, confused that it was ice not water; knowledge, hidden to the living but released to the dead, was telling her there should be a boat to take her safe across.

"Where is the ferryman?" she said, "I must pay him." She pulled a wedding band from her finger, stared at it then threw it away in horror and disgust. Her hands went to cover her breasts, her nakedness. "I am ashamed, I am unclothed."

"Birth-clad you came into the world, Mary, there is no shame in the naked body." All the same, Tiola removed her cloak and placed it around the girl's shoulders.

Mary gathered it close, grateful; she was cold, shivering.

Tiola put her arms around her, held her and whispered that all was well, that the horrors and the fears were over. And noticed a chain around the girl's neck. She touched it.

"Mary, from where did you get this?"

Mary lifted it, peered at the acorn dangling there, bewildered. "I – I do not know. I found it in the water, I think."

Worry was soaking through Tiola. Why did Mary Ormond have Jesamiah's acorn? What had happened?

"He said I could have it to pay my way."

"Then you must use it so. Throw it onto the ice as you pass over."

Mary regarded Tiola with wide, solemn eyes that spoke more of her ordeal than could any words. In return, Tiola kissed her forehead and guided her to the frozen water where the Gentle Ones were waiting to take the girl into their compassionate protection.

Hesitating, Mary touched her hand, "He is a good man. Cherish him."

"I will. I do," Tiola answered.

Seventeen

Sitting on the bank of the river that wandered behind Archbell Point, through a haze of tears, Tiola watched the sun rise. She now understood Jesamiah's despair and so wanted to be with him, to cleanse them both from the stench of brutality, but until the evil that was in Teach was defeated, she would not be able to communicate with the one she loved beyond her own life.

"I am not proud of what happened this night," Charles said suddenly appearing, seated beside her. "That girl was treated ill. She should not have died as she did."

Tiola jumped to her feet, fists clenched at her sides, anger blazing in her eyes. "Jesamiah was trying to save her, how dare you condemn him!"

Charles frowned up at her; "You misunderstand me. Teach should not have abused her. I am proud of Jesamiah, but he should not have taken the risk of doing what he did. He baffles me. I do not understand him."

It was not sufficient to cool Tiola's outrage. "Had you been a father to him then perhaps you would. Had you loved him, then perhaps you would not be baffled. He is a kind, generous man."

Charles exhaled slowly, a mimicked reflex of when he had been alive, for he had no living breath. "He is a pirate. He kills, he steals."

About to shout again, Tiola backed down. Charles was right. "Yes, he was a pirate. And he does kill and he does steal, but he is not possessed by evil. He is capable of being a good man."

Charles sat a while watching the sun's rays stabbing into the paling blueness and the last stars disappear. "We do not know," he said, "when we plant our seed and watch a woman's belly swell, what angel or demon will be born." The sun rose higher, warming the world with its smile. "Please. Sit, Witch Woman. I long to talk to you but it is difficult for me to say what is in my mind when you are so fired with wrath."

Tiola sat, although not close. Something was worrying her about Charles Mereno, but she did not know what. Not for the first time she wished she had been granted the gift of reading minds or seeing the future. She could communicate with Jesamiah by thought – he was the only living human this had ever occurred with – and it was often easy to guess intentions by the subtle movements of body language, the way an eye flickered or a muscle twitched. Mereno displayed none of these telltale signs. Like Jesamiah he had taught himself to give nothing away, to not make those indicative changes.

As the daylight strengthened, Charles Mereno spilled out his guilt to Tiola: told her what he had done in the past, how he had drunkenly abandoned Carlos and his bride when they needed him most. "Jesamiah has put me to shame; he did not become sodden with rum and consider only himself. He tried to save an innocent this night. That he failed is not his fault."

Charles chewed his lip for a while, considering what to say next. "Carlos was my dearest friend; I also loved the woman he took as wife. Although it was not me she loved in return, I promised to look after her if ever anything happened to Carlos. It was a promise I did not expect to fulfil for many years. Certainly not on their wedding night. She never spoke again after what they did to her. She barely ate, refused to leave her room. She became a wild thing if ever I tried persuading her, so I soon stopped trying. When the child was born she would have nothing to do with him, and when he was two years old she hanged herself."

He plucked a blade of grass, shredded it. "I had no affection for the boy. I left him in the care of servants and sailed away, returned to piracy. The boy, Phillipe, blamed me for her death."

"But he was a child, how could a two-year-old blame you?"

"No, no, I mean when I eventually returned. He blamed me for everything. And he was right to do so, for it was my fault. It should never have happened." He gazed across the tranquil river at the leaves stirring in the breeze.

"When I returned I brought a new wife and our baby. Jesamiah. I truly thought it would be a new beginning, that the past was ended, that we could start again. I thought the jealousy Phillipe felt for Jesamiah would pass. I should have told Phillipe who his father was and how he came to be born. But I did not. He had no idea why I preferred Jesamiah to him. Is it any wonder there was such hatred?" He plucked another blade of grass, then another.

"You promised to look after his mother, you did what you could. Why did you keep her son? Why did you not place him in an orphanage, or a monastery?"

"You ask me that; you of all people? Would you abandon an innocent child?"

Tiola shook her head. No, she would not.

"I had an obligation to his mother. I could not just send him away. You see, before he was born I had hoped he was Carlos's child, and for her sake I thought it best to maintain that I was the father, that I was her legal husband. She had married Carlos in secret, no one beside me and the men who abused her that night knew the real story. Her servants later discovered that del Gardo, her own brother, had raped her, but they knew nothing of the rest of it. Nothing at all."

There was a long pause. Tiola sat silent; waiting, realising there was more of the confession to come.

"Bad enough," he said, "that her brother defiled her and that the boy could have been born of incest, but I knew from the day he came into the world which one of them had sired him. Phillipe was Edward Teach's son."

Her turn to gasp, then hesitate, consider. "You could not have known that for certain, Charles."

"Oh, I knew it; when I returned with Jesamiah there was no denying it. The resemblance was unmistakeable." He groaned; an agonising sound of despair. "I had my precious baby, Jesamiah, in my arms. I so loved him, that tiny little man. His fingers curled around mine; his beautiful dark eyes so full of trust." Charles's voice choked. "And as I showed him to Phillipe I never thought to hide my pride. I looked into Phillipe's eyes and saw Edward Teach looking back at me. From that day I knew I had to make a choice: destroy Phillipe or shut myself away from my son. I chose the latter. I did not love Phillipe, I despised him. How then could I openly love Jesamiah? For his sake, apart from ensuring they were both fed, clothed and had an education, I turned my back on the both of them."

"You allowed Phillipe to make his life a misery." Tiola's contempt was audible.

Charles shook his head. "Yes, Jesamiah had a tough time, but life is tough. Tougher. And because of Phillipe he has learnt to survive. No amount of love could have taught him that. He learnt how to endure and when something worse occurs, he will know how to endure that as well."

"Worse?" Tiola almost laughed. "Could there be anything worse than those childhood years of pain and torture?"

Charles Mereno got up, walked to the trees where the sunlight was not yet penetrating.

"Oh yes," his voice was receding, growing fainter as the shadowed trees swallowed him, "there is much worse. There is Edward Teach."

Eighteen

Someone kicking his shin woke Jesamiah. He had eventually curled up to sleep on the quarterdeck, out in the open where it was colder and damper but smelt fresher. Irritably, for his head was pounding, he opened one eye. The man standing there blotted out the early morning sun, which was behind him. His face was in blackness, a halo of light around his head. But this was no angel, unless it was the Fallen Angel himself. The Devil.

"I been thinkin'," Blackbeard said.

Good for you, Jesamiah thought.

"A'cause o' thy stupidity we could be 'avin' the whole of Bath Town baying fer us'n blood by tha morrow."

More than likely, Jesamiah also thought.

"I'll o'course tell they it were thee who drowned 'er. They bain't goin' to suspect me, 'er'usband, be they?"

Sighing heavily Jesamiah crawled to his knees then his feet. "No, I suppose not. What do you want me to be doing then? If it involves killing someone, forget it. I make it a rule not to kill people 'til after I've fed me belly." Jesamiah moved around. He did not like squinting into the sun, not being able to see Blackbeard's eyes.

"Killin'? Nay, nay, all I want thee t'do is get this ship underway. I've decided to shift anchorage. We'll drop down to tha Ocracoke." He yawned and stretched, filled his lungs with fresh air then spat over the side. No sign of a body floating there; it was possible the incoming tidal current had already taken it up river. To Bath Town. It could be bobbing, even now, against the uprights of the bridge. Or washed up on Governor Eden's front lawn. Teach thought that was funny and guffawed.

On the other side, this could put an end to the lucrative little business venture he was running. Best be gone, then he could feign surprise and grief, make out she had run away from him. Must have met with ruffians. Curse them. Perhaps it would be a good idea to leave her clothes in a heap somewhere ashore? He knew just the place. "Make way then, Acorne, if'n thee please."

He turned around and stamped off below, leaving Jesamiah disconcerted. The crew consisted of twenty-six men. All of whom were drunk. *Adventure* was a sloop; minimum crew would be five or six hands. Could he rouse those who were sober enough to set sail? He scratched at his beard growth then under his armpit, aware he was beginning to stink as bad as the rest of them. Did he have time to strip off and have a quick swim? It would take the buggers twenty minutes at least to wake up enough to cast off. Probably twice that to find their way to the mooring ropes! And he could always use the excuse he was searching for the corpse.

Swim first, get underway after. He peeled off his clothes, secured a length of cable and tossed one end over the side – in case there was no one to help him aboard again.

The river was cool and refreshing, made him feel clean and cleared his head. He waded among the reeds for a short way, found only a bucket with a hole in it and four dead rats. Of Mary, nothing. Jesamiah was hit by a fresh wave of grief and guilt. He had not meant her to drown; had wanted only to save her further degradation and certain death at Teach's hands. What else could he have done? They were only yards from the shore. Why could she not have splashed her way to safety?

"Halloo! Ahoy!"

Turning quickly, Jesamiah's foot slipped in the silt and he toppled backwards into the water, arms flailing. A jolly boat came alongside, the young man rowing, reaching down to offer a hand.

"I apologise. I did not intend to startle you."

Jesamiah stood up, realised the water only came as high as his knees and waded in deeper. Modesty did not bother him, but it was difficult to shout at someone for being a bloody fool when standing naked in a river displaying tool and tackle. "Who the bugger are you?"

"Jonathan Gabriel. I want to speak to your Captain. I want to become a pirate."

"Do you now?" Jesamiah's answer was gruff. This boy could be no more than eighteen years old. What sort of romantic nonsense had he heard about Teach? How would he feel about joining this crew if he knew what had happened here last night?

"I need the money, Sir," Gabriel said. "So I can get wed."

Swimming towards the ship Jesamiah made no answer. He grasped the trailing rope and hauled himself up to where the ladder cleats started – the lowest four were missing. On deck, he dried himself with his shirt and began to dress. What a surprise, no one else was up and about yet.

Jonathan Gabriel's head appeared above the rail. "Are you the Captain's first officer? Will you take me?"

"No I ain't, and no I won't. Get yourself home."

"I cannot do that. I would seem the fool if I did."

Ah, so there had been some bragging and tomfoolery in Bath Town?

Over-indulgence at Teach's wedding probably. Perhaps it would learn this boy a valuable lesson to sail with them as far as the estuary, then set him ashore with a clip round the ear and a hefty boot to the backside.

"Very well. Know anything about ships?"

"Not a thing, Sir. I am a tailor's son."

Jesamiah strolled towards the quarterdeck, stepping over lengths of discarded cordage, broken cleats, empty bottles and other piles of stuff he had no intention of identifying. And snoring men.

"You'll have to learn bloody quick then, won't you?"

He kicked two men awake, put his hands round his mouth and roared his first order aboard the *Adventure*.

"All hands! Get your shitty, pox-riddled pieces on deck! Now!"

He had to go below, do a good bit of kicking and prodding – and throw a few buckets of cold water around – but after thirty minutes had most of the men assembled. Not one of them was sober. Bleary-eyed, mouths like a parrot's cage, hangovers as heavy as a ton of rock, but on deck.

Nineteen

Several times at breakfast Tiola had glanced sideways at Perdita. She ate virtually nothing and the signs that she had been weeping were clear, even to the blindest fool. Tiola counted Governor Eden as the head of the list in that category. The matter of Perdita's marriage to Tobias Knight had arisen at the wedding. Knight had come right out with it, publicly announcing the forthcoming arrangements. Nobody had thought to ensure that Perdita had been pre-warned of her engagement, she had found out from a delighted family on their return to Archbell Point.

Tiola assumed the tears, the obvious sleepless night, were for the devastation the girl felt, but come mid-morning when everyone was soundly dozing in various chairs or beds after an extensive luncheon, she went in search of the girl. Found her where she guessed she would be, in the lovers' trysting place in the clearing beside the river. Perdita was sitting beside the tumbledown hut, her back against the rotting wood of the wall. It only took Tiola to sit beside her and take her hand for the story to flood out, accompanied by fresh sobs of despair. Perdita was desperate to confide in a friend.

Jonathan had gone. Outraged that another may steal the one he loved, he had left a note to say he had taken ship with a crew and would be back in a month or two with a fortune.

"He has joined Teach," Perdita wailed, the sobs choking her throat. "I know he has. He will be caught and hanged and then what shall I do?"

Comforting her was difficult, for she was probably right. The fool! Oh the silly, stupid fool!

"I was going to speak with you," Tiola said, annoyed with herself that she had not done so before now. This was her fault. Had she spoken, this would not have happened. "When my husband comes for me…"

"Husband?" Perdita whipped her head up. "You said husband?"

Another confession. "*Ais*. I did. Jesamiah had some personal business to attend here. We took the opportunity to marry in secret. And before you say it, we were wed in the way of my belief, beneath the witness of the stars. When he comes to fetch me I intend to ask if he will take you and Jonathan to Williamsburg. I have some money aboard his ship – I would like to purchase a tailor's shop for you both."

Perdita was almost speechless. "You would do that for us?"

Tiola nodded. "No couple who are in love should be parted. All we have to do is persuade your foolish *amour* that life as a pirate is not a good choice." She patted Perdita's hand. "Jesamiah will find him, look after him, I am sure."

Relieved, and with too much on her mind, Perdita asked no awkward questions. She twisted the linen handkerchief between her fingers. "I must marry Jonathan. I cannot wait to become Mr Knight's wife next May." Said in a rush, "My flux has not come."

Ah!

Tiola smiled, said tactfully, "It is only a few days since you lay with Jonathan, my dear."

"I know, I may just be late but I have never been so before. Usually to the hour I start to bleed."

With gentleness Tiola laid her hand above Perdita's womb and searched with her Craft for the energy of life. It was there, minute, very new, barely more than a spark, but there.

Perdita placed her hand over Tiola's. "It is only a matter of days, but I am certain that I am with child. Please do not say that I could not possibly know this, for I do. I carry my beloved Jonathan's son. And I will have this child and wed no one but his father."

From beyond the trees, in the direction of the house, a woman's scream rose hysterically in pitch – Elizabeth-Anne? Tiola jumped to her feet. "Stay here. I will go."

"Do you think it is the babe?" Perdita was also standing, anxious. "Elizabeth-Anne may need us both."

"No!" Tiola said too sharply. She took Perdita's hand, squeezed it. "Please, trust me. Stay here for a few minutes, then follow slowly." She smiled, touched the girl's belly. "Just in case. We want nothing to startle your child."

A cart was drawn up on the gravel drive before the front door. Everyone from the house was gathered around: the women, the servants, even the men were weeping.

Without going near, Tiola knew what burden lay there. Someone had found Mary Ormond's body.

Twenty

With the wind against them and after several hours of laborious tacking, the *Adventure* had sailed less than halfway down the Pamlico River.

Jesamiah had asked, cajoled and ordered Teach's crew into working as a team, but had given up. Trying to explain they would not miss stays so often if they all hauled at the same time and in the same direction was like squeezing blood from a stone. How in the love of God these men had ever managed to capture a Prize, he did not know.

When Teach himself ambled on deck, beard combed and looking as fresh as a daisy sprouted in the middle of a pigsty, Jesamiah hoped the men would rally a little. When they had to tack again and a scuffle broke out for'ard, he realised it to be a forlorn hope.

"Why the Navy is so damned scared of you I cannot imagine," he grumbled after Teach had stared at the flapping sails and tapped the hourglass a few times. No sand trickled from the top to the bottom, for the glass was cracked and damp had got in. The fine-powdered sand was a dark, solid mass wedged into the narrow centre. The thing was useless.

"Thee bain't seen us in action, have thee though?" Teach was now staring at the shore, not particularly interested in what his men were or were not doing.

"I am not certain I wish for that pleasure. Do any of these imbeciles actually know what 'haul' means?"

Edward Teach was not listening. He called for Israel Hands, who came running up from below.

"Cap'n?"

"Did any one of thee stop to think about water?"

Hands scratched at a louse in his hair. "We had full kegs a few days ago."

"A few days? A few days! There bain't be more'n two kegs of green muck down there! We bain't shipped water fer more'n a month!"

Israel Hands shouted back at him, "It ain't my job t'see t'the water! You shot Black Nero, it were 'is job to keep an eye on the bloody stuff!"

"An' it bist thy job to replace him!"

Laconically, Jesamiah folded his arms and leant against the taffrail. "You can either stand there and argue, Teach, or do something about the fact that we will be hitting the bank in less than five minutes."

Looking up sharply, Teach saw Jesamiah was right and issued a string of orders at full voice.

Ten minutes later, Jesamiah had to admit that perhaps this slovenly crew did have something in them after all. One broadside from Teach and they scuttled like beetles from beneath an up-ended rock. Another fifteen minutes; with a minimum of fuss, they were moored and the men were swaying the empty water kegs ashore and heading into the woods in search of a freshwater stream, which Teach said they would find beyond a stand of trees. Israel Hands, Jesamiah noticed, was carrying Mary Ormond's clothing.

Quiet settled on the river when every one of the men had gone ashore. Jesamiah took the opportunity to explore the ship; he had intended to have a thorough inspection, but after twenty minutes came back on deck where Teach was sitting, dozing.

"Finished pokin' and pryin', have thee?"

"I've seen wrecks in better condition than this sloop."

"I had a perfickly good ship 'til thee ran her aground."

"You and your men scuppered the *Queen Anne's Revenge*, not me. From what I've seen of their slovenliness, I'm not surprised you lost her."

"They bain't lubbers, Acorne. Tell 'em as what be needed an' they get on with it. They as don't need wet-nosed nursing. We'll get a better vessel soon as we can, but we bain't keen on thy kind of orders aboard the *Adventure*." He did not add that he hoped, soon, to hold the proud claim of being the new captain of the *Sea Witch*.

Jesamiah nodded. It was so on many a pirate ship where the captain took command only during a Chase. Decisions were made democratically with a vote taken after general discussion; the men working together with the barest of effort, able to sail a ship whether drunk or sober. That was the allure for many of them: the freedom to do as they pleased. Although here, aboard the *Adventure*, it was a false freedom. The men could do what they wanted – as long as Teach approved.

"I keep 'em tha wrong side of sober deliberate," Blackbeard confided, pulling the sea chest he had been sitting on out from the encroaching shade. He removed his coat, sat, tipped his face to the warmth of the sun. "Don't get as much lip that way."

"You mean sober, one or two of them just might find the courage to oppose you."

Teach made no reply.

Jesamiah was inspecting the box where various pennants and colours were kept. Most of them were ragged and stained. He shoved them back, not bothering to fold them neatly. A couple of seams along the decking were splitting open, he noticed. "When did you last have the men holystone this deck?" he asked; then, "And are you aware the rudder chain is loose?"

"Got any more comments?"

"Aye. Not one of those lazy buggers has bothered coiling the anchor cable correctly, the thing's rotten and you've more rats and fleas in your hold than ballast."

"A few rats don't bother me."

"Don't bother me either, but it ain't good t'be havin' so many."

"Leave it, Acorne, or I might decide t'shoot thee now instead o' later."

The men were returning. Making a lot of noise, but without much fuss the filled kegs of water were brought aboard and stowed. Teach stayed where he was, soaking up the late afternoon sunshine, but even though his eyes were apparently closed Jesamiah had the feeling he was watching every movement. A feeling confirmed when one of the last kegs to be swung aboard was dropped. It fell to the deck and split open, water sluicing everywhere.

"Who let this boy aboar'?" Teach questioned as he got up and swaggered down into the waist. He stopped before Jonathan Gabriel and poked his shoulder, "What I be wantin' with a tailor? Eh?"

"I want to become a pirate."

"Then thee'd best learn not t'let go o' tha bloody rope and lose all tha bloody water, eh Archangel?"

"I did not let go. It broke. The thing was rotten. And my name is Jonathan Gabriel."

Watching from the quarterdeck Jesamiah had to admire the lad's audacity.

"Archangel. Show me thy hands."

Again Jesamiah gave the lad his due, he did not hesitate but held out his hands, showing the backs and palms. "I am not afraid of hard work Captain. I can haul a rope along with the rest of them."

Blackbeard nodded and began to walk away, but then Jonathan Gabriel made a fatal error. He pointed to Israel Hands. "Why did that man over there hide Mary Ormond's wedding gown beneath a tree? Will she not be wanting it?" He glanced around, puzzled. Innocent. "Why is she not here? I heard you brought her aboard."

The crew froze, all eyes looking towards Blackbeard walking back towards Jonathan Gabriel, his boots a slow, tread on the deck; *thump, thump, thump.*

"Show us thy hands again, boy."

A cold dread twisted in Jesamiah's stomach, he was on the verge of calling out, but he kept quiet. Him and the boy against this rabble? There was nothing he could do for the lad. Not without getting himself killed.

Without hesitation, without realising the grave danger he was in, Jonathan Gabriel held out his hands.

"I have no trace of shakes or trembling, Sir. A firm grip and agile fingers."

"Thee be tha lad a'courtin' tha Guv'nor's stepdaughter."

It was not a question but Jonathan Gabriel answered as if it were. "I am. I love her, we are to be married."

"Are thee now?" Teach shook his head, his eyes narrowing like a snake's before it strikes. "I think not, Archangel. I don't hold with whores who refuse me my pleasure. An' she 'as a lesson t'learn, that 'un."

Moving fast, faster than anyone would credit a man of his size and bulk, Blackbeard's hand shot out and grasped the boy's right arm, dragged him, spluttering a protest of alarm, to the nearest cannon. With his free hand Teach lifted an axe that had been left on the deck, raised it and brought the blade down twice, severing the hand at the wrist.

Jonathan screamed. Jesamiah too, "*No!*" but Teach was insane and possessed not a half ounce of pity. He neither heard nor cared. Gripping the boy's left arm, ignoring the lad's frantic writhing and desperate kicking he struck off that hand also. Blood from the arteries was fountaining grotesquely over the deck, the cannon, Teach, the men nearby. Jonathan was shrieking, the sound soaring louder in pitch and fear as Teach hefted him over the side. A splash. The noise stopped.

The river turned red as Jonathan Gabriel tried to swim away, his lifeblood pumping from him with every desperate stroke. Stunned, gorge rising into his throat, Jesamiah watched as the tailor's attempts to get away became feebler. He went under and did not come up again. The blood spreading on the surface eased. Stopped.

"Rufus."

"Aye Cap'n?"

"Take them two trophies t' tha great cabin. I've a use fer they."

"Aye Cap'n."

"An' Rufus."

"Cap'n?"

"I has a task for thee, once tha sun sets."

"Aye Cap'n."

The men were silent, not one daring to make comment or show disapproval, for if he did he would be next. Teach was aware of the silence, though, of the hardness in their eyes. It would not take much for them to turn against him. He had to keep them loyal, keep them yoked and there was only the one way to do it.

"Thee did well getting' tha water lads, but who wants t'be drinkin' water eh?" He swaggered to the nearest scuttle hatch and kicked it aside. "Least, not when we have rum in tha hold! Break it out, m'lads! Break out a keg or two!"

There was a cheer, a shout of approval. Two men hurried below, within moments two kegs were on deck, broached, and they were dipping pewter mugs into the liquor within. Toasting Blackbeard for the fine captain he was.

Jesamiah remained at the taffrail and glared with hatred at the man who was making himself comfortable again on his seat in the sunshine. "What kind of monster are you, Teach?"

"The 'I be alive he be dead', kind," Blackbeard answered from beneath his hat. "No one makes a fool o' me Acorne. No one. Remember that."

Twenty One

Sunday 3rd November

"Something unpleasant has happened."

Tiola was becoming used to Charles Mereno appearing from the shadows without warning, but she had been lost in private thought and was short on patience. She did not hide her annoyance at his intrusion.

"What? More unpleasant than a young girl's brutal rape and death? Please Charles, do what you need to do and be gone. I have the living to care for, I can no longer attend the dead. Please go."

Charles Mereno leant one shoulder against a tree trunk, folded his arms, crooked his head to one side. He was a handsome man, even in his older age with the grey hair that had once been a fair-haired red; the wrinkled and rumpled skin. The traces of his son, Jesamiah, were there too, in the shape of his chin, the set of his jaw. The way he stood there, as Jesamiah often stood. The only thing missing was the acorn earring and a flutter of blue ribbons. "You do not mean that."

"I am afraid I do."

He raised his hand, fiddled with his earlobe, exactly as Jesamiah did with his earring.

Despite her impatience, Tiola smiled at the unconscious similarity. She relented, put down the book. It was not engaging and she had not read a single passage for over half an hour. "Very well. What has happened?"

"I am not easy with Jesamiah being aboard that ship."

"Nor am I, but neither you nor I can do anything to alter the situation." She paused, stared at him. "Or can you? Why are you still here, with me? Why are you not doing what you came back to do?"

"Because the time is not right. He is not where he has to be."

Tiola lifted her head slightly, frowned. Again the feeling that had been nagging her raised its awareness. There was something wrong, something Charles had not told her.

"Edward Teach must be destroyed," he said.

"*Ais*. But I cannot do it."

Mereno moved away from the tree, stood beside the bank, his hand resting where, in life, the hilt of his cutlass would have been. He cast no shadow, though the sun was bright. "Teach does not deserve life."

"No, but it is not for me to judge him. And even if it were, I still could not kill him. Only his creator has that right."

The water was rippling, little eddies and flurries stirred by the breeze. It was clear here, Charles could see down to the bottom like peering into an upside down world. The other River, the one he had sat beside for so long, long a time had been dark, as black as night and as cold as the touch of death. He bent down, smoothed his hand through the water, scooping some of it up and watching as it ran through his fingers, the sun turning the cascade into sparkling, vibrant colours. He had noted what she had said.

"Jesamiah will fight Blackbeard, do you know that?"

Tiola bit her lip. *Ais*, she knew that. "As much as I love him," she said with an ache in her throat and her heart, "I am not his keeper. Jesamiah will do what he wants to do. What he has to do." She looked up, her black eyes flashing a defiant challenge. "Do I chain him in a hold? Lock him in a prison? Or do I endure his chosen paths of freedom?"

Charles shrugged, it seemed they all had to endure, one way or another.

"A package has arrived for the girl, for the one they call Perdita," he stated. "You should go to her. Jonathan Gabriel is dead."

He watched Tiola gather her skirts and run, the book forgotten. To the trees, to the river and the dappled sunshine, he said, "Would you set aside your rules and laws, my dear, if you knew that the taking of a life was the only way to end all this? I am dead. I can do only what I have come back to do. Nothing more. When the time is right, when Time itself stops, I must take the life of my son. If I could change the past, if I could do other things to put right these sorrows, do you not think I would? With all my heart, God help me, so I would!"

Approaching the house it was plain there was something amiss. Elizabeth-Anne's distressed sobs could be heard from the open drawing room window. A servant was being violently sick in a flower bed. Eden was striding down the drive, hatless, without the walking cane he usually carried.

Tiola hurried through the front door that had been left flung wide. Nicholas Page was in the hallway, ash pale, his hand over his mouth. At his feet an opened, discarded package. Tangled string, a length of tarred canvas. All of it stained. Brown stained.

He saw Tiola, looked at her helplessly. "We do not understand. Why? Who would send this – this hideousness to Perdita?" Nicholas Page ran a hand over his head, knocking his wig askew. He gestured at the strewn packaging. "I offered to clear this up, but I find I cannot do so. I…I…" He shook his head, covered his mouth with his hand and fled, pushing past Tiola and bolting through the open door. She heard him retching outside.

Tentative, Tiola peeled back one corner of the canvas reluctant to discover what lay within. For all her wisdom, for all her Craft and Knowledge, her capabilities, she gasped and backed away, her hands going to her mouth, the nausea rising from her stomach. She sat down heavily on the first stair, put her head between her knees while the sickness swept through her and the world reeled in a cry of revulsion.

I would rather be condemned to Hell for murdering that bastard than live, knowing had I shot him, someone else would remain inviolate. Alive.

Perdita's words reverberated inside her skull. Tiola closed her eyes as she fought down the churn in her stomach. But even with her eyes closed she could see what was in the package. Could see what Perdita had found upon opening it.

Hands. Two male hands severed at the wrist. Distinctly recognisable from the tailor's calluses on the fingers.

Twenty Two

Friday 8th November

The Ocracoke. Bordering the entrance to Pamlico Sound; the waters here were suitable only for ships with a shallow draft. The channels were narrow and likely to change. It was a notorious graveyard for shipping and an ideal place for pirates.

Ocracoke Island was an expanse of marsh, sixteen miles long and not very wide, with a few wind-twisted trees, heaped sand dunes and not much else. Except for the bones of men and ships. Two vessels lay at anchor, riding low as the evening tide ebbed outward. Teach's sloop *Adventure*, and a twelve gun brigantine.

Not a soul was aboard either one, the crews were ashore enjoying themselves. Fires fuelled by gathered driftwood burned brightly, dotted here and there along the spit of land that many claimed God had forgotten existed. The smell of roasting fish and pelican wafted with the wind. At one fire a group of men were singing raucously; at another, a squabble over the last portion of meat. Where the clumps of scrubby marsh grass gave way to a stand of wind-tortured oaks, some men were fornicating with the few whores who had been aboard the brigantine, brought here especially as part of the entertainment. Not far away, more than a handful of men were raucously sodomising each other.

The Ocracoke marshes were open, and bleak. Even with a gregarious rabble of pirates deep into their drunken celebration of carousal, the place was dismal. The group of men around Edward Teach's fire had finished their meal and were talking while passing the rum around. Bones sucked dry of the marrow lay everywhere, tossed into the sand. The fire was the largest, built carefully in the lee of a series of dunes that gave some shelter from the intrusive wind. The flames rose and fell, flickering blues, yellows and greens as the salt in the wood caught and burnt.

Beside Teach sat the only man he had ever respected; Charles Vane. Vane had a price on his head at a value similar to Blackbeard's for he was wanted personally by Governor Rogers of Nassau. He had thumbed his nose at Rogers in the summer when the Governor had first arrived from

England to take up his position of authority. Amnesty had been offered but Vane refused the prospect and destroyed a naval ship as he fled the harbour. There had not been much support for him from the pirate community who had been pleased to see the back of him. He was a cruel, vindictive man who cheated his crew of prize money. Those who went against him he delighted in punishing by the barbarity of keelhauling. He and Blackbeard were a matched pair.

Beyond an initial scowl, Vane had ignored Jesamiah since stepping ashore several hours ago. Ignored also his own quartermaster, seated next to Jesamiah and sharing a bottle of rum. John Rackham, known as Calico Jack, the fancy dandy of the pirate brethren. Rackham also detested Vane.

"You want to sail with me, Jack?" Jesamiah asked, returning the bottle back to him. "I can offer you a better life than the one you have with Vane."

"Will you make me a captain?"

"No. *Sea Witch* – when I get her back – is mine."

"Then I thank you for the offer, but I have an idea to get my own vessel and my own captaincy."

"Jack, that will lead only to the noose. Take amnesty and life. A long, quiet life."

Jack Rackham drank a few gulps, handed the rum back. "So why are you here, eh? Amnesty means a long quiet life of tedious boredom. Nay, give me the short but merry one, Jesamiah." Jack winked and nudged him with his elbow. "The ladies prefer a pirate in their bed, you know. They enjoy the added excitement."

Jesamiah's thoughts did not exactly tally with Rackham's theory. He did not need the added excitement of saying he was a pirate to pleasure a woman. Aside, so far, since signing Governor Roger's book of amnesty he had been flogged, threatened with torture, sent spying in Hispaniola, and was now charged with spying on Blackbeard. Amnesty? It was not proving restful or pleasurable, and was certainly not tedious or boring! He drank, swallowed; said grimly, "Aye, I've heard that a man as he swings on the noose and evacuates his bowels and piece can be pretty excitin' for those watching."

"You're turning into an old maid, Jesamiah Acorne."

Jesamiah grinned. "Nay, just a married one."

Rackham raised his eyebrows in surprise. That Acorne had a wife was news to him, though there had been rumour of him being with a handsome black-haired lass. "Wife?" he asked. "When did this happen?"

"Not long ago. Before I got myself too deeply into this damned mess." Jesamiah tossed more wood on to the fire, eyed Teach and Vane roaring at some jest one of them had made. "I tell you Jack, this ain't no life. Not once you find a good woman to love and to keep you warm at night."

Rackham shook his head in disbelief and upended the bottle, disappointed to find it empty. "I like bedding the lasses too much to have just the one. A wife ain't for me."

For answer, Jesamiah just smiled. He liked Jack Rackham, an honest man – as far as a pirate could be honest. They had shared a few adventures in the past, and a few bottles – and more than a few women.

Getting to his feet, Rackham went to relieve himself, returned with another two bottles, one each.

"I thought Stede Bonnet was to have come?" he said to Israel Hands, seated on his other side. "Why is he not here I wonder?"

Overhearing, Vane growled contempt. "You're soft you are, Rackham. As soft as a spent prick. It don't matter about Bonnet. If he ain't interested in joining us then he can go kiss his arse and be damned. I never trusted the drunken sot anyway."

"Thee's never trusted anyone," Teach observed dryly, "not even thy own quartermaster over yonder." He pointed at Rackham.

"That's because he's a traitorous little runt."

Rackham was on his feet, pistol in hand waving it unsteadily. "You take that back, Vane, you turd! It ain't my fault the men want me as captain instead of you! You've been bloody useless these past months. I'd make a better job of it than ever you will." Worse the wear for drink he waved the pistol again.

"Gentlemen, gentlemen!" Jesamiah stood and with a placating smile removed the weapon from Rackham's hand before he shot himself, or someone else, in the foot. "We are here to discuss business, not kill each other." He was also concerned that Stede Bonnet had not arrived, but was glad of it. Another vicious brute he would rather not renew acquaintance with. "We all know Bonnet is not especially good at navigation. I expect he's got lost further down the coast." Jesamiah did not add that for the same reason he was surprised Vane had got here. But then, Vane relied on Jack Rackham to navigate.

"We as don't need Bonnet," Blackbeard announced, "Us'n can doos what I have in min' without him."

Rackham sat down again, Jesamiah also. This was it then, the Grand Plan. The reason they were all gathered here.

"I have a plan," Vane announced, cutting in. "We need to unite, work in consort."

Teach growled, did not look too pleased at being verbally pushed aside, but like it or not, Vane was the most prominent pirate in the Spanish Main. He had a good ship, an adequate crew. Teach's glory had peaked at his successful siege of Charleston back in the spring. And then he had lost his ship. The *Queen Anne's Revenge* had been his great pride, he had done very little of note since losing her. What could he do with a sloop that was falling to bits?

Vane announced his proposal. "I intend to reinstate Nassau as a place fit for pirates. Show this Governor Rogers he's bitten off more'n he can chew."

Jesamiah roared with laughter. Perhaps not the best reaction; Vane was not amused.

"You think I am jesting, Acorne? You see something funny?"

Sobering, Jesamiah attempted to collect himself. He had been alarmed when first learning of a meeting of pirates here on the Ocracoke – Teach had obviously had this planned for some while, and it was exactly the sort of thing Spotswood needed to know about. It occurred to him, sitting here trying not to laugh any louder than he already was, that perhaps Virginia's Governor had already got wind of this grand parley? If he had, that would explain his anxiety and the need to employ a reliable spy. Were these men sitting here not such greed-bound, drunken fools, both Spotswood and Rogers would have had justifiable cause for concern.

He said, quelling his merriment, "It would have been a good plan, Vane, if you had not flapped your tongue."

"Don't know what you are talking about," Vane countered.

"Don't you? You mean you have completely forgotten that you personally sent a message to Rogers telling him of your intention? That you and Teach here and one other pirate – I assume you meant Bonnet – were going to kick his arse? Told him to prepare for war?"

Silence.

"Well?" Teach asked, glowering at Vane. "Did thee blab?"

Vane got to his feet, started waving his arms about. "I might have done. I might have let a few things slip. What of it? I have got Rogers worried. He is no match for us. We sail in there, claim Nassau harbour as ours."

Jesamiah crowed again. "Oh aye, you got him worried! So worried he sent for Navy reinforcements and has ensured every cannon on the fortress walls is in prime working order. You expect to attack an armed fortress with one brigantine and a leaking sloop? Rogers has Nassau battened down as if there's a hurricane coming!"

"Aside," Blackbeard interrupted, "I bain't interested in Nassau. I hunts these waters. I has deals made, and tha whole o' tha Ocracoke and Pamlico Sound here as mine. No skulking Navy frigate be goin' t'get me here."

Jesamiah chewed his lip. He was right there. If Spotswood wanted to attack Teach he would have to be drawn out from these shallows into open water.

"I propose," Blackbeard spoke deliberately slowly, his cold gaze going from one man to the next. "I propose we blockade Hampton Roads. Get Spotswood t'capitulate t'us. We cut off his shipping supply – his precious town'll be dead within tha month."

Yet again Jesamiah guffawed with laughter. "You are both barking mad! Your sloop will probably disintegrate in the next gale to hit her, and the Chesapeake is not exactly Charleston Harbour, is it? You did a good job there with a blockade, I'll grant you – but Spotswood is no blustering housemartin. And he happens to have two well-armed fully crewed Navy frigates at his disposal. How are you going to fight them with your handful of men?"

"I have seventy in my crew when they are all mustered!" Blackbeard roared back. "Good men."

"Rubbish. You are left with twenty-bloody-six and six cannon. Against frigates? Against an army commander who distinguished himself at Marlborough?"

"The rest o'me men are at Bath Town. They'll join us when I sends fer 'em. We canst do it, Acorne. Despite your scorn, *Adventure* be a fast lit'le whore. Vane has tha most vicious crew on all tha seas, and Bonnet has brawn if no much brain. We wait, we pick off them frigates one at a time then sweep in. It'll work, I'm tellin' thee. It will work."

"But Bonnet is not here is he? And we'll need quality vessels for what you have in mind."

"Then quality sloops we will has." Teach nodded once, curt, and poked a finger in the air towards Jesamiah. "Thee will get 'em fer us."

"And just how am I going to do that?"

Teach leered, his version of an amused grin. "If thee be wantin' to stay alive, Acorne, thee'll think o'summat. All I want is'n excuse t'kill thee, an' I be right eager fer thee t'oblige me."

Jesamiah made a pretence at scowling and huffed, puffed and tutted for the next half hour. Inside he was chuckling with delight. Teach had no intention of attempting to do away with him while there was a possibility of getting his hands on *Sea Witch*. And going off to fetch two seaworthy sloops was just the excuse he needed to be gone from here without rousing suspicion. It could not have worked out better if he had planned it himself!

Twenty Three

Saturday 9th November

For Perdita Galland, the atmosphere at Archbell Point was desolate. The sun shone but its brightness was an intrusion. Sunshine was for happy days, not for the ending of a young girl's world.

Fishermen had found a body floating in the Pamlico River. A male with hands severed at the wrists. He had been identified as Jonathan Gabriel, although the corpse was bloated and fish had eaten at his face.

On that same day Governor Eden had discovered Perdita's affection for the boy and had beaten the truth out of her. Abruptly, his repugnance at the boy's murder had altered to outrage at his stepdaughter's disgrace. Locked in her room, the punishment of confinement had not bothered her. She welcomed solitude where she could sob in abject misery and her heart could break in desolate privacy.

Elizabeth-Anne had been weeping for almost the entire week, her woe increasing when she became certain that the distress would harm her baby. Tiola had reassured her the child remained healthy, and there was no sign of imminent labour. The reassurance did not stop the tears.

The shouting had been renewed this morning. Governor Eden had sent for his stepdaughter and given her a sharp interview. Her marriage to Knight was to take place within the week. On her knees, Perdita had begged and pleaded, but his mind was set and the dowry was agreed. She would be wed before any possible sign of a child should show. Knight would know nothing of her whoring. Nothing at all. She would forget Jonathan Gabriel, never think of him again.

Tiola was at a loss for what to do. She so wanted Jesamiah to come and take her away from here – so wanted this child to be born so that she could leave. But the babe had not dropped; it would probably be at least another week yet. No one was in any doubt that Jonathan's death had been at the hands of Blackbeard. There was no certainty for the reason, but it was assumed the boy had known something of Mary Ormond's drowning. The speculation was that he had gone to confront Teach. None but the Eden household knew the full truth.

Sitting on the porch, idly rocking in a chair, Tiola was deep in thought. Should she interfere and take Perdita's pain away? She could do so but all the girl had left were her memories, what right had Tiola to remove them, no matter how deep the present pain? She looked up as a shadow fell across her: Perdita, pale, thin, haggard and so, so sad.

"You should have let me kill him when I had the chance," she said, her voice so low it was difficult to hear.

Tiola rose, went to take her friend's hands but Perdita stepped aside. "I wish to walk by the river. Forgive me, Tiola, but I want to be on my own."

"Of course, but Perdita, I am so sorry. I cannot say how sorry I am."

"Then say nothing. Sorry is such a short word and its necessity will soon no longer be needed." Holding the wooden banister rail Perdita went down the three steps and on to the lawn. She smiled briefly up at Tiola. "It was not your fault. The blame is with Teach. I hope someday someone puts a bullet through his black heart." She scuffed a tear aside. "I want to be beside the river, where I shared happiness and love with Jonathan. It is the one place where I can always be with him, and no one can take him from me."

Tiola watched her go, the girl's head bowed, the sun lighting her hair, dancing a shadow at her feet.

What good have I done here? Tiola thought. *Evil broods in this place and it will not be cleansed until Teach is dead.*

Twenty-Four

"Ahoy! Ahoy there *Adventure*!"

Jesamiah peered groggily over the rail into the brightness of the midday sun. A brig was hove too, carrying a decent amount of cargo by the look of her.

He had opted to sleep aboard the sloop for there were fewer flies and it was far away from Vane. He did not trust that man any more than he trusted Teach. Either one of them could have slid a knife between his ribs while he slept. For all that he liked Jack Rackham, Jesamiah did not trust him either. He was prone to getting wild ideas that he never thought through until the consequences were too late to do aught about.

He yawned, scratched at his backside, peered again over the side as the shout came again.

"*Adventure*! Ahoy!"

"What do you want?" he called grumpily. No one ashore appeared to be awake, even though the sun was at its zenith. Huh, hardly surprising, the drinking and carousing had gone on until almost dawn. He doubted any one of them would regain their senses for several days yet. "What is it?" he repeated. "If you want Teach he's over there." He jerked his thumb over his shoulder. "I'm the only one aboard."

"Well I ain't coming no closer – it's a deep enough channel here, I ain't risking running aground."

Jesamiah raised his hand, a partial wave, partial salute. "Fine. Do what you want, mate."

"I have news."

Rubbing his forehead – he had a pounding headache, he had, after all, partaken of his own share of the rum – Jesamiah hauled himself to his feet and propping his arms on the rail, made a flimsy attempt at appearing interested in the occupants of the brig bobbing on the tide thirty yards away.

"I'm Sam Odell, Teach knows me. Just come up from Charleston."

"Oh aye?"

"Four armed sloops under the command of Charleston's Governor

Johnson attacked Worley, killed him and twenty-five of his crew."

"Worley? He was new to piracy, weren't he? Prowled the Florida coast?"

"Aye. Johnson tried and hanged 'em all there and then on the spot."

Jesamiah shrugged. He did not know Worley and it was the risk they all took when they signed to go on the account.

"There's more," Odell called across the sparkling blue of the flooding tide between them. "Stede Bonnet has also been caught."

That got Jesamiah's attention. "You're jesting!"

"As sure as I'm standing here it is the truth. Four days ago. He put up a pretty pleading – said his men were responsible for any attacks, not him. He's a cowardly scammer-bag that one." Odell spat over the side. "Good riddance to him I say. He claims he always shut himself in his cabin and would have nothing to do with no acts of piracy! Not a soul believed a word of it. He is to hang. God rot him I say. Tell Teach. Once Bonnet's despatched I reckon they'll be after him as well."

Jesamiah watched Odell's handful of crew competently negotiate the brig towards the Pamlico River, going to Bath Town, probably. Where Tiola was. God, but this was ridiculous, he had to do something to stop all this nonsense. Give Spotswood what he wanted – the opportunity to finish Blackbeard off. This idiotic plan to blockade Hampton Roads was ideal. If Teach even attempted to enter the Chesapeake those Navy frigates would have him – perhaps it was best to encourage the proposal, and make out that he was going to fetch those sloops?

Stede Bonnet captured and to hang? Well, well. Serve the bugger right. Jesamiah had never liked him.

Twenty-Five

Tiola waited on the porch for most of the afternoon, only going indoors to attend Elizabeth-Anne, see she was comfortable and offer her a herbal tea to help her rest. As the sun began to set, the concern that had been gnawing at her increased. Finally, the unease growing to fever pitch, she fetched her cloak and followed the route Perdita had taken across the lawns and along the foot-worn path that threaded through the bushes and shrubs.

At the river Tiola paused. Did she have any right to intrude? The girl was entitled to her grief, but she was also entitled to the comfort of a friend. Setting off up the path, Tiola guessed Perdita would have gone to that tumbledown shack in the clearing. The poor girl had probably sat there in the sun and cried herself to sleep, not noticed the fading day. Probably did not care.

The woods were quiet. There was no wind. No leaf rustled, no bird sang or called. Utter silence, as if Nature were holding her breath.

She found the glade, found Perdita's cloak on the grass at its edge, crumpled as if she had lain there a while. The door to the little hut was closed. Deep evening shadows were already darkening the trees; half the glade was almost invisible now the sun had gone. But Tiola could see. In even the blackest night her Craft gave her vision that was as clear as day. She stood there, clutching Perdita's cloak to her breast, the tears of despair trickling down her face. She should have realised what the broken-hearted girl had meant when she had said she was going to be with Jonathan.

With love, compassion and the sadness of bereft regret, Tiola climbed the lower part of the tree as Perdita had done, reached out and cut the rope that made the noose around her neck.

It was no good trying to revive her. Perdita had hanged herself hours ago.

Twenty Six

Sunday 10th November

Hell, Teach maintained, was nothing to fear. It was Heaven, he claimed, that scared the shite out of him. All that praying and confessing. All those do-gooders and holy singing angels.

"Give me tha Devil," he roared as he stood on the beach on Sunday morning, "give me tha lust and tha greed o' tha Devil!"

Vane had started the tirade. News of Stede Bonnet had unsettled them all, several of the men wanted to take a vote to leave, to sail across to Africa, lie low for a while.

"None of us fancy going to Hell, Teach!" Vane had cried. "Not even you, were you to admit the truth."

"I bain't afeared of nothin'. 'Specially not Hell. It be a fine place for men who call themselves men." That said, Teach had promptly set about proving it.

Common practice to clean a ship's hold of rats and fleas by lighting pots of tar and brimstone and leaving the noxious sulphurous vapour to fumigate the closed space. Not common practice for men to sit there amidst the suffocating stink and smoke, but that was what Teach insisted on. To show them what Hell was like and that he, Edward Teach, Blackbeard, the Devil's own, could tolerate the foul conditions better than they could. And when Teach got an idea into his head, no matter how ludicrous, his men did as he bade them. Or died.

Blackbeard sat there on a barrel at the head of the circle, like a king on his throne, his pistol – primed and cocked – was set across his lap, his threat taken seriously that the first one to run would be shot. One by one the pots were lit, began to burn giving off a red smoke.

Jesamiah frowned. Sulphur did not usually burn that colour, Teach must have added something else to the pots.

It was not too bad for those first few minutes; the smell was most unpleasant, but used to the acridness of gunpowder, to which sulphur was added, it was bearable. There was one lantern set on a keg in the centre of the circle, its flame a patch of yellow, but all else in the darkened hold was obscured as the red smoke began to turn into a heavy, noxious fug, burning like all the fires of hell. Jesamiah grimaced as the smell became gut-wrenchingly putrid. It was like having a length of burning match stuffed up his nose.

Seated a little to Blackbeard's left he could hear rats squeaking and scratching, desperate to get out. They would not have much luck. There were no holes in the hull and the scuttle hatch was shut tight. They were all to suffocate down here, rats and men. Loosening his shirt, Jesamiah pulled the collar up across his mouth and nose, held it there with his hand. It helped his breathing a little but did nothing to stem the watering of his eyes. Several of the men had taken the faded bandannas from their heads and had tied them across their faces. Teach was just sitting there, arms folded. Was he human? Surely he could not be?

Shutting his streaming, stinging eyes Jesamiah tried to concentrate on something else, something pleasant. Tiola. He was beginning to think he was never going to see her again. And he had not even enjoyed his marital rights! What was she doing now? Was there any sign of this wretched babe emerging into the world?

They had managed a few shared words over the last days. Sad, grief-stricken words mostly. Poor Mary, Jonathan, Perdita. It was all tears and death and dying. Curse Edward bloody Teach! Jesamiah wanted to be with his wife, to make love to her; did not want this constant killing.

Several of the men were coughing. Jack Rackham was muttering a prayer and whimpering. He was a good sailor and a fancy dresser, with his love of finery and the calico cloth, but he was not the bravest of men. Vane was swearing under his breath between gasped splutters.

Gibbens started up to his feet, but the click of Teach's pistol made him sit again, his body bending over in great coughs.

"This is ridiculous, Teach! You'll damn kill us all quicker than any bloody Navy battle! You enjoy your creation of hell if you wish. I have had enough of it."

Israel Hands. He had been with Teach from the first. From the days several years back when they had jumped ship from the Navy and started a more profitable life of piracy under the command of Benjamin Hornigold. Hornigold had taken amnesty, was one of Governor Roger's advisers along with Henry Jennings now. Perhaps they had been right to see sense? Israel Hands had been the only one to remain as Teach's true friend, no matter what he did. But this was going too far. They were all going to die down here in this dreadful stink of brimstone. Someone had to make a break for it and Teach would shoot any one of his crew without a second thought. But Hands? Would he shoot his friend?

"Thee leave here, Israel, an' I mean my word. I'll shoot thee."

His eyes running with tears, breath choking in his suffocating lungs, Israel shook his head, "Then shoot me Teach. I don't particularly care anymore." He went up the ladder and began pushing the hatch cover aside.

With utter calmness, with no apparent reaction to the stench or smoke, with no qualm of conscience or remorse for the ending of a friendship, Teach levelled his weapon and fired. The bullet slammed into Isiah's knee, shattering the kneecap. He shrieked – and every man leapt to his feet and bolted for the hatch, the first ones there scooping Hands up and carrying him out to the fresh, clean air. Jesamiah and Charles Vane among them.

"The man's insane!" Vane spluttered through gasps for breath, his mouth opening and closing as if he were a fish. "Utterly stark, staring mad! If he thinks I am going to sail with him he has another think coming! Bugger knows what he will dream up next!"

He never even looked at Israel Hands who lay groaning on the deck losing blood and consciousness. Instead, Vane was gesturing wildly for his men to start climbing down into the longboat. "Are you coming, Rackham? I am leaving. Teach can keep his hell to himself."

Jack Rackham, Calico Jack, hesitated.

"You are welcome to stay with me," Jesamiah said as he used his knife to rip a Spanish flag into strips to bind around Isiah's shattered knee. "I'll be leaving here soon too. Come with me?" Rackham was a little naïve, perhaps, a little too much in love with the simple life, but a good fellow. Fun.

Vane was in the boat, ready to give order to push off. The tide was on the flood; if they hurried they could set sail and negotiate the shifting channels and hidden sandbars without too much fuss. "You coming, Rackham?"

Apologetically, and with a grin that made him look more like a naughty boy than a fearsome pirate, Rackham spread one hand. "I'll not get my own ship with you, Jes. I'm sorry. And anyway, you have your wife. You'll not be wanting a whoremonger like me around her, will you?"

That was true. Jack Rackham could coax a woman into his bed faster than an anchor dropped. "You take care then, Calico Jack." Jesamiah shook hands with his friend then turned his attention to saving Israel Hands' leg. He doubted he would be successful.

Except for the rats Edward Teach sat alone in the hold. The air had started to clear once the hatch had been opened, but there was still enough smoke and foulness to create the hellish fire and brimstone illusion he had intended.

"Thee bist all cowards!" he bellowed. "Lily-livered dregs! Not one o' thee be fit t'sail with me! I be Blackbeard tha Devil's own! Tha most notorious pirate on tha Spanish Main!"

"Except you are not, are you, Edward? Vane is more notorious than you. Few of your men are prepared to stay loyal, and your ship is a leaking hulk. You are finished, Edward. Finished."

There was another in the hold. A figure sitting where Acorne had sat. Their appearance was alike, same facial expression; same build. For a moment Teach thought it was Acorne, damn him. He should have shot him long before now, but then, he did dearly want the *Sea Witch* for his own, and as much as it galled him to admit it, he was not going to get her without Acorne's initial aid.

The man sitting there was not Acorne. It was his father. Charles St Croix Mereno.

Blackbeard chortled. "So, this be where thee ended up? In tha pits of Hell!"

"No Edward, I am not yet there. You are invited there ahead of me. The arrangements are made."

"I'ave a pact with tha Devil. I bain't goin' t' die."

"I am sorry to disappoint you, Edward. You have been misinformed."

Teach swore, slapped his thighs, started coughing, his face turning puce as he struggled for breath. He was choking but he made himself turn his back on the phantom, walk triumphant, with dignity, up the ladder. Only in the privacy of his great cabin did he throw open the stern window and take in great gulps of air. He refused to notice that his hands were shaking.

Twenty Seven

Monday 11th November

"I take it this daft idea to attack Nassau has been abandoned?" Jesamiah asked as he ate breakfast. Technically it was luncheon as it was well past noon, but no one had been awake before midday to cook or eat. Except for Jesamiah himself. He had been up and about since before dawn.

Teach only grunted an answer as he chewed, not about to admit that his lungs felt as if they had been set on fire.

"And Hampton Roads? Are we still to blockade there?"

Again a grunt. When he did finally speak, Teach's voice sounded as though it had been rubbed with gravel. "What have thee done with Hands? Buried him?"

Jesamiah finished his coffee, wiped crabmeat from his moustache. He was becoming a little bored with crab, fish, and pelican. A fine piece of beefsteak would go down well. Or roasted lamb with potatoes. Or pork with crisp crackling. Finch was a curmudgeonly old basket, but he could cook, and Jesamiah was missing his steward. And his crew. And his ship. And his wife.

He nodded towards a stand of trees. "Yesterday evening I ordered Gibbens and Caesar to hold him down while I sawed his leg off. It was not a job I enjoyed, especially as your surgical equipment is blunt and rusty. I stayed with him all night. By some miracle he is still alive. I suggest you send him to Bath Town. He can receive proper medical attention there. Or a decent Christian burial."

Another non-committal grunt.

"If he survives, Hands will turn evidence against you, you know that, don't you, Teach?"

Blackbeard sniffed, tossed his picked-clean meat bones to the fire. He would have to send the men to look for more wood soon. "Nay, 'e won't. Even if 'n he do, they as 'ave t'catch me first."

Leaning forward, Jesamiah rested his elbows on his knees and linked his fingers, rubbed his thumb over where the T of Tiola's name was starting to show through the tar – how he missed her. Had enough of being without her. "So what are we going to do? Sit here and wait for our beards to turn grey?" When he received no response, continued; "The *Adventure* is past her prime. What if I could get us two decent sloops? We could cruise across to the African coast. Commandeer a new flagship for you. Something even better than your *Queen Anne's Revenge*? There's plenty of slavers just right for the picking over there."

Teach croaked contempt. "As I recall, thee were none too 'appy when I suggested getting us as such afore."

Jesamiah scratched at his beard growth. "Well, I've been thinking on it since then. As it happens I know where a sloop is moored. Rightfully, she's mine. All I have to do, in theory, is walk in and claim her. Complete with crew. For the second, well, I think I can find something suitable at Hampton Roads."

Teach snorted through his nose, not wanting to admit that Jesamiah had the upper hand. He was annoyed with Vane; the unreliable sot had let him down. Together they would have been invincible. He had no intention of forming a lasting partnership with Acorne, he was too squeamish and anyway, Teach did not like him. Not that he liked Vane, but at least Vane did not pull disapproving faces when someone got shot. Nor did he trust Acorne. Not an inch.

Jesamiah linked his hands behind his head, stretched, feeling the pleasure of easing stiff muscles. His shoulder barely hurt now. He certainly seemed to heal fast these days – did Tiola have something to do with it? Probably. He was tired, it had been a long night nursing Hands. He doubted the man would be alive by the time a pilot took him up to Bath Town. He hated amputating limbs. One of the worst tasks a captain had to do if there was no surgeon aboard. There again, maybe Hands had no wish to live, with only one leg what was there for him? Another reason why Jesamiah had not slept, he had spent a good part of the night wondering what he would do if he lost a limb. Maudlin thoughts that befitted this bleak place that was the Ocracoke. He had to get away from here! "I had a vague idea about retrieving my sloop when I discovered *Sea Witch* had gone. I intend to go after her, and I have a suspicion they may've taken her across to Africa. No one steals my ship and gets away with it. But I can't get her back on me own, savvy?"

Teach rubbed at his chin, thoughtfully.

"I intend t'shoot thee when I be ready to, Acorne."

Leaning back on one elbow, Jesamiah stretched his legs out on the warm sand, batted a fly away from his eyes. He tipped his hat over his face, lay down, his hands clasped over his chest. He needed to sleep. "Not if I shoot you first, but I'll not be doing that 'til you've helped me get my ship back."

"If I send thee off t'get these sloops, how canst I trust thee t'come back?"

From beneath his hat, Jesamiah said, "Oh I will be back. Cross m'heart an' spit in yer eye, I promise you, I will be back." He sounded convincing, but then, Jesamiah's easy-come lies always did.

Twenty Eight

From the seclusion of the trees Charles watched Jesamiah climb into the gig, the men of Blackbeard's crew chosen to take him and the unconscious Israel Hands to shore near Pilot Point were sullen and resentful. Their mood would change if Jesamiah treated them to a drink in the tavern there. Whether they would return to Teach was another matter.

Charles was pleased Jesamiah had gone, for this was the place where land became sea and sea became land. The Ocracoke. It was here that he should have found the peace he craved by fulfilling his appointed duty.

Twice he had drawn his pistol, had aimed. Twice he had not found the courage and had uncocked the hammer. Yet again he had failed.

Is this my hell? *he wondered.* Forever condemned to fail in my duty? To not have the guts to pull a trigger?

Twenty Nine

Wednesday 13th November – Virginia

"No. I am sorry, Alicia. The last tobacco crop was not sold, consequently there is not much money, and no one will take that tobacco as barter. It is not acceptable quality. I do not even know if I will be able to purchase what we need for next year's crop." Samuel Trent appeared stressed and harassed. He had known la Sorenta was in a run-down state, but had not realised until he had studied the ledger books quite how bad it was. Phillipe Mereno had barely done a thing since old Halyard Calpin had died. The manager he had put in Calpin's place had been next to useless. It was not surprising all the money had gone; Mereno had been living on the accrued capital from the sale of his wife's Bahamas sugar plantation and had set nothing aside for the running of his own. La Sorenta was close to bankruptcy and here was Alicia demanding three hundred pounds to spend on a new wardrobe for the approaching Christmas season of balls and celebrations!

"No," he repeated, "I cannot give you what is not there to give." Alicia stood inside the office utterly stunned. It had been Charles Mereno's office, then Phillipe's, although he had rarely used it; and now Trent had marched in as bold as you please to claim it. For a full two minutes she said not a word, and then erupted into a demon fury. She swept the ledger books from the shelf above the desk, tipped papers to the floor and stamped on them. Was about to tear a chart from the wall when Samuel launched to his feet and stopped her. It had taken him three days to fashion that estate plan, he was not about to see it ripped up.

His action infuriated Alicia even more. "Let go of me! How dare you? You have no right to be here, no right to tell me what I can or cannot do. You have no right to anything. No right!"

He released her arms, stepped away. "I have every right, Mrs Mereno. Jesamiah…"

She stamped her foot and screamed. "Jesamiah? Jesamiah! I hate Jesamiah, I loathe him! This is all his fault. Everything is his fault."

Samuel Trent was a placid young man who had no experience of women. Rather than keeping quiet and letting her rant, he attempted to point out the truth, that it was her husband who had been at fault. He was assaulted by another ear-piercing scream.

"If you do not like the way I am trying to save this plantation from ruin, lady," he finally yelled back, "I am not forcing you to stay. No one, least of all myself, would wish to keep you here against your will. Take your personal possessions and go." He surprised himself at his forthrightness, was almost on the verge of apologising when Alicia cut in.

"Very well. I have no intention of remaining where I am not welcome. I will leave in the morning." With a swirl of petticoats she left the room. Samuel sighed, started picking up one or two papers, dropped them again and conscientiously went after her.

"Mrs Mereno, Alicia, I can probably give you enough tobacco worth about fifty pounds sterling." To him it seemed a lot of money: a naval sea captain's annual pay.

She swung around and threw the first thing to hand at him. A flower vase. He ducked and it smashed against the wall behind him.

"I could not even buy an undergarment for fifty pounds!" She exaggerated of course, but in a temper she was not prepared to be reasonable. She stalked away, leaving Samuel bewildered. He did not understand women at all.

She spent the evening fitting as many clothes as she could into trunks, securing her jewellery into a casket and ensuring the entire seventy-two piece silver dinner service was packed carefully into layers of straw in wooden crates. There was nothing Samuel could do to dissuade her. Nor could he, the next morning, do much to stop her loading her baggage on to the estate's sloop, the *Jane*, especially when she stated she was only borrowing it.

"But where will you go? Alicia please; be reasonable. What will I tell Jesamiah when he returns?"

Her answer shocked Samuel, but made the crew of the *Sea Witch*, most of them lounging beside the river fishing, a few aboard completing the routine daily tasks, laugh out loud. Samuel had heard Jesamiah use the word, a particularly descriptive blasphemy, but had been totally unaware that a woman would know it, let alone utter it. Nor did he believe Rue when told it was Alicia who had taught it to Jesamiah in the first place.

Standing on the jetty, Samuel watched the current of the Rappahannock take the *Jane* and Alicia away. He felt a sense of failure; perhaps he was not as good at running an estate as he had thought? He had certainly handled that contretemps badly.

"I am going to Williamsburg," Alicia had announced yesterday, "to open a brothel."

Yesterday, Samuel had not believed her. Today, watching her sail away, he was not so sure. "I did not do very well there, did I, Rue?" he confessed. "But there appears to be no money to spend on non-essential things like dresses, ribbons, lace and finery."

Rue chortled and slapped Samuel's shoulder. "One thing you must learn about women, *mon ami*, there must always be money to spend on the essentials such as dresses, ribbons, lace and finery! To keep a woman 'appy it is the luxuries of life you cut down on – *le petit* things, like food and bills!"

Mr Janson eventually came up with a logical suggestion.

"Why not see that lawyer fellow in Williamsburg? Mebbe he knows where there's some more money? Someone's 'as t'see 'im at some time anyways t'sort out the legal muddle 'bout this place, don't they? No reason why you can't be makin' a start, is there?"

It was a good suggestion, but Alicia had taken the estate's only sloop and Samuel had not the gall to beg a passage aboard any Urbanna ship. The whole town would be wanting to know why, and he was not prepared to admit failure in public – not yet.

Rue let him stew on the problem for half the day, then relented. The crew was getting bored sitting around. A short voyage down to Hampton Roads would be something to pass the time. Providing they temporarily changed *Sea Witch*'s name and again issued her with suitable papers, registering her as the official property of la Sorenta. No one was particularly keen on being mistakenly arrested for piracy.

Thirty

Saturday 16th November

Rumour had already reached Williamsburg and the ears of Governor Spotswood that Blackbeard was anchored in the Ocracoke inlet. Less than a day's sail away. Too near for comfort, and too near to be tolerated.

Of Acorne there had been no word – nor had there been any message from him. General opinion among the Governor's entrusted 'pirate committee' was that he had returned to piracy and would be seen no more. Spotswood and Lieutenant Maynard were visibly disappointed. Their judgement had plainly been well out of kilter.

Their meeting on the afternoon of the fourteenth day of November was held in secret – ostensibly, the four men had met to play cards: Captain Ellis Brand of the *Lyme*, Captain George Gordon, Maynard and Spotswood. Anyone peeping through the window of the Governor's private parlour on the first floor would have wondered why there were no cards on the table, only a chart of the North Carolina coast spread across the flat surface.

Spotswood chewed the end of his pipe. It had remained unlit this past fifteen minutes. "So," he said at last, "do we admit Secretary Knight and listen to what he has to say? Or do I send him away; grant him audience on the morrow?"

"I believe we should at least hear him out, Sir. He has been reliable in the past and may have more pertinent rumour."

"As reluctant as I am to admit it," Brand replied, "I agree with Captain Gordon. I have no liking for Knight and I am aware, as are you, it is probable that he has been extremely selective in what information he has passed to us. He is a weasel of a man if you ask me. His only interest is in feathering his own nest. But it could be possible that Blackbeard has at last outstayed his welcome in Bath Town. It was a bad business that with his wife, poor lass. There's many folk would now gladly see the back of the rogue whatever the truth of the matter. If so, then aye, let us hear what Master Knight has to say."

When he entered, Tobias Knight was gushing and obsequious, his speech liberally patterned with reverent 'my lord', 'your honour' and 'my dear sir'. When Spotswood remarked that to date Bath Town had appeared to have openly welcomed the pirate Blackbeard, Knight had a ready and plausible answer.

"What could we do, Governor? He held us to ransom. If we had not co-operated with his vile and devilish wishes he would have turned his cannon on us! Look how he treated Charleston. We have only just recovered from the Indian troubles. Surely you do not expect us to blithely let our homes be burnt down, our women raped, our men enslaved?"

"No, I do not," Spotswood answered formidably, "but neither do I expect you to ask him to dine at your tables and offer him a daughter of the town in marriage! I expect you to fight back, damn it!" Clenching his fist, the Governor struck the desk he was sitting at.

"Fight? With what?" Knight was indignant with his answer. "We have hardly any militia, and the few we do have carry arms that saw better days fifty years ago! We are not Virginia, Sir – we do not have the King's patronage. We do not have excessive crops, rich plantations and chests of gold to spend on elaborate palaces or for fighting pirates who outnumber us three to one!"

"He has a point, Governor," Maynard commented.

"We beg aid from Virginia to destroy Blackbeard before he re-enters the Pamlico. We do not want him back in Bath Town."

Conceding to the sense of that, the discussion moved on to what could be done. Knight confirmed that Blackbeard was lazing at Pilot Point with several other pirate ruffians. He had no idea of their plans of course, but given the proximity to Virginia, it did not take much of a leap of imagination to guess.

"We need to take steps," Spotswood decided, "some secret, some public. Let it be known I am to offer a handsome reward – £100 to the person who can capture or kill Blackbeard, £59 for his officers and £25 a head for his crew. Dead or alive, I will accept either."

"I think a two-pronged attack on Pilot Point," Captain Brand added, spreading out another chart marking the Ocracoke and the North Carolina coastline of the Pamlico estuary. "Gordon here to take the *Pearl* and attack by sea – pen these buggers where they are. I will lead my men along here," he indicated the coastal route, "land and attack from the rear. The pirates will have nowhere to go."

"But are not some of those waters rather shallow?" Maynard asked dubiously.

"Our cannon can fire quite adequately from deeper water," Brand assured him, "those scumbags will probably surrender as soon as they catch sight of us. Everyone knows pirates are a cowardly lot when cornered."

It was a good plan – to be kept secret lest word reach the pirates. Tobias Knight was given the task of returning to Governor Eden with a request that he was to muster the North Carolina militia and bring them downriver to partake in the final demise of Blackbeard.

Spotswood himself escorted Knight to the main stairs, watched him descend and go out through the front door. He returned to his office, shaking his head. "Alas, Gentlemen, I fear most of that little performance was charade. Eden has allowed Blackbeard to get out of hand and now has no idea how to curb him. But he will not fight. Oh no, he wants us to do his dirty work in case we fail. That way he can claim innocence of the whole affair."

Captain Ellis Brand grinned. "But we will not fail, will we, Sir?"

They at last played several rounds of cards. Only Maynard, being dealt four bad hands in a row, had his doubts. The plan would not work. Down to his boots he knew it would not.

Thirty One

North Carolina

Luncheon in grand houses was a modest meal; cold meats, pastries, fruit. It was a modern way of thinking, as only the well off could afford three meals in the one day. For the poor, breakfast at dawn and a dinner half way through the day had to suffice, with perhaps a hunk of bread and maybe some cheese before going to bed with the sundown. But the rich could afford tallow and beeswax for candles and so could dine by artificial light. With the day extended into the night, and it being a long time between breakfast and the evening pleasantry of dinner, the partaking of a midday meal had become a popularity.

The house at Archbell Point had been in subdued mourning, the grieving made all the worse by Eden's refusal to acknowledge Perdita as kindred. She had shamed him in the eyes of the community and the Lord, and as Governor and temporary spiritual leader, he had refused to permit her burial in holy ground. She had an unmarked pauper's grave outside the church walls and none save Tiola and Nicholas Page had attended her burial. A pall of gloom hung over the house as if it were a suffocating fog. The one thing that relieved Tiola's sadness and sense of failure was that the depression was caused by these outside events, not from the Dark seeking her out. Unless she used her Craft, she would remain undetected – although the Malevolence was out there, lurking, waiting, sensing that there was something, somewhere, and drawing the Dark inward.

Elizabeth-Anne was not hungry. She nibbled some cold beef, but set it aside and then tried bread and honey. It made her feel nauseous. She had not slept, from grief, from discomfort, the two marching side alongside.

Tiola was watching her carefully and when the mother-to-be winced and attempted to stretch a niggling pain from her lower back, interpreted the signs. She said nothing until the gentlemen had left the table to collect their guns for an afternoon of shooting.

"My dear," she said, reaching across to rest her hand lightly atop Elizabeth-Anne's, "I do believe your son has at last decided to rouse himself from his bed."

Thirty Two

Virginia

A week to get to Hampton Roads – an entire week. The frustration had annoyed at first, but Jesamiah had employed the time wisely while waiting at Pilot Point near the mouth of the Pamlico River for a suitable Chesapeake-bound vessel. The Point was expanding into a small hamlet, more than just an anchorage for ships awaiting an experienced pilot to take them up river. Besides the pilot's house and offices, there were now chandlers' stores, two taverns, and a barber's. Jesamiah took advantage, had a professional haircut, shave and hot bath. Paid extra to have his clothes laundered as well, so it was a clean, fresh young man who paid his passage and stepped aboard the *Judy James*, heading for the Chesapeake, Hampton Roads and then to Annapolis in Maryland.

He'd also had a stroke of luck while skulking in the pilot's office waiting for the fellow to sort a payment disagreement down by the jetty. Rifling through some promising looking charts, he had found an architectural plan for a house. He had slipped it into his copious pocket, along with several other items that could be of use in the future – old habits lingered for an ex-pirate – and realised he now had the perfect disguise for getting to Williamsburg unnoticed. No one would recognise him if he were to assume the guise of an architect eagerly seeking patronage in the blossoming town. He purchased a leather bucket box, some more parchment and played his part well. Two people aboard the *Judy James* asked to see his designs; he showed them the one he had stolen and spoke convincingly of porticoes, cornices, foundations and load bearing walls – while having no idea what he was actually talking about. But neither did they so it was no matter.

The *Judy James* was a good little craft, short in the beam, but sprightly at sea. Jesamiah spent a while with the captain, trying not to show that he was an experienced sailor, although it must have noticed for Captain James remarked how at ease he seemed, even though the wind was not being kind and the Atlantic was somewhat rough. Jesamiah shrugged it off by saying he had inherited his sea legs from his father. A true-enough statement, but a low chuckle from behind his shoulder unsettled him. When he spun around, no one was there. He was still hearing his father's voice then.

Captain James had not noticed anything amiss and had continued praising his ship, explaining that the craft proudly carried his mother's name; a remarkable woman who had faced down a bear and an Indian, and as a girl had explored the forests near Jamestown. She lived in Williamsburg – the Captain offered to give the young, ambitious architect a letter of reference. "For you never know," he had said, "my mother may be able to help set you on the right path."

Jesamiah was gracious, thanked him; regretted that perhaps in other circumstances this Mistress Judy James would have been a delight to know. Privately, he doubted she would be keen on welcoming a man who, last time he was in Williamsburg, had been about to hang.

Another delay had been the sailing time. Few ships sailed from, or entered, Pamlico Sound in the afternoons, only early mornings or at dusk, notwithstanding the run of the tide or the vagaries of the wind.

"Pirates, you see," James had explained. "Blackbeard himself lurks among the marshes of the Ocracoke. If he spots us then, *pshht*, we are goners." He had drawn his thumb across his throat in a gruesome manner. Jesamiah had added a suitable gasp of horror to those of the other passengers.

"But we'll be safe in the mornings and at dusk. The buggers are too drunk to wake with the sun and too busy getting drunk with its going down."

The pirate in him had immediately made Jesamiah realise that there was a fortune to be made by attacking at dawn or dusk. Still, he was no longer a pirate. He did not need the information. All the same, he looked with interest at another merchant ship sliding inward to the Pamlico as the sun began to warm the day and the *Judy James* skipped cheekily past the Ocracoke and the rabble of snoring scumbags.

Nearing Hampton Roads he had almost had a change of plan. Tiola, after these days of silence, spoke to him.

~ *Luvver? I think Elizabeth-Anne is in labour.* ~

~ *Thank God for that! I'll turn around as soon as I can and come and get you.* ~ *And I'll forget Blackbeard and get out of here*, he added to himself.

~ *No, I have a feeling that labour will be long and slow, and I will want to remain here for a few days, to see all is well.* ~

He had been going to argue, but ahead was the harbour and as the *Judy James* heeled landward he studied what vessels lay at anchor; several fishing boats and two sloops; the *Ranger* and the *Lady Annapolis*. Was puzzled to see two he knew well – his own *Jane* from la Sorenta and his beloved *Sea Witch*, clearly renamed again as *Sea Siren*. Explanation was soon uncovered, for he found Rue easily; there were only two taverns. An exchange of information had to be brief; Jesamiah had no fancy to walk or hire a horse. Once the *Judy James* had unloaded the cargo destined for Williamsburg it would be taken there by wagon. He had about half an hour before it left, three quarters at the most.

He took advantage of the short wait by going across to the *Sea Witch*, listening to Rue's various accounts as he did so. Samuel Trent and Alicia Mereno, it seemed, were in Williamsburg. How fortuitous. Jesamiah would have his chance to give the strumpet the spanking she deserved.

As soon as he set foot on the deck he felt a thrill of elation; the men aboard cheered, glad to see him, and *Sea Witch* shifted slightly. Anyone else would have said the tide was turning or a wind was getting up. Jesamiah knew better. He touched a stay, a light caress with his hand. The tingling warmth in his fingers felt like a welcoming greeting. Hurrying to his cabin he batted Finch aside. He knew exactly what he wanted and did not have time to listen to a litany of complaints. "I want clean clothes, some fresh powder and flints for my pistol and some money, nothing else. Go on, Rue, you were saying?"

Jesamiah listened as he stripped off his old clothes – becoming ragged now, despite laundering – and replaced them with new. "Are the men happy about sailing to England when this mess I'm embroiled in is done and buried?"

Rue nodded. They were. Many of them, those who were Navy deserters or had been press-ganged had not seen their families for years. And the novelty of Virginia was already wearing thin. It was not a welcoming place for those on the wrong side of the law.

"We loaded the 'ogs'eads of tobacco as you asked, though much of it is poor quality. We are keeping silent on our cargo – I'ear there are rules about exporting the stuff?"

Pushing his mahogany table aside, Jesamiah flicked the square of carpet back. With his knife he prised up a loose plank of the deck, reached into the black hole beneath and brought out a small wooden chest. Said to Rue, "I'll claim I'm taking it to Cadiz if anyone asks. No one bothers about trash going to Spain. But I don't want you hanging around here too long, Rue. Take the *Sea Witch* to Pilot Point beyond Pamlico Sound, will you? When I join you, we will collect Tiola and leave this damned coast. Sail into the Pamlico at dawn or dusk. I have it on good authority it's a wise thing to do, but be cleared for action, just in case."

Rue's face lit into a broad smile at the prospect of Tiola coming aboard. "*Oui! Certainement*! Miss Tiola is ready to come 'ome? *Bon, bon!*"

Jesamiah opened the chest. Inside were various small canvas bags and pouches. He took one out, tossed it to Rue. It was heavy and it chinked. "Not quite, but she will be by the time I've done. Take this and share the coins between the men, they deserve some pay. I'll be wanting the *Jane*. Send those landlubber daisies that crew her back to la Sorenta, I need experienced men who know how to shoot straight and don't mind being shot at. Volunteers though." Jesamiah emphasised the words, "Only volunteers." He laid two more bags on the floor and slid two small pouches into his waistcoat pocket.

Rue was observing him quizzically. Concerned. "I like not the sound of that, *mon ami*. You are expecting a fight?"

"A battle. Wait for me at Pilot Point. You'll hear the outcome. If it is not favourable you will look after Tiola for me?"

The answering nod was slow, not because Rue had any doubt about caring for Tiola, quite the opposite, for he looked upon her as a daughter, but Jesamiah was implying that he might not be surviving this. "Does Miss Tiola know of what you are to become involved in? A fight, per'aps to the death?"

Jesamiah replaced the plank, stamped it down and kicked the carpet over it. Shoved the table to where it should stand. He shook his head. "Nope. Nor is she going to."

Originally he'd had no intention of keeping his promise to Teach. He would take word to Spotswood, fulfil his side of the bargain and then be gone, but those few quiet days aboard the *Judy James* had caused a change of mind. There had been shocked talk of Mary Ormond's death and the tailor's mutilation. The scandal of the other girl's suicide, even though it had been hushed up. And Tiola's own grief. It was something she had let slip that altered his plans. *When he attacked me that night*, she had said.

~ *What night? What do you mean?* ~ Jesamiah had immediately leapt in with questions, but she had made little to no reply.

~ *It was nothing,* ~ she had said. ~ *Nothing.* ~

Jesamiah had already learnt that *nothing*, where Tiola was concerned, usually meant something big. Teach had to be dealt with. And sailing north towards the Chesapeake, Jesamiah had realised that he could not trust the Royal Navy to deal with it efficiently. And if the bastard had indeed attempted to assault Tiola then he had no intention of letting someone else put a bullet through his bloody head.

Thirty Three

The wagon set its passengers down near Bruton Church opposite the Market Square, then trundled off towards the Sir Christopher Wren College. Hefting his bag of dunnage over his shoulder, Jesamiah stood, getting his bearings and deciding what to do.

Williamsburg, as a capital, was only nineteen years old. The Virginia Colonists had abandoned the previous location at Jamestown after their statehouse had burned down for the fourth time. The new site, known then as Middle Plantation, had already been expanding into a prosperous neighbourhood of stores, taverns and houses, and with its church, college and the William and Mary Hospital, the area had already cultivated a prestigious air. No one had objected to the founding of the town, nor its naming for the man who was, then, its King.

Mid-afternoon. There were a few stalls set up, quite a bustle of people milling around. There was a population of about one thousand, or so Jesamiah had heard, although whether this included the black slaves or not he had no idea. Would slaves – black or white – count as population? The number of people almost doubled during Publick Times, but that was over, visitors had gone. Any poor soul locked in the gaol would now have to wait for the next quarter session of Court for trial. Relieved he was not one of them, he strolled eastward along Main Street, glancing briefly up the grand, tree-lined avenue of Palace Street. Should he risk being open and simply march up to the palace and demand to see the Governor? Without credentials it was unlikely he would get one foot in the door. Ironic. In shackles he had walked right in, as a free man, he dared not approach those fancy wrought-iron gates. He would have to get word to Spotswood somehow, but according to the law, in Williamsburg he was a pirate due to be hanged. No, he would stick with his alias of Joshua Oakwood and await a suitable opportunity. One would come, they always did. Although sometimes you had to go after them under full sail and with cannons loaded and run out.

He bought some cheese from a stall, nibbled at it as he wandered on, leaving the busy market behind. Main Street was a broad thoroughfare that swept along for one mile on an east-west axis. The first Governor of Williamsburg, Nicholson, had known what he was doing when he had drawn up the basic plans for what was to be the grandest town in all the Colonies. So much of it was new: it all had an air of fresh paint, fresh-cut wood and pristine cleanliness, although the smells and quality of buildings changed along the back streets, where there was a jumble of small houses, ramshackle stores, and shacks and sheds for the slaves to live in.

Jesamiah decided to find a tavern and a room for the night. He did not much fancy sleeping under a hedge. He chuckled as a thought came to mind. How would the bear-fighting, Indian-chasing Mistress James react to a pirate curled beneath her shrubbery? Had he known where she lived he might have been tempted to find out. On the larboard side, rain was in the air and a warm dry bed appealed more to his sense of comfort.

He skirted around a fresh pile of horse manure and crossed the street. The *King's Arms* appeared clean and comfortable, but expensive. The *Raleigh*, opposite, would suit his pocket more. As Jesamiah Acorne he could well afford luxury; as Joshua Oakwood the architect, he could not.

The *Raleigh* was one of the older taverns, built before Williamsburg became the capital. It certainly looked as if it had stood here for eternity. Inside, the dim gloom was a fug of pipe and candle smoke, men sat in groups around tables made from barrels sawn in half, the rushes spread on the floor had not been changed in months. The place smelt of damp, rot and mould. The woman behind the bar had a pleasant smile and cheerfully served Jesamiah his request for rum.

"Any chance of a room for the night?"

"Certainly. We ask for payment in advance though, young sir."

Jesamiah set two silver shillings on the counter then added another. "A single room? At the front, overlooking the street?"

The smile did not waver. "Yes Sir. Our best."

He added another shilling to the pile. "Clean sheets and hot water?"

The woman scooped up the money. "Top of the stairs, first door on your right." Taking the rum, Jesamiah nodded his thanks and went upstairs.

The room was at least tidy. Sparsely furnished with essentials only, as musty as downstairs and the sheets a dull yellow and slightly stained, but he had slept in worse places. A lot worse! He tossed his coat, hat, cutlass and pistol onto the bed and pulled the only chair up to the sash window. Tried wiping the grime from the glass with his elbow; some came off, most was on the outside. With a bit of persuasion the window opened. He peered out. Riders passed by; a wagon loaded with hay, another, piled with furniture; a carriage with a pair of handsome chestnuts. Mothers walked with their children, husbands with wives; young couples, the elderly leaning on walking canes. Men about their business. Women shopping. Slaves of all ages and both sexes everywhere.

Sitting down, he propped his feet on the low windowsill, sipped his rum and pondered how to get to Governor Spotswood. Find an open window? Climb in? Wait by the gates for the Governor to come out, catch his attention? Or could he approach John Redwood, the gaoler? He frowned; that man coming from the *King's Arms* looked familiar. Where had he seen him before? The man headed east down Main Street, walking quickly. Jesamiah forgot about him.

Would it be an idea to visit this lawyer fellow of his father's? Probably, except he did not know who he was or where to locate him – beyond somewhere here in Williamsburg. There would be dozens of lawyers, where did he start? Why had he so stupidly thrown that letter of his father's away without reading it first? If nothing else of importance it would have had the lawyer's name on it!

He would have to try and find him to sort out la Sorenta. He had already decided to leave the estate permanently in Trent's hands. If the lad made a profit, then all well and good, if not, he did not particularly care. He had no need of the income; had done well enough without it thus far. He would give Trent five years to turn the estate around, if the boy failed, then he would sell the land and be done with it. As for Alicia…She could do what she wanted, stay or go. It was her choice, although from what Rue had said, she had already decided not to stay.

That woman approaching the *King's Arms* was just like her. Even to the sassy swagger of her hips. Jesamiah moved his feet to the floor, leant forward to see better. It *was* her! He stood, shoved at the window to open it further. It refused to budge. He scrubbed at more grime. Who was that man with her? Not Trent. It was the fellow who had left the tavern a moment ago – suddenly Jesamiah recognised him. Knight. Tobias Knight – and he was the one who had greeted Alicia so curtly that first day at la Sorenta, the one who had ridden off in a huff. Tobias Knight: Secretary to the Colony of North Carolina, right-hand man to Governor Eden and Edward Teach's friend. Well, well.

There was no reason to query his being in Williamsburg, there must be a lot of communication between the two colonies. But had Spotswood not said something about Blackbeard always being one step ahead? What if that was because somebody fed him titbits of relevant information? That was not to say it was Knight who tattled, but it was certainly a possibility. Why was he accosting Alicia?

Jesamiah tried to lean out, cursed the window for not opening wider.

Knight had her arm in a fierce grip and was shaking her so violently her head was lolling. Several bystanders were taking a curious interest then turning away, not wanting to interfere, assuming it was a domestic squabble. Alicia tried to shrug Knight aside but he only tightened his hold and thrust his face closer. Even from this distance, Jesamiah could interpret the nasty sneer etched on it. What was it Trent had said? Alicia had needed money. Was that why she had hidden the Letter of Marque, hoping to sell it or something?

Money! Knight was a money-grubbing shark. Ah, things were starting to make sense.

Unsure whether to stay and watch what happened, or buckle on his cutlass, put on his coat and go and intervene for the fun of it, Jesamiah's decision was made for him. A man appeared from nowhere – from the side street presumably. In a flurry of arms and legs he laid into Knight, swatting him three times with three well aimed punches. Left and right to the face, the third to the belly. Knight crumpled, blood welling from his nose. A crowd had gathered, the women twittering like sparrows, the men grunting disapproving noises, but making no move to stop the fracas. Samuel Trent – for that's who it was – grasped Knight by the collar and the seat of his breeches and bundled him down the steps, across the street and plunged him, head first, into the horse trough directly below Jesamiah's window.

"And bloody stay away from Mrs Mereno, else next time you will get more than a bloodied nose and a dunking, you scumbag!" Brushing his hands clean then straightening his cravat, Samuel strode back to the *King's Arms*, looped his arm through Alicia's and escorted her inside.

Jesamiah smiled, sat down again and returned to his drink. He had not thought Trent had it in him! Good for him, the lad had spirit after all!

Knight hauled himself from the trough amid amused laughter. He did not see the funny side, apparently, for when someone offered a hand to assist him he gruffly knocked it aside and squelched off down the street, leaving a dripping trail in his wake.

It was brave of Samuel Trent to take him on, but a man like Knight would not notice a few punches from an untried boy. Especially a man who had an established friendship with a pirate and the ear of a Governor. But then, Trent also had an established friendship with a pirate – who had the ear of a Governor. If he could only get close enough to bend it!

~ *I do not like this. There is something deeper going on.* ~

"Too right there is!" Jesamiah was out the door and descending the creaking stairs before he realised he had answered his father's disembodied voice without a single thought.

Thirty Four

Main Street had cleared of onlookers, the incident forgotten, people were about their business. Jesamiah crossed over, avoiding two wagons, and walked in through the open doors of the *King's Arms* tavern: definitely a place of higher quality and resources. He went to the counter and asked for Master Samuel Trent.

A barman answered him, more intent on drying a pile of washed glasses than passing time with someone of less than wealthy appearance. "You have just missed him. He left a moment ago."

Damn. Jesamiah leant an elbow on the counter, considering. "Well, where may I find Mrs Mereno?"

"Friend, are you?"

"Not that it is your business, but no, I am a relative. Her brother-in-law."

The man set the glass down, picked up another; began polishing. "Top of the stairs. Room four."

Jesamiah touched his hat, bounded up the stairs two at a time. Room four. He knocked.

"Who is it?"

Mumbling "It's me," in an approximation of Trent's higher pitched tone, Jesamiah heard her footsteps on the far side, a bolt withdraw. The handle turned, the door opened slowly. A frightened pale face peeped out.

"Samuel? Is it you – Oh!" Alicia tried to slam the door. Jesamiah was quicker, he rammed his boot into the gap, pushed it wide; her strength no match for his.

She shrieked and fled across the room, grabbing up a poker from beside the fireplace as she went. Brandishing it with both hands, she held it high. "Do not come near me! I will strike you, so help me I will!"

Jesamiah shut the door. Stood a few feet inside, shoved his hands into his pockets. "Put it down, Alicia, I've come to talk, not fight."

"Go away! Leave me alone, you brute!"

Taking his hat off and skimming it to the bed, Jesamiah ambled to the armchair, sat. "Me? A brute? It was you who tried to get me hanged, if

I recall, by stealing my Letter of Marque."

She still held the poker, although its weight had caused her to lower it a little. "How dare you suggest such a lie, I…"

"Oh, belay it, Alicia. I know the truth. I heard most of it from Sam when he came to get me out of gaol, and Rue's filled in the rest," he lied. Both men had told him only parts of the story.

"Sam? Sam!" Alicia strutted over to the fireplace, set the poker into its rack and faced Jesamiah, her bunched fists on her hips. "Samuel? You have the nerve to talk to me of Samuel Trent? You gave him my home. My furniture. You gave him everything – including my money!"

"No, I gave him the opportunity to manage an estate which I am not interested in managing. Your home, your furniture remains mine, though I do not want them either. As for your money, from what I gather, there is none for me to give. Your husband squandered it all. Do not blame that on Sam, or on me. And from what I have just witnessed, you ought to be grateful to young Trent. It takes guts to stand up to a man like Tobias Knight."

She glowered at Jesamiah. How did he always manage to know everything? Damn him. Suddenly, the fight went out of her. She slumped, her head drooped, her shoulders sagged and tears began to fall. If he had been told the situation then he knew how stupid she had been. And the trouble she was in.

"Oh Jesamiah. What am I to do? I do not want to return to the streets as a whore, I truly do not."

Jesamiah went to her, put his arms around her, drawing her head to his shoulder. Held her while she wept. This woman was an utter bitch when she wanted to be, was selfish, arrogant, stupid – but God help him, he had always been fond of her. Why, he did not know. Maybe because she had spirit, because she fought for what she wanted and did not accept 'no' for an answer? It was tough, surviving.

"Ssh, ssh," he coaxed, stroking her back, placing a light kiss on her head. "Hush now, we'll sort something."

"How?" she sniffed, her face buried in his shirt. "I have no home, no money and I am being blackmailed by a weasel who threatens to expose me." She looked up, the cosmetic paint she wore smudged on her cheeks and around her eyes. "He accosted me just now. Threatened me again. He is vile, utterly vile. If I do not pay him tomorrow he will tell everyone. And then I will be summoned before the Council and punished as a woman of ill-repute. They will flog me in public. I could not bear that. Oh I could not bear it Jesamiah!" She was crying again.

Jesamiah pulled her closer. *So that's what is behind all this,* he thought. *Blackmail.* "And me?" he murmured. "How did I fit in?"

She wept a little more, sniffed a few times. Delving into his pocket, Jesamiah produced a handkerchief that was not too grubby.

"I thought it would frighten you if they locked you away for a few days.

I was going to ask you for money, and in return find your letter. Only when I went to the gaol in Urbanna, you were not there, they were already bringing you here to Williamsburg. And," she blew her nose, handed him the kerchief back, "and I did not know what to do."

With her arms around him Alicia felt the security of his strong solidity. Jesamiah was a rock, an oak. He smelt of tar and sweat, of leather and hemp and the sea. She had always loved Jesamiah, since the first day in Port Royal when she had seen him come ashore, a cock-sure young whelp little more than a boy, in search of fun and sex. He had found both with her. Her first husband she had been fond off – he had not known she had been a whore, nor had Phillipe, her second. Phillipe had been a mistake. And Jesamiah? Had she really been so stupid that she had nearly caused him to hang? Yet now, with Knight after her, she would be the victim and harshly punished.

"I'm sorry," she whispered, "I did not mean to involve you, but I did not know what to do. I still do not know what to do. I have nothing to pay Knight with. I asked Samuel to give me some money – I said I wanted clothes – but he refused."

Very gently, Jesamiah prised her away from him and set her at arm's length, his hands on her shoulders. He looked at her red-rimmed eyes. "That is because Samuel has no money to give you. The estate is broke, thanks to Phillipe. And you, you silly goose, should have done the obvious thing and told me right from the start what was happening."

She wiped at her damp cheeks, smudging the cochineal colouring even more. "I could not do that. You would have laughed and told me to not be so silly. I did ask you for money when we were in Nassau and you told me you would not let me have one penny."

Jesamiah sat on the bed, patted it for her to come sit beside him. What she said was true. He would have laughed. Had he said no to even a penny? Probably. They sat a little apart, their bodies not quite touching. At last he plucked the courage to ask, "And what of the child?"

She raised her head, her frown quizzical. "What child?"

"The one you said you carried. My child."

She drew in her breath. Her hand went to her slender stomach, flattened and trimmed by her tight corset. Child? She had forgotten all about that.

"Will you make me your wife? Give a child of mine your name?" She did not know why she asked; she already knew his answer.

He stood, walked over to the window, stared down into the bustle of Williamsburg's Main Street, across at the tavern and his room, at the window he had left open.

"I cannot, Alicia. I love Tiola and I married her some days ago." How many days, he could not remember. Too many, that was for certain.

He turned back to Alicia. "I'm sorry. I will support you though, I'll give you all the money you need. I will not abandon you or the child. You have my word."

He meant it; she could see and hear that he did. She shook her head, sighed. Confessed. "There is no child. I made it up."

He turned again to face the window, said simply, "Oh."

To Alicia's ears the disappointment in that one word was heartbreaking. He wanted a child? Actually *wanted* a child? She half rose, her hand stretching out, sat down again. "Well, you have a wife now. I am sure there will soon be children. A whole shipload."

"I have been bedding Tiola for some while now. I lived with her for seven months in Cape Town. I think I might be incapable of siring a babe."

How like Jesamiah to take the blame for himself and not lay it on the woman he loved. Alicia felt tears welling again. She had hurt him with this pretence, God help her, how could she have been so cruel? She put her hand to her stomach again, her frown deepening as she tried to think. When had her last flux come? It was always unreliable, often late, the flow light and only lasting two days or so. It rarely inconvenienced her, which meant she never kept track of the dates. It suddenly occurred to her that she would have to wait a whole month around to be entirely certain about not carrying a child. Should she say there could be a possibility? No. She could not, for the last thing she wanted at the moment was to be pregnant.

"There is nothing wrong with your seed, Jesamiah. I told you, you impregnated me that time at la Sorenta. It may be that your wife has deliberately been stopping her womb from quickening. She is, after all, talented in that area is she not? Very probably she had no intention of permitting her belly to swell until you married her."

He twisted his head, smiled at her. "Do you think so?"

She had absolutely no idea, but Jesamiah Acorne was not the only one who could lie convincingly. "Yes," she said. "I do think so."

"I'd better have a word with her then, hadn't I?"

"I'd make them sweet honeyed words if I were you. And stop leaving her behind. And…" Alicia paused, considered him longingly. He was so beautiful – but he was not for her. "And stop cavorting in other ladies' beds."

He shrugged. "You mean no more whoring?"

"No more whoring."

"Not even with you?"

"Especially not with me."

"That's a bit of a bugger. I was going to suggest we go to bed so that I could give you some sort of payment."

She closed her eyes, said calmly, hoping he would not read the lie behind her lips, "I do not want to go to bed with you, Jesamiah. Now, or ever again. I am a respectable widow. I am no longer a whore."

When she opened them again he was standing directly in front of her. He reached out, put one finger under her chin, tipped her face upward, leaned in and kissed her. It was a long, sensuous kiss.

When he broke away he said, "Then I will just have to think of another way for you to earn some money – a reward perhaps?"

He stepped back, retrieved his hat. "Give me an hour. Get your best gown and prettiest bonnet on. You are going to get me into the Governor's palace." And he was gone, the door closing behind him. She looked out of the window, saw him hurry across the street, go into the tavern opposite.

The smooth-talking whoremonger! He'd had no intention of taking her to bed. None at all! Surprising herself, Alicia found that she was laughing.

Thirty Five

North Carolina

Elizabeth-Anne's baby was *occipto posterior*, a medical term which Tiola did not use aloud to the labouring mother. The baby's back was to his mother's back, which meant his head was not fitting into the cervix very well, which in turn meant the contractions were of irregular strengths. They grew stronger as the afternoon wore on, becoming a succession of small contractions interspersed with huge, agonising ones as Elizabeth-Anne's body tried to push the baby to a better position. Some of the waves of pain came in pairs, a stronger one wearing off into a smaller cramp. Then a gap when it almost seemed as if everything had stopped – but another big one swamped the woman and she cried out, fearful that she and the child were not going to survive.

In a normal birth the baby 'dropped' into position before labour began, sometimes days before, occasionally only a matter of hours. The head would dip in and out of the pelvic brim, fitting into the space between, reducing the size of the visible bump becoming more uncomfortable for the mother. The dipping had still occurred, but with her experience, even without her gift of Craft, Tiola could clearly see that Elizabeth-Anne's bulge was too high, almost under her breasts. Tiola did not need to feel with her hands to realise the foetus was back to front and was going to make this birth difficult.

Massaging Elizabeth-Anne's back, Tiola deliberately kept cheerful. The poor woman had suffered dull, aching back pain for the past four weeks.

"I want to push. If only I could push it might ease this pain."

"No, please believe me, if you pushed this early it would make things worse. Ride through the feelings, dear-heart, just ride through them." Tiola dare not explain that with the contractions not working properly, the cervix was not dilated enough to allow the child to pass through. With incorrect pressure it would swell and eventually, birth would be impossible. The only result: death for mother and child.

There were so many things that could go wrong but Tiola retained her reassuring smile. If the waters broke, labour would become more painful, blood loss could be greater than was safe – or the foetus could try to turn in the pelvis and become stuck. Tiola had performed a caesarean twice in the past. She had saved one infant, lost both mothers. She massaged her sweet-smelling oils into Elizabeth-Anne's back, thighs and belly and murmured a small spell to ease the worst of the pain. Teach, she knew by her own gift and by what she had heard, was the other side of Pamlico Sound, camped on the Ocracoke, far enough away for her to use all her skills and Craft, but there was a residue of the Dark lingering here in Bath Town. An echo of Malevolence attempting to find her. She needed to be careful, to use what she had sparingly. Even with her Craft, whether the mother and child were safe from the cruelties of nature, she did not yet know.

Thirty Six

Virginia

At first Jesamiah had thought Alicia was not going to come, but the words 'a reward perhaps' had lured her. Alicia would never change. Money would always be her first love.

"Have you any idea where Sam is?" was his first question. "And where is Knight staying?" was his second.

Main Street was emptier now, people with homes to go to had gone to them, stalls and stores had shut for the night. The sky was almost dark, several stars were growing brighter. The lamplighter was coming down the street lighting the torches in wall sconces and lamps hung upon walls, attracting moths and night insects. From the taverns and those few places still open, yellow light spilled outward to pool on the pavement. Alicia wondered how much this reward was to be.

"Samuel was to meet with the estate lawyer to see what can be salvaged from the mess your brother left. Then he was going to dine. Beyond that I do not know. I am not his wife, nor his keeper. Nor do I know or care about Knight." Her answer was curt. Already she was wondering what she was doing walking along Main Street after dark with Jesamiah. What if Knight was to accost her again?

Jesamiah did not want to meet with Samuel. For two reasons: one, he thought it best to leave the lad to cope on his own and not feel he was being examined, and two, he did not want a repeat of Sam begging to join him. When he returned to face Blackbeard it would be a fight to the death, and he had enough to think about without feeling responsible for an untried lad.

"Phillipe was not my brother, Alicia."

"So you said. I do not believe you."

"Too bad. It happens to be the truth. Which lawyer was Samuel seeing?"

"A local firm: Masters Stealit and Spendit."

He chuckled. If she was making jests she had forgiven him his earlier teasing. "Seriously, Alicia, I need to know." As he asked the question, the name came into his head.

~ Richard Faversham. ~

He repeated it aloud and Alicia scowled. "If you already knew, why ask me?"

"I did not know, I guessed. I must have seen a sign somewhere." He found it so unsettling to hear his father like this. Was he watching every move? Constantly following behind? Jesamiah resisted the urge to look over his shoulder. Yet again he so wished that Tiola was with him, or that at least he could talk to her about the way he was being haunted. But she was busy with Elizabeth-Anne and a baby which, from what she had implied hours ago now, was reluctant to come into the world.

They walked on in silence, crossed Colonial Street – Jesamiah had to pull Alicia back as a carriage rumbled by taking the corner a little too tight and coming too close.

"Some people ought to learn to drive," he muttered. "Are you all right?"

Although slightly shaken, she nodded. "I thought for a moment it was Knight, come to finish me off."

Jesamiah put himself between her and the roadway, any carriages or wagons would have to go through him first. "I was going to have a word with you about Knight. You know he will want more money if you pay him this time, don't you?"

Glum, she nodded.

"It would be better to call his bluff."

"What? Tell him to announce to the world I was a convict and a whore?"

A scrawny she-cat shot past, followed by a dog in pursuit. The cat resembled the one he had seen that morning when he had been taken to the palace, although somewhat skinnier. "Well, you could do that if you wanted, though I would not advise it."

She scowled at him, saw he was laughing. "This is not a humorous situation Jesamiah. I am in trouble."

He stopped walking, trundled her around to face him. "Why do you not blackmail him in turn? Buy his silence? Threaten him?"

In exasperation, she raised her arms in the air and walked on. "Those are the most unhelpful suggestions I have ever heard. What? Shall I frighten him by saying his hair is turning grey or his wig is unfashionable? Or his belly is becoming too big to button his waistcoat?"

Jesamiah trotted to catch her up, grasped her arm. "No. You tell him unless he leaves you alone you will inform Governor Spotswood about a certain close acquaintance."

"And that will worry him?"

"For fok sake; button your mouth and listen! Knight will not want Spotswood knowing he and Blackbeard are partners."

Her eyes widened, the first spark of hope in weeks cheering her. "Are they? You are sure of this?"

"Yes. I have suspicions about Knight that if true, will send him scuttling like a crab for deep water. If you can get me into the palace I will be able to confirm what I think."

Alicia continued walking, considering the implications of what Jesamiah had said. It would be so good to get the better of the odious man. "But I will not always be here in Williamsburg. What if he goes to la Sorenta? He is a violent man."

"I thought you said you don't want to go back there?"

"I do not. But what choice have I? I am homeless. I am penniless." They were at the palace green, one or two benches made from fallen logs were set to the side – a way to make people sit and admire the grand building dominating the far end. Jesamiah sat Alicia down, seated himself next to her.

"If you could do what you wanted, what would it be?"

She answered immediately. It was something she had thought of often these last months. If she were free, if she had her fortune to do with as she pleased. "I would buy a plot of land and build a tavern here in Williamsburg; a reputable place for gentlefolk, not a disorderly house – no whores or rag-a-bones with an itch in their breeches. I would run something like the *King's Arms* – only even better. Hold balls and entertainments. Cook good meals, have clean rooms with clean linen. My establishment would be known through all the Chesapeake as Virginia's finest accommodation."

Jesamiah was surprised at first, but then, on second thoughts, perhaps not. Being a tavern keeper was one of the few things outside of running a bawdy house that a woman could do in her own right. And yes, Alicia would be good at it.

"And how much would this buying a plot of land cost? Two, three hundred pounds?"

She pursed her lips, calculating. "To buy and build and furnish? Oh, probably at least three hundred pounds of tobacco. Three hundred and fifty pounds of it if I wanted to be sure of the first year. After that I would start turning a profit." She sighed, folded her hands in her lap. The palace at the end of the tree-lined green looked pretty all aglow with light shining from every window. "I would site it either behind the Capitol Building or here near the palace. I know it is somewhat rough at this end of Main Street at the moment, but give it a few years and mark my word, things will be different! Aside, land is slightly cheaper this end. I could not really afford the Capitol."

"But that's where the best clients are?"

"Of course."

"So five hundred pounds would set you up nicely?"

She stood, tiring of the conversation. "Yes, but I have not even got one ounce of tobacco with which to barter, so there is no point in dwelling on unreachable dreams, is there?"

Jesamiah stayed where he was. "I am talking pounds sterling, not tobacco weight."

"No one uses actual money here in Williamsburg," she retorted scornfully.

"Well I do. Please, Alicia, sit down. I ain't said all I want to say."

She stood for a few more moments, tapping her foot and sighing impatiently, then flounced down beside him.

From his pocket, Jesamiah pulled two sealed letters. She saw her name on one, made a grab at it. Jesamiah snatched it aside, held it high. "Uh, uh, hear me out first. This one is for you. It states all the things you are entitled to."

She tried to reach it again, but he held it even higher. "If you do not listen to me, Ma'am, I will destroy it and you will be left with nothing."

She huffed, impatiently folded her hands into her lap.

"This," Jesamiah continued, "states that you may take whatever is yours from the house. I warn you, I would have expected my father to have had an inventory, so do not try to take anything that was there before you moved in. It also states that unless you are satisfactorily making your own decent income – which does not mean whoring – then…"

"Huh. What chance have I of an income that does not involve lifting my skirts?"

"…As I was saying; unless you have an income, you are to receive an annual allowance from the estate, *if* there is sufficient to support it."

She sniffed.

"You could at least say thank you."

"Thank you." She did not sound particularly grateful.

"This other letter is for the lawyer. He is to see to it that Samuel Trent becomes the permanent estate manager of la Sorenta – and Samuel is to answer to him annually with the accounts if I am not here." He paused, studied the night sky, the familiar patterns of the stars. How were Tiola and the babe? Was she really stopping herself from having his child? Could she, would she, do that? Was Alicia really not pregnant? And then his thoughts returned to tomorrow and the day beyond. Five, six days maybe, and it would all be over. By Friday he could be up there with the stars, a dead man, peering down at the living world.

"Also in this letter, I have instructed the lawyer to tell you everything if I do not come back. Someone should know the truth about my father and Phillipe. It might as well be you. He was your husband, after all."

"What do you mean, you might not come back? Where are you going?"

Jesamiah puffed his cheeks, glanced again at the stars, "Very possibly somewhere far away and not very pleasant, darlin'. Maybe a bit hot and smelly I should think, if a past experience in a hold is anything to go by." He slapped his hands on his thighs, stood. "Come on, let's see if you can get me in to the Governor without anyone hanging or shooting me."

"You will make sure I get paid for doing this won't you?"

"I will, darlin'. I will." He handed her the two letters, made sure she put them safely into her poke.

He whistled as he strolled towards the wrought-iron gates, Alicia looking as beautiful as ever on his arm. It was bravado. The sound a man makes as he walks to the gallows and does not want the watching crowd to know he is scared to death.

Thirty Seven

North Carolina

The vow of the midwife was that she would give all her energy to the mother and child she was delivering until she was certain they had made safe passage through the arduous journey of birth. It was a vow that no conscientious midwife would query or ignore, but there were occasions when Tiola needed some of that energy for herself. She too had to survive. Tiola was usually able to bring a healthy babe into the world through a relatively comfortable birth. By and large the mothers needed no particular assistance beyond the help of a friend or relation. Tiola, as midwife, was there to anticipate problems and deal swiftly and efficiently with emergencies. But even with her skill and care, women died.

It would have been good to have Perdita here helping, with her calm manner, her soft voice and gentle smile. Tiola thrust the thought aside as she massaged Elizabeth-Anne's feet and legs, not wanting tears to come. The three lives had been lost: Jonathan, Perdita and their child. Then there was Mary Ormond – she did not want to lose these two as well.

Elizabeth-Anne was propped on the bed by pillows and cushions. The contractions had become stronger, but the baby was no nearer to being born. It was night outside. Tiola had watched the sky fade into purple then dark blue. One diamond of light shone brighter than its companions. Venus. She could not be thinking of where Jesamiah was. What he was doing.

Another contraction shuddered through Elizabeth-Anne, followed quickly by another. Her waters had broken in a gush of fluid half an hour ago. Unless Tiola was touse her Craft to its full extent there was nothing more she could do to help, except hope that the woman had the courage and strength to keep on pushing her baby out, and that the boy wanted to help get himself born.

Thirty Eight

Virginia

Alicia, Jesamiah had always been convinced, could charm the birds down from the trees. That might be so, but the footman at the palace obviously did not know of it, or he was the wrong sort of bird. A turkey not a turtle dove.

"I have told you, Ma'am, Governor Spotswood is at dinner. He will not be seeing you, nor no pip-squeak architect. Go away and come back Monday." He glanced again at the man with her. An architect, he'd said, but his face seemed familiar. The footman had seen him somewhere but could not place where. It was the eyes he recognised. There was something familiar about those dark eyes. And aside, why would an architect be wanting to see the Governor on a Saturday evening?

"Sir, I am Mistress Alicia Mereno. I am a personal friend of the Governor's. I assure you he will be most displeased were he to discover you attempted to turn me away."

"Then I will take that risk. I know he will be even more displeased to have his dinner disturbed."

They were at least inside the entrance hall with its array of fearsome weaponry. They had got this far but it seemed they were going no further.

From upstairs, Jesamiah heard a woman laugh and then a man's voice – Spotswood. All Jesamiah had to do was run across those few yards of black and white tiled flooring, turn left and dart up the stairs. Half a minute? Less? More? How long would it take this footman to get out a pistol, cock and fire? Not that long. He needed a diversion, something to distract this obstinate fellow. He put his hand in his pocket. Felt the pouches he had put there when aboard the *Sea Witch*. Smothered a grin. Diamonds were rare, and precious. He had acquired them a short while ago, one of the two perks of his spying assignment on Hispaniola. The other, had been the chance to make love to a beautiful woman.

"I think we're getting nowhere, Alicia. We will do as the man says; come back Monday."

He slid his arm through Alicia's before she could protest and started for the door. Leaning close, said quickly; "I'm going to distract him. What you get, you keep. Savvy?"

He whirled, thrust out his hand as if to strike the footman a blow to the face. The man staggered backwards a pace and raised his arms as Jesamiah threw something at him. The flickering light from the many candles glittered on a shower of sparkling, twinkling diamonds that sprayed from his hand and fell like tinkling rain to the floor. Alicia cried out and fell to her knees, scrabbling to gather up as many of the beautiful gems as she could – the footman, too, was on his knees, shoving her hand aside as he groped for his share.

"They are worth a lot, Alicia!" Jesamiah shouted as he sprinted for the stairs. "Better than tobacco for barter, eh? Call your tavern *The Acorn*!"

The footman realised his mistake, hesitated, anxious to collect the diamonds for himself, as anxious not to let the scoundrel anywhere near the Governor, which would certainly mean his dismissal. Out of duty he had to stop him. He pocketed a good handful of the glittering beauties and shouted for help – but Jesamiah was already up the first flight of stairs, around the bend and halfway up the second; was almost at the top.

"Governor!" he yelled, desperate, for this was his only chance. "Governor, it's me, Jesamiah Acorne! I must see you!"

Alicia ignored the both of them. She opened her poke bag and sweeping her hand backwards and forwards across the floor scooped up as many diamonds as she could.

Thirty Nine

Sunday 17th November

"Were I you, I would leave Virginia."

Groggy, roused from sleep, Knight lifted his head from the pillow. He blinked, squinted into the room that should have been dark; light from the lamp in the corridor was streaming in through the door. It was ajar; he was sure he had shut it. Pushing the covers aside he half rose, froze immobile as he realised a pistol was pointing at his head.

"As I said; were I you, I would leave Virginia and stay left. You ain't welcome 'ere, Knight."

Raising hands that were trembling, Knight uttered a few squeaks of alarm then stammered, "Who are you? What do you want? I have no money. I have nothing for you to steal."

Jesamiah sat on the end of the bed, being careful to ensure that the light remained behind him so that his face could not be seen.

"Of course you have no money, Mrs Mereno has not paid you what you asked her, has she?"

Knight was wondering if he shouted for help, would anyone come? Jesamiah guessed his thoughts. The man had given them away by flicking a glance at the door and opening his mouth.

"No one will come. Everyone's asleep and the porter downstairs will be expecting the other half of the payment I made him." Jesamiah leant forward slightly. "I told him not to worry if you made a noise. He thinks I'm a sodomite come to pleasure you."

Knight blanched.

Tempted to start unbuttoning his breeches to frighten the man thoroughly, Jesamiah thought better of it, he was limited for time. He'd had a job climbing out of the first floor window at the palace, and would find it damned more difficult to get in again. At least he'd had no bother getting to see the Governor. Their talk yesterday evening had been most interesting, the one planned for later this morning promised to be similarly so.

"Now," Jesamiah said, "about you leaving Virginia. The Governor does not – yet – know you are a touch too friendly with Edward Teach."

Knight began to bluster. Jesamiah clicked the hammer on his pistol to full cock. "No good you protesting, mate, I know what I know. I am prepared to keep m'knowledge to m'self though. On one condition."

"I need no conditions. I have done nothing wrong."

"No? Shall I tell Spotswood about the tunnel between the creek and the Governor's cellar? That it extends to your cellar? I wonder what he would find if he were to look?"

Noticeably, Knight remained quiet.

Jesamiah stood, walked backwards to the door. "If you are still here come sunup, Knight, I will tell Spotswood everything. And if I ever – ever – hear of you threatening Mrs Mereno again, you'll wish I had, 'cause hanging for treason will be preferable to what I'll do to you. Savvy?"

He opened the door wide, slipped out; closed it. By the time Knight had struggled from the bed, stubbed his toe, found the doorknob and opened it again, the corridor outside was empty.

Forty

North Carolina

Sunday morning; dawn was yet a way off. Elizabeth-Anne had been in labour for hours – more if you counted the niggling pains that had started early the previous morning. She was tired, the baby too. Both had almost had enough. Another massive contraction swept in like the surge wave of a bore tide and Elizabeth-Anne screamed.

"Help me! Oh help me! I cannot go on. I cannot do this anymore. Just stop it. Please, I beg you, just stop this pain!"

Tiola heard voices outside, Nicholas, anxiously calling his wife's name. Had she been anywhere else Tiola would have let him in. It was nonsense not to allow men into the birthing chamber. They were there at the begetting, damn it, perhaps to witness this end of things would keep their cocks in their breeches a little more often.

Gripping Elizabeth-Anne's hands, Tiola stroked her sweat-damp hair. "You can do it, dear-heart, you are doing it. Follow your body, stop trying to go against the pains, go with them. When each one comes push with it, push it down, push it out. You are delivering your baby. He is nearly here, believe me he is nearly here, it is nearly all over!"

Tiola looked into the woman's exhausted eyes and breathed lightly on her face, murmured *"hie…esshh,"* and spoke a few soft, chanting words. She rarely used her Craft during a birth as she never knew who was near, who was watching, who – what – was listening. The quickest way to be discovered as a witch was to use her ability during a birthing, especially if the birth went wrong. But Elizabeth-Anne was near exhaustion and it would be a while yet before the child came. Tiola could at least give her some respite, a chance to rest, to rekindle some strength; and the best way do so was to rake away the pain. And trust that her interference went undetected.

Forty One

Virginia

Governor Alexander Spotswood was as furious as an enraged hornet. Tobias Knight of North Carolina being the object of his rage. The Governor had summoned everyone relevant in hunting down Blackbeard to be at the palace an hour after sunup on the Sunday morning. Messages went out to the Captains Gordon and Brand and Lieutenant Maynard of the Navy, Jesamiah Acorne and Tobias Knight. Except Tobias Knight was nowhere to be found. His room was empty, his clothes gone. On enquiry, it was discovered he had taken a horse before dawn and left Williamsburg. Why, no one seemed to know.

Apart from his secretive midnight sojourn, Jesamiah had spent the night sprawled warm and comfortable as a guest at the palace. He had quite liked the luxury. The mattress was filled with goose-down and the palace boasted a bathhouse – of which he had taken full advantage before breakfast. All he had needed was Tiola to share the bath and the bed. Next time, perhaps? If there was a next time.

"Just how much did you tell Knight?" he asked, unfolding his arms and getting to his feet. "How much of your plan does he know?"

Spotswood growled. The two captains blustered a bit, not committing themselves and not wanting to answer a man they saw as a knave. Maynard was the one to speak up.

"He knew all of it. He knows the Governor put out a public decree of reward as a ruse to detract from the fact we are to sail secretly after Teach and capture him."

"I see. And in what inappropriate ships are you intending to sail?"

Captain Gordon was indignant. "How dare you insult us? You are a scurvy, ignorant vagabond; a degenerate pirate! What know you of ships, of tactics? Governor!" he faced Spotswood, hand outstretched, appealing, "I beg you to remove this dog. He cannot be trusted."

Slamming the desk top with his hand Jesamiah roared his anger. "It is Knight who cannot be trusted, and you are the one with your head stuffed up your arse, Gordon, not me!" Incensed, he swept several books to the floor. "The Navy has one hundred and twenty-four commissioned vessels. Just ten of those are stationed here in the Americas. Six are in the Caribbean under command of Commodore Vernon, one patrolling up near New York, one for New England and two here in Virginia. Have you any idea how many pirate ships there are? Do you really want me to tell you? Do you really want me to show your ignorance to the Governor?"

Gordon had never liked Jesamiah Acorne. He saw him as a threat to his authority. "You are remarkably well informed. How do you know this information?"

"Because it ain't a fokken secret and I ain't fokken stupid!"

Spotswood interceded before the two took the argument further and started calling each other out. "Captain Acorne, you tread on the Navy's pride, though I see your point, and I personally think the Navy's pride deteriorated some while ago." He held his hand up to silence Gordon's protest. "I accepted Captain Acorne into this venture because I also believe he knows what he is doing. I suggest we grant him the courtesy of at least hearing him out?" He gestured at Jesamiah to continue. "But, Acorne, please, temper your words. It is, after all, Sunday."

Apologising, Jesamiah asked, quietly, "How do you intend to get close to Blackbeard Captain Gordon, Captain Brand? Where did Knight tell you he was anchored?"

"Pamlico Sound. Near Pilot Point," Maynard responded. He shared Jesamiah's opinion of Gordon, though he would not express it aloud. Ellis Brand was competent, but too cautious. He spent too long weighing the pros against the cons.

Jesamiah spread his arms, palms upwards. "Well, there you have it. Knight is playing you for fools."

"How so?" Captain Brand had not liked Knight, had thought him untrustworthy, though given the seriousness of the situation, and the person who verified his suspicions, he was not elated to discover his assessment had been correct.

"Teach is settled on the Ocracoke, where you will never get those ships of yours anywhere near cannon range. He will wait for dark then slip out with the flood tide – and you would not be able to stop him. He can sail for miles over those shallows with a rising tide. You will have to stick to deep water."

Lost in thought, steepling his fingers against his lips, Spotswood sat considering. He took some snuff, sneezed; blew his nose. "Knight said Teach was gathering other pirates. That he intended to make Pilot Point his base – build a fortress and hold the whole of Pamlico Sound to ransom. That would severely affect our trade as well as that of North Carolina. Knight said he had come as an emissary and that the Colony needed our help to rid them of Teach. I take it none of what he said is true?"

Jesamiah shrugged. "I do not know all of it, but aye, Teach has been talking to other pirates. Vane, Rackham. Bonnet was supposed to have joined him."

"Bonnet wept like a babe when they took him to his hanging. He pleaded for mercy and screamed for a pardon. The crowd pelted him with filth for his cowardice. Or so they are saying." Gordon's sneer was contemptuous.

Ignoring him – he was not interested in Stede Bonnet, alive or dead – Jesamiah continued, "I have a suspicion that Teach intends to call in others. He thinks I am with him, he is waiting for me to return. He intends to create mischief one way or another." He pulled up a chair, sat, "I would guess that Eden and Knight have had enough of him – I have already told you of the foul deeds that have happened. But the pair of them have been hauled so high with Teach they know not how to shorten sail. If they initiate a fight and Teach survives – well, they already know how vicious he can be."

Spotswood took more snuff. After several sneezes said, "So they get me to do the deed? If it goes wrong they will plead innocence."

"You said it Governor."

Spotswood sat back in his chair. "So, Acorne, you have a better plan?"

Jesamiah nodded. He did.

Later, while Maynard was rousing John Brush to open the armoury and fill a wagon with muskets, pistols and grenados, Governor Spotswood privately asked Jesamiah two questions. He expected truthful answers to neither – if indeed he got an answer at all.

"Did you have anything to do with Knight's inexplicable departure?"

Looking pained, Jesamiah laid his hand over his heart. "Me? Why would I be involved? How could I have done? I spent a peaceful night in your guest bedchamber. And very pleasant it was too, compared to the previous accommodation you offered me."

Spotswood chewed his lip, nodded sagely, not believing a word of it. "Then you have no thoughts on how several of my carefully tended blooms got broken last night and footprints were all over my flower beds?"

"None at all."

"And Acorne."

"Sir?"

"From where did those diamonds come?"

"Diamonds? What diamonds would they be, Governor?"

Spotswood produced two from his waistcoat pocket. "These diamonds."

Whistling at their obvious value Jesamiah shook his head. "I have no idea, but I suggest you put them away and keep them for something useful. New flowers perhaps?"

"I am not open to corruption, Acorne."

Jesamiah touched his hat in salute and headed for the door; "Glad to 'ear it, Guv'nor. Glad t"ear it."

Forty Two

North Carolina

Tiola moved to sit beside Elizabeth-Anne who was naked and lying on the bed on her side, her knees drawn up. The pulsations of the last contraction rippled beneath the sweat glistening on her skin. Somehow, together through the long hours, the two women had worked to get this far, and there was not much further to go.

As Sunday morning had dawned, Tiola had coaxed and encouraged, massaged and caressed. She was not going to lose this child, nor his mother. She put one hand on the woman's in-drawn knee. They were nearly there. It was nearly over.

"Good, now breathe my dear, pant, that's it, short breaths. I can see the crown. We are almost there. Elizabeth-Anne, we are almost there!"

She waited for another contraction to ease. "Let's get you up – that's it, we need to give your bones a chance to spread for the head to pass through."

Elizabeth-Anne grasped Tiola's hand as she shifted position and sat back in the middle of the bed, her bottom resting on her heels. Tiola massaged the skin around the birth canal, rested her fingers lightly on the cap of the baby's head to hold him back a little, to give the perineum time to stretch naturally without tearing.

"Pant," she said. "He has kept us waiting all this time, now he insists on hurrying!" She panted with Elizabeth-Anne; "*Hah; hah; hah.*" The baby's head rotated, showing its wet, slanting forehead, and the perineum slipped over his face as easy as anything. The head was out. Tiola felt like shouting with joy, but all was not safe yet.

"One more push!"

Not losing the momentum, her body trembling, Elizabeth-Anne pushed downward for one more surge – and the baby was out, sliding into Tiola's outstretched hands as she deftly caught him. Another term for the midwife – baby catcher.

"A boy!" Tiola cried, elated, peering quickly over its tiny, wet, mucky body to see in an instant that all the parts he was supposed to have were there. She laid him down, tied off the cord near his abdomen, making sure she bound it tight. She fetched a bowl, cut the cord and let the mother's end drip into the utensil. The dark blood was not Elizabeth-Anne's, she would come to no harm. This was placental blood and allowing it to flow a while would help the afterbirth come away the easier. She laid the baby next to Elizabeth-Anne, covered him and his mother with blankets and efficiently cleaned away the mucus from his nose and mouth. The little fellow was already crying, indignant at this frightening world, but the room was warm and comfortable, as would he be soon.

Elizabeth-Anne remained on her knees a while, staring down at him, her unbound, tangled hair flopping over her face. She reached up, tucked a strand behind her ear. Giving its normal warning of a rush of fresh blood the placenta was delivered, straightforward and quickly. Tiola was there with the bowl, she caught it, checked it had come away in one piece, that there were no tears left inside the uterus.

Overwhelmed with emotion Elizabeth-Anne barely noticed. She said nothing as she rolled over and gathered her baby to her breast, hushing him within her embrace, her kisses and her love. Tiola closed her eyes in prayer to the Great Mother who cared for all Her children.

She sent the servant running for clean bed linen – the girl had been useless except for fetching and carrying. She had spent most of the time squatting in the corner with her skirt over her head, refusing to look at what was happening. Tiola bustled outside onto the landing. Nicholas was waiting there, sitting on the top stair, his head in his hands; he leapt up as the door opened.

"My wife? My child?"

"Both are well. You have a son. Give me but a moment to tidy away the residue of women's work and you may come in."

Tiola hugged him, pleased, sharing his delight. "Be proud of your wife, Nicholas, she has laboured hard for you and your son this day."

Forty Three

Virginia

Pleased that Rue had made sail in *Sea Witch* as he had ordered, Jesamiah set to at Hampton Roads with Robert Maynard to commandeer a second sloop. He already had the *Jane*, and her volunteered skeleton crew as his own vessel, the second one he had in mind he had seen at anchor close to where *Sea Witch* had been. The *Ranger* would be ideal for their purpose, and she had still been there, idling at anchor.

"Teach is expecting me to return with two sloops," Jesamiah had said to the men in Spotswood's office. "If Knight gets word to him of your plan, then he will also be expecting two Navy frigates. I propose I sail in with the sloops as near as I can get. If he spots us too soon I can play-act, confirm the Navy is wise to him. It might buy us a bit of time, at least get us nearer. With sloops," he had added, "we can get in close. With frigates, we cannot."

"And who will man these sloops?" Brand had asked.

"The *Jane* is mine, so I will have my men. You can put who you like in whatever other vessel we can acquire. As long as they are volunteers and they know what they are doing."

"And what if Blackbeard sees through your scheme?" Captain Gordon had been scathing, reluctant to admit Jesamiah had the right of it. "What if he slips out, as you said he might, and attacks Virginia? How do we defend ourselves?"

Not wanting to confide that Teach might be less fearsome than they thought – at the last count he had only eighteen men left, assuming those who had taken Jesamiah and the injured Israel Hands ashore had not returned – Jesamiah had a simple answer to Gordon's question. "Why not remain here with the *Lyme* and the *Pearl*. Use them and your valuable experience to keep guard over the Chesapeake. Also, if you were to stay with the frigates, if Knight has told anyone of what you had previously planned, they will be none the wiser that we are about to attack. No one will notice us sailing away in two sloops. They *will* notice you leaving, Captain Gordon."

Gordon had liked the idea. It meant he did not have to become involved in any unpleasant fighting. Maynard too was pleased. Gordon was more hindrance than help. They would do better without him.

Brand had offered his own suggestion. "Are there not some of Blackbeard's men remaining at Bath Town? If the *Lyme* or *Pearl* were to drop me off higher up the North Carolina coast as soon as may be – and return straight-way back here to quell any rumour, I could take my men overland, be in Bath Town at roughly the same time as you reach the Ocracoke. Cover your rear."

Jesamiah failed to see the point, but he had held his tongue. Let the Navy think they were being useful and they would stay out of his way. There may well be some pirates remaining in Bath Town – the wounded Hands for one, but most of them would have melted away as soon as their captain had sailed out of sight. They were the ones who wanted to stay alive, who'd had enough of Blackbeard's devilry.

Having to keep the new plan secret, Jesamiah and Maynard realised they could not simply march to Hampton Roads and demand the owner of the *Ranger* give her up. Jesamiah had the solution to that also. He bought her. A scatter of gleaming diamonds tipped from a second pouch sealed the deal within five short minutes.

The only man to be suspicious was the armourer, John Brush, as he tallied the number of boxes of muskets and small arms being taken on board both craft. He had recognised Jesamiah as soon as he laid eyes on him. A quiet word from Lieutenant Maynard had silenced him – helped along by Jesamiah placing two diamonds into the armourer's palm.

"One for you, one for your daughter," he had said with a smile.

For himself, Jesamiah had driven a hard bargain with Spotswood. He would provide the ships, the men to crew the *Jane* and the knowledge and experience to get close to Blackbeard. Virginia would supply the weapons, the crew for a second ship – and agree that Jesamiah could have a quarter of whatever they found aboard the *Adventure* when the fighting was all over. No one had said anything about maybe not being alive to collect what was due.

Jesamiah knew for a fact that there were at least a dozen chests of gold dust in Teach's hold. Three of them would be enough to reimburse his outlay. And nor did he intend to stick to an agreement of a mere quarter! He had a rough idea of where Teach had hidden his own secret cache. Somewhere the Navy would not think of looking.

His men from the *Sea Witch* had been waiting aboard the *Jane*. Good men, though a couple Jesamiah had been tempted to refuse, but he had not dared suggest they stand down. Sailors, especially those aboard a pirate ship, were proud men. Thirty-three in all; among them, Nat Crocker, Finch, Joe Meadows, Sandy Banks, Isiah Roberts and Crawford. Twenty others and seven Navy Jacks made up the number. The *Ranger* had another twenty-five. With Jesamiah and Maynard they tallied sixty men. Teach had eighteen under his command, unless more had joined him since Jesamiah had been away. It was possible. Maybe Vane and Rackham had come back? There was no way of knowing until they arrived and could see for themselves. And even if Teach did have fewer men, he had cannon, the Virginians did not.

Jesamiah had not been sure about taking Crawford, he could be sullen and did not like taking orders, but he was good in a fight and a crack shot. In the end, Jesamiah let him stay.

To Finch, he had said, "You are not coming."

"An' why not?"

"Because I say so."

"You expect me t'let you go off by yerself? T'get yerself killed?"

"I said no."

"Why not?"

Close to losing his temper, Jesamiah had shouted, "Because for some utterly stupid reason I care about you!"

Finch had chewed his gums a little then spat a globule of spittle into the sea. "So you don't care about these others then?"

"Of course I do!"

"Well then."

His hands going as if to throttle him, Jesamiah had given up. "All right, but I'm warning you; if you get killed you'll have me to answer to."

Finch had grinned. "Aye Cap'n."

The one other disagreement: Maynard had insisted on being aboard the *Jane*, leaving Midshipmen Hyde from the *Lyme* to command the *Ranger*.

"It is my orders, Jesamiah; I am sorry," he had said.

"Spotswood don't trust me, eh?"

"Would you trust you?" Robert had asked cynically.

Jesamiah had laughed. Admitted, "Nope. Never trust a pirate, except to trust that you cannot trust him."

There were no cannons, only the minimal essential supply of food and water; nothing in excess, nothing that was not necessary. No one took any dunnage aboard. No clothes, no personal possessions. Just weapons. They needed to be light. The last thing they wanted was to run aground in the shallows of the Ocracoke under the baleful stare of Blackbeard's guns.

At three in the afternoon of Sunday the seventeenth day of November, with men, ammunition, weaponry – including grenados – but little else aboard, the two sloops set sail from Hampton Roads bound south for the Ocracoke, off the North Carolina coast. For some of them it would be their last voyage; their last fight.

Forty Four

North Carolina

Clean sheets, a clean gown for Elizabeth-Anne, her hair brushed, the babe swaddled in a blanket; Nicholas sat on the bed with the little one gathered in his arms, a joy of wonder glowing on his face. The serving girl had made up the fire.

As, many miles away, the *Jane* and the *Ranger* were preparing to set sail from Hampton Roads, Elizabeth-Anne was propped against the pillows, her eyes closed. She had slept a little, had drunk some tea and swallowed a few mouthfuls of broth. The child had suckled at his first essential milk, but soon he would need to be fed again. Tiola had not insisted; there was no immediate hurry. The boy was asleep and Elizabeth-Anne would benefit from the rest.

Tiola was tidying away the last of the soiled linen, and felt Nicholas look up at her. She smiled across the room at him; at the perfect picture they made, the father with his son in his arms, the mother peacefully recovering. Only she was not. Tiola frowned. Elizabeth-Anne was pale and her breathing was coming in small gasps. Something was wrong!

Dropping the linen to the floor, Tiola was there at her side.

"What is it?" Nicholas asked, but Tiola hushed him, her fingers around Elizabeth-Anne's wrist, counting the pulse-beat that was drubbing as if it were the summons of war drums. Elizabeth-Anne was sweating, yet her skin was cold to touch; white, almost translucent.

Tiola ripped back the bedclothes. The clean sheets, the clean gown, Elizabeth-Anne's thighs and legs were saturated with blood.

Forty Five

Virginia

The *Jane* was much smaller than the *Sea Witch*, and Maynard's frigate, the *Pearl*. A sloop this size, when handled by merchantmen would require as a minimum, no more than a third of the thirty-three hands presently on board. Rigged fore and aft, the single mast was stepped one third of her overall length aft of the bow. Stripped of all that was unnecessary she seemed spacious, although Finch had already been grumbling about the cramped conditions below.

"Ain't room to swing a rat, let alone a bloody cat."

"Remind me again why I agreed you could come?" Jesamiah had commented wryly.

The wind was gusting, but there was no need to adjust the amount of sail, the *Jane* could take the strain. She was proving to be a good little craft. Maybe his brother had done something right after all in acquiring her? Jesamiah walked up the steeply sloping deck to join Rob Maynard at the weather side, noting that it took him more effort than he would have expected. These weeks of sitting around in various gaol cells had not helped with the flabbiness of his muscles, though his weight had improved for the better. The poor diet of corn mush had been beneficial in one way. Grabbing the rail atop the bulwark, he grinned at Maynard who had one hand jammed on to his hat to keep it in place. Jesamiah had left his below, but now the threaded blue ribbons and the hair escaping from its tied queue were flogging about his face, stinging against his skin like miniature whip lashes. His coat flapped about his legs and he had to shout to make himself heard.

"She's handling well – if we can keep this up we'll be at the Ocracoke by Wednesday."

"Don't tempt fate, Acorne! We've a long way to go yet!" Maynard cupped his hand around his mouth to be heard; what with the wind, the thunder of the spread of canvas and the slap of the water against the hull he was having a hard job of it.

Jesamiah peered over the rail at the water churning past. They were making seven knots at least he reckoned. Above, the sky was as blue as a robin's egg. He tipped his head, smiled. It was good to be aboard a vessel again, racing southward through the rollers of the Atlantic, although he would have been happier to be aboard his own *Sea Witch*. Still, she should be there at Pilot Point, waiting for him – if he managed to survive what lay ahead. Spray surged over the bow, soaking the men for'ard. Jesamiah could see them laughing, their mouths open, heads tossed back. Even Crawford had joined in. They too were pleased to be doing something positive, to be at sea.

"They seem a cheery lot," Maynard observed. "I am amazed at the discipline you hold over them. They offer you minimum respect yet make no argument when you give a disagreeable order."

"That is because we work as a team, as brothers, not master and slave. I give no order that is not necessary, and if any man dislikes the way I do things, he is free to leave at the next port. We have no floggings aboard my ship."

"So how do you handle insubordination? It cannot just be an anarchic free for all."

Jesamiah was watching the wake foam away, the sun gleaming on the churned water. Over to leeward, half a mile away, was the *Ranger*. He had already told Maynard he was impressed by the choice of Midshipman Hyde to command her. The man knew his job.

"Discipline?" he answered. "I get most of it by earning respect. They know I know what I am doing, that I am fair, and they will get a share of whatever prize we win."

"And if they go against you?"

"Like I said, they have a choice to sail with me or not. Anyone pushing his luck too far loses that choice."

Nat, at the tiller, adjusted the *Jane* a point and her sails cracked, the mast bending under the weight of the wind pressure.

Jesamiah looked Maynard square in the face. "If any man riles me, he gets two warnings."

"And if there should be need of a third?"

The answer came as straight as the look. "He don't get a third. I tip him over the side."

A stronger gust of wind took Maynard's disapproving reply away with it.

"They make the rules," Jesamiah responded, "I don't write 'em. It's the price of being free men. Work together or not. Their choice. Do you get such a choice in your Navy?"

Maynard stared ahead not wanting to answer. It seemed disrespectful to his king and the captain he served. All the same, he had to admit he was enjoying himself for the first time in months, being here with Acorne.

"You can go below if you wish, Rob, I'll take this watch."

"No, I'll stay a while." Maynard laughed, added, in case Jesamiah took his intention wrong, "Too excited to miss out on anything!" Nearly losing his hat he took it off and tucked it under his arm.

"There's another reason the men are in a good mood," Jesamiah said, thinking that perhaps he ought to be honest. He liked Robert Maynard, was grateful to him for the consideration he had offered. "There's prize money aboard the *Adventure*. Gold dust mainly, a few chests of pieces of eight; another of gold coins. You'll find it all stowed in the aft locker in Teach's cabin. There's a false floor. If you look at the outside of the locker then compare the depth with the inside, you'll see what I mean."

"Gold?"

"Aye, gold. Enough for you to retire on, mate, even after dividing it into the agreed shares."

"I will get my provision of the hoard from the Admiralty." The answer was rigid with disapproving starch. What Jesamiah was suggesting bordered on piracy.

"Will you? You sure of that? Look at Woodes Rogers! Think how little he got of the considerable prize money he collected: a mere handful of coin and the dubious reward of being made Governor of Nassau? And they call us pirates! You'll not see a penny of it, Rob, believe me."

It was a sad thing to have to say, but Maynard did believe him. He nodded, hesitated, said, "I have a sweetheart back in England. I would so like to have the money to be able to make her my wife."

Jesamiah slapped his shoulder. "You live through this, Rob, you'll be rich enough to buy yourself a whole harem of wives. Just make sure the plunder is taken quietly and put somewhere secure. Give your men a decent share to keep them quiet and lay low for a few months. Then find a reasonable excuse to buy yourself out of the Navy. The rest of your life will be yours to do with as you will."

Finch had come on deck to announce he had managed to make something that vaguely resembled coffee. He overheard the last comment, had to add his own farthing's worth. "Wives? You don't bleedin' want to be buying wives – better to bloody sell 'em, not buy 'em!"

Forty Six

North Carolina

Blood loss was the major cause of death after childbirth. Tiola knew it only too well. In the right way of things, after the birth and expulsion of the placenta the uterus contracted until it was hard, like a ball. If it did not, the empty womb would be as an open wound with a flowing blood supply and nothing to stop the bleeding. The reduction of the uterus stopped the blood flow, but if it relaxed, failed to harden, there was no compression to the wound site and the mother haemorrhaged. And went on haemorrhaging until she bled to death.

Tiola padded Elizabeth-Anne with towels, but no sooner was the blood mopped up than more soaked through. As it clotted it looked like lumps of raw liver had been dumped on the bed. Tiola was covered in it, her hands, her gown, her face. Her hair. She looked like something out of a macabre theatre play, but she was not able to clean herself, not even to wipe her hands, for she was racing against time, and against Death.

She could see its pitiless shadow in the corner of the room, waiting. She was not afraid of Death – Death was benign, not evil or cruel, for every living thing had to die and move on to the next existence. It was the manner of its summons that brought the pain: the corruption of hatred that committed murder; the brutal unexpectedness of natural disasters, fire, flood, famine. And the waste of a woman dying in childbed.

No mother having gone through labour deserved to die in this way, so Tiola battled to keep her in the world of the living. She had the right to enjoy her son, and he to have a mother to love him. Too many good people had died; Tiola was not going to allow it to happen to another.

Elizabeth-Anne was conscious, Tiola had laid her flat, raised her legs, told Nicholas to hold her hand, talk to her. Keep talking to her. There had been nothing to feel inside Elizabeth-Anne, no hardening lump, only a wet, sticky mass as if Tiola was plunging her arm into a morass of mud. That at least told her the problem and she knew how to deal with it – if only she had time!

She had her hand on Elizabeth-Anne's abdomen and was pushing it in and down, rubbing in a circular motion, hard and firm. At first it had seemed as if nothing was happening. Elizabeth-Anne was pale and faint, her body trembling and so cold, but Tiola kept rubbing, around and around and around; pressing hard, pressing firm, on and on, around and around. The bleeding continued, seeping out of the mother's womb as if someone were wielding a pump. When Tiola pushed hard, over to the left, the blood streamed faster. She was the one operating the pump handle! Push down, blood squirted. Push down, more blood. But Tiola kept on with her hand regardless, working to stimulate the uterus to contract. Elizabeth-Anne was moaning piteously for the motion was painful, but there was nothing Tiola could do about that, except rub and rub and rub, hard and strong.

"Am I going to lose her?" Tears were streaming from Nicholas's eyes. The baby was crying in his cot, abandoned and forgotten for the moment. The serving girl, as useless as before, stood by the door, her hand stuffed in her mouth, weeping.

And there it was! A small hard lump, the size of a shilling piece forming beneath Tiola's pressing hand. She kept rubbing, could not stop. If she did, the uterus would relax again and all this effort would be wasted. "No," she said to Nicholas, panting as she rubbed and pushed. "I am not going to lose her. I am not."

The hard lump became the size of a guinea piece, was expanding, but still she kept on. The bleeding had eased, but she would have to continue for a while yet. She wiped her arm across her face, smearing more blood. Her arms were aching, her fingers stiff and she looked as if she had butchered a pig.

"Nicholas, put your hand here, do as I have been doing. Yes, press down, rub in circles."

"But it hurts her!"

"It will hurt more if the bleeding starts again."

Tiola lifted the crying baby, hushed him and roused his mother. If Elizabeth-Anne could feed him the flow of breast milk would help to seal the bleeding. The poor woman barely knew what she was doing, but Tiola held the child and guided his tiny mouth onto the nipple. Once he was sucking she called Nicholas to come, help his wife and child, and she took over the rubbing.

She was exhausted, her energy drained by the need to remain outwardly calm and in control while the fear and panic shot about inside her. Tiola was almost asleep, her eyelids were drooping, her hand working automatically. All she wanted was her bed...but she kept rubbing, pressing downward, going around and around. Nicholas helped his wife move the child to the other breast, a small whimper escaping the boy's milky mouth as he protested.

"He will be a boy to be proud of," Tiola remarked, "though I wager he will lead you a merry dance as he grows."

And then she felt the lump reach the size of a man's clenched fist and all the tiredness, the fatigue, the feelings of hopelessness fled. The bleeding had stopped. The womb was contracting, and when she looked into the corner of the room, Death courteously acknowledged her victory, and was gone. The relief was overwhelming. Tiola closed her eyes and made no attempt to wipe away the tears that trickled from beneath her lashes. But when she opened them again, she caught a movement in that same corner. Another shadow: one that was not neutral or benign. The squatting presence of the Dark.

Anger, the aftermath of anxiety, replenished Tiola's flagging energy. She stretched out her arm, fingers splayed, and sent a flare of light scudding after the Malevolence, sending its unwanted presence and sniggering spite away.

As dusk settled, Tiola crawled into her bed; the blood had been washed away but her body ached with weariness. Elizabeth-Anne was safe in the care of her husband, and the newborn slept, contented. The Malevolence had gone.

~ *Jesamiah?* ~

He answered her call immediately. ~ *Sweetheart? You sound tired.* ~

~ *I am. I nearly lost her. After all this, I nearly lost Elizabeth-Anne.* ~ She felt Jesamiah's presence, the feel of his arms, his body pressing close. His breath, his smell.

~ *But you didn't? She is safe and well?* ~

~ *Ais, mother and son are asleep.* ~

~ *And so should be the midwife. Go to sleep, sweetheart. I love you.* ~

She was drifting, may have slept a minute or two. ~ *Jesamiah?* ~

~ *I'm still here.* ~

~ *But where is here? I am afraid. The Dark is near you, I can sense it.* ~

~ *I'm fine. Go to sleep. I'm where I like to be. At sea. Go to sleep.* ~

Drowsy, Tiola did not realise what he had said, did not understand his meaning. She slept, but it was a troubled sleep. She dreamed of blood. Covering her hands and soaking into her clothing. Blood seeping into the deck as Jesamiah lay dead on a ship that was not the *Sea Witch*. This was a smaller craft with torn and battered rigging that moaned in the desolate wind of the open marshes. And throughout the dream came the black presence of the Dark.

She awoke, screaming Jesamiah's name. Screaming that Edward Teach could not be killed. Like her, his immortality was protected, except, his protection came from the hatreds and evils of the Dark.

Teach could not be killed until the Malevolence was sent from him. And no living human could do that, only an Old One of Wisdom. But Jesamiah did not know it. He was going to kill Edward Teach, Blackbeard, but had no knowledge that Teach could not be killed!

Forty Seven

Tuesday 19th November

Charles Mereno was having doubts. What if Phillipe had not been Teach's child; had been sired by Carlos after all? Would it have made a difference? Possibly. Would it alter what he had to do now? No.

He ought to have been truthful to the Witch Woman, for she had been kind and had helped as much as she could. But then, she was under the impression that all he wanted was to explain; make amends. He had deliberately misled her. She would not have helped had she known his ultimate intention.

This ritual, this cleansing – whatever name you put upon it – was it a test? Another doubt: what if he was wrong? What if this killing that he was meant to do was not for the peace he so craved but was some foul manipulation by the Devil to damn him forever? Hah! He was already damned, so what did that matter! No, he had to believe what he had been told – even if he was as mad as Teach, and the words he had heard were those of his own insanity.

Where land became the sea, and the sea became land, where one was not the other…he had to take the life of his begotten son. His son. The boy he had sired. The boy he had abandoned to face his own fate.

"I taught you to sail," he pleaded to the keening wind and the roar of the sea as he stood at the tip of the Ocracoke and watched the dawn send her strands of light into the sky. "I taught you to load and fire a pistol, to use a cutlass. I ensured you could understand a sextant and chart a course. I taught you all those things a seaman needs, yet you despise me."

He had himself been abandoned. Was that why he had not been the father he should have been? He was wrong to be bitter, for his mother had loved him and the stepfather who had given him the name of St Croix had treated him as his own. But it had hurt as a child, as a youth, being aware that his natural father had not wanted to know him.

Except, what he had believed had not been the truth. Only when Jesamiah was about to be born had Charles discovered the truth: that his father had not even known of his existence until it was too late. His mother had not told the man she had loved all her life of the son she had borne. She had not wanted to hold him to her out of obligation, condemn him to a loveless marriage – for her lover had given his heart to another. And so she had set him free. Charles' eventual knowing of his father's ignorance had not smoothed those years of bitterness though. And now, here he was paying the price for his own blinkered selfishness. Had he not been drunk that night when a good man was murdered and a good woman violated, had breeches been kept buttoned, he would have no need to be here, doing this. Ah, the consequences arising from one misdeed!

More thoughts. More questions.

Why had Jesamiah not read that letter? Why was he denying his father this last chance to explain? Jesamiah had always been so damned obstinate. What about when he had tried to send the boy to England, to school? It would have been an opportunity to get him away from Phillipe – but would he go? No!

Jesamiah had been a brave boy. He had never tongue-tattled, had taken punishments for things he had not done without whining. Had masked his tears and hidden his fears.

"I was so unfair to the boy," Charles mumbled to himself. "I should have defended him. But it is too late now. Too late."

The sky was turning blue as the sun rose. It would be a while for them to come down from the Chesapeake, for wind and tide were against them, another day yet, two?

"I wanted you to turn on Phillipe," Charles said to the wisps of mare's tail cloud building in the east. "I wanted you to prove to me that you could defend yourself; that you could fight back. But you did not, Jesamiah, did you? Why did you not?"

And then the answer occurred to him. Jesamiah had not had anything to prove. The proving that he was brave enough to fight back was not what he had needed. He had wanted only fairness and justice and the love of his father – and his father had denied him because he, Charles, had been afraid. It was himself, Charles Mereno, who should have done the proving!

Teach had always claimed that he had sold his soul to the Devil and Charles had readily believed it. From when he had first taken him on as a midshipman, there had been something different about the boy, and that same difference had been there in Phillipe's eyes the day when Charles had brought Jesamiah home. It had been deeper than hatred or something born of sibling jealousy. The madness of evil?

Oh yes, Phillipe had been Blackbeard's son, and had Jesamiah fought back he would have been destroyed. He had survived only because he had submitted. He had endured until he had gained the strength and courage to retaliate. Endured until he knew he would win.

Unlike his cowardly father, who had shut his eyes and hidden, pretended not to see; lain there, drunk, while evil was done.

Forty Eight

Wednesday 20th November

Three captains refused to accept Tiola as a passenger, on account that it was too risky to take a woman aboard. Too unlucky! Many a sailor insisted a woman would bring bad fortune to a voyage.

~ *I am coming to the Ocracoke,* ~ she had told Jesamiah. ~ *I have to come.* ~

~ *You are not*! ~ he had answered forcefully. ~ *You will stay away.* ~

She ignored him, did not bother explaining why she had to be there: because Edward Teach could not be killed by a mortal hand until the protection of the Dark was forced from him. She had resolved to walk the fifty miles to the coast when she overheard a man grumbling that Captain Odell was intending to set sail. Odell was known to be friendly with Teach, and no one trusted him.

"He's had a job getting a crew," she heard the sailor remark. "I for one intend to stay out the way 'til he's gone. I'm not getting mixed up with no piracy schemes."

Odell was a canny man: he had a nose for business and was not afraid of following the scent. Teach could no longer come openly into Bath Town, not after what he had done. Piracy, stealing, plundering, rape – even murder was acceptable when it was strangers who suffered. But not when it was their own. Not a pretty young girl and a popular young man who had been born in North Carolina; whose savage deaths had left their respective fathers childless. Blackbeard had overstepped the mark and the tide of opinion had turned against him. Odell was from Charleston, he was not a Bath Town man and he intended to capitalise on that swing of opinion. Teach would be wanting to offload his ill-gotten cargos somewhere new and Odell intended to make his fortune by becoming the replacement middleman. All he had to do was convince Blackbeard that he needed a new partner.

Several men who should have crewed for him did not agree with his thinking, so when Captain Sam Odell left Bath Town Creek, he had several kegs of best rum in his hold and six men and a boy as crew. The boy knew little of sailing, but was willing to learn and jumped to it when told to hold this or pull on that. Men saw what they expected to see, and what they saw was a quiet lad with a beardless chin, a lanky figure and slender hands. Tiola was adept at making men see what she wanted them to see. It did not take a skill of Craft to bind her breasts, wear a boy's breeches and shirt; braid her long hair into a queue and lower her voice to a lad's unbroken timbre.

She would not be aboard long enough for them to discover any different, and by midday – evening if the wind slowed their passage down the Pamlico – they would be in the waters of the Ocracoke, where, somehow, she had to find a way of stopping Jesamiah getting himself killed by Teach.

Forty Nine

Thursday 21st November

The *Jane* and the *Ranger* dropped anchor at the northern end of Ocracoke Island where trees would partially hide their masts. Teach, assuming he was where Jesamiah had left him, was sixteen miles away at the other end. It was mid morning and they had no intention of moving further down until the evening. Once they did move there would be need for stealth and as much quiet as possible, with a minimum risk of running aground. The aim was to attack Teach at first light, going in with the flood tide before he realised they were there.

All the men were weary. The voyage had been as fast as they could make it and not one of either crew had shirked any portion of the work. They went ashore to relax for an hour, to eat, sleep, to check and load their weapons. Every man had at least two pistols and a musket. The grenados were placed in baskets ready for use, the Colours were laid ready. All they waited for was the sun to start sliding down the sky towards the horizon.

Fifty

Once the sun had begun to set, Tiola had managed to stay near Sam Odell's brig – she had spent the afternoon with two of Odell's men on what, on the Ocracoke, was termed as 'inland', snaring wild birds for supper. They had caught a fair few, and with campfires blazing, the evening had been heralded by the smell of roasting meat. But even staying out of the way she was aware that Blackbeard's interest had been drawn to her.

He had no fancy for boys; that she did know. Had he recognised her face? She dared not use her Craft to alter her appearance – she passed well enough for a boy without it. Unless someone ripped open her shirt or caught her relieving herself in the bushes, she was safe. Normally, even if they did, she would have used her ability to make them instantly forget what they had seen. But so close to Teach, she had to be careful. She could hear the whisperings of the Malevolents that possessed him. They were aware that something was not right; she had only to use her Craft once and they would have her. It was not that she was afraid, not for herself, but she could not kill Teach, to do so was against all the laws of Light. Another would need to do that – and for the doing she first had to defeat the Dark at the right time and in the right place. Neither of which was here as evening settled. And so she suppressed her Craft and stayed out of sight as much as possible.

Teach and Odell had eaten their fill and the drink the merchant had supplied was rapidly swamping any empty space in their bellies. Once it was full dark Tiola had made up her mind to slip away. There were not many places to hide on the Ocracoke, but not one of those men getting steadily drunker would bother tramping several miles in search of a missing boy.

Teach looked at her again. She tried to duck her head, pretend she was busy, but he called to her. "Boy. Oi, boy, come thee over here."

Reluctant, she padded on bare feet across sand that was warm from the day's sun. She stopped a few yards away, kept her gaze downcast.

"They tell me thee caught an' cooked these birds."

"Aye, Sir."

"Speak up boy, let us see thy face!"

Nothing for it, she would have to brazen this out. She lifted her head, but did not look direct at him. Instead, she shifted her line of sight to a vague point above his shoulder. Eye to eye, the Malevolents would link to her.

"Thee be a pretty boy, bain't thee?" Teach observed. "How old be thee then?"

"Thirteen, I think, Sir, though as I cannot count beyond ten I cannot be certain." She mimicked the Carolina accent; dared not allow any trace of her own Cornish burr to taint her voice.

Teach peered at her more intently. "Where've I seen thee before then, eh?"

She had been expecting the question, had her answer ready. "I've seen you many a time, Sir. I come from Bath Town, I've been pesterin' my Ma to let me join your crew, but she were a bit dipsy about that. Said I'd be better off askin' Captain Odell here. Which I did an' he were good enough t'take me on."

It worked. Teach was losing interest. "Thee want to be a sailor then, boy?"

Again she put eagerness into her answer, "Oh aye, Sir! That I do!"

"Well then, get thee up an' over them dunes there, and keep thy eyes peeled fer sign of a Navy frigate. There'll be a moon risin' later, thee may just see somethin' that'll be o' great use t'all o' us. Off thee go."

Tiola gave a little hop and a bow as an excited boy would do, then turned and ran, her heart pounding with relief.

"A frigate?" Odell queried. "You expecting company?"

Teach generously topped up his guest's tankard. "Nay, I b'lieve it t'be all piss an' wind, but tha lad may'n well be useful – just in case I be wrong." He pulled a letter from his pocket, handed it to Odell, who squinted at it in the flicker of firelight.

He could make out only a few words, "'*If this finds thee yet in harbour – Make thy way up as soon as –*' signed," he squinted harder, "'*thy real friend.*' By Gad, Teach, this be a warning! Is it safe to stay here? Who sent it?"

"Tobias Knight, a jellyfish of a fool. Bain't no Navy boats goin' t'get close t'us 'ere."

"Strikes me you might be the fool, Teach."

"What's that? Thee callin' me stoopid?"

"Course not, but I do not want to get involved in no fighting."

"Thar's bain't goin' t'be no fightin', only drinkin' and thee's fallin' behin' me, ol' mate – thee's fallin' behin'! Hie there, Tom, where be that fiddle o' thine? Give us a tune eh? A lively tune fer us t'sing to!"

Fifty One

They had let the sloops drift in; Nat Crocker pushing the tiller over and Skylark whipping the mainsheet off the cleat, the line running through his rough hands. At the right moment, Jesamiah, standing forward in the bow and leaning so far over he had almost tumbled, had frantically signalled for the anchor to let go. The *Jane* had come to rest on the opposite side of the island to where Teach was anchored; the *Ranger* a short way behind her.

In the darkness Teach's exact position was uncertain, but the singing, the laughter and carousing from his camp was enough to guide them. As quietly as was possible the sails came down, a cold meal was passed around and men settled to sleep, but when the moon rose – not quite a half moon – Jesamiah whispered to Maynard that he was going to take one of his men to see exactly where Teach was and what he was doing.

"Are you mad?" Maynard hissed back at him. "We know roughly where he is. That will suffice."

"I don't do roughly, Rob."

"Then I will come with you."

"Don't be daft. If I get caught I can bluff my way out. You will be horribly murdered. Aside, someone has to stay here in command."

Jesamiah took Skylark with him. Slipping barefoot over the side, they half swam, half waded for the shore. They had daggers only, nothing on them that could chink or clatter. Keeping their heads down they ran up the narrow beach and over the sand dunes. Even this short way inland the smell was different; the scent of earth, of foliage and warm sand cooling after a day in the sun. The chirrup of insects, the sound of the wind whispering through the marsh grass, the sigh of the sea. The moon gave sufficient light as they ran, crouching low, their shadows leaping beside them, appearing like grotesque beasts keeping pace.

The laughter was louder, the clink of bottles, a man belching. Teach's wild guffaw. A fiddle began to scrape a tune and several of Teach's men began to sing – more laughter, and the hollow stamp of feet on the sand.

Jesamiah signalled to drop to their bellies and he and Skylark squirmed forward up another dune, found themselves peering down at three camp fires, men sprawled around in various poses, several dancing raucous jigs in the space between, many of the rest already in a drunken sleep. There were two boats at anchor here on the inner, sheltered side of the island, protected by the shoals and sandbanks. The *Adventure* and another Jesamiah did not recognise.

"Odell," Skylark whispered into Jesamiah's ear. "The *Cormorant*." He recognised her immediately, for he had painted her likeness several times when keeping watch at Bath Town.

"How many in Odell's crew?" Jesamiah asked.

"Hard to say; differed. Nine maximum. They won't fight. Odell's a trader, not a pirate."

"An' it don't look like Teach has got any more men than when I was last 'ere."

A shout went up from around the fire, instinctively Jesamiah and Skylark ducked down, but it was only two of them squabbling. Jesamiah recognised them, Gibbens and Red Rufus.

"If only I had a pair of pistols. I'd take those two buggers out right now."

"Not a good idea Cap'n."

~ *He is right, luvver; you would be dead before you could reload.* ~

Tiola?

~ *I am here, to your left.* ~

Jesamiah motioned for Skylark to pull back, squirmed around and studied the tree over to his left. He had not noticed her, could not even be certain she had been there a moment ago, but it seemed as if she was stepping out from the very trunk itself as she showed herself.

"What the...!" he bit his tongue, he had almost shouted at her. ~ *What the fok are you doing here?* ~

~ *I could ask the same.* ~

~ *Aye, but you'd not get a bloody answer!* ~ He was cross because he had been startled, and the crossness rapidly shifted to anger as fear set in. This was no place for his wife! ~ *I told you to stay away!* ~

~ *And I told you I had to come. It seems we do not listen to each other.* ~ She was teasing, laughter was in her voice. Jesamiah could see nothing funny.

Signalling with his hand, he indicated that Meadows was to go back to the sloops. He pointed to Tiola then himself. Skylark nodded, grinned, his teeth flashing white in the moonlight. Then he was gone, running low over the dunes. If he wanted to know how Tiola had got there, or ask questions, he would have to bide his time and wait.

Jesamiah grasped Tiola's arm and half marched, half dragged her northward, away from Teach and the two sloops. There was a generous stand of trees that he remembered about half a mile away. He'd slept there a couple of times when he had wanted a respite of privacy. Few of Teach's men bothered wandering far from the shore. Walking required effort and effort was something they shied clear of.

"What are you doing here?" he snapped when they could talk, though in little more than a whisper. "Are you trying to get yourself killed?"

"Are you?" she answered with equal indignity. "You cannot kill Teach without my help."

"Oh aye? Learnt to shoot now, have you?"

It was no good arguing. Tiola released her bottled anger, calmed and centred herself. "What possesses Teach protects him. Like me he can die, but it will not be easy to kill him."

With her anger faded, Jesamiah too calmed down, although his fear for her safety was hammering at his heart. "So you will help us finish him? Use your spells?"

She laid her hand on his chest, dipped her head, scared to look at him, to tell him the truth, but she had to. "As soon as I can I will drive out the Dark, but I cannot kill him, Jesamiah. You know I cannot."

He stepped away, turned his back on her, his anger spilling over the edge again. "You abort babies. That's killing, ain't it?"

That hurt. She was on the edge of crying. There had been so many cruel deaths, and her frayed emotions were shouting at her to put an end to Teach now – but she could not. She could not kill unless her own survival depended upon it.

"I rarely terminate a pregnancy, Jesamiah. When I do it is because the mother would not survive if I did not. I sometimes have to choose to end the life of a babe during birth, but it would die anyway, I merely hasten its end. And it is not a choice I make lightly."

He hunched his shoulders, folded his arms, said, "Then let's do it now. You do what you have to do and I will do my part." He pulled the dagger from his belt, its blade glinting in the moonlight.

She shook her head. Men were going to die – Jesamiah too maybe – but there was nothing she could do to prevent it. Nothing. "I cannot. Until the balance shifts, I will not possess enough power to defeat him. If I tried now I would also die, the Dark and the Light are of equal status, Jesamiah. What I send out will return threefold if I am not careful with my control. I must wait until there is a fluctuation of Existence, then transform the negative energies into positive. And I can only do that when I am summoned, and Time becomes right."

"Summoned? Who by?" Jesamiah demanded. His anger, his frustration, building. He did not understand a word of what she was talking about, but understood that she was trying to tell him there could be extreme danger for her. He had a sudden feeling that he did not want to hear an answer to his question.

Tiola put her hand on his arm, said quietly into his mind, *~ By the stopping and starting of Time, and by one who cannot die, for he is already dead. ~*

"My father. My bloody father?"

She nodded.

Charles Mereno had not been honest with her, she was well aware there was much that he had not said, and she had sensed his presence here on the Ocracoke from the moment she stepped ashore. Just why he was here, what his intentions were, she had no idea. That they were interlinked with Edward Teach did not take much guessing. But was there something else? There was something troubling Charles Mereno, something deeply distressing him. But what?

Jesamiah walked away a few paces, stood in the cradle of silvered moonlight, his head bowed, tired, worried. Uncertain. "I've already told my father, several times over, that I do not want to know. The past is done, closed. I want only the future, Tiola." He turned slowly around, looked so vulnerable, so sad. "All I want is you, my wife."

"I am here, and I promise I will keep myself safe, if you will promise the same?"

He looked at her, she was so beautiful, even appearing as she was, a ragged-dressed, barefoot boy. Was she really his? Or was this some wicked faery trick of an illusion to make him believe he was the luckiest man alive?

"That is not a promise I can make," he said sadly. "I cannot hang back and expect my men to fight for me."

Tiola was quiet a moment. No, he could not, and if death was his fate, then…She released her breath in a quivering shudder of acceptance. He would die one day, that was a certainty. One day, she would be without him until they met again in the next world. That was his fate. She had no control over fate, the future or destiny. But she did have control over the here, the now.

"Make love to me," she said, "so we can be as one for this night."

He had no need to answer, no need to say that maybe this could be their first and only night as husband and wife. He did show her how much he loved her, though. Showed her in the way he knew best.

Fifty Two

Friday 22nd November

As the last stars faded the two sloops weighed anchor and crept towards the channel that took them to the other side of the island. Jesamiah had made it his business to study the lie of shoals and deeper waters while he had been here with Teach, but all the same, they asked Frank Blake, one of the Navy crew who had known this area for most of his life, to pilot them in. There was very little wind, and the dawn sky promised a fine, sun-rich day. What wind there was came in little gusts that sent the spindrift skimming and waves bouncing like skittish horses, but the flurries were few and far between. It was frustrating, the *Adventure* was in sight but they were almost becalmed, they could not get at her! And any moment now someone from over there could awake and see them.

Maynard decided to send out the small boat to sound the depth, and to run out the sweeps. "We'll row in."

"They'll hear us," Jesamiah warned.

"Aye, but with our oars and the boat going ahead, we may be on them before they gather their wits."

It was a risk. Jesamiah shrugged, but he did not countermand the order. He did not have a better one.

Sandy Banks and Crawford went in the boat with a few of the Navy men, everyone else in the *Jane* took the sloop's oars, save for Nat and Maynard at the tiller and Blake forward in the bow. Even Jesamiah took hold of an oar and prepared to help pull. Maynard raised an eyebrow, said nothing. All the same, Jesamiah answered the thought.

"I ain't afraid of hard work. That's another thing we do different to the Navy. We all put our backs into it when we need to."

With the *Ranger* following under oar behind, they made slow progress forward. The strategy did not last long.

Gibbens awoke, needing to urinate. He stood, streaming his water against a bush, his rum-sodden mind not taking in that there were two sloops pulling towards the *Adventure*. Two sloops? Was this Acorne? Had he got those boats then? Already? That was quick work. He stood there, frowning, the thoughts struggling through his inebriated brain. If it was Acorne, why would he be rowing in? Why not wait for the tide and the wind and sail in as any of them did?

Then he realised. This was not Acorne! Without bothering to button his breeches, but clasping the waistband in his hands, he ran, shouting and bellowing the alarm, waking everyone.

The way of pirates: they could be filled with more drink than a keg full of rum, but when action was needed they took no second thought. Those with muskets fired off shots, others ran through the shallows, swam the last few yards and clambered aboard their ship. Teach, Gunner Norton, Jimmy Baker and the Negro, Caesar, were already aboard with the captain. Edward Teach had opted to sleep in his own bed, in his own cabin, not on the sand that irritated and itched when it got inside clothing.

As men came aboard, Caesar handed out weapons and the pirates ran to the rail, took aim. The *Jane's* small jolly boat received the force of two volleys. The third was from one of the cannons, which whistled its shot across the water and fell wide in a plume of spray. With more men wounded than were unscathed, Nat ordered the boat back to the sloop. He had a flesh wound, Crawford too. Another cannon shot would have them sunk.

Sam Odell had stayed ashore. He scurried with his crew into the dunes and they hunkered as low as they could get, hands over their ears and heads, wanting no part of this. The boy who had been with them yesterday was completely forgotten.

"Cut the anchor cable!" Teach yelled, "Get them sails up! Morton, why bain't them cannons reloaded!"

The odds were in the attackers' favour – sixty men, two sloops, against nineteen in one boat. But Teach knew these waters well and he was not incompetent. With the flurries of wind, and some of the men at the sweeps, he headed for the narrow channel between the sandbanks, knowing exactly where it lay. This was his hunting ground, this was where he lured ships by making the vulnerable and innocent think the water was deep.

Maynard ordered the King's Colours to be hoisted, and set off after him, as before, the *Jane* going ahead, the *Ranger* following. The sails of all three were worse than useless; the creak and splash of oars and the grunt of men pulling the only sounds. Jesamiah was standing beside Maynard, anxiously watching the varying hues of the water ahead and gauging what was deep, what was shallow.

Jesamiah was not happy about sailing under the King's flag, but he had made a bargain and he intended to stick with it. He wanted no mention of his or the crew's names to be written in the logbook, which Rob Maynard kept with meticulous detail. As far as legal records went, Jesamiah Acorne did not exist. All he wanted was his rightful share of treasure and recompense for damage to his sloops. If he lived he would take the reward and go. If he died, the prize money was to be sent to la Sorenta. To where he had also ordered Tiola, should she be left on her own. Tiola had not acknowledged his order. If she were left on her own…she did not know what she would do, where she would go.

Blake called out a warning – they were too far to starboard. And a bullet tore through his throat. The blood from the severed artery sprayed in an arc behind him as his body toppled from the bow into the sea. Almost at the same instant, the *Jane* and the *Ranger* ran aground.

Teach guffawed loudly then hurled a torrent of abuse, the still, almost windless air carrying his gruff voice clearly. "Damn thee for villains! Who bist thee? From where'd thee come? Blast thy eyes!"

"You can see very well from our Colours you knave! We are the King's men!"

Teach ignored Maynard's bold words. "I can see thee, Acorne! Damn thee and may the Devil take thee for a cursed traitor!" He had a bottle in his hand. He raised it in the air, crowed, "I give thee no quarter, Jesamiah Acorne! D'thee hear? No quarter t'none o' thee or I'll see thee in Hell!" He drank from the bottle and then hurled it at them to seal his macabre promise.

Jesamiah raised a pistol and fired at Teach, a wild shot, for the distance was too great. "I expect no quarter from you, Teach!" he shouted, "and you shall expect none in return!"

Finch was raging at the men to lighten the load – they had to get afloat. The drinking water went overboard, then he sent men down to haul up the ballast, send that over, his blustering and swearing motivating them to shift their arses. What little was left of the food – the stove, the wood to burn in it, the coffee, even the cups and drinking tankards went. About to start on hammering at the bricks of the stove's chimney, the rising tide rocked them loose, and encouraged by Isiah Roberts, with some more heaving and pulling, the *Jane* floated free. A moment later, the *Ranger* too was afloat. The men cheered. The fight was on again!

They put their backs to it and rowed. The *Ranger* was a little way behind. Teach had brought the *Adventure* around slightly. Her guns had been loaded with swan shot, nails, and pieces of old iron. He fired a broadside. The resulting damage to the *Ranger* was catastrophic. Midshipman Hyde was killed instantly, his head half severed. Five of his men died outright also. Ten more wounded. With more than half her crew dead or injured, the *Ranger* ran aground again and stuck fast. There was no one to pull her off this time.

For a moment Maynard did not know what to do. With one broadside half his attacking force had gone. Jesamiah yelled for his best shots to come forward – Sandy Banks, Joe Meadows, Crawford, Nat Crocker..

"Shoot at his jib," Jesamiah ordered, "concentrate your fire on those fore halyards. If we cripple her we can force her aground."

They rested their muskets on the rail, took careful aim – nothing haphazard, nothing left to chance – and fired, reloaded, fired. Teach was returning fire with pistols and muskets. His guns were at last reloaded, were being run out – another broadside, but he was not so lucky this time. Some tore holes in the sails, some gouged great splinters from the rails, but most of the shot fell short. Crawford fell back, a bullet through his shoulder; Sandy Banks screamed, dropped his musket. Blood burst from his eye as a bullet tore into his face. Other men fell writhing on the deck. Jesamiah, Nat and Skylark took no notice. They fired again and by sheer luck, the *Adventure*'s halyards snapped, the jib tore free and she slewed into a sandbank. Teach was stuck fast.

With no wind to clear it, smoke hung in a great pall between the two sloops. Those men who were not dead were coughing, their eyes watering from the stink and sting of gunpowder. Jesamiah's ears were ringing from the gunshots; his hearing impaired, sounds were suddenly muffled, distant.

In the lull of firing, he hurried aft ordering the more seriously wounded to be taken below. On strict command he had told Tiola to stay down there. Strict orders. Bad enough having her aboard, but he would not allow her on deck. Would not. With wounded to care for, not really knowing where to start with their terrible injuries, Tiola had no opportunity to disobey.

Maynard found Jesamiah for'ard. "We're drifting towards the *Adventure*, with one man on the tiller we'll come straight up against her. Get your men ready to board."

"No!" Vehemently, Jesamiah disagreed. "If we're drifting let's make Teach think we're done for. Let him come to us. Get everyone below. Just you and me up here. When we are alongside, we can give Teach a warm welcome."

Fifty Three

Jesamiah had not noticed that a bullet had nicked his arm. He felt the first twinge of pain as he grasped the tiller and encouraged the *Jane* to keep drifting in the right direction. Maynard, next to him, was half slumped over the binnacle box. He had enough blood on him from helping the wounded below to look convincingly dead.

Unaware of the ruse, unaware that he was not about to be boarded, Blackbeard retaliated as the *Jane* bumped alongside. Most of his crew were alive and relatively unscathed, for the *Jane*'s small arms had not been as effective as his cannon. His men tossed grenados made of bottles filled with gunpowder and scrap iron to the *Jane*'s deck, a quick-fuse in the bottle's neck to ignite it. They exploded on the *Jane* with loud bangs and more smoke, but aside from those already dead her decks were empty, and little damage done. The noise abated. There had been no retaliatory fire. The smoke began to clear.

Teach waited a moment. There was a man slumped over the tiller, another, blood covered, draped over the binnacle box. Bodies were scattered around, two had been decapitated, severed limbs had streamed blood everywhere. It was a charnel house. He grinned.

"We've knocked 'em on the 'ead, m'dears!" he cried, and stepped across into the *Jane* with most of his men: his boatswain Garratt Gibbens, Phillip Morton, Thomas Gates and Red Rufus, among them.

Save for the flurries of wind and the cry of gulls overhead, it was eerily quiet. Teach walked towards the nearest scuttle, poking at bodies with his foot as he passed. He had found time during that first flight after cutting his anchor cable to dress in his usual imposing manner: two pistols hung from his baldric tied on by ribbons – there had been others, but fired, they had been discarded. Twined into his beard and hair, slow match fuses were burning and smoking. With his grimed face, tall stature and bulging eyes, he looked a fearsome sight as he strode across the *Jane*'s bloodied deck, although it was only his own men who saw him. And Maynard; peeping through the crook of his arm covering his face. Another yard…One more…

And Maynard sprang upward. Yelling like a wild man, his pistol raised, he aimed, fired, point blank at Teach.

Teach already had a pistol in his hand – loosed a shot as Maynard's bullet thudded into his shoulder. It was enough to knock his aim askew and his bullet flew wide, but not enough to kill him. He barely felt its impact. At the same instant, Jesamiah moved, fast, away from where he had been slumped over the tiller, and adding his roar to Maynard's frantic yelling, urged the men of the *Jane* to come up from below, to attack.

The men, many already bloodied and wounded, appeared from the scuttles, weapons raised, screaming and chanting a war cry of "Death to the bastards!" All was noise and chaos; pistols popping, blade ringing against blade, shouts, grunts, cries.

Jesamiah met with Gibbens. Both of them had pistols that had been fired in the frenzied rush – Jesamiah's had taken down one of Teach's men; Gibbens' shot had gone wide of the mark – they had their cutlasses out, met, parried, broke apart, met again. Jesamiah's foot slipped on blood on the deck, he went down on his backside. Gibbens moved in for the kill but Nat Crocker was there, behind them. He was using his pistol as a club; brought the butt down on Gibbens' head. There was an audible crack, the pirate fell, unconscious. Another man – Nat turned, used his feet, his elbows, anything, to fight, to defend himself. Jesamiah came upon Red Rufus, someone else with whom he had a score to settle. Jesamiah's cutlass swung upward; Rufus tried to parry with his own, but he was not as fast, not as agile. The cutlass – a killing weapon, heavy, lethal. His belly slit open, Red Rufus lay dead.

Skylark ducked under an axe that was scything downward, brought his dagger up and plunged it into his opponent's groin – but Skylark fell also, his face contorted in a grimace of agony, a bullet lodged in his thigh.

Maynard could not believe his bad luck. He had shot Teach at close range but the man stood there and fought on like a fury! In disbelief he saw another bullet slam into Teach, going clean through his side. The big man stumbled, but that was all. It was as if he could feel nothing, as if he had no blood inside him to shed. No earthly life to lose. Was he truly protected by the Devil?

Enraged, more than a little afraid, Maynard raised his cutlass and attacked. Teach merely laughed and stepped aside. The blade came down and shattered in half, broken on impact with his cartridge box, the edge tearing across Maynard's hand, cutting the knuckles open to the bone. With the back of his hand Edward Teach delivered a blow to Maynard's face and contemptuously swept him aside. He turned with a leer of triumph to face Jesamiah. He had another loaded pistol raised, was aiming straight at Jesamiah's heart.

And Time stopped.

This was the place. The place where the land became the sea and sea became the land. Where one was not the other and all was not as it seemed.

Charles Mereno stood between Blackbeard and Jesamiah, he too had a pistol raised, was pointing it at Edward Teach. The bigger man with the black hair and the bushed beard slowly lowered his weapon, the hint of a questioning frown wrinkling his forehead. After all these years of taunting, was Charles St Croix Mereno to finally find his balls and turn against him?

Not taking his attention off Teach, Charles spoke to Jesamiah. "I wanted to make it up to you," he said sorrowfully, "but you would not let me. You would not listen to what I wanted to tell you about Phillipe."

"And I did not – do not – want to know about him now."

Teach looked from the ghost of the father to the living son. Derision spread across his face. "'Ee weren't thy brother, Acorne. Thy father 'ere had no doin' with plantin' 'is seed in the whore who birthed that boy. Any one of a dozen men could've sired 'im. Did thee know that?"

"He knows," Mereno said. "I told him on the night that poor young wretch you took as wife was used so ill."

Teach cackled, a sound drenched in madness. "An' did 'ee tell 'im I were one o' them dozen men?"

"I did. I told him Phillipe was your son."

Teach laughed again, a great cheer of mirth. "I 'ave sons an' brats all o'er tha place. In ev'ry port I doos reckon. Bain't acknowledged a one of em, an' I bain't as startin' t'do so now." He hoiked spittle into his mouth and spat the saliva to the deck. "There again, fer many a reason I bain't happy with thee, Acorne." He raised his pistol, pointed it at Jesamiah's head and cocked the hammer home. "Thee 'as turned traitor t'me and my men. I casn't be havin' that, now cas'n I?"

He pressed the trigger. It clicked. Nothing happened.

Charles stared with hatred and loathing at Teach, a smile that was more of a sneer touching the corner of his lips. "You are losing your touch, Edward. That pistol is not loaded. You have already fired it."

With a grunt of annoyance, Teach threw the weapon at him.

Jesamiah shivered, felt suddenly frightened. There had been no clatter as it had fallen, harmless, to the wooden deck. There was no sound at all, only their own three voices. Everything was still. It was like looking at a frozen tableau – the scene could have been a painting, one of the pictures Skylark created. Nothing moved. Not the clouds, the gulls, the sea, the tattered sails. The men, in various poses, stood like carved statues. Even the blood on the motionless deck was not running or dripping. This was unreal! A dream maybe? One of Tiola's spells? He wondered if he had been wounded or killed and he was looking as a dead man on those who were alive. But if that was so, as Teach was moving then he was dead with him, and he did not want to be in the same place as that misbegotten whoreson. And Tiola was somewhere below with the wounded. Surely, she would not have let him die here, alone?

"Jesamiah?" Charles said, his anguish returning, so sad, into his voice, "why did you not let me explain?" He lowered his pistol, slowly twisted round to face Jesamiah.

"Evil is here, son; to counter it I have to do what I have to do. But I so want to say I am sorry. So want to say I love you and that I did what I did, will do what I do, out of love for you. I got things wrong, I made mistakes." He faltered; steadied his nerve."I would that you could forgive me, though I do not deserve it. Because of my stupidity I was not a good father, but never, never doubt that I loved you, Jesamiah. With all my heart, I have always loved you, my dearest son."

What could Jesamiah say? What could he answer? His childhood had been a misery because his father had never protected him. But he had got through it, he had survived, and perversely it had made him a better person because he was determined not to be like Phillipe, or like his father.

"I wanted you to listen," Charles repeated, a harder note coming in his words."I wanted to tell you why, but the sand has run through the hour glass, and Time will wait no longer." He raised the pistol, but not at Teach. He was aiming at Jesamiah.

Jesamiah stood very still; as immobile as the men frozen in Time. He did not look at the gun, only at his father's saddened eyes. He was a dead shot, Charles Mereno. At this close range he would not miss once he pulled that trigger. It would be quick, instant: a better death than hanging.

"I no longer have questions about the past, Papa, nor care about the answers. You are dead, you are gone. Phillipe is dead. Neither of you can hurt me any more."He half smiled; flicked a glance at the pistol."At least, I thought you could not. Why kill me? What have I done? It's him,Teach, who has evil in his heart. Not me."

With infinite sadness Charles answered, "Please find it in your heart to forgive me. Edward Teach traded his soul with the Devil to become a midshipman aboard my ship. Unless the Dark is chased from him he cannot be killed. But you can, and for my peace, for yours, I have to do this. I am so sorry. So sorry."

Charles cocked the hammer home, pulled the trigger, and fired at Jesamiah as the last grain of sand dripped through the hourglass, and Time became right and jolted back into its solemn, measured, tread.

Fifty Four

Tiola was coming up through the scuttle. The men fighting for their lives were not aware that a small area of the deck had warped into a different dimension where time had ceased. Below, caring as best she could for the wounded and the dying, she had sensed the unbalanced shift and fled up the ladder, coming too late, just too late, to save Jesamiah. She ran, heedless of the fight going on around her as suspended Time became right again, and the gun in Charles Mereno's hand fired. Jesamiah was falling. His head struck the tiller and blood spread beneath him, pooling on the deck.

Here it was, her nightmare dream. The one word tore from her as a single, long, gut-wrenching cry of grief. "Jes…a…mi…ah!"

She threw herself over him, covering his body with her own, her tears falling like a burst of summer rain, her arms going around him, trying to make him sit up, trying to make him come alive. Trying to keep him warm and with her.

She heard the snigger: the humourless giggle of the Malevolents behind her.

~ *He is dead, Witch Woman! He is dead! And you are not so clever as to bring the dead back to life, are you? We have won! We have him*! ~ The giggling shrieked in a cacophony of macabre hilarity.

Tiola stared up at Teach, her dark eyes a depth of impenetrable black as he stepped forward, his last pistol aimed at Jesamiah's head.

His ugly, satisfied smile was repellent. "Let us make sure 'e be dead, eh?"

In a blur of movement that no human could have made, Tiola was standing astride the man she loved beyond her own life. Head erect, her fingers linked together at her waist, her eyes turning into pools of a glistening blackness that sparked with flecks of gold and silver. As the balance shifted into flux, energy crackled from her body and a great mass of power built and built behind her, swelling and expanding. She stood there, the Old One of Light with her gift of Craft, magnificent and omnipotent.

Slowly, very slowly, she brought her arms out and up, palms uppermost, forming a great circle of power in the air; a circle of bright, white fire trailing where her hands passed, building and building in density. The Circle of Light. At the zenith above her head her fingers touched and joined. The Power invoked; the Circle complete.

Her voice was potent in its commanding chant:

Light enclose the Circle,
All to fill the Air;
Coursing through the deep Earth,
Within the Fire flare.
Light upon the Water
The River and the Sea,
Spirit become the Circle
Protecting him and me.
Power to my Circle,
Power to my Might
Power to my Ageless Craft
Dark shall fear my Light!

The sky had turned black, the rage of the Dark Energy appearing like storm clouds banking overhead. Thunder split the sky, the rage of the Malevolence unleashed. The only light was Tiola's circle, the white fire that burned but gave no heat.

"You cannot harm me!" she cried to the swelling rage of Darkness. "I have formed the Circle and it cannot be broken!"

The Dark expanded in the sky, thicker, denser, boiling and swirling in its anger, but held at bay by the burning circle, came no closer.

Tiola turned her head slightly with a mixture of contempt and hatred towards the loathsome reptile that was Edward Teach. But for all her disdain, she also held compassion. The Dark had used him, had sent the Malevolents to feed on his vile greed and arrogance. To gorge and bloat and consume, leaving behind nothing of the man, only the sinister control of the Darkness of Evil.

"I cannot kill you for it is forbidden," she said, "but I can and I will drive out the Dark and those it sends to devour! I can and I will drive out the false promises of its minions, those which claim to protect and keep Death cowering in the shadows. I can and I will defeat the evil of the Dark that threatens those I love and cherish!"

The Darkness above and around roared its fury and howled its rage, a sound like the cannons of a battalion firing a sweeping broadside. But it was impotent against her.

"I can and I will destroy this Malevolence of the Dark!" And Tiola hurled the Circle of Light from her, thrusting it away with both hands. With all the strength she possessed she cast it, not at the broiling clouds of the Dark, but direct at Edward Teach.

He flung up his arms, screeched in fear, warding the blaze of Light off, trying to stop its terrible force from touching his face, his body, his hands. He staggered backwards, tripped, half fell, breath gasping in his lungs as the blaze tore into and through him. The Dark fled and the canker that had inhabited Teach fled with it, racing across the sky as a hare bolts from the hounds. The Circle of Light flared once, and vanished. The sun shone again and the equilibrium of Life and Death returned to its course of balanced stability.

Teach was on one knee. He had dropped his pistol. Desperate, he reached for it, his fingers scrabbling to close around the butt, to lift the weapon, cock it, aim. Maynard was trying to rise to his feet also, his head was spinning from the blow Teach had dealt him, blood trickling from a gash across his eyebrow. Men were fighting hand to hand. Kicking, punching and biting. Not much sound now, except for the thud and thump of blows and the groans of the wounded and the dying; the cry of gulls wheeling overhead, the sound of a wind hurrying, belatedly, across the marshes.

Blood was soaking through Teach's clothing, matting his beard and hair; the fuses entwined there had sputtered out. He pushed himself up, stood swaying, his vision blurring, dazed, bewildered and disorientated. This was not how it was meant to be. He could not die. He had been promised, promised that Death would not come for him. But Death stood there, bold and brazen before him.

"I have come for you, Edward," Charles Mereno said, bending to pick up Jesamiah's cutlass and to step in front of Teach. "I did a great wrong when I was a young man. Because of lust I got a woman with child and I spurned her plea for help. They said she was a Dark Witch and that she had conjured the Devil to protect her son."

He stood before Teach, the cutlass blade pressing into the pirate's throat through the matted blood-soaked beard.

"And that child became a monster who found me, his father, and deliberately set out to make my life and the lives of others a misery of despair. I knew, when first I saw you, Edward Teach, that you were my son."

Charles glanced at Tiola who was kneeling beside Jesamiah, cradling him, her tears spilling, her power gone, faded. "I had to raise Phillipe as my own; it was my duty to do so. I knew, to my shame, that he was my grandson. I tried to deny it, to ignore him. Out of cowardice, hid away and did nothing to stop the wickedness. But now at last I will find peace by ending what I so selfishly began. I must destroy the son I so foolishly and carelessly created."

He drew the cutlass back and struck, slicing the blade through flesh, sinew and bone, severing the head of his firstborn, illegitimate son, Edward Teach, with the one blow.

Fifty Five

The aftermath of battle was a mess. The sea around where the two sloops, *Adventure* and *Jane*, drifted was tainted red by the blood draining through the scuppers. More than half the men were killed; most of the others wounded. Among the dead, Nat Crocker and Sandy Banks. Wounded, badly but not mortally, Isiah Roberts, Joe Meadows – Skylark, and Crawford. Finch, though he had fought as fiercely as the next man, had not a scratch on him.

No one knew who had killed Blackbeard. The fighting had been confusing and intense; there had been so much smoke that for a while it had seemed as if the very sky had turned black, split only by a blast of flame from cannon fire. That the *Jane* carried no cannon, and none aboard the *Adventure* had been loaded, were facts that no one, except Tiola, realised or understood.

They found twenty cutlass slashes on Blackbeard's body, with five gunshot wounds, and although they marvelled at his great strength at attempting to cheat death, none felt sorry for him as they tossed his corpse over the side without word or prayer for his passing. The tide was on the turn and his remains swept in and out, bumping against the side of the *Jane* as if seeking its severed head, which Maynard had hung as a trophy from the bowsprit.

Those pirates who survived were locked, defeated and broken, in the hold. All of them were wounded. They would be taken to Williamsburg, tried and hanged without mercy.

Before the tide fell too low and dusk encroached, the *Jane* and the *Ranger*, with the *Adventure* as a Prize, limped away from the Ocracoke towards Pilot Point on the Pamlico River, leaving the corpses of those pirates who had died to the fish and crabs to devour. Their own dead would receive honoured burial.

Tiola was relieved to see the *Sea Witch* waiting there, as beautiful as ever she was. They took the *Jane* alongside and transferred the wounded of Jesamiah's crew to their rightful ship, and with subdued farewells and promises to return the boats to la Sorenta, Maynard sailed on to Bath Town where Captain Brand and his men were waiting, not needed. The fight was over.

Under Rue's solemn, guiding hand, the *Sea Witch* weighed anchor and set sail, bound for England as had been Jesamiah's order.

Jesamiah himself was an exasperating patient. He grumbled about the stitched wound that throbbed and ached at the back of his head, he mithered about the bruising to his chest and the pain of the broken collarbone in his right shoulder. But of his father he said nothing, not even after Tiola had tried to explain the why of it all, in an effort to help him understand.

The thoughts were there, though. As *Sea Witch* ploughed her way through the rough Atlantic rollers he remembered those days when, as a child, he had been alone with his father. He realised now, that they had been good days; days when the both of them had set aside grief and torments and had taken pleasure in each other's company. Realised too, as he lay there in his bed those first few days, watching the glittered reflection of the sea or the night shadows shape-shift on the low beams overhead, why the things of his childhood had happened in the way they had.

It had begun with the passing lust for and abandonment of a serving woman, and as with the neglect of all mistakes, the one had led to another and the injustices of retribution had marched too close. Out of guilt, Charles Mereno had taken on a lad as midshipman; a lad whom he had realised from the first was his bastard son. Because of guilt over his drunken and cowardly inability to prevent the death of a friend and the rape of a woman by that son, he had brought up the resulting child, Phillipe, as his own. And Jesamiah had paid the price of it all.

The ghost of the man who was Jesamiah's father had made those mistakes in life, but in death had tried to ensure that his son, Jesamiah, stayed alive. Deliberately, he had taken aim at the bronze buckle of the baldric belt strapped across Jesamiah's shoulder; enough to wound, but not enough to kill. Enough to put him out of the fight against Teach; a fight he could never have won.

Only once did Jesamiah speak of his father to Tiola. They had made love – gently, for the sake of his shoulder – and after, in the brightening dawn that was peeping through the salt-grimed stern windows, he had said, "The fathers in my family have not done so well, have they? I would, were I to be a father, learn from their mistakes and be there, always, for my son. Were I to have one."

Tiola had smiled, had kissed him in the way that only a wife who loved her husband could. And had said nothing.

Charles Mereno turned away from the River and walked towards where the sea lay flat and calm and blue beneath a sun-warmed sky. He thrust his hands deeper into his pockets and whistled a jaunty tune. He wondered if he would meet his friends again, the crewmen he had called brothers – his closest friend, Carlos. Surely they were here, gone ahead?

Peace, he realised, was contentment and happiness. There was only one thing that slightly bothered him. Something the Witch Woman had said when she had accompanied him back to the River.

"It is unwise to bring the Dark too close," she had said, "for the Dark does not always reveal the truth. We hear what we think we should, or want to hear, but guilt can whisper falsehoods. Unlike the Dark, the Light would never command. The human will is free to make its own choices."

Walking across the heather-clad moor, the sound of the bees busy and a lark trilling high in the sky, he wondered what she had meant. And then it occurred to him.

Had his actions, from that very first day when a black-haired boy called Edward had asked to serve aboard his ship, been nothing more than a guilt-burdened assumption? Had resemblance to a woman he had once tumbled, and then forgotten, been naught but an illusion? He would never know the truth, not now. It no longer mattered; he had put right a wrong. And with that knowledge the burden that had followed him beyond the grave lifted from his shoulders.

He walked on, whistling, content, knowing he had done his best for the one truth that was, without any doubt, certain. He was proud of, and loved, his son. Jesamiah.

Author's note

I like to think of my *Sea Witch* series as stories that are akin to a typical sailor's yarn – some bits are accurate, others are blatant fantasy, but most of it is not quite one or the other. The trick of a good yarn is to blend the reality with the imaginary so it all becomes plausible, and belief is suspended in deference to enjoyment. I hope I have achieved that.

Had I intended to write these books as serious fiction, as with my other historical novels, I would have been scrupulous with the facts of history, but these sea adventures are a blend of reality and fantasy so, with my apologies, I have gone for the character of the story rather than attention to fine detail. That is not to say the historical parts are entirely inaccurate though!

With editing assistance from my good friend and maritime author *par excellence* James L. Nelson, my nautical scenes are as correct as I can make them; any errors are my fault not his. I do confess that I have taken liberties with *Sea Witch* herself, however, for a couple of things about her are not quite right. Her rigging and copper-clad bottom are a few years in advance of her time. This was a deliberate decision on my part as I wanted to model her on the tall ship the *Rose*, a replica of which was built by another friend of mine, John F. Millar of Virginia. Fans of sea-stories may know the *Rose* in her alter ego part of HMS *Surprise* in the movie *Master & Commander*. I feel justified with this 'poetic licence' as the *Sea Witch* is, after all, a major character in a fantasy adventure novel, and I do state in the first book of the series, *Sea Witch*, that she is a new-built ship – so who is to say when the new designs first took place as innovative, unrecorded, experiments?

In *Bring It Close* many of Blackbeard's scenes happened – but without Jesamiah and Tiola of course. Blackbeard did take sixteen-year-old Mary Ormond as his 14th wife, and she did suffer the abuse I described on their wedding night – although her ultimate fate is my invention as we do not know what became of her. So too, did the fate of Jonathan Gabriel occur, although the name and character detail is made up, as is Perdita's; all we know is that Blackbeard took his revenge on a girl who spurned him. Her reaction to the horror has various unsubstantiated accounts, I have merely chosen to use one of them.

Governors Eden and Alexander Spotswood existed, as did Lt Robert Maynard and Tobias Knight; their parts concerning Blackbeard's demise are also accurate as are the dates for that final battle in the shallows of the Ocracoke. Eden was implicated in a subsequent investigation, as was Knight, but both were clever enough to be acquitted. Some reports mention that Maynard disappeared a few months later – others say it was a year or so. It was said he had died, but given that very little of value was officially retrieved from Blackbeard's ship, the *Adventure*, I think this is unlikely. Maynard would have been able to search at leisure, and the Royal Navy was known for its extreme slowness – and gross unfairness – in paying out prize money. It therefore does not take much of a leap of imagination to work out what happened to Maynard – or where the bulk of Blackbeard's treasure hoard went!

Blackbeard himself had a variety of names, he may have changed identity, or it was common in the Eighteenth Century to have alternative spellings for the same name. He was known as Edward Teach or Thatch, but it seems he came from Bristol, England, so I believe the difference in his names is accountable because of his West Country accent.'Teach' could have been pronounced as something like "T'ach" – Thatch.

But 'Blackbeard' is his more infamous name.

He did indeed live at Bath Town, North Carolina for a few months as a 'respectable' citizen and had Governor Eden eating out of his hand. North Carolina was not as wealthy as the prospering Virginia and corruption was rife throughout all the Colonies. The initial plan hatched between governor and pirate could have worked beautifully, if only Edward Teach had stuck to it.

The crew members I have named (Garrett Gibbens for instance) were his real crew – we know their names because they were captured and hanged at Williamsburg. Israel Hands was arrested in Bath Town, seriously wounded from being shot in the knee by Teach. He gave evidence against those men captured and was pardoned. Legend says he ended his days begging in the streets of London. The only crew member of note whom I made up is Red Rufus. Sam Odell was indeed at the Ocracoke – he had to prove he was an innocent bystander, even though he had spent the night drinking with Teach.

I used several textbooks for my research – and found it most frustrating when they differed in detail. The Midshipman who commanded the *Ranger* in the attack against Blackbeard, for instance. In one book his name was Baker, in another, Hyde, so for the final word I stayed with UK maritime expert David Cordingly.

Anyone visiting Colonial Williamsburg in Virginia can see the gaol (jail), the courtroom in the Capitol Building, John Brush's house, and the palace for themselves. I have researched the detail as well as I could (with the kind help of my friend Judy) but inevitably there will be a few discrepancies. You will not find the '*Acorn*' tavern that Alicia will be investing in, for instance, but the *Raleigh* and the *King's Arms* are certainly there (though the *Raleigh* is of a much better standard now!) I hope to return Jesamiah to Williamsburg one day – he will have to see how Alicia is getting on, after all, and I need an excuse to go back to do more research!

La Sorenta, a few miles north of Urbanna along the Rappahannock River is entirely fictitious, as are most of the 'incidental' characters. My apologies to the ancestors of any 'real' people if I have not portrayed them in a favourable light – the necessity of drama in story telling, I'm afraid.

For those who are interested, when he is talking to Governor Spotswood, Jesamiah mentions various territories and towns named after monarchs, and that the king at the time, George of Hanover, (George I) had no such honour. As far as I am aware he never did. The Colony of Georgia was named after his successor, George II. And George III, of course, lost it all towards the end of the century when the American Colonies rebelled and fought the War of Independence. Which, contrary to general belief in the UK, did not start with the famous Boston Tea Party where a cargo of tea was thrown into the harbour. Tea was involved, but the animosity between America and England was because of smuggling tea as contraband. As a minor historical note of interest, in revolt against the British Government's heavy import duty of tea the American settlers resolved to drink coffee instead. It remains the favoured US beverage to this day. The original *Rose*, mentioned above, played an important part at the outset of the War. She was very effective against the Colony Smugglers in and around the Chesapeake – too effective, for rebellion against her constant prowling soon occurred.

One pedantic little note to those readers who tut over the minutiae of historical detail – it is perfectly correct for Jesamiah to have called Blackbeard 'Sleeping Beauty'. The original story (Sleeping Beauty – *La Belle au Bois dormant* – The Beauty Asleep in the Wood) was written by Charles Perrault and published in 1697.

My apologies for my attempt at portraying Teach's Bristol accent. I took advice from a noted English Dialect book – so any laughable nonsense is not entirely my fault. Charles St Croix Mereno may appear again in Voyage Four – *Ripples in the Sand*, but should you wish to discover more about Jesamiah's grandfather, Alexander, you will find him in my editor Joe Field's own excellent novel of the English Civil War – *Rogues & Rebels*. I heartily recommend the read. Thank you Jo for allowing me to steal Arabella and Alexander's son. The book is out of print at the moment, but I am hoping Jo will consider putting it on Kindle.

Had I realised when I set out to write this series how popular Jesamiah was to become, maybe I would have considered writing these books as straight historical adventure – but then maybe fact and fantasy has a tighter blend of authenticity than we realise? Or perhaps there is a Parallel Universe where things happen similar to our existence, but not quite the same?

In my imagination things once happened as I have written them. To me, Jesamiah Acorne, Tiola Oldstagh, *Sea Witch* and her crew are very real, they exist – but not in this world.

No one knows for certain the full detail of any event that happened in the past – for instance, a charming rogue of an ex-pirate could indeed have insisted on having his name left out of the official records concerning the demise of the man known as Blackbeard.

And please let me know if you find a blue ribbon hanging mysteriously on a bush, branch or gatepost. It seems Jesamiah has taken to leaving them in unexpected places for his growing crew of loyal fans to find…

Helen Hollick
2011

Glossary

Aback – a sail when its forward surface is pressed upon by the wind. Used to 'stop' a ship.
Account – see On the Account.
Aloft – up in the tops, at the masthead or any where about the yards or the rigging.
Articles – Each man when coming aboard 'agreed the Articles'. Some pirate ships were run on very democratic lines, the crew elected their captain, agreed where to sail, divided the 'spoils' fairly etc. Most rules were sensible things like no naked flame below deck; each man to keep his weapon clean and ready for use; and no fighting aboard ship.
Bar – a shoal running across the mouth of a harbour or a river.
Bare poles – having no sail up – the bare mast.
Belay – to make fast or secure. Also: 'Stop that'. 'Belay that talk!' would mean 'Shut up!'
Belaying pin – a short wooden rod to which a ship's rigging is secured. A common improvised weapon aboard a sailing ship because they are everywhere, are easily picked up, and are the right size and weight to be used as a club.
Bell (Ship's bell) – used as a clock, essential for navigation as the measurement of the angle of the sun had to be made at noon. The bell was struck each time the half-hour glass was turned.
Bilge – the lowest part of the ship inside the hull along the keel. They fill with stinking bilge water or 'bilge'. Can also mean nonsense or foolish talk.
Binnacle – the frame or box that houses the compass.
Bo'sun – short for boatswain, usually a competent sailor who is in charge of all deck duties.
Bow – the front or 'pointed' end of the ship.
Bowsprit – the heavy slanted spar pointing forward from the ship's bow.
Brace – rope used to control the horizontal movement of a square-rigged yard.
Brig – a two masted vessel square-rigged on both masts.

Brimstone – formerly the common name for sulphur.
Broadside – the simultaneous firing of all guns on one side of a ship.
Bulkheads – vertical partitions in a ship.
Bulwark – interior wall of ship.
Cable – a long, thick and heavy rope by which a ship is secured to the anchor.
Cable's length – a measure of 120 fathoms or 240 yards.
Capstan – drum-like winch turned by the crew to raise or lower the anchors.
Careen – the process of beaching a ship, heeling her over to her side and cleaning the underside of weed, barnacles and worm; making essential repairs to the part of a ship which is usually below the water line. A careened ship will go faster and last longer than one that is not.
Cathead – vertical beam of timber protruding near the bow, used for hoisting the anchor.
Cat o'nine tails, or 'cat' – a whip with many lashes, used for flogging.
Caulk – to seal the gaps between planks of wood with caulking – see oakum.
Chain shot – two balls of iron joined together by a length of chain, chiefly used to destroy, masts, rigging and sails.
Chandler – a merchant selling the various things a ship needs for supplies and repairs.
Chanty/shanty – a sailor's work song. Often lewd and derogatory about the officers.
Chase – or Prize. The ship being pursued.
Cleat – wooden or metal fastening to which ropes can be secured. Can also be used as a ladder.
Clew – the lower corners of a sail, therefore Clew up – to haul a square sail up to a yard.
Close-hauled – sailing as close to the direction of the wind as possible with the sails turned almost 90°.
Cordage – rope is called cordage on board a ship.
Colours – the vessel's identification flag, also called an ensign. For a pirate, the Jolly Roger!
Courses – lowest sails on the mast.
Crosstrees – wooden platform partway up a mast to keep the shrouds spread apart.
Dolphin Striker – a short perpendicular gaff spar under the cap of the bowsprit for guying down the jib-boom. Also called a martingale.
Doubloon – a Spanish gold coin.
Fathom – a measure of six feet of water.
Fore or for'ard – toward the front end of the ship, the bow.
Forecastle – pronounced fo'c'sle; raised deck at the front of ship.
Fore-and-aft rig – sails set length wise not at right angles (square-rigged) to the hull.

Flukes – the broad parts or palms of the anchor.
For-and-aft – the length of a ship.
Forestay – the rope leading from the mast to the bow.
Fother – to seal a leak by lowering a sail over the side of the ship and positioning it so that it seals the hole by the weight of the sea. The canvas can be.
Futtock –'foot hooks'.
Futtock shroud – short pieces of rope which secure lower dad-eyes and futtock plates to the top mast rigging.
Galleon – a large three-masted square-rigged ship used chiefly by the Spanish.
Galley – ship's kitchen.
Gasket – a piece of plait to fasten the sails to the yards.
Gaol / gaoler – pronounced 'jail' and 'jailer.
Grape-shot – or grape, small cast iron balls bound together in a canvas bag that scatter like shotgun pellets when fired.
Grenados – early form of hand grenade.
Gunwale – pronounced gun'l; upper planking along the sides of a vessel. 'Up to the gunwales' – full up or overloaded.
Halliard or halyard – pronounced haly'd. The rope used to hoist a sail.
Hard tack – ship's biscuit. Opposite is soft tack – bread. Hatch – an opening in the deck for entering below. Hawser – cable.
Heave to – to check the forward motion of a vessel and bring her to a stand still by heading her into the wind and backing some of her sails.
Heel – to lean over due to action of the wind, waves, or greater weight on one side. The angle at which the vessel tips when sailing.
Helm – the tiller (a long steering arm) or a wheel which controls the rudder and enables the vessel to be steered.
Hold – space below deck for cargo.
Hull – the sides of a ship which sit in and above the water.
Hull down – a vessel when it is so far away from the observer the hull is invisible owing to the shape of the earth's surface. Opposite to hull up.
Jack Ketch – the hangman. To dance with Jack Ketch is to hang.
Jollyboat – a small boat, a dinghy.
Jolly Roger – the pirates' flag, called the jolie rouge – although its original meaning is unknown. The hoisted flag was an invitation to surrender, with the implication that those who did so would be treated well – and no quarter given to those who did not.
Keel – the lowest part of the hull below the water.
Keelhaul – an unpleasant punishment – the victim is dragged through the water passing under the keel, either from side to side or bow to stern.
Knot – one nautical mile per hour.
Landlubber or lubber – a non-sailor.
Langrage – jagged pieces of sharp metal used as shot. Especially useful for

damaging rigging and killing men.
Larboard – pronounced larb'd; the left side of a ship when facing the bow (front). Changed in the 19th century to 'port.'
Lee – the side or direction away from the wind i.e, downwind.
Lee shore – the shore on to which the wind is blowing, a hazardous shore for a sailing vessel particularly in strong winds –can easily be blown on to rocks etc.
Leeches – the vertical edges of a square sail.
Letter of Marque – Papers issued by a government during wartime entitling a privately owned ship to raid enemy commerce or attack enemy warships.
Lubberly – in an amateur way, as a landlubber would do.
Luff – the order to the helmsman to put the tiller towards the lee side of the ship in order to make it sail nearer to the direction of the wind.
Maroon – a punishment for breaking a pirate ship's articles or rules. The victim was left on a deserted coast (or an island) with little in the way of supplies. Therefore, no one could say the unlucky pirate had actually been killed by his former brethren.
Mast – vertical spar supporting the sails.
Molly Boy – a homosexual prostitute.
Oakum – a material used to waterproof seams between planks on deck etc. Made of strong, pliable, tarred fibres obtained from scrap rope which swell when wet.
On the Account – or the Sweet Trade; a man who went 'on the account' was turning pirate.
Piece of eight – a Spanish silver coin worth one peso or eight reales. It was sometimes literally cut into eight pieces, each worth one real. In the 1700s a piece of eight was worth a little under five shillings sterling, or 25p – this would be about £15 today. One side usually had the Spanish coat of arms, the other two lines symbolising the limits of the old world at the Straits of Gibraltar, the exit into the Atlantic Ocean from the Mediterranean. In later designs two hemispheres were added between the lines representing the Old and New Worlds. Pieces of eight were so widely used that eventually this sign was turned into the dollar sign – $.
Privateer – an armed vessel bearing letters of marque, or one of her crew, or her captain. A privateer is theoretically a law-abiding combatant.
Quarterdeck – the highest deck at the rear of a ship where the officers stood and where the helm is usually situated.
Quartermaster – usually the second-in-command aboard on a pirate ship. In the Royal Navy, the man in charge of the provisions
Rail – timber plank along the top of the gunwale above the sides of the vessel.
Rake – when a ship sweeps another with a broadside of cannon.
Ratlines – pronounced ratlins; ropes beneath the yards on which sailors would stand while adjusting the sails.

Reef – (1) an underwater obstruction of rock or coral. (2) to reduce the size of the sails by tying them partially up, either to slow the ship or to keep a strong wind from putting too much strain on the masts.
Rigging – the ropes which support the spars (standing rigging) and allow the sails to be controlled (running rigging).
Round shot – iron cannon balls.
Rudder – blade at the stern which is angled to steer the vessel.
Run – sail directly away from the wind.
Sails – in general each mast had three sails. See diagram at the front.
Sail ho! –'I see a ship!'The sail is the first part visible over the horizon.
Scuppers – openings along the edges of a ship's deck to allow water to drain back to the sea rather than collecting in the bilges.
Scuttle: 1 – a porthole or small hatch in the deck for lighting and ventilation, covered by the 'scuttle hatch'. Can be used as a narrow entrance to the deck below.
Scuttle: 2 – or scupper – to deliberately sink a ship.
Sheet – a rope made fast to the lower corners of a sail to control its position.
Sheet home – to haul on a sheet until the foot of the sail is as straight and taut as possible.
Ship's Biscuit – hard bread. Very dry, can be eaten a year after baked. Also called hard tack.
Ship of the Line – a war ship carrying at least 50 guns.
Shrouds – ropes forming part of the standing rigging and supporting the mast or topmast.
Sloop – a small, single masted vessel, ideal for shallow water.
Spanker – a square sail wide at bottom and narrow at top attached to a boom that projects straight back from the mizzenmast along the axis of the ship.
Spar – a stout wooden pole used as a mast or yard of a sailing vessel.
Spritsail – pronounced sprit's'l; a sail attached to a yard which hangs under the bowsprit.
Square-rigged – the principal sails set at right angles to the length of a ship and extended by horizontal yards slung to the mast.
Starboard – pronounced starb'd. The right side of a vessel when you are facing toward the bow.
Stay – strong rope supporting the masts. Stem – timber at very front of bow.
Stern – the back end of a ship.
Swab – a disrespectful term for a seaman, or to clean the decks.
Sweet Trade – see On the Account.
Sweeps – long oars used by large vessels.
Tack / tacking – to change the direction of a vessel's course by turning her bows into the wind until the wind blows on her other side. When a ship is sailing into an oncoming wind she will have to tack, make a zigzag line, in order to make progress forward against the oncoming wind.

Tackle – (pronounced 'taykle') An arrangement of one or more ropes and pulley-blocks used to increase the power for raising or lowering heavy objects.
Taffrail – upper rail along the ship's stern.
Tompions – muzzle-plugs to protect the bore from salt corrosion etc.
Transom – planking forming the stern.
Trim – a term used for adjusting the sails as the wind changes.
Waist – the middle part of the ship.
Wake – the line of passage directly behind as marked by a track of white foam.
Warp – to move a ship by hauling or pulling her along on warps (ropes); also the name of the ropes which secure a ship when moored (tied up) to a jetty or dock.
Weigh anchor – to haul the anchor up; more generally, to leave port.
Widow maker – term for the bowsprit.
Windward – the side towards the wind as opposed to leeward.
Yard – a long spar suspended from the mast of a vessel to extend the sails.
Yardarm – either end of the yard.